ALSO BY PATRICIA O'BRIEN

Fiction

Good Intentions

The Ladies' Lunch

The Candidate's Wife

Non-Fiction

*I Know Just What You Mean: The Power of
Friendship in Women's Lives*

Staying Together

The Woman Alone

The
GLORY CLOAK

A Novel

Patricia O'Brien

A TOUCHSTONE BOOK
PUBLISHED BY SIMON & SCHUSTER
NEW YORK   LONDON   TORONTO   SYDNEY

obr

TOUCHSTONE
Rockefeller Center
1230 Avenue of the Americas
New York, NY 10020

TOUCHSTONE and colophon are registered
trademarks of Simon & Schuster, Inc.

For information regarding special discounts for bulk purchases,
please contact Simon & Schuster Special Sales at
1-800-456-6798 or business@simonandschuster.com

Designed by Jan Pisciotta

Manufactured in the United States of America

1 3 5 7 9 10 8 6 4 2

Library of Congress Cataloging-in-Publication Data
O'Brien, Patricia.
The glory cloak : a novel / Patricia O'Brien.
p. cm.
"A Touchstone book."
1. Alcott, Louisa May. 1832–1888—Fiction. 2. United States—History—Civil War,
1861–1865—Medical care—Fiction. 3. United States—History—Civil War,
1861–1865—Hospitals—Fiction. 4. United States—History—Civil War,
1861–1865—Women—Fiction. 5. Nurses—Fiction. I. Title.
PS3565.B73G56 2004
813'.54—dc22   2003061708
ISBN 0-7432-5750-2

FOR ROBERT M. PEAK

1954–2003

Loved and gone too soon

The
GLORY CLOAK

Prologue

NOVEMBER 1997

"It's getting too dark to see anything," complained the man in the yellow hard hat, peering through the gloom of the old building. "Let's finish in the morning."

"Can't. Demolition starts at seven," answered his companion, stepping carefully over a yawning hole in the floor as he gazed at an ancient ladder propped up by the crumbling stairwell. He could see that at least two of the rungs were broken. "Have to inspect the top floor. That's my job."

"You get on that thing, you're crazy." The first man removed his hat and wiped his brow as he eyed the ladder. "The shoe store guy who lived downstairs said it's been boarded up for fifty years at least."

"All the more reason to check it out."

"What are you going to do when you get up there, pull the boards off with your bare hands?" The first man cupped the hat under a sturdy, muscular arm, his voice impatient now. "I know you inspector types are keen on history, but this is the most decrepit wreck on Seventh Street." He waited for an answer, and when none came, he pulled his hat back on and turned away. "Look, I'm out of here; union rules. Gotta pick up my wife. She hates waiting. You know how it is."

The other man said nothing, his attention suddenly caught by a gap in the ceiling directly above him. He barely heard the echo of the construction foreman's footsteps retreating, for his eye had caught a glint of something above the ceiling timbers. Carefully he mounted the ladder, holding his breath as he tested each rung. This was beyond duty, he thought, as one cracked under his weight. His fascination with Civil War vintage buildings would get him yet.

Reaching the top, he hesitated, then thrust his hand blindly through the opening. His fingers closed around a rectangular object that felt like a piece of tin. There was raised lettering on it and he drew it closer, squinting to read in the gloom.

Missing Soldiers Office
3rd Story, Room 9
Miss Clara Barton

"My God," he muttered. With a great heave, he pulled his body through the opening, landing on a bare wood floor. A room. Confused, he looked around. A room that was unexpectedly bright, for the two narrow windows were not boarded up. Long, limp strips of faded gold and silver wallpaper hung from the walls, exposing yellowed plaster. The smell of ancient newspapers and disintegrating fabrics made his nose itch, and he held back a sneeze. On the wall, slightly askew, was an awkwardly nailed-together frame of red pine, holding what appeared to be a letter written in spidery, faded ink:

To the Friends of Missing Persons:
 Miss Clara Barton has kindly offered to search for the missing prisoners of war. Please address her at Annapolis, giving her the name, regiment, and company of any missing prisoner.

Signed
A. Lincoln

This time a soft whistle broke from his lips. Jesus, he was standing in some sort of time capsule. An almanac rested on top of one of the cabinets, and a neatly stacked pile of newspapers lay next to it. He could make out the year on one of them: 1868. A faded paisley purse lay limply on the windowsill. Next to it were a couple of apothecary bottles and a scattering of ink pen points. Boxes of documents on the floor had been pushed up against the walls.

The entire room had a busy, cluttered look, as if the occupants had simply stepped out and would be back any moment. The man began to explore. Carefully he opened a desk drawer to peer inside, and spied an empty envelope. He was caught immediately by the name of the addressee: Louisa May Alcott.

"What's this about?" he said aloud, starting at the sound of his own voice. He decided to touch nothing more, eager now to get out and contact his boss. There would be no demolition here in the morning if he could raise the alarm fast enough.

As he pushed the drawer closed, a piece of paper wedged in the cracks of the wood slats loosened and fell to the floor. He bent to retrieve it. The words written on it, still sharp and clear, were in a sprawling, agitated hand:

> *I cannot believe you would give up, turn your back on love; I cannot believe it! You've been hoping for this all your life. Henry could not offer it, but it is offered to you now. What truth do you speak of, Louisa? You want me to understand your torment, but have you thought of mine? Oh, this pain! What have you become and what*

The words stopped in mid-sentence. Carefully he placed the note back in the drawer and closed it, strangely moved by the writer's evident anguish. He took one last look around, thinking he could almost hear the rustle of heavy silk skirts and the sound of voices, both laughing and weeping. He shook his head, a bit sheepish about such imaginings. Time to go. Gingerly, he lowered himself back through the floor, feeling for the top rung of the ladder below.

December 1997

The Washington Post

FOUND; MISSING LINK OF
CLARA BARTON'S LIFE
U.S. to Preserve D.C. Building
Where Worker Discovered Home,
Office of Famed Civil War Nurse

The federal government reversed a decision to demolish a downtown Washington building after historians confirmed the top floor was the apartment and office of famed Civil War nurse Clara Barton. In November, a huge cache of personal papers and her government files on missing soldiers were discovered in a closed-off portion of the three-story building near Seventh and E Streets NW . . .

Chapter One

He was so little, the colored boy wedged in Abba's oven. I couldn't believe
my eyes. He sat with his knees to his chin, shaking like a blob of jelly, and
after a horrified moment I shrieked and slammed the door shut.

Louisa flew into the kitchen, swooped me up and clapped her hand
over my mouth. She smelled of cinnamon apple tea. "You naughty girl,"
she hissed. "You were told to stay out of the kitchen. Why do you pay so little heed? We could go to jail if he were found."

I bawled in mortification. I adored Cousin Louisa. She was the nicest
of the Alcott sisters, even though at eighteen she was ten years older than
I and almost a grown-up. She put on wonderful plays and I didn't want
her to be angry with me. She paused in the act of giving me a good shake,
and I could see she was trying mightily to control her temper.

"It's all right, Susan, don't cry," she finally said. "He has to stay in
there until dark and we don't want to be making a fuss over his presence.
Don't be afraid."

"He won't be cooked, will he?"

"No, no, you silly little goose. He will be taken somewhere safe."

I was getting more interested now, and dying for another peek. "Why
does he have to go?"

Louisa's chin, already square and formidable, grew even more so as she
replied. "Because he is escaping slavery, which is an abomination. You hear
me, Susan? Say it."

"Slavery is an abdom——" I faltered. I could see the Brown girls watching from the doorway, and hoped their father would not come storming in
the room, for he was a glowering man with fierce eyes and dark hair that

stood straight up in front: his hair is as much afraid of him as I am, I thought.

"It is evil."

I nodded, clutching Louisa's hand.

She softened and smiled at me with a hint of forgiveness, so I dared to ask more.

"Can he play with me before he leaves?"

"He won't have time to play."

"But I want to be his friend," I said, thinking of those sad, fearful eyes.

Louisa leaned over and kissed the tip of my nose. "I will be your friend, Susan," she said. "I promise . . . if you obey me."

"Oh, yes," I breathed, delighted. "Always."

And so, on a fine spring day in 1850, it began—a pledge of friendship that took us through thirty-eight years, warming my life even through pain; now she is gone and I sit here alone at my desk, wondering how to make sense of it all. Out the window, at the end of the short gravel walk from my shop to Main Street, the postman is stuffing yet more tributes in the mailbox, for I have promised to help dear Anna, now the only sister left, answer the overflow. After doing his best to tie the lid shut with a strand of rope, he catches a glimpse of me and mournfully tips his hat. All of Concord is mourning Louisa. Not just Concord; the entire country. Especially the children.

And I am left to face my own life—my loves and jealousies— lived so often in counterpoint to an adored friend who lived mainly in her head and on paper.

I want Louisa to be remembered for her good character and sturdy heart, beyond her success and fame—and certainly beyond her father's trumpeting praise of her as "Duty's faithful child." But I also must trace the path that led us through the tantalizing possibilities she brought to life. What hopes she floated out onto the water! Her sailing ships were fragile vessels of paper filled with life and passion that I cheered on, time after time, wanting back something they could not always give.

I loved Louisa, perhaps more than anyone in my life. As a child, she thrilled me—she was tall and thin, with gray eyes both fierce and funny, and moved sometimes awkwardly and other times with swift, sure grace. Her clothes always had an indifferent, patched-together look that I, kept harnessed by my proper parents in proper clothes, envied. She was so free and buoyant, she was once able to convince me that if I flapped my arms industriously enough, I would be able to fly. "Can *you?*" I asked, mouth falling open. "Of course," she said solemnly. "But I'm too busy writing my play to show you right now."

As I grew and changed, I saw her more for the complicated dreamer, the woman of many moods, she truly was. Through everything, my love never wavered.

And yet I betrayed her. Even though our friendship survived, nothing changes that fact.

"Susan, we have endured," she whispered from her deathbed. Was it but a week ago? How can that be, when her voice still echoes in my head?

"Oh Louy, we have. But at times it was a terrible journey," I replied, clinging to her hand.

"Our own Pilgrim's Progress."

I managed to smile, remembering how she would outfit her sisters and me with hats and sticks and lead us from the City of Destruction in the dark cellar to the Celestial City, which was just the dusty attic stocked with fruit and candy rewards. But Lou would dramatize the hazards along our way so vividly, my childish heart would thump with fear.

"I was most afraid of the lions and the hobgoblins," I whispered.

"You were brave, Susan. We had no choice, you know." She tried to smile, then coughed and pulled the quilt to her chin.

What did she mean, I wonder? Now I open the top drawer of my desk and stare at the letter waiting there that must be answered. The request for information from the earnest Ednah Dow Cheney, now clearly determined to become Louisa's biographer. It is time to pick up the pen and take a stab at being Duty's faithful child, at least this once.

March 1888

> *Dear Mrs. Cheney,*
>
>   *I pray you will bear me no grudge for not addressing earlier the topic of your letter, but I needed to allow my own grieving to ease before replying. I understand the importance of your questions, but I do wonder if I offer anything that will be of value to you for your biography of Louisa.*
>
>   *In the time we served together as nurses in Washington during the war, there were indeed people who played a larger role in her life than most suspect. Yet that is often true, would you not agree? Especially for someone as celebrated as Louisa.*
>
>   *You ask about us. In truth, our friendship was not a conventional one with a predictable trajectory. It produced a shared lifetime marked by loss and missed opportunities as well as by joy. Do forgive me, but our small story is not one that fits comfortably into the image the world has of the author of Little Women.*

I hesitate, then scratch out all but the first two sentences. Mrs. Cheney is too eager to know what happened at Union Hospital. Are there words adequate to convey that experience? I know why soldiers do not want to talk about their wartime adventures, for my own nightmares of pain and death haunted my dreams for years. War leaves memories one can neither face nor forget.

But that is not what pricks her curiosity. Industrious, conscientious writer that she is, her letter asks the question directly. Did Louisa ever find a man she loved? If so, who was he? And what happened? She looks for clues to Louisa's sadness, and she knocks at the right door, but I do not want to let her in. It is a burden I would be tempted to share, but only with one person, and that one person is certainly not Mrs. Cheney. Yet she persists, telling me I owe the story to history. If it isn't told now, she says, Louisa will become folklore, forever blended with her greatest creation, Jo March.

I lay down my pen. It is easier now to go back to staring out the window at the mailbox. Too easy. I am only putting off the inevitable, for although I can avoid Mrs. Cheney, I can no longer avoid my own questions. The memories will shake loose and choose their own course; there is nothing now I can do to stop them. Oh, how painful it is to face what I must ask of myself—did I lose or find myself through Louisa? Did she consume me or set me free?

So I will start. At the cemetery.

I don my cloak and trudge up Main Street, past Monument Square, up Bedford Street and into the graveyard, wondering what self-punishment I am inflicting to make this journey yet again. My step slowing, I turn onto the narrow, winding path that takes me up the ridge, the cold, hard ground unyielding beneath my boots. A meandering rise, up past the Thoreaus and the Hawthornes, remembering, hearing; stopping at the Alcott plot. The two fresh coffins of Bronson and his daughter are still above the ground. They will remain here for now, for the earth is still too frozen to put them to final rest.

If I concentrate, I hear whispering back and forth. Even the faint echo of Bronson calling across the path to Nathaniel, still trying to break through the man's dark reticence as he was wont to do in life. Their homes were not much farther apart than their graves, and now they lie as neighbors for eternity.

I look to the right, to the next plot. I can hear Henry Thoreau's monotone as he discoursed on the wonders of communing with bullfrogs and Louisa's enthralled responses as she tried to tame this rude, clumsy man whom even Harvard could not civilize. He was certainly a sagacious observer of worms and plants and weather, but she saw more than that, and yearned for him to notice her. When I was a child, perhaps nine or ten, I saw only a cold, remote boor who chewed with his mouth open. I would sit spooning my soup when he came to dinner, watching him talk and slurp, and wonder why Louisa was all moony-eyed as she leaned forward to catch every word he spoke. I took to imitating his slurps, following each of his with one of mine, playing my own sly game. May started to copy me one night and I giggled, then choked, with disastrous consequences. Bronson's disapproval was daunting, but it was Louisa's hurt glance that truly chastened me.

We would laugh about that, now. If we could.

It takes a few moments to traverse the narrow path upward and reach the Emersons, Concord's royal family. Here the first crocuses are emerging, which is fitting, for this is the grandest spot on the hill. In life, Mr. Emerson housed his friends and dug into his pockets to give them money, and none was helped more by him than the philosophizing, work-scorning Bronson. And none more mortified by that kindness than Louisa.

And yet she lived to please her demanding father, even as he lived on the money of others and on her reputation. How should I think of the man? Indeed, Bronson was without band or rivet. But his vague mysticism was frequently contradicted by a furrowed brow and glaring eyes when someone challenged his will. Especially his daughter. Will I ever understand the power he exerted over Louisa? Oh, she would roll her eyes about him, but when he clutched her hand on his deathbed and pleaded, "I am going up, come with me," it took only two days for her to obey. If she had not, I believe he would be scolding her from beyond the grave for not dying on his timetable.

I am too harsh. What is the use of nurturing anger? Wasn't that what Louisa and I had to give up to remain friends? I stand before their graves tasting the sour energy of indignation, but it withers in the face of the memory of this dear family, these dear people, my dear Louisa, all gone. Only Anna remains.

We were third cousins, connected primarily by the abolitionist politics of Bronson and my father. My parents and I lived in New York and visited the Alcotts at least twice a year through my childhood, our visits never lasting more than a fortnight. How I looked forward to them! As an only child, that energetic household of four girls enthralled me. My father and Bronson would huddle with like-minded men in the parlor, arguing over how best to fight the Fugitive Slave Act. The men would shout and argue, but the only visitor who scared me was John Brown. Even my father seemed a bit nonplussed by his fire.

On one of those evenings, I think when I was nine, my thoughts turned back to the little boy I had found hiding in the oven.

"What happened to him?" I asked Louisa before drifting off to sleep.

"He's safe in a new home," she assured me. "Just like the colored man Papa was talking about tonight."

"The one called Shadrack?"

Louisa nodded. "That should teach the government not to try to ensnare a Massachusetts man. They'll not find him now." There was both pride and a touch of nervousness in her voice, for anyone aiding a fugitive was subject to a thousand-dollar fine and six months in jail. I shivered in my bed, wondering what jail was like.

Through those days, my sweet, scattered mother would try to help Abba Alcott make cakes and pies, but she would often wander away from half-worked dough to pick flowers for her hair, singing all the while. My mother—unlike Louisa's—never really finished anything. Even her kisses were but promises, coming close to my cheek and then floating away like feathers in the wind.

My cousins were my favorite playmates. Especially Louisa. She was so wonderfully daring, so full of fun. I followed her everywhere, trying to imitate her free and easy stride, her hearty laugh—everything. No boy could be her friend until she had beaten him in a race. And no girl, unless she liked climbing trees and leaping over fences. Louisa taught me that rules for proper behavior were sometimes absurd and there was joy in breaking them. Around Louisa, I felt less fearful of adult disapproval. Sometimes she would go dark and gloomy, remorseful for some giddy adventure frowned upon by her father, and I would be bereft. But she always brightened again. Once when I was ten she marched me out to her favorite tree, pointed to an alarmingly high branch, and announced it was time for me to learn to hang by my knees. "I can't do that," I said, aghast.

"You wait, you'll be immensely proud of yourself when you succeed," she declared, proceeding to climb the tree and move out onto the branch. She swung herself backward, swaying lazily in the breeze. "Come *on,* Susan," she commanded.

I climbed, twisting my foot on a gnarled protruding root, beseeching her sympathy for my youth, my timidity, my awkward-ness. Anything to keep from following her out onto that branch. And yet something made me go on. Didn't I want to be just like Louisa?

"Oh, stop complaining," she said calmly, swinging to and fro.

I inched outward, trying to tuck my skirts tight beneath my locked knees. With a deep breath, I swung backward.

"See? You're doing it."

"I can't. I'll fall on my head."

"Pretend you're a little monkey. You are, actually."

"I am not. And if Mama sees me, she'll scold me because my britches are showing." I gasped out the words. It was hard to talk, hanging upside down.

"It's worth it. Feel the breeze. Pretend you're hanging by your tail."

My knees were aching. I couldn't hold on much longer. How could she be so serene?

"Can you do handsprings?" she suddenly asked.

"No," I managed.

"I'll teach you. Let's go." She swung upward, grabbing the tree limb with both hands. I did the same, clutching a small branch for balance, wobbling to a sitting position. I climbed slowly down the tree, still dizzy with my own audacity.

Louisa jumped to the ground and brushed off her skirt. "Good job," she said, as I scrambled down behind her. She started to laugh. "I'll tell you a little secret, Susan. You're the only one who's taken my challenge."

"I *am?*"

"Don't look stricken. Aren't you proud of yourself?"

"Well, I'm willing to take chances," I said quickly.

"I like that. I'd say you are quite daring."

And that was that. I was full of pride and more determined than ever to keep proving to Louisa that her scrawny, undersized cousin was not a timid child.

Anna, the plainest of the four sisters, had quite a lovely singing voice, and although she was a bit prissy—being the oldest—she had the patience to listen in a way I learned to value. Once I showed her the sketchbook held with twine that Mama had fashioned for me after catching me sketching one of her lovely ball gowns. "You have quite an eye for fashion detail," Anna said, paging through my childish drawings. She gazed at me thoughtfully. "Here," she said, handing me a modest gown. "Take this old frock and remove all the stitching in the bodice."

I thought I had heard wrong, but she laughed at my surprise and urged me on. Then she jumbled the pieces and said, "Now put it together again, but give it a different neckline." What fun I had! "See? You have a skill," she said when all was done. "You now can cut through fabric without trepidation and make it be what you want."

I found that knowledge quite dazzling, although Louisa hooted down all domestic skills. The tomboy who could throw herself into a stack of dry leaves with a whoop and a holler and care not a fig what anyone thought had little use for needlework. And oh, the plays! After the time of my unfortunate peek into Abba's oven, Louisa wrote a grand one about helping escaping slaves, which she insisted we act out each time I visited—although, truth be told, I tired of being assigned the part of the little colored boy and always worried someone would fire up the stove with me in it. Louisa was always writing wonderful stories. "I will be a famous writer, wait and see," she would declare, and I believed her totally.

Beth rarely acted, but she would provide musical accompaniment, as she was the only one able to pick out tunes on the wheezy old piano. She always seemed remote and ethereal to me, sitting there, smiling, a blue or pink ribbon bobbing in her curly hair. I overheard Mother whisper once to my father as Beth played, "A bit of a wind could blow that child away."

May, of course, the baby of the family, was the flippant one the adults loved to spoil and, from the start, my competition for attention. She teased me constantly about my nose until I caught her drawing picture of noses one day—fine, Grecian noses, none of which looked remotely like her own. "Well, mine looks more like those pictures than yours does," I declared. She covered the page with her hand. "It does not," she retorted. "Well, I think it does," I said, "and that means you are envious of me, and that's a sin!" With this righteous declaration, I flounced off, mightily pleased with myself.

But May and I would put aside our differences when it came time to be part of one of Louisa's productions. What fun we had! Louy would retreat to the barn to write a script and then run to the house, hair flying, calling to us to come learn our lines and choose our costumes. She would stand in the loft, arms on her hips, and give a summary of her latest splendid tale with such fervor I would hang on every word. None of us ever questioned the fact that Louy always got to play the dashing hero or, if she so chose, the passionate, enterprising heroine. Why would we? She was always the best on play night, striding to the center of the parlor stage in front of the Emersons, the Channings, and the Hosmers, and whomever else Abba could cajole into coming, her voice ringing clear and strong as she saved threatened damsels and denounced dastardly villains.

"Oh Louy, I love Ernest L'Estrange, he's so romantic," Anna breathed, her plump cheeks flushed with color. It was the day we began rehearsing "The Curse of Castille," Louisa's best play ever, I thought. The hero she created was indeed thrilling, so thrilling that the Queen of Maltonia, denounced as a witch after falling in love with this strange commoner, refuses to betray her lover even as she is about to be burned at the stake. L'Estrange gallops into the flames on his horse, cuts her bonds with his sword, and swoops her up into his arms.

"He cradles her body with great tenderness, holding her with manful strength," Louisa said breathlessly. "Then she wraps her arms around his neck and shivers at the feel of his lips on her throat as they gallop away to safety." She spread her arms out wide and bowed before her enthralled audience of four. "The end."

"Wonderful, so exciting," sighed Anna, as we all clapped. "How do you make him so real?"

"He's the perfect man," Louisa announced. "He is strong and virile, and kind and true. He's the man I would love if I could find him!"

Beth giggled, pale hand to her lips. "I thought you never wanted to marry," she teased.

"I would give my heart to the right man," Lou retorted. "But I suspect he doesn't exist, so I've just had to make him up."

"Well, old Henry isn't Ernest L'Estrange, that's the truth," murmured May, trying to keep her voice low enough so Lou wouldn't hear.

But Louisa did hear. She cast one of her most forbidding frowns at her sister for this disparaging mention of Henry Thoreau. "I'll not stand one word against Henry," she said. "He comes closer to the grand design of what a man should be than anyone."

May wiggled impatiently. No one understood Louisa's fascination with the chilly, awkward Thoreau.

"He's too short," May said, undeterred. "And I'd be afraid he'd kiss me with asparagus in his teeth. Has he kissed you, Louy?"

"May! How dare you?" Louisa demanded angrily.

I kicked May with my foot, alarmed that Louisa would cancel our play and send us all back inside. "She didn't mean it," I said. "Please, let's keep going. It's a lovely play, and all the parts are wonderful! May, say you're sorry."

"I'm sorry, Lou, I'm just having fun. Anyway, I'm tired of practicing my lines. Let's choose costumes—we have some new ones that Marmee sewed last night." May skipped over to a basket of fabrics by the barn door and plunged her hands in. "Oh, look, green doublets with plush puffs! From Marmee's old draperies, aren't they? Who wears them? Ernest L'Estrange? I want to wear them." She looked fretful, then her face cleared as she spied a large, wicked dagger made from tin. "Ooooh, can I carry that? I'm the villain, won't that work well?"

Louisa, back in the spirit of the day, handed it to her with a flourish just as I spied a garment stitched of red and green silk. I pulled it from the basket and held it up. It was a perfectly splendid cloak with an upright collar and a grand sweep of fabric that took my breath away. There were no goods of such quality in the Alcott home, even I knew that. Abba must have been given the material, perhaps by Mrs. Emerson. Come to think of it, it did look like a gorgeous comforter I had once spied on the Emerson bed.

"I love that," said Beth, her eyes shining.

Louisa, in the act of reaching for it, hesitated as she glanced at her little sister. Beth had one of her headaches that day, but she had loyally rehearsed as Lady Suzette with great eagerness, and Lou didn't want to deny her anything. "Then it is yours to wear," she said.

Beth took the cloak, stroking its folds. It was unusual for her to express a desire for something. She wrapped it around her body and was instantly swallowed up, her slight frame almost disappearing inside its splendor.

"It is pretty on you," offered May, with surprising generosity.

Beth laughed, removing the wrap. "Oh girls, it's too much for me. Lou, you're the only one who can wear this and do it justice. You have the flair for it."

"No——" Lou began to protest.

Beth was firm. "It's your cloak. It's your *glory* cloak. You will do wonderful things wearing it, I am sure of it."

"Who is the weaver of tall tales now?" Lou said with a comical smile. But she took what was surely the grandest ever of our costume props and draped it over her shoulders, not all that reluctantly. It looked truly regal.

"Louy, you are the King of Everything," I said shyly.

*   *   *

When the typhoid epidemic hit in 1858, my parents ruled out all visits. I would stare out the window of our New York home each morning watching the death carts clatter by, masked workers stopping to pick up victims shoved out to the street—sometimes wrapped only in sheets—by families hoping to clear their houses of infection. As it worsened, we never left our house. I didn't worry when Mother first took to her bed—she always did during her monthly—but when I found my father lying on the floor and the servants gone, I knew. Within one week, both were dead. I pinned a ribbon on my mother's bosom and combed my father's hair before wrapping their bodies in our very best damask table-cloths. Then I hauled them out alone, weeping, expecting to be next with none to take care of me.

The epidemic finally ended. At the age of sixteen, although alive through no divine intercession I could perceive, I was spun loose of my moorings. An elderly spinster aunt who lived upstate first took me in, but I found no comfort in a home dominated by religion and righteousness. Aunt Hope confiscated immediately upon my arrival all items of "frivolity," which included not only all my mother's pretty things but my treasured sketchbook and package of charcoal, declaring I was not to be distracted from a responsible life. I soon learned that meant I was to be on my knees night and day thanking God that I had a roof over my head. I would have felt more grateful if Aunt Hope had believed in lighting a warm fire once in a while, but she considered cold toes and fingers somehow purifying. Some three months after my arrival I mustered the courage to protest, and she responded calmly.

"You've been spoiled, child," she proclaimed as we sat in her dingy parlor, inhaling dust from the heavy folds of her ancient, velvet drapes. "Your parents are dead, and God wants you to accept that. No more moping about, no pining, no weeping at night. Do you hear me? Not only is your protracted mourning unhealthy, it hinders your spiritual development. We must work on that. Now make the tea and we will pray together."

I cast about in my mind for an escape. Who could I turn to? Where was the warmth and love that I craved? Only in Concord.

That night I wrote to Louisa, scribbling a long letter smeared by tears, begging for rescue. Posting it secretly was difficult, but post it I did. I resolved not to let Aunt Hope consume me with her unending prayers.

Weeks went by. I checked the mail daily. Had Louisa forgotten me?

And then one cold October night there was an unexpected, sturdy hammering at the door. Aunt Hope opened it with caution, and when I heard the booming voice of Silas Forrest, owner of the hay fields next to the Alcotts' old place in Concord, I knew Louisa had not abandoned me.

"Madam, I'm here at the behest of Mr. and Mrs. Bronson Alcott to collect Miss Susan Gray," he announced in awkwardly formal fashion. "She's to be brought home to Concord, begging your pardon. Per her own wishes, I may add."

Aunt Hope turned to me, with something in her eyes I could not identify at the time, and know now was a form of hurt. I had a brief glimpse of her fragile, spinster-dry heart. She had done only what she was capable of, and the fact that it fell far short of what I needed did not spare her. "You want to leave?" she asked.

"Yes," I said.

"Then you shall," she said, crisp as a cracker. The shift was speedily arranged. There were few necessary good-byes. I took time to nuzzle my aunt's ancient hearth cat, the only warm body in that home, and then packed my bags as quickly as I could, my heart light.

"I wish you well," Aunt Hope said after Mr. Forrest had loaded the carriage. "The Alcotts are the only other relatives you have who will take you, and you are probably delighted they are rabid abolitionists."

"Yes, ma'am." I stood on the porch step, pulling at my shawl.

"What is it, Susan?" she asked impatiently.

"I want my sketchbook."

"Your *what?*"

"My book with my dress designs. You took it, and my mama gave it to me and I want it back."

Silas Forrest sat poised in the driver's seat, saying nothing. I stared at my aunt and refused to budge.

"Trash, your mind has nothing in it but trash," she muttered. She picked up her skirts and retreated to the library. I saw her open a drawer, caught a glimmer of my mother's diamond brooch, and then saw the blue leather cover of my precious book in her hands. My heart began hammering. She stalked back to the porch and thrust it rudely into my hands. "It is time for you to go," she said.

"I want my charcoal."

This time she said nothing as she returned to the library. Again I saw the glimmer of what could only be my mother's brooch as she opened the drawer. But when she withdrew a small chamois drawstring bag and brought it to me, dropping it disdainfully into my hand, I felt whole.

"Thank you," I said.

"So, that godless mother of yours managed to teach you some manners." She stepped back from the buggy, lacing her hands tight in front of her stomach. Clutching my sketchbook and charcoal, I climbed quickly in. Mr. Forrest tipped his hat to Aunt Hope, spoke softly to his horses, and we were off. I could not believe it. I was free. Louisa had saved me. I did not turn to wave good-bye.

Silas Forrest was not much of a talking man, and I traveled somewhat lonesomely, for he would not answer my questions about the family I so eagerly looked forward to joining. They'd had some "hard times," he said, but it wasn't for him to gossip, and they would tell me all. But he did volunteer one thing that kept me warm through that long journey. "Miss Alcott told me to take good care of you, that it's high time someone did," he said. That was worth the extra shawl I lacked to shield me better from the cold.

We stopped at an inn that night and reached Concord the next day near dusk. The Alcotts had moved to the outskirts of town since my last visit, and I squinted into the waning light to see the new home they called Orchard House. It was a simple brown clap-board house with a gabled roof and a center dormer over the entrance, set back from the road against a gentle slope of maple and oak trees. It looked inviting. I could see warm lights within, and my heart was beating fast as I ran up the path, aching to hear the laughter of the girls and smell the comforting cooking from Abba's kitchen.

The door flew open and there was Abba Alcott, comfortable, round Abba, standing in the passageway, her arms flung open in greeting. "Welcome back, dear," she said, her eyes soft and quite wet. "Such sad circumstances for you, and for us."

Behind her stood Louisa, looking much more grown-up than she had a year ago, and I suddenly felt shy. She seemed less tall to me, but her chin was surely as stubborn as my father's, something I hadn't noticed before. Her long, dark hair was parted severely in the center now, pulled so tight that a thin ribbon of pink scalp shone through. Nothing about her looked delightfully scattery, and I caught no liveliness in her eyes. No signal for fun. What had I expected? Furtively, I arranged my face. My parents were dead; what was wrong with me that I had half-skipped into this house, ready to play?

I glanced past Louisa and saw Anna in a plaid dress, her much more rounded body looking eerily like her mother's. May stood in the shadows, pulling on yellow curls and chewing on her finger-nails. She, at least, reacted the way I had expected: not exactly welcoming, but with wary curiosity.

"Where is Beth?" I asked.

Abba sank against the door frame, shoulders heaving. With a cry, Anna rushed forward to hold her mother up. What had I done? May made a face, turned and fled. Only Louisa stepped forward and spoke to me directly.

"We've lost her, Susan. She died but a few months ago."

"Oh, I'm so sorry!" I burst into tears, knowing already that any-thing bad that happened to this family happened also to me. I longed at that moment, overgrown child that I was, for the beloved old rag doll that Aunt Hope had taken from me and tossed out when I first arrived at her home. I wanted to hug it now for comfort. But suddenly, Louisa was hugging me.

When she spoke, it was directly to her mother. "I think, Marmee," she said, her voice breaking slightly, "we now have a new sister to love."

Abba pulled herself straight, drying her tears. Louisa's words had produced the intended effect, and Abba rose to her duty. "Forgive me, Susan, dear. Our loss is still raw, but yours is even more so. Louisa, take her into the parlor, and I will bring in some apple cake."

"Don't worry, we are very happy you are here, especially me," Louisa whispered as she took my hand and led me forward. "Let's go say hello to Papa, who is in full gab. You know, one of his philosophical discourses."

We stepped into a small room with cream walls and dark pine floors. The floor was covered by a round braided rug, frayed at the edges, and Beth's old spinet stood against a wall at the foot of a back stairway. Resting against the outside parlor wall between two windows was a green horsehair sofa. On it, I recognized what we used to call Louisa's "mood pillow." In earlier years, when the pillow leaned at a comfortable angle, that meant Louisa was ready to laugh and play, but if it lay flat, we were supposed to tiptoe by and leave her alone. Tonight, it stood straight as a soldier snapping to attention.

The parlor flowed into a dining room, where a meal at the large cloth-covered table had obviously just been consumed. Bronson Alcott sat at the dining room table, bald on top with stringy gray hair, wearing knee breeches and a stained cravat, gesturing energetically as he argued with a portly companion whose nose had a strikingly prominent beak. I vaguely remembered seeing him before.

Bronson turned toward me without as much as a simple greeting and demanded: "We are discussing the role of women, which is, at its purest, to give moral example. Do you agree?"

"I don't know," I managed.

"Then hear my words, child. Women are more pure than men because they lack the malevolent passions." He redirected his gaze, now self-satisfied, toward his companion. "And that, my friend, is why they are in charge of shaping morality."

"I don't see why women should be responsible for men," I said. I had blurted the first thing that came to mind and immediately saw I had startled Bronson.

The other man chuckled and folded large hands over his waist-coat, tipping back in his chair. "A spirited response, my dear." He cast a slyly triumphant look at his host. "So much for your notion of the self-sacrificing nature of women, Bronson," he said.

"Susan—" Lou gave my hand a squeeze. "You remember our neighbor, Mr. Emerson, don't you?"

I nodded, mortified. The benefactor of the Alcotts; how could I forget him? My father had warned me often about my impetuous mouth. I wanted to tell them quickly I *was* properly trained, not someone without manners; that I had a tendency to say what I thought, but, please, I *knew* better.

"Papa, Susan's been traveling a long time and is quite tired, I'm sure," Louisa said. "I'm going to take her upstairs and tuck her in."

Bronson surveyed me like a befuddled shepherd faced with a balky lamb. "Ah, yes, of course. Welcome. Your father was a fine man, and we will miss him." He gave me a wintry nod and a pat on the shoulder, then turned back to Emerson.

I stood numbly by as they deplored Southern talk of secession from the Union, until Louisa picked up the plate of apple cake Abba had silently set down and beckoned me to follow her. We climbed the narrow staircase in the front hall to her bedroom, where I took off my boots. Louisa pulled the newspaper out that lined them and tossed it away without comment. She tucked the boots into a small closet and handed me a flannel nightgown to wear as I stood shivering in the unfamiliar room. "Oh dear, you look like a scared mouse, Susan," she said as she sniffed my hair, then wrinkled her nose. "Well, I'm glad you're in a house now that can spare soap and water for washing. You were always such a tidy little creature, scrubbing your face and hands after our plays, pinning all that curly hair up on top of your head."

"I've hardly thought of it for many weeks, and wouldn't care if it were never washed again, as long as I could be here." I wiggled into the nightgown, savoring the soft comfort of the well-washed flannel. "I thought I would die in that gloomy, sour place. What would I have done if you hadn't saved me?"

"You're a resourceful girl, although I suspect you would have been glum forever and missed us dreadfully," she said with a smile. "Instead you get to confront Papa and Mr. Emerson and reshape the woman question for the Transcendentalists. Aren't you the fortunate one?"

"Was he angry just now?"

"Papa? Our dear old Plato? No, no, it does him good to get pulled up short once in a while. I've been performing that task since I was a child. And paying the price, of course." She smiled again, somewhat ruefully.

"You were wonderful at not being good all the time," I said, settling my bottom on the bed next to her. "I still remember the night you drank his cider in back of the barn and got tipsy."

"Now why would you remember that? Thinking of it makes me headachy and dizzy all over again."

"You couldn't walk straight," I offered.

"Must you remind me?"

I giggled. I felt warmer; less uncertain. "I emptied two basins for you that night to save you from discovery."

"Oh, Father knew when he saw his wild daughter looking ashen and clutching her stomach. But he never said anything. He did show tolerance." She picked at the rim of lace around her cuffs in an absentminded way. "You bring back such adventurous memories, dear. I'd like to feel that daring, that buoyant, again. But we all have to grow up and put youthful pleasures aside."

Her sober tone made me think of my own sudden somersault into maturity. My eyes filled with tears. "I miss my parents," I said, surprising myself with the blurted words.

"Of course, you do."

"Aunt Hope said I was mourning too much."

"Aunt Hope is an old bag of wind, and knows nothing. You miss them as I miss Beth."

I thought of quiet, timid Beth, who had been so easy to overlook. As a child I had thought of her more as a musical ornament, a pretty, frail girl who seemed happiest at the piano. She used to sneak me extra cookies.

"Do you remember when the five of us were sleeping in the attic that time when the wool-carder came running naked through the orchard . . ." I began timidly.

"Oh, goodness. Beth spotted him first, didn't she?"

"Under the full moon, dancing away."

Louisa began to giggle in that wonderful, throaty way I remembered. "What a hoot that was! That skinny, spindly man, loping among the trees . . . I can't remember Beth laughing more."

My voice tripped over the question, but I had to ask. "How did she die?"

Louisa's smile faded. "She was always frail, you know," she said.

I nodded, remembering how Lou would never let any of us quarrel with Beth, and how Abba was always running out to the barn on chilly days to drape an extra shawl over Beth's thin shoulders.

"The doctor called it consumption, but I think it was the aftermath of scarlet fever. She wasted away, slowly, day by day, and we could only watch, unable to do anything. We began bundling her each night in front of the fire, for she wouldn't stop sewing. She wouldn't rest. We would sit after dinner and watch her stitch away, making small remembrances for her friends—a pen wiper, a needlebook—until one night she put her needle down for the last time, saying it was too heavy." Louisa covered her face. "We put her to bed and she was gone within days."

"Oh Lou, that is unbearably sad."

"I know it is, but she was too good to live."

"Lou"—my literal streak won out—"goodness didn't kill her. Sickness did."

"Yes, of course, but why is it the truly good people who do no wrong to anyone are snatched away? I'm trying, trying to understand."

I nodded, unable to speak, thinking of my poor mother and father.

"She was so gentle, never prone to moods or anger—oh, I wish I could be like her. If I could be, if I could approach life with her sweet gentleness, I wouldn't fear death." Louisa had pulled her knees to her chest, rocking back and forth. "I might even welcome it."

I could not believe my ears. This, from Lou, my bold friend who loved life with such passion? "Don't say such a dreadful thing," I pleaded. "It's wicked, Lou. Why would you say such a thing?"

"Oh dear, I've forgotten how you drink in my every word." She reached out and squeezed my hand. "Don't worry, I'm not thinking of doing away with myself, but I do so want to be a better person. I have a terrible temper and such an impetuous nature, I tend to spoil things. I can't indulge myself anymore. Papa can't seem to make any money, and when he does, it disappears. I need to support this family, do you understand? But I hate being a teacher. I want to do it with my writing—and that means disciplining myself and becoming more serious."

Did I sense then that *my* Lou was already disappearing? Alarmed, I threw my arms around her.

"Spoil? *Spoil?* That isn't true! Was it impetuous to heed my plea and bring me here? To help a poor girl with nowhere else to turn? No, no, it was a warm and compassionate thing to do, and if that's what you call your 'impetuous nature,' I love it. I will repay it with loyalty all my life!"

She hugged me back, one of those great bear hugs unpoisoned by complexity that one remembers forever. "I rescued you because you are my dear little friend, and I couldn't leave you in such an unhappy place. I don't mean to frighten you. You know my dramatic nature; please don't be alarmed. But I'm sadder than I can say. How do I explain? When Beth died, a vital link in this family was taken away." Her eyes filled with tears that spilled down her cheeks. "We Alcotts are so woven together, the absence of one person alters us. But I'm going to fight. I don't want anything altered, I want us to stay as close and safe with each other as we've always been."

"I can't be Beth, but I will be a good sister, I swear I will. And things will get better."

"They will, I believe that, too. See? You've already raised my spirits. We have to support each other, don't we? If we do, maybe we can survive our losses together."

Her voice was so warm and serious, I hurried to answer. "Yes," I vowed. "Yes, yes."

She kissed the tip of my nose, just as she had that long-ago day in Abba's kitchen. "Now go to sleep. First thing tomorrow morning, we wash your hair."

Chapter Two

I hardly saw Louisa in those first few weeks. She spent most of her time in the bedroom, writing, and although I tried a variety of ruses to coax her out, none seemed to work.

"Louisa, help me get this latch undone!" I was in the attic, struggling to open the trunk that held all our theatrical costumes and props, feeling quite miffed that she wasn't there to help me haul everything down for our usual evening theatrics. The lid came up partway and I spied a shimmering garment of red and green. My heart quickened. Wasn't that the glory cloak? How wonderful that it was still here! I fingered the soft silk, wistful for the times it represented.

"What are you doing up there, Susan?" Ah, *this* had worked. I peered down and saw her standing, hands on hips, looking up at me from the bottom of the attic ladder.

"It's Saturday night," I said. "We always put on plays on Saturday night."

"You would remember, wouldn't you?" There was a note of regret in her voice. "I'm sorry, we don't really put on plays anymore. All my good ideas dried up. Now please come on down."

"Rubbish. You just don't want to do it." I wiped the dust off on my apron and climbed down the ladder, feeling quite put out. I was learning that living here permanently was not the same as visiting, and I hated to see how much things had changed. I had a home again that would not be snatched away, which was immensely comforting, but the sense of play I had loved in this family had not survived Beth's death. I felt guiltily bereft. No frolics anymore in the evenings? No ghost stories? I yearned for those delicious evenings when Louisa would give us all the shivers and then blow out the candles and make us sit in the dark to hear the end of some truly scary tale.

Louisa was frowning when I stepped off the last rung and faced her. "Susan, I can't do playful things anymore. I have to work on my writing, and try to sell as much of it as I can. Will you not accept that?"

"You can't spend *all* your time poking away at your stories."

"Would you like to read them for me? I mean, as my critic?"

"Are you serious?"

"Yes. You're as much of a bookworm as I am."

It was true; I did love stories, and I was flattered. "Well, yes, I would."

She smiled. "We have several bargains, don't we? I like this one. But now you must let me work to fulfill it." She edged away, blowing me a kiss. "Now go downstairs and visit with Abba. She misses you."

I found Abba in the kitchen, her face flushed with the heat of the oven. She deposited a tub of apples in front of me on the table. "Here, be a dear, pare these for me, will you? Tonight we'll have apple crisp for dessert."

I caught the wise glint in her eye and was mollified. But I yearned to do adventurous things again with Lou. I thought of how victorious I had felt when I first hung by the knees from a high branch, skirt above my head, ragged drawers exposed to the world. Why did childhood have to end? I wanted the old Lou at my side, urging me on to do other daring things, but it was not to be. Sometimes she was in Boston, teaching or working as a governess—jobs she loathed. When she was home, scribbling away, I would peek into the room and try to coax her outside—until she sold a small book of fairy tales for thirty-two dollars to *The Saturday Evening Gazette*. After that, she was in a fever to sell more. "I can't stop now," she declared.

Still, every now and then she would indeed hand me a batch of pages to read. I did so a bit shyly, even dutifully, and found myself amazed by one lurid, passionate tale after another.

"Susan, take a look at this," she said one afternoon, handing me a stack of pages. "If I don't have time to act in plays, at least I can write about someone who does."

I scanned the title—*Marion Earle; or, Only an Actress!*—and flopped onto the bed. I was soon absorbed in the story of Marion, a kindly actress who takes in and shelters an unmarried young girl named Agnes and her baby. Marion then falls in love with the dashing Robert Leicester, unaware that he is the man who wronged her young friend.

But the day of their wedding, Agnes, who knows only that Robert is marrying some unknown woman, forces her way into the ceremony and holds her baby aloft, crying for justice. Marion insists that Agnes step forward and take her place at the altar with a shamefaced Robert while she, "motionless and white as a marble image, stood with the child upon her arm, looking straight before her with eyes that saw only utter darkness."

Dastardly man, I thought as I turned the page, thoroughly absorbed. He'll come to no good.

And of course he disappears after the wedding, leaving Marion and Agnes to raise the baby—reappearing three years later to collapse with a life-threatening fever on their doorstep. Marion nurses him back to health and reunites him with Agnes and their baby. Then she dies.

"Oh dear," I said, as I finished the final page.

"Don't you like it?" Lou asked.

"Oh, it's a capital read!" I said.

"I know it's a potboiler, of course—"

"It's quite exciting and people will surely love it. Such friendship between the two women!"

Louisa beamed.

"But why does Marion punish herself so? Why does she break her own health and die while taking care of that awful, weak man?

And, um, well, there is a great deal of activity——" Alarmed, I saw Louisa's smile fading.

"Susan, it's just a sensation story. I'm writing it to make money, and I do *not* think there is too much activity." She frowned and chewed on her pen, thanked me, and then gently suggested I leave her alone so she could continue working.

I said no more, realizing I wasn't expected to invest myself in her stories, just read them. I was her special audience of one; not a critic, I thought as I left the room.

"You're wasting your time," May announced in the hallway. She had emerged from her room, paintbrush in hand, a blotch of yellow paint on her nose. Her grubby painting smock made her look quite industrious, and, now that Louisa was paying for art lessons, she daily proclaimed herself a real painter.

"I'm helping her. And she can't work all day and all night," I protested.

"Of course, she can," May retorted. "You see what's happening. She lies in bed and thinks up whole plots and then scribbles away without eating or talking for days. Who wouldn't? By the way, that silly old Henry is courting Ellen Sewell, did you know that?"

"No," I said, astonished.

"Well, he's mooning about, and Lou is devastated. She can't bear the idea of spending her life cleaning houses or drilling math into the heads of sleepy children, and she can't bear watching Henry's flirtation. So that means losing herself in work. She received thirty dollars for her last story, isn't that fine? I'm going to succeed, too. She'll be a famous writer and I'll be a famous painter. What will you be?"

"I'll be the one who wipes the paint off your nose," I said.

"Oh bother, you're just jealous!" May turned on her heel and disappeared back into her room. I wanted to run after her and tell her I was just lonely, but instead I went downstairs and curled up on the horsehair sofa, feeling quite sorry for myself. Everybody was too busy for me. Abba was either toiling at home or helping care for poor families; May was too dazzled with her daubing; and

Anna, well, Anna was constantly mooning over an insurance man named John Pratt. Anybody could see she was smitten, although Louisa had grown quite cross when I had suggested as much the Sunday before.

The old green sofa became one of my favorite solitary resting places. In the days that followed, I began reading some of Bronson's books while curled up there, my toes tucked beneath Lou's mood pillow, and found the hours flying by. I was deep into *Plutarch's Lives* one afternoon when the front door suddenly flew open. Anna burst into the vestibule.

"Susan?" She looked around. "Are you alone?"

I nodded, a bit mystified. The usually placid Anna stood there another moment, seemingly struggling with some decision, then moved swiftly into the room and sat next to me.

"I'm going to be married," she whispered.

"Oh, my goodness, that's wonderful," I said, flattered she had taken me into her confidence, but confused at her agitation.

"John is the most wonderful man in the world," she hurried on. "I know this will be hard on Marmee, and Lou so detests marriage, but it is all I have ever wanted. You'll support me, won't you?" Her voice had turned pleading.

"Of course," I said. "But why are you worried? Surely your mother—"

"Oh, she'll hate to see me go. We're a bit of a queer lot, I guess. Or at least some people seem to think so," Anna said. She leaned closer, whispering again. "Do you know what I heard that dreadful Mrs. Hawthorne say? Well, she isn't dreadful, but she is very critical, truly. I overheard her tell a friend at the post office that we Alcott sisters are no longer girls. And she questioned why we continue to live at home and live unmarried, arrested lives. That's what she actually said: 'arrested lives'!" Anna's cheeks turned pink.

"That's rubbish," I said. "Why would she say such a ridiculous thing? It's—"

"It's dreadfully unfair, of course. But, well, it's always been hard to go outside of the family circle. I'm not terribly brave." Anna let out a deep sigh. "I love my family dearly but I love John, too, and I want to be away from the contention and disagreements of home. I want a peaceful life."

I understood. In a family where everyone said what they thought with little self-censoring, Anna shrank from the slightest friction. Any bickering or stomping up the stairs, and Anna would flee the house. But to leave for John Pratt? I loved romance, to be sure, and it was uncharitable of me to think that John Pratt seemed bland and boring. They met at a corn-husking party, and Anna said she knew from the very first ear of corn that he was the man for her. How could I not cheer her on?

"I'm sure you will be very happy," I said, and squeezed her hand.

"Thank you." She squeezed back. "I so want Louisa to find happiness, too. I hear Ellen Sewell has rejected Henry's proposal of marriage. What do you think of that?"

My eyes widened. "Oh, my goodness, is it true?"

"The best gossips in town say so," she said with a smile. "Do you think Lou will brighten when she hears?"

"Without a doubt," I predicted.

"My dear sister—perhaps she has something to hope for again." She looked at me somewhat diffidently. "May I ask a favor, Susan? Will you help make my wedding dress? I'm neither young nor pretty, but I would love something beautiful—maybe of silvery gray."

"You would trust me?" I was immensely flattered.

"Susan, didn't I teach you to sew?" She gave me a quick kiss on the top of my head and jumped up. "Now I'm going to tell the rest of the family."

She disappeared upstairs as I began imagining what the wedding dress would look like. First, I would construct an artful bodice, nothing ordinary; I would use antique lace; and then . . . I sighed. Finally, I had something fun to do, something quite grown-up. My earlier petulance felt embarrassing. How nice that it was Anna, peaceful Anna, who coaxed me out of it.

Then came the storm. First I heard murmuring voices, then shouting from upstairs. Then crying. And finally, Louisa came thundering down the stairs. She strode to the front door, on her way out, when she spied me in the parlor. "Susan, get your coat and come walk with me," she demanded.

Only too happy to oblige, I was soon scrambling to keep up with her long stride as we headed back into the woods.

"How can she do this? What is *wrong* with my sister?" Louisa burst out. "We have only just lost our Beth, and this family must stick together! What does she think she is *doing?*"

"But she loves him and she's twenty-seven," I offered.

"He's too ordinary! Anyhow, she doesn't need a man to take care of her. I can take care of everybody, so there's no need for her to willfully break up the family!" Louisa threw herself down by a thick oak tree and buried her head in her hands. I had never seen her so upset.

"I don't understand," I ventured. "Isn't that what most women want? To get married, I mean?"

She hoisted herself up on her elbows. Leaves were stuck in her hair, giving her a slightly wild look. "Why?" she demanded. "Love is nonsense. Look what marriage does to women. Why should any of us want it? Marmee has been worn to a nub through years of hard work and worrying about money. I don't want that for my sisters. Why doesn't Anna see I can take care of her? Why is she doing this to me?"

"She isn't doing anything to you," I protested. "You are much too hard on her. It isn't fair."

"Don't you scold, I just need you to listen. Doesn't she *love* me?"

"Well, I *am* listening—" I started, and then stopped. For the first time I heard the pain in Louisa's voice, not just anger and indignation. Her question hung between us, buttressed by a sudden, sad, frightened look in her eyes. I realized it was from the heart.

"Of course, she loves you," I replied, stunned.

She blinked, and the frightened look faded. "You must think me crazed," she said finally.

"No, no, you were taken by surprise," I reassured her. But I wondered, did Louisa want *nothing* to change? She was standing up against love and marriage like a defender of the North Bridge. If she truly rejected such a destiny for herself, did that mean no one else in the family could marry?

Her mood was relaxing. "But Susan, even if I *am* being unfair, don't be bossy. That's my role, remember?"

At least her voice sounded normal again.

"I'm not trying to be bossy, I just know Anna is happy, and maybe if John becomes comfortable enough to speak up more, you'll like him better. He's timid, a bit. But so was I, isn't that true?"

Louisa, still prone and poised on her elbows, gazed at me speculatively. "You've got some of the same impulsiveness that plagues me. But I see what Marmee means when she says you have an old head on young shoulders. You're saying I can't force Anna to do what I want her to do."

"I'm not that young. I'm sixteen. Anyway, that *is* what I'm saying, but you are free to boss me back." I wanted more than anything to shrink the decade of time between myself and Louisa.

There was a glint in her eye. "All right, I accept your invitation. If I am to be more charitable to Anna, can you not be more charitable to May?"

"Why?" I said. And immediately, shamefacedly, corrected myself. "How?"

"Just stop teasing her about her nose."

I thought of May wearing that ridiculous clothespin on her nose when she slept, futilely trying to pinch it into a more elegantly Grecian shape, and giggled. Hand to mouth, I nodded my head. "I will," I said. And then, as lightly as possible, I added, "I have some news for you."

"What is it?" she asked, immediately alert.

"Henry and Ellen are no longer courting, I hear."

"Truly?" Her face flushed.

"Anna heard it. Ellen turned him down."

"Oh, my goodness." She turned her face slightly away.

"So there's hope after all," I said teasingly.

Her color was still high as she turned back to me. "I can't imagine what for," she said. But her step was almost buoyant as she stood and took my hand; together, we headed back to the house.

The next morning I came downstairs expecting a more sunny Louisa, but I saw her sitting by the parlor window staring out, looking quite dejected.

"Is something wrong?" I asked, hoping no other sudden family flights from the nest were in the offing.

She sighed with great heaviness. "I must face the truth, Susan. My work is no good; it's just trash. James Fields was right."

"What?" I was not prepared.

"Remember when I showed him my story about the time I went out to service? I should have listened to his advice."

"Mr. Hawthorne's publisher?" I groped for the connection.

She nodded. "I was stupid enough to try to write about something real that happened to me. About the time I took a job in Dedham."

I vaguely remembered. Lou had gone to work as an old lady's companion and was forced not only to scrub floors and clean fireplaces but to fend off the woman's brother until she finally marched out—and was paid a measly four dollars for weeks of hard work. "What did Mr. Fields say when he read the story?" I asked.

She cleared her throat, stared at me over imaginary glasses and harrumphed in a deep voice: "Stick to your teaching, Miss Alcott. You can't write."

"What a rude boor!" I said with great indignation. "How dare he?"

"He said my characters were too one-dimensional."

I could hear the hurt in her voice, and knew well enough by now how sensitive she was to criticism, how quick to despair. Why was this depressing her now, so long after the fact? I rushed to reassure. "I don't care how important a personage he is, he was wrong," I declared.

She seemed not to hear. "I'll tell you what the problem is. The problem is that I overreach. I want too much."

"You want to be a successful writer. Why does that mean 'you overreach'?"

"I am not talented enough. I can't expect more than I have."

"Why *not?*" I was beside myself, now.

"I feel like a fool, writing away. But I can't let go of the dream that someday I might write something truly wonderful. Is that stupid and vain?"

"Of course not. You'll do it! You'll be respected and you'll be rich and your mother won't lift a finger anymore and May will travel the world, and we won't be just eating apples for sweets." I put on enough of a comical face to coax a laugh. Her mood lightened and together we headed for the kitchen to help with breakfast; she, purged of self-doubt for the moment and I, imbued with the knowledge I could give comfort as well as receive it.

"By the way," she paused at the doorstep and smiled. "You were right about my little story about the actress. There *was* too much activity."

"No matter, you sold it," I said cheerfully.

Did I truly think she would become rich and famous? I don't know. But from then on when she handed me stories to read, I spoke up firmly about what I liked and disliked.

I also began to understand the fragility of her confidence. My wonderful Lou was a creative person, but what she created were people and ideas. When I drew Anna's wedding dress, I could go to the dry goods store and hold up different fabrics to see how they draped—I could touch them, move them, shape them—fabric doesn't disappear. It glows with quality if it rests, unused, on a shelf. It is tangible. But who fully trusts the imagination? If ideas are offered to the world and rejected, who is confident that trying again is the brave thing to do or simply an act of empty arrogance?

*   *   *

After some flustered soothing of her mother and Louisa, Anna decided to postpone her marriage. "Just to give them a little more time to get used to the idea," she told me with a sigh. The delay gave me time to sketch dozens of designs for Anna's dress, sitting in the parlor, with Anna watching over my shoulder. We would giggle and dream and go together to the dry goods store to hunt for just the right lace edging. I entertained my own dreams and fantasies during those months, but they were threaded with vague anxiety. If Anna's determination to marry was seen as such a defection, what other transgressions might be seen the same way? What if I ever said or did something they deplored? I thought back to the lonely, frightening final weeks of my parents' lives, and tasted the fear of abandonment again. Once again I heard the relentless ticking of the old hall clock in my family home, hating it; wanting time to stop; wanting to hold off the inevitable. Kneeling by my mother's side on the last morning of her life, I wept because I could no longer coax a bit of gruel or even water between her lips. "Poor baby," she had whispered, "who will take care of you and love you, my darling? I fear your fate will be harder than mine."

Oh Mama, Mama, I thought as I bent over my sketchbook. With the Alcotts, that won't be true. Surely.

Louisa was standing in front of the fireplace, deep in thought, wearing the dress I made for her to wear to Concord's 1859 Autumn Ball, a grand affair Anna had somehow coaxed her younger sister into attending. I had happily volunteered to fashion both their dresses. Louisa pretended not to care about clothes, but she did consult me warily on occasion, and paid me the compliment at one point of saying, "You do have a way with fashion, Susan, and I certainly do not." But she was a balky subject, one who would shift and complain as I knelt with a mouthful of pins, trying to fix a hem. We fired off at each other on these occasions, but she would eventually settle down and was indeed interested in how she appeared in the looking glass when her gown was complete.

"See? Look how pretty you are," I said that night, as she slowly twirled in front of the glass, stiff as a marionette.

"I am not pretty, and I don't like the feeling of clothes that constrict me and make me breathe short and stumble over my feet," she declared. She moved away to stand in front of the roaring fire. "Fashion makes me feel like a plumed hen."

I must have looked hurt, because she hastened to reassure me. "You've made a lovely dress, and it is wonderful. It's just that I so often wish I had been born a boy!"

I laughed, for this was the "glorious complaint," as I had dubbed it one day after years of hearing it, especially after a day of running and jumping and swimming. I stopped suddenly, sniffing the air.

"What is that awful smell?" I said.

Louisa jumped forward and turned to look at her dress. "What an idiot I am—look what I've done. My sash is burnt."

"Maybe you did it on purpose. You don't want to go because you're afraid Henry won't dance with you." May raised a saucy eyebrow.

I gritted my teeth at her tease as I inspected the damage. But in truth, I feared that, too. Nothing seemed to be happening between them. A long-ago scene from one of my childhood visits flashed through my mind.

Bored as only a child can be and feeling daring, I had secretly followed Lou and Henry around Walden Pond one day—he in his wide-brimmed straw hat, striding so fast even Louisa with her long legs had to trot to keep up. He did indeed look like a stork, I remembered thinking. I had been about to give up my pursuit when Louisa suddenly stopped, clutched his hand in hers, and, in a quick, theatrical gesture, laid her head on his breast. I slapped my hands to my mouth and giggled. She was playing the role of Bettina again! We had just acted out Goethe's *Correspondence with a Child*, and she was reenacting it with Henry as Goethe! Oh, that was funny. Henry seemed to freeze in place, but then gently put her away from him. He turned his head to where the sun glinted against the water. "Look," I heard him say, his voice thin as a goat's bleat. "There's a blue heron."

Louisa followed his gaze, her face hidden from me, and I barely caught her words. "A lovely sight," she murmured in an unnaturally muted voice. I retraced my steps, thinking how blessed Henry had been with the appearance of the heron—and being careful not to crunch any leaves on the path.

Later that night, the oil lamp in the room extinguished, Louisa spoke softly from her bed. "I saw you spying on us today," she said.

I was chagrined. "I'm sorry," I whispered.

"I know you think Henry is a stick, but he is not an object of mockery."

"I wasn't mocking him, I just don't understand what you find so *enthralling*."

She sighed, a deep, heavy expiration of breath. "There are feelings you are too young yet to know about."

I bridled. "I'm not a baby, I know more than you think."

"But you have not yet found a kindred spirit."

I lay there, absorbing her words, a tingle of expectation working its way down my spine. *This* was interesting. "You love him?" I asked.

"His spirit. His mind. That's what I love."

"Well then, will you marry him?"

"No, no—" she seemed flustered. "Of course not. I can't imagine why I would. He's been my teacher since I was a young girl. He's simply magnificent, Susan. His heart is quiet and observant, unlike any other I've known." She stopped, struggling to put her thoughts into words. "He makes me realize what I could be if I were a better person. He is fine and pure and connected to nature, and . . . completely self-sufficient."

My brain went stubbornly to his pushing her away at Walden Pond. "Well, I don't see why, if you love him, you can't marry him."

"I don't think you understand. Anyway," she sighed, "I am too wild and queer."

"You are not wild and queer, your father just makes you think you are."

Louisa pulled herself up on one elbow, and I could sense her staring at me through the gloom. "Papa is far from perfect, and he has trouble holding a job, but he does love me and everyone in the family, and I'll thank you not to fault him for every sad thought I have about myself."

"I'm sorry," I said for the second time that night. Louisa might deplore her father's fecklessness, but she would brook no criticism of him from me. And I hadn't asked my real question, which was why, if this was such a pure love, did she seem to become someone else when she was around Henry? Someone not as funny; someone who might enjoy breathing short in a corset. She was playacting, I was sure of it, and that confused my childish reasoning, for I knew her as strong and brave and true.

"Susan! Susan, aren't you listening? Is her sash fixable or do I go by myself?"

I blinked. May stood before me, dressed and ready to leave for the dance, hands on her hips, alternately staring at me and glaring at her sister. I gazed at the piece of burnt material in my hand and realized I had been daydreaming again. "I'll just stitch the bow smaller, that's all. See?" My fingers flew. "It's almost done."

"It isn't that I don't want to go," Louisa said to May in a placating tone. "I'm just a clumsy oaf, that's all. If things were fair, Susan would go in my stead." She shot me an understanding look, and I smiled. Bronson had decreed I wasn't old enough for such a sophisticated event. I suspected it had more to do with the cost, but I also wondered, at times, whether he had some need to hold me separate from the core of this loved household. I sensed exclusion from no one else, not even the irritating May, who would on occasion show me how to hold a paintbrush and daub brilliant flowers onto her precious scraps of canvas. And she and I had begun to play checkers with each other in the evenings, something we both enjoyed.

"What kind of man do you want to marry?" she asked one evening in the midst of a slow game. "Someone like Henry?"

"Oh no," I said promptly. "I dream of someone quite different."

"Tell me," she coaxed.

"Someone handsome and funny who laughs a lot and likes to dance and treats me like a queen." I blushed. This was more than I had intended to say.

"That's how I feel, too. Someone exciting, right?" She sighed. "Like Ernest L'Estrange. Not like that spindly, ethereal Henry. I can't imagine why Lou still moons over him all the time."

"She loves his cerebral nature."

"Can you imagine having him touch you? Oh, I know I mustn't poke fun, but can you?"

I giggled in spite of myself. "No," I said.

"What about Noah Williams? He's quite handsome and pleasant." I saw the wicked look in her eye as she tossed in the name of one of the town's more eligible bachelors.

"Much too sure of himself," I said calmly. "And his laugh is shrill."

"I agree. Isn't that fortunate? We share something in common."

"But I'm better at checkers." I made a swift move on the board and May grimaced when she realized I had won the game.

"Oh bother, Susan. You're as aggressive as Lou. Let's play one more, please?"

Contented times. All seemed right in my adopted home as I waved good-bye to my "sisters" on their way to the dance. I felt safe at last.

I awoke later that night to the sound of excited voices downstairs and footsteps running on the path outside. It wasn't the lighthearted chatter of the girls coming back from the ball. Something else was happening.

I jumped from bed and pulled on my wrapper, then went to the head of the stairs and peeked down. May and Louisa were there; Anna and John as well. But there were others gathering, a cluster of solemn-faced townspeople. I saw Mr. Emerson and Mr. Hawthorne; Bronson was ushering them all into the parlor. Louisa, looking frightfully pale, glanced up and saw me. To my relief, she hurried up the stairs.

It is strange how time seems to stop at the moment of a life-changing event. The smaller details register first: the cacophony of voices drifting up the stairs; an ugly tear in the hem of Louisa's dress; an itching that began in my scalp and spread to the palms of my hands.

"What's wrong?" I whispered as the voices in the parlor grew louder.

"Do you remember John Brown?" she asked.

"Of course," I said, with a shiver. Bronson had always admired Brown, though others in town dismissed him as a reckless firebrand. As far as I was concerned, he scared me as much now as he had when I was eight years old.

"He raided a place in Virginia called Harper's Ferry. Crazy, noble man! He took the federal armory, intending to arm the slaves for a revolt. A mob tore him down, and even cut the ears off a freed slave fighting alongside of him. He's in jail now, and will be tried for treason." She was having trouble breathing.

"But what he wanted to do was a good thing," I said, loyal abolitionist that I was.

"Yes, but suicidal, for the government in Washington fears he may trigger a slave uprising. He'll be hanged, wait and see."

"That would be terrible," I said.

"Father says it could be the match that ignites war."

It was the first time I focused on the central word that had become part of our dinner-table conversation, argued up and down and back and forward as we passed the potatoes and beans.

The trial was swift. And Louisa's prediction came true, only three months later. The day of the hanging, bells tolled throughout Concord, cutting harshly through the crisp winter air. The people of Concord met at the town hall and we all bowed our heads in both prayer and despair. We were shaken to the core, and everyone spoke now of the possibility of war in somber tones. The world

was shifting beneath our feet in a way none of us could yet understand. Louisa reached out to Henry as we left the church, and I
saw him sigh heavily, shake his head, and move away. Her cheeks
reddened as she turned back to me.

Much later, after all were asleep, I awoke to find Louisa gone
from her bed. I crept downstairs and found her curled tight in
Bronson's chair in his study, her face tight with suffering and stained
with tears.

"We will prevail," I began with some timidity, touching her
shoulder. Was she crying about the hanging, I wondered, or Henry's
slight?

She shook my hand away with a tiny gesture of impatience. "I
know we will, at least I hope so. But that's not why I'm flooding
the place with tears. What a mess I am!" She buried her face in her
hands. "I'm a fraud. All this day I've bowed my head and mourned
Mr. Brown, but I've been hiding something."

I was baffled. "What happened?"

"I'm happy, tremendously happy. Can you believe, on this day,
I would say that? Can you imagine such sacrilege?" She uncurled a
fist and showed me a crumpled letter. "The *Atlantic Monthly* magazine bought that new story I sent last month and they are paying
me fifty dollars. Finally, a chance to be taken seriously as a writer!
But I have no right to be so happy on this terrible day; it is
wicked."

"Well, I think that's nonsense. It would be wicked not to appreciate your good fortune," I said with great firmness.

"Said with admirable certitude, Susan." She smiled faintly.

"You've worked hard, and you deserve this."

"Thank you. You helped make it happen, you know. Your suggestions were good. But surely it's wrong to be both happy and sad
at the same time."

"What you really mean is: Is it wrong to be happy for yourself
when others are mourning?"

"Yes."

"To think otherwise could be to invite the sin of hypocrisy."

She studied me. "How do I announce my news at so sad a time?"

"Tell people tomorrow; they will be happy for you. And I know you will do it with sensitivity to the sorrowing mood. But now? Now you exult. You will be famous and successful, you will, and nobody will stop you. Why don't you share this news with Henry?"

"No, no; oh, I wish I could."

"Why not? The two of you are back to spending time together, strolling about."

She paused for a long moment before answering. "Yes, but we hardly talk. Or I hardly talk. I listen and try to respond with just the right words so he won't pull away and be silent. He does that, I'm afraid. You saw him today. Oh Susan . . ."

The hunger in her voice took me aback. It was different from the stalwart adoration of the past. "What is it?" I asked.

She looked away, her face flushed. "I want him to truly see me. I . . . I want him to offer some intimacy—to hold me, perhaps share a kiss. But he's so elusive."

Never had we had so intimate a conversation.

"If he pulls away from you when you speak, then perhaps this is not a good match."

"I'm trying to be what he wants me to be."

"And what is that?"

She sighed. "A less expectant person. Sophia says her brother thinks love cannot be expressed in words, that to do so, to divulge love, even to the beloved, is to no longer love."

"Truly?" I was astonished.

She nodded. "It seems Ellen questioned his love because of this. He told his sister that she should have known his heart, that once love is expressed, it evaporates."

"Oh, what nonsense!" I blurted.

"You think it is? Do you?"

She was truly asking my opinion. "Yes, I do," I said. "Love must be shared to be understood. It cannot be left to shrivel like a dead leaf on the vine."

"It is hard because I truly love him. No one understands why, and I'm not sure myself."

"Well," I gazed at my friend, who seemed partially to be talking to me and partially to herself, "unless he changes, there is no path to follow, I fear."

Louisa nodded slowly, looking past me with sorrowful eyes. "I still have my writing," she said, again half to herself.

"You will always have that," I said. "And Lou, you will always have me."

She smiled, her gaze still faraway. "I know, dear. Now it's time to go to bed."

Chapter Three

Our daily routine became predictable. Louisa, always the restless sleeper, would rise early and I would rise with her. While the rest of the family slept we would go to the kitchen and make our morning coffee. Louisa would nibble at some buttered bread and drink the coffee, then she would fill a basin to wash. After that she would silently brush her long hair and tie it up, while I folded some black grapes inside an old damask napkin to take back upstairs. I knew she was thinking of what she would write that day. Then we would tiptoe up the stairs, wrapped together in comfortable silence.

For the rest of the day, Louisa scratched away with her pen at her desk in the bedroom while I sat on the old mahogany sleigh bed, reading and amusing myself trimming hats with scraps of ancient ribbon and lace. She loved tart gumballs, and kept a tidy supply in a low drawer, which we would share in the afternoon. Two for you, and one for me, she would say. Ah, no, I wrote well today, so it is two for me, and one for you! We would laugh and reach for more.

It was a comfortable room. The walls were of the same cream-painted pine as downstairs, and the wood floor was covered with a red-and-gold carpet of floral and checkerboard design that had belonged to Abba's mother. Louisa's desk faced out toward the front of the house, which meant we could see through the window all who came up and down the path. Our two beds took up half the space, but there was room for a large, circular table that was usually cluttered with books and remnants of snacks Abba would bring up during the day. The fireplace added winter warmth, made even cheerier by May's painting above the hearth of an owl perched on a branch. She produced it as a surprise one afternoon while Louisa was in Boston. I must say, although I thought May a bit sly with her symbolism—she called Louisa a "wise, old owl" behind her back—I loved that delicate, feathery little creature. It gazed into the room with wise, bright eyes, almost as if it knew that serious work was being done here.

The duty I claimed for my own during those pleasant days was guarding Louisa's privacy. Monday would come, and she would closet herself with pen and paper through almost the entire week, speaking hardly a word to anyone. Nothing could pull her from her desk when she was writing. No walks, no talks; nothing. I fended off visitors, family quarrels, distress over unpaid bills; anything that might interfere with her churning out stories.

Even I was not fully aware at the time of her prodigious output. By the summer of 1860, Louisa announced she had two books half done, nine stories simmering, and, as she wrote to busy Anna, now married and pregnant, "stacks of fairy tales mouldering on the shelf."

But not many were selling. When a letter would arrive from *The Atlantic Monthly* or *Scribner's,* we would all pretend a casualness we did not feel as Louisa ripped it open. Sometimes it was good news. Usually it was not, and she would fold the letter, stick it into her pocket, and march upstairs, not to be heard from again until dinnertime.

Indeed, no one else in the family was earning much money. I had a small inheritance from my parents that Abba declared must not be touched until I was twenty. And even though Bronson was that year named superintendent of schools in Concord, the pay was meager. Still, as Louisa pointed out, he was, finally, at the age of sixty, getting attention for his radical ideas about learning. His reports to the town ran sixty-seven pages, filled with worthy ideas. Children should learn to write by such practical methods as keeping journals and writing letters; spelling should be learned with definitions and derivations. How commonsensical it sounds now!

I soon came to realize how truly generous the Alcotts had been in taking me in. Their resources were lean and my presence only stretched them further, which struck me as so unfair. I was eighteen now, I thought, and quite grown-up. Why couldn't I help?

That question was in my mind the morning I sat down with a piece bag and tried idly for the first time to make a bonnet. I had a vague idea of crafting something ringed in spring flowers that might amuse the girls if I sallied forth in it at dinnertime. I stitched and molded, becoming increasingly absorbed, experimenting with different weights of horsehair inside the flowers to give them shape. Why, it looks quite good, I told myself, holding it up when it was finished. Immediately I began another one, excited now. I could do this. The second one would be even better.

"Look, Louisa," I said, sailing into our room just before dinner-time with the second bonnet on my head. "Do you like it?" I tried a fancy pirouette and stumbled.

Louisa smiled indulgently. "You made that, Susan? It is quite polished and fine. You have a very good design sense, dear." She turned back to her desk in a gently dismissive way.

"I have a wonderful idea for making money," I persisted. "Why don't I make a dozen of these and market them in town? What do you think people would pay for them? I have so many ideas!"

"Oh, I don't think so," she said quickly. "No, no, that wouldn't work."

"Why not?"

She hesitated. "Susan, we're not tradespeople. The Alcotts don't engage in selling goods. Father would never hear of it."

"Well, what is selling stories?" I retorted, stung. "Aren't you taking money for what you write? How is it different?"

She laid down her pen with a frown. I could see she was getting cross. "It simply is different. You'll have to understand that. If you want to do something creative, why don't you paint, like May?"

"I don't want to paint. I've always loved sketching designs, but my fingers itch to make them real, and I know I can make beautiful bonnets, I know I can," I said. "It's a different thing, but it's still creative."

Louisa was standing now, still frowning, but peering out the window, not looking directly at me. "I'm sorry to disappoint you, I really am. You shouldn't worry so much about trying to make money. I'll provide for this family. Oh, where is the post? He's late again!"

"You're always saying the postman is late. You're always waiting."

She smiled with an aura of distraction. "I know, I know. Why don't you run into town for fresh bread? Get it hot, right from the oven, then we'll share a treat together. Nice, thick slices with Abba's jam."

"All right," I said, giving up. I took off my bonnet and, with regret, put it carefully on the windowsill. It truly had been fun to make.

I tromped off to town knowing I had been gently diverted, but by the time I returned home with a supply of fragrant, hot bread from the bakery, I felt better. I brought the loaves to Abba in the kitchen for cutting, and was surprised to see her in a somber mood.

"Didn't I get enough?" I asked.

"Of course you did, dear. But the post came with another rejection while you were gone. Louisa is very upset."

I climbed up on a stool next to the wood chopping block where Abba had begun slicing the bread. "That's five this week," I said.

Abba nodded and sighed. "She works hard, and she will succeed, but she can become dreadfully discouraged. My poor child, she takes on all the burdens, more than she should have to." Abba took a whack at the bread, digging the butcher knife so deep into the wood, she had to struggle to pull it away.

"Oh, we're talking about Lou." I turned around at this new voice to see May bouncing into the room. "Wouldn't it be wonderful if she fell in love? Not with old Henry, but with someone who deserved her and loved her back. Wouldn't that be wonderful?"

She hopped onto the stool next to me, reaching for a slice of bread.

"She pushes off eligible men," Abba said softly. "I don't know why, for she is a grand girl and deserves someone who appreciates her."

"Well, I'm going to marry a rich, handsome man, you wait and see," said May. "I won't be living in some dilapidated little place, like Anna and John."

"May!" Abba stared at her youngest.

"Well, I'm only being honest, and I know you feel the same way about their house. You said so."

"John will do fine, their marriage is young. What I said is, marry a man who can provide for you. Otherwise it's a lifetime of hard work and worry. It's—" Abba stopped herself and went back to cutting the bread. May and I shared a quick glance; Bronson's unspoken faults filled the room.

"Louisa needs something to encourage her, something to give her more confidence," I said.

"Yes, she does. But what can it be?"

"I have an idea." I hesitated, wondering if what I was thinking sounded too childish. "Abba, remember the beautiful cloak you made for our plays? That wonderful red-and-green one of silk?"

Abba looked puzzled for a moment before her brow cleared. "Ah yes, I remember. You girls loved it. That was years ago."

"It's still in the costume trunk in the attic, I saw it there. Remember the very first time we pulled it out of the costume basket, May?"

May nodded, a faraway look in her eyes. "It was almost as special as my dagger."

"Beth loved it at first sight, so Lou gave it to her to wear, but Beth gave it back. She said it was Louisa's glory cloak."

"My Beth said that?" Abba spoke softly, hands still, poised above the sink.

I was getting excited. "Yes, and you know what she told Louisa? She said, 'You'll do wonderful things wearing it.'"

The three of us considered that in silence.

Abba spoke first. "Then we must haul it out and present it to her," she announced. "And I'll make a cap to go with it."

It took us only a few minutes to unlock the trunk and pull out the glory cloak. It still shimmered beautifully. Abba quickly fashioned a little green silk cap while May dug out a red grosgrain bow to sew on it, and I stitched up the edges of the cloak, frayed from its many trips across the boards on Louisa's shoulders.

In a few hours we were ready. The three of us went to Louisa's room and found her sitting in a corner, staring out the window.

"My dear child, we have something for you," whispered Abba.

As Louisa turned, I held up the cloak and gave it a great swirl.

Her eyes widened. "My goodness, where did you find that?" she asked.

"In the trunk of hopes and dreams," I said dramatically. "Lou, you must put it on. It's your glory cloak!"

I thought she might think it a joke, but she didn't. She took the glory cloak and swung it over her tall, sturdy shoulders. With a grand gesture, she tied the looped sash at the neck and stood tall, once again the King of Everything.

"And now, your crown," Abba said as she placed the green cap on her daughter's dark hair.

Louisa took an elegant, sweeping bow as we laughed and clapped. There was high color in her cheeks now, and a sparkle in her eyes. "Thank you, worthy subjects, you have brought me strength. I will wear this when I write from now on, for inspiration."

"And courage," I offered.

"And faith," May said with surprising vigor.

Abba smiled, her arms wide. "And love, dear. Never forget love."

"My, we're getting soppy!" May sputtered.

Oh, we shared a wonderful laugh over that.

*   *   *

"Look at this, will you?" Louisa said, handing me a sheaf of manuscript. She brushed back a fold of the glory cloak, which covered
her like an airy cocoon. "It's a novel. Tell me what you think."

It was a gloomy afternoon a week later, and I was surprised at
the weight of the pages suddenly in my hands. The words were
spread out in great indecipherable loops and scrawls, and my heart
sank. It would be a long, slow read.

Not so. Soon I was totally absorbed in Louisa's tale of Sylvia, a
woman who impulsively marries the wrong man because she fears
the one she truly loves does not return her feelings.

When he reappears and finds her married, he demands to know
why she did not wait for him. She has no answer and, struggling to
stay true to her husband, bids him farewell. Sylvia then seeks out a
friend to ask a question: If fate had given her the proper timing,
which man *should* she have married? Neither, replies her friend, declaring that Sylvia suffers from the affliction of "two contending
spirits in one body." She should be doomed to a life alone.

> . . . *so Sylvia, living in the shadow of a household grief, found*
> *herself detecting various phases of her own experience in others.*
> *She had joined that sad sisterhood called disappointed women; a*
> *larger class than many deem it to be, though there are few of us*
> *who have not seen members of it. Unhappy wives; mistaken or for-*
> *saken lovers; meek souls, who make life a long penance for the sins*
> *of others; gifted creatures kindled into fitful brilliancy by some*
> *inner fire that consumes but cannot warm. These are the women*
> *who fly to convents, write bitter books, sing songs full of heart-*
> *break, act splendidly the passion they have lost or never won; who*
> *smile, and try to lead brave uncomplaining lives, but whose tragic*
> *eyes betray them, whose voices, however sweet or gay, contain an*
> *undertone of hopelessness, whose faces sometimes startle one with*
> *an expression which haunts the observer long after it is gone.*

If the town band had tootled its way through the parlor, I would
not have lifted my head, for *Moods* took my breath away. It would al-

ways be Louisa's dearest creation. She immersed herself in it, exposing herself in a way she never would again. I have wondered many times, what if she had received for *Moods* the respect she deserved? Perhaps she would have continued to explore the depths of the human heart. What if the young Henry James had not humiliated her with a review mocking her writing skills and her understanding of human emotion? Such a useless imagining of alternate outcomes!

"You like it?" she asked when I finally came back to the room.

"Yes, oh yes. Very much."

"Tell me why," she demanded.

"You make me believe in these people, and I so want Sylvia to have a happy love life! And her love for Adam is so . . . so passionate and from the heart. Do you think most women have contending spirits in their bodies? I mean, do you?"

Her fingers fluttered, unsure of direction. "Why do you ask?"

"Because I'm wondering if you are Sylvia, filled with wanting. For true love."

Louisa's face did not change expression as she came to me, gently taking the manuscript from my hand. The red bow on her cap had tipped, but this was not the moment to point that out.

"No, there's no connection."

"Why doesn't Adam promise to marry her if she leaves Geoffrey? I don't think he loves her enough to claim her, and she has to give up so much. Can't there be a happy ending somehow?"

"Susan, this is a story, not real life. It is my queer funny brain producing fantasy."

"I know that, but the reason it is good is that your true heart is in it. I can see it; I can see it when Sylvia blames herself for her passion. But I don't see why she has to renounce *all* love because of that. It's like you and Henry—"

"Oh, you can be tiresomely childish. The woman you read about isn't me, it is Sylvia." Louisa was impatient now. With a flick of her hand, she flung off the glory cloak and let it slip to the floor. She hugged the manuscript protectively to her chest and walked out of the room.

I followed her, determined to explain, chiding myself for being so blunt. How delicate the task of criticizing my friend's work was!

"Lou, wait," I said.

Louisa paused at the top of the stairs, her right hand cupping the banister post. The house was quite still. A soft breeze flowed to the hall through an open window in Abba's bedroom. I could hear through the window the faint sound of someone priming the pump in the side yard; Abba must be drawing water for dinner.

She turned and faced me, this time with a sheepish expression on her face. "Why do I stomp away from you? You saw what it was immediately. I had to write it."

"Tell me what you mean," I coaxed.

"Well, I've freed my mind about love. Finally."

I tried to line my words up in proper order, but they spilled out too quickly. "I should think you would allow Sylvia more happiness," I began.

"She finds happiness in renouncing Adam."

"There is no happiness in renunciation. She's afraid he will dominate her, at least that's how it seems to me."

"Susan, are you still so trapped in childishness that you can't see how unwise a forbidden love can be?"

"You've called me childish twice, now. I'm not a child."

She seemed to relax slightly. "You're right to speak up for yourself. I value that in you, Susan. I'm sorry, I'm feeling . . . anxious."

Encouraged, I tried again to express my thoughts. "You see, I would want the man, not the denial. Not the self-sacrifice."

"Well, dear, may you find him. That's all I can say."

"Louisa . . ." I wanted this to end well. "I admire your book immensely."

This time she turned and gave me a hug. Gratefully, I hugged her back.

The signs of war were everywhere by 1861. You could sniff its pungency in the air; see it in the worried faces of people gathered at the rail station each morning to seize copies of the *Boston Herald* before they were all sold. Even Ephraim Bull, our esteemed developer of the Concord grape, became more impassioned about the coming war than about horticulture, and took to giving speeches at the station without either his trademark wig or his silk hat. The eccentric Miss Peabody, infamous for wearing her blouses inside out, was also there every day, more scattered than ever, but an ardent supporter of the Union.

Bronson had a routine. He strode to the station each morning to wait with the others, returning each time with the precious paper tucked under his arm, stovepipe-thin legs churning agitatedly up the path. "War will soon sweep over us," he had announced only one year ago, the day after Mr. Lincoln's election, as he dropped the paper on the table. We gathered around and stared at a sketch on the front page of Lincoln being burned in effigy at a South Carolina courthouse.

It became a macabre game to count the secessions. South Carolina—leaving several dozen Union troops cut off from reinforcement or help within the walls of Fort Sumter in Charleston Harbor. Mississippi, Florida, Alabama, Louisiana, Georgia. We could do nothing but wait as the nation was slowly torn in two.

Will Banning, a diffident youngster with unruly blond hair who worked at J. W. Walcott's coffee and tea store on the Milldam, suddenly disappeared one day without a good-bye to anyone. We learned later his family in Georgia had ordered him home. Abba had been quite fond of the boy. Each time she visited the store, he would slip an extra spoonful of tea into her order with a wink and a nod. She was very upset.

"Our men will be seeing him again soon enough," Louisa said sadly. She pointed out the window to a pair of young farmers bundling hay across Lexington Road. "They'll all meet again on the battlefields, Marmee." Abba turned white and burst into tears.

In the midst of this eerie tension, this waiting, Bronson continued to host the weekly open house that had become a gathering place for his fellow Transcendentalists. The men would gather around the table, sipping coffee from the green-rimmed china cups Abba so cherished, the ones inherited from her mother that whispered of long-gone luxuries. We would arrange ourselves in the parlor. May would sketch and I would sew, hardly attempting to follow the often incomprehensible discussions favored by Bronson. Louisa was usually the only one truly listening, but only, as she told me, "when all those musings become tainted with enough reality to throw an anchor."

The meetings took on an increasingly sharper edge as the siege at Fort Sumter dragged on. The men would inevitably begin to discuss what Mr. Lincoln should do—abandon the fort or dig in and defend it? With what perils for each choice? Bronson would try vainly to steer his beloved conversations back to a more lofty plane, but it became harder and harder to do, and fewer and fewer of his colleagues, impatient with him, were showing up.

But when the Confederates finally launched their devastating attack of Fort Sumter, it no longer mattered. Within twenty-four hours, cockades appeared everywhere and flags flew from every house and church steeple. The farmers on the other side of Lexington Road put down their scythes and donned uniforms, and soon all the men of the town were drilling daily in formation on the town green. I wandered the town, shocked. Could this be true? Yes. We were at war.

Chapter Four

On the nineteenth of April, one week after the fall of Fort Sumter, the Concord Artillery of the State Regiment, Massachusetts Volunteer Militia—such a lofty, official designation—was ordered to Washington immediately.

The very next morning the men who herded livestock and shod the horses and sold caps at the dry goods store lined up at the rail station, crisp in their blue uniforms, their young, solemn faces almost unrecognizable, as we all clapped and cheered and cried our good-byes.

"Get a Reb for me, boys!" yelled the usually taciturn Silas Forrest.

"You do us proud!" shouted a red-faced Mr. Bull.

Red, white, and blue were everywhere—on cravats, hats, and handkerchiefs—and a cluster of earnest children played drums and fifes in noisy unison. I thrilled with pride. The predecessors of these men had fought the Redcoats at the North Bridge, and now the Concord Artillery was off to war again. Had the Minutemen been as young and vulnerable-looking as these boys? How many would come back? I thanked God guiltily that there were no brothers in our household.

"I can't stand doing nothing," Louisa muttered at my side as the last of Concord's men boarded the train.

"There's plenty for us to do," Abba said firmly. She had already organized a group of Concord women for daily sewing sessions. Socks needed to be knitted, shirts sewn for the troops, bandages rolled and prepared—and Abba seemed filled with purpose and energy for the job.

"Oh, sewing and all the other rubbish. Why can't I enlist? Why can't women fight, too? It's not enough. I've never wanted more to be a man." Louisa yanked her shawl tight and turned, stalking off the platform, once again the glorious L'Estrange; this time, thwarted from galloping into the flames.

"Should I go after her?" I asked.

"No, let her be," advised Abba. "We mustn't fuss too much over her moods. She gets over them."

"But she needs me," I said.

"You don't always need to be a sounding board, dear. I fear sometimes there is too much leaning on you."

My eyes widened. Louisa leaning too hard on *me?* Surely it was the other way around.

"You are young," she said, seeing my bafflement. "Save your energies for the right moments." We stayed and waved until the train pulled away and then walked together back to the house.

Abba and I had grown closer over the span of those first few years. I did not think of her at that time as a substitute for my mother; I saw her more as an anchor, I suppose. An anchor to identity, for she gave me family. And she was of sturdier stuff than I had realized during all the happy visits when I, like everyone else, took her nurturing presence for granted. She gave me glimpses of fire, sometimes unexpectedly. With her hands deep in suds as she washed the perennially dirty pots and pans in her kitchen, she confided to me one night that Bronson had once called Louisa a devil.

"Did he mean it?" I asked in awe.

"He always believes his own pronouncements," she said with something more than resignation. What she did not tell me, but I learned later, was that he had called her a devil, too. Bronson, mild-mannered to the world, was not a man who tolerated defiance in his family. I suspected Abba had managed to smother the fires in herself for the sake of the girls, and wondered what price she paid.

*   *   *

The next deeply felt blow for our town was not war news. Not the feared dispatches that would tell us of the fatalities suffered by the Concord Artillery. Those missives of death would come soon enough, but there was another event that shook us all deeply.

It was spring, the month of May, the time when we all breathed easier, freed, we thought, of the fears of influenza for another year. It was not to be. I glanced out the window one Saturday and saw Henry's sister, Sophia, running toward the house, skirts hiked up, boots still stained from shavings on the floor of the plumbago shop the family ran in back of their home.

"Mrs. Alcott! Mrs. Alcott! Please help!" she cried, banging on the door. I unlatched the door as the family came running. Sophie fell into Abba's comforting arms, sobbing that Henry, only forty-four, whose frequent colds and raspy cough we all took for granted, was suddenly very ill. He had tried to bring a batch of finished pencils from the shop to the house and dropped them all, too weak to hold them, she said. He had fallen in the grass, and it had been all she could do to drag him into the house. He breathed, but shallowly.

"No, no," Louisa whimpered, resting her head against the door frame. Abba reached for her own coat and pulled a shawl over Louisa's shoulders, taking her by the arm. "We'll go together," she said.

In Henry's remaining weeks, Louisa hardly left his side. I would come with Bronson, bringing cider and apples, and she would be stroking his forehead. What was there to be done? Every day, morning and evening, Sophia frenetically dusted the shelves that held his collection of arrowheads and bird's nests, claiming they must be pristine when he was well again. Although distraught, she kept resolutely working, a practical woman who counted dollars and cents and knew she had to keep production going in the shop. I wondered how one family could have produced two such different siblings.

On one soft spring evening when the azalea bushes along the road to town were in bloom, I walked Louisa home from the Thoreaus'. I was worried for her, as much as for Henry.

"You aren't eating enough," I said. "You must stay strong."

"Susan, I cannot believe I will lose him without knowing if he loves me." Her voice was hoarse. "He lets me touch him, something I have yearned for. But I'm cursed with my longings. This, this isn't how it was to be, not how I dreamed it."

I held her hand, not knowing what else to do.

He died the next day, on May 6, with Louisa kneeling at his bedside, holding his hand. He whispered to her that Nature seemed to be taking a long time to finish the job. Nature, his friend, was playing a cruel trick.

Louisa came undone. "Never to hear him play the flute again, to see him climb a tree to peek at a bird's nest or watch fish swim into his hands. That incredible, lovely man, how can he be gone so soon?" she sobbed.

I linked my arm through hers to give support as we walked that sunny spring day behind the coffin to the church, listening to the church bells toll his forty-four years. Henry had not wanted a funeral, but Mr. Emerson insisted. It wasn't just Concord that wanted to pay homage, he declared; it was Boston, New York, the world. The church was jammed. Truly, if fish could have wept, the waters of Walden Pond would have swelled with tears. Sophia spoke of how this gentle brother taught her patience by inviting her to watch with him the evolution of a brilliant moth, and Mr. Emerson said he had, in the space of a short life, "exhausted the capabilities of this world."

Then came the long trek up to Sleepy Hollow, where we stood watching Henry's coffin descend into the ground, between his father and his brother, with none yet of his neighbors to keep him company but our lost Beth Alcott across the path. My first trip to Sleepy Hollow cemetery, and not the last.

In the months that followed, Louisa sank into despondency, and I watched with worried sadness. So many links were gone from her carefully cherished life—Beth, Henry, even Anna. Had her heart been stricken a mortal blow? Oh, she was in there somewhere, I knew she was!

Yet she was not writing, and eating only indifferently. The war was worsening, and the dreary, boring act of sewing for the soldiers was driving her wild.

"Have you heard about this ferocious woman, Clara Barton?" asked the red-haired wife of the Unitarian Church pastor one morning as we sat sewing with a group of women in the parlor.

"Ferocious?" Abba looked puzzled at first. "Ah, the woman who single-handedly found supplies to feed all the soldiers camped out in the Senate Chamber. The entire Sixth Massachusetts. Amazing. Why do you say ferocious?"

"Because I hear she's making generals tremble in their boots. She absolutely will not let any of them get in her way. Now she's put together her own distributing agency for dispensing supplies. I hear she was the only one feeding the wounded at Bull Run, isn't that shocking? So persistent! Badgering the men in charge for permission to drive her supplies to the battlefield—"

"Oh, that sounds truly fine and brave," I interrupted, enthralled. "What a splendid way to help. I wish I could do the same."

"Which only makes what we're doing more futile," Louisa said. She dropped her needle and held up the blue shirt she had been sewing as if it were no more than a dirty rag. With one hand she ripped out the basting holding the sleeves to the bodice, tossed the fragments of cloth on the floor, and threw what remained of the shirt against the parlor wall. It hung there, draped over Beth's piano.

Sophia Hawthorne, not one to take breaches of decorum lightly, pursed her lips in tight disapproval and glanced at her daughter, Una. Mrs. Hawthorne did not think her precious child should be exposed to anything so graphic as raw anger. The gossip in town was that she had stopped speaking to her own sister because she had made the mistake of showing Una a tract depicting a naked slave girl on the block. Mrs. Hawthorne declared to one and all that such a horrifying depiction of absolute nudity was an "exaggeration," leading Abba to murmur that Mrs. Hawthorne seemed more upset by nudity than slavery. This morning, Abba simply lowered her eyes, waiting for Louisa to get her temper in check—to no avail.

"This is made-up women's work. *Stupid* women's work! Look—" Louisa grabbed a copy of the paper and held it high. Her cheeks were so flushed, I feared a fever. "Women are passing as men and joining the fight. Why do we sit here? What good are we? We can do more! We can—"

She stopped at the sight of her mother's bowed head. I stitched quickly, clumsily, sticking my finger. Abba was being humiliated before her neighbors.

Without a word, Louisa walked over to the piano, picked up the discarded shirt, and sat down again in her chair. She stared at the garment for a long moment before she picked up her needle again and resumed sewing. My heart went out to her, knowing that by now she was silently berating herself for her outburst, and so unnecessarily, I thought.

"I feel much of the same frustration," I declared as calmly as I could. "Women should be able to do more."

Mrs. Hawthorne sniffed, but Louisa cast me a quick glance of gratitude. And in truth the restlessness she had expressed was also stirring in me.

The war was going badly, with defeat after defeat, but not until news came of Antietam did we understand how badly. The details were shattering. Thousands of Union men under the direction of General Ambrose Burnside had died trying to cross a small stone bridge—wave after wave of bodies going down; charge after charge continuing, until the bridge became soaked in blood. And who had won, we asked? The results were inconclusive. Only later did we understand it could have been a decisive turning point in the war if General McClellan had not refused Burnside's plea to send reinforcements.

Louisa was beside herself, not only with the horrible news but with its political aftermath. "Can you believe Mr. Lincoln wants to *pay* for the slaves?" she demanded at dinner, stabbing her fork into her plate. "He's so afraid to abolish slavery, he will pay the slave-owners, as if for property! How can he do this?"

"Isn't it because he's afraid he'll lose the border states if he frees them all?" I asked.

"It's much more complicated than that." And as she did so often now, she pushed back from the table and left the room.

Abba sat silently for a moment, then put down her napkin and turned to me. "I'm sorry, dear. She isn't herself."

I shrugged my shoulders, only slightly stung by Louisa's huff. She would apologize later, but it wouldn't change her low mood; that was the bad part.

"I think it would be good for Louisa to get away from here for a while," Abba said. "Why don't the two of you go to Boston for a few days? It would be a pleasant outing, I suspect." A smile played at the edges of her lips. "I don't think Lou's sewing will be missed."

I loved the idea, and took it immediately to Louisa, who brightened in the most heartening way. And so we made our plans. We traveled to Boston together in October, and indeed Lou became less gloomy and crotchety the closer we came to joining the quickened pace of the city. Her face was still pale, but what I had come to think of as her "duty look"—pinched lips and fur-rowed brow—had faded away. Her spirit was almost light as we stepped from the train. And I? I was thrilled to be in Boston. Con-cord is so provincial, I told myself. This was the hub of the uni-verse; surely good things would happen to us here.

We walked that very morning all over the city, tiptoeing through the Old North Church, quite taken by its austere simplic-ity; ducking our heads to clear the low rafters of Paul Revere's home; then visiting the nearby basement workplace of a small group of energetic women working on pottery wheels, their sleeves rolled up, their eyes steady, their hands so skilled, we could only watch in awe. "It's amazing they've made this a business," Louisa whispered as we watched. "Isn't their work attractive?"

I gazed at the mostly blue and white pottery lining the shelves in their cluttered workplace, and could only nod agreement, excited by the purposeful energy of these women, imagining myself among them—not making bowls and platters, but hats. I fantasized admirers crowding at my window, and people digging into their pockets to buy my creations. Someday I'm going to have a shop, I promised myself. Someday I will sell the work of my hands, just as these women were doing with theirs.

We went next to the Boston Common, my first sighting in years of that breathtaking expanse of lawn and lake laced with graceful paths that flows to the city below the Statehouse. The foliage had turned, and the trees were brilliant with orange and yellow. The air was bracing and I yearned to breathe deeply, regretting the constrictions of the fashionable corset I had in a burst of vanity worn for this adventure.

What a lovely day it had become! We laughed and chatted as we strolled, poking fun at the antics of two young boys rolling their hoops, and had just begun wondering where we would stop for lunch when Louisa suddenly halted and grabbed my arm.

"Susan," she said, pointing. "What do you think that is?"

Ahead was a strange contraption made of heavy iron, mounted on a brick post in the center of the walk. A few people slowed as they walked by, and then hurried on. It was round, with three evil-looking prongs jutting to the center, and hinged in the back with a brass clasp.

"I have no idea," I said.

We moved closer. Louisa peered at the inscription and caught her breath. "It's a slave collar," she said.

I stared at the evil thing, trying to imagine a human neck held captive by those pointed prongs. I saw the rivet where the chain was to be hung that would link each captive to the next. I tried to imagine the degradation, the flouting of all morality, that would allow one human being to lock this thing onto the neck of another. I suspected Mrs. Hawthorne would have hustled her daughter past *this* display as quickly as possible.

We turned away and walked slowly out of the Common, the crisp pleasures of the day fading.

"Women cannot stay out of this war," Louisa declared.

"No, they cannot. We have to do more."

"I hate the constraints on us!" She quickened her stride.

"I read something about the government needing nurses," I began.

"So have I." Her pace slowed.

"Well, why not the two of us?" The audacity of the idea took my breath away. "Can't we inquire about nursing commissions?"

Louisa came to a full halt. A governess behind her wearing a fussy lace cap stumbled, then cast her an irritated glance as she pushed past with a perambulator.

"I must confess, I already have," she said.

"You have?" I was delighted—finally, the adventurous Lou I knew was surfacing.

"There's a woman named Dorothea Dix who's been put in charge of recruiting nurses for the hospitals. I hear she's quite arbitrary, an unlikable sort, but she has the power to *recruit*. It's all very official and real, not made-up work at all."

"Who cares if she's an unlikable sort? There must be a place for us—they *need* us." I knew my words were true as I spoke them, and felt an incredible exhilaration.

Lou looked at me doubtfully. "I'm plain enough to meet her standards, but I'm not sure about you. You've become quite pretty, almost as pretty as May, which may be why you annoy her so frequently."

"If that's supposed to be a prelude to saying I'm too young, I'll tell you right now, Louisa May, don't even *think* of going without me." My heart began thumping hard against the infernal corset.

She laughed. "Susan, you should see your face—my, oh my, your eyes look like they could throw daggers! You do get fierce sometimes. I wouldn't go without you, don't you know that?"

"If there are problems, we can solve them," I said. Oh, I felt fierce all right—for adventure, for high purpose, for something new and exciting—and I knew in my heart *this* was what we should do.

"Well, unfortunately you *are* too young." Louisa reached into the folds of her skirt and pulled out a wrinkled circular, putting it into my hands. "Read this."

It was indeed a recruiting plea, calling on able-bodied women of the North to volunteer their services as nurses, and I read it with growing excitement. Then I reached the final paragraph:

> *No woman under thirty years need apply to serve in govern-ment hospitals. All nurses are required to be very plain-looking women. Their dresses must be brown or black, with no bows, no curls, no jewelry, and no hoop skirts.*

"They won't take me," I said, pushing the handbill back into her hands.

"There are ways to get around it," she hastened to say. "We'll hide your age, that's what we'll do. You must look haggard and plain, and act like me. Exaggerate. Pretend you have stiff bones, and when they give you the application, peer at it as if you need spectacles. I don't, of course, but pretending to age would help. We can do it, Susan."

"We will," I said with full fervor. I believed it now: I was not going to be left behind. "We will do some good, instead of sitting with our needles and sewing away in stuffy Concord."

Louisa chortled and swooped me up into an exuberant hug. "Oh, you are like me, I've always known. We're leaving Concord together, Susan, we're going to have a splendid adventure. You and I, we are going to escape that town of reflected history and trans-planted geniuses!"

How good my memories are of that day. We tromped back through the Common, thrilled now by the energy around the recruiting tents, knowing the patriotic music being played in the bandstand spoke to us in a new way. And even though our decision was to alter the direction of both our lives, there was a glory to it all. For on that sunny morning on the Common, I felt I had put childhood behind me.

*   *   *

"This is nonsense. I cannot believe you are ready to desert your family for an adventure in Washington."

Bronson dropped his fork upon hearing Louisa's announcement that we had enlisted and were only waiting for our commissions to serve in Washington City. Head lowered, I picked at the last of the summer's canned vegetables. Abba stared at her cooling tea. May had slipped away as soon as she sensed her sister's planned confrontation with Bronson, unwilling to witness her father's wrath.

Louisa sat straight as a schoolmarm. "Father, I would never desert my family, and you of all people should know that. Our country needs soldiers, but it also needs nurses."

His thick eyebrows flew upward and his voice grew deep and thunderous. "You are needed *here*. Where is your sense of responsibility?"

My fingers laced together in a protective gesture of containment that I prayed would stop my tongue. I risked a glance at Abba and saw a flash of anger in her eyes. Bronson was thundering against Louisa's patriotic resolve with the purpose of keeping her under his control. And why would he not, given the fact she was the primary breadwinner in the family? Her income as a teacher and writer would be sorely missed. Was there never to be any theme allowed to her but self-sacrifice?

"I cannot sit here and pretend Sumter did not fall, nor do I think you can, Father," Louisa said with spirit. "And surely I needn't remind you of what Mr. Emerson said here, just last week at our table, that it is impossible to extricate ourselves from the times in which we live?"

"That is quite true, and that means being wary of their dangers. The morals of the women in Washington are rumored to be questionable. It is not a safe environment for proper women."

"I find it hard to believe you would put forth such an argument," Louisa protested. "My morals were taught by my parents and are too deeply rooted to be endangered."

"You are not a trained nurse," Bronson shot back.

Abba raised her chin high. "And who, my dear, ministered to our sweet Beth with better skill and attention than Louisa? Can you name another?"

Bronson fell silent. I could hear the clock ticking loudly in the dining room.

"I do not want you in danger," he said finally. His face turned sorrowful. I sensed him crumbling.

Louisa's tone softened in response. "Come now, Pa, you know the stir in the air to which your old Lou is responding," she cajoled. "I need to help; I can't bear having nowhere to direct my energy. There will be income to keep all snug here while I'm gone. I've fed Mr. Leslie enough tales for his newspaper to keep food on our table, I can assure you of that."

Bronson turned his attention to me. "Susan absolutely cannot go with you," he said. "She's much too young."

"Papa, Susan wants to go, and I wouldn't dream of going without her. This is something we want to do together." She reached under the table, grabbed my fingers and squeezed.

"Don't you have an objection to this wild plan?"

It was a question I had anticipated and I felt quite proud of my instant answer. "No sir," I said, "for I feel the same fire to serve. And I wouldn't go without Lou."

"Then I see it is done." Bronson threw down his napkin, pushed back from the table, and strode off with heavy steps to his study. What a strange, heady feeling it was to thwart his will. For once.

Una Hawthorne actually helped us pack. She was a good sort, fun to be around when not under the thumb of her mother. She was thrilled when she heard we had signed up, thrilled and, I think, wistful. *She* would never have such an adventure. She marked our clothes with ink and made sure Louisa packed her brass inkstand and a copper teakettle—this took some negotiating, because Louisa insisted on filling up space with multiple copies of Dickens, assuring me that the wounded soldiers would be eager to read. "I can't imagine anything better than reading to them at night," she declared.

"But shouldn't we include the nursing pamphlets?" I asked.

"We'll be given instruction," Louisa said with great confidence. "We need to think of keeping the soldiers jolly, so they will not despair of home."

I watched her with amusement. She was literally bouncing around the room, gathering things, joking, nibbling from time to time on a piece of lemon cake on the mantel. Some cake crumbs had drifted over the ledge, sticking to May's painted owl, giving it a decidedly comical look. We were laughing about that, picking the crumbs off, when May came to our room and crept onto Lou's bed, eyes misty, folding herself into the position of a mournful supplicant.

"What will I do without you, Lou?" she implored. "And without you, Susan? I must sew my new silk frock for the dance next week without your supervision! How can I do it? Please, look at the silk—is it the right color?" She held out a folded piece of blue boiled silk like a matchgirl begging alms.

I unfolded the material for inspection. No flaws, I reported. I reassured her that it would wonderfully complement her fair complexion and take her gracefully through any number of dances. And not to worry; Abba would supervise the sewing in my stead.

We stayed up and gossiped and chatted with May, only a little guilty about the need for a full night of sleep before our journey of the next day. In truth, neither of us would have slept well that night under any circumstances, so we eagerly took the opportunity to be, once again, a small band of girls enjoying each other's company in the old way. And although our numbers were sadly reduced by two, we didn't talk about that. Instead, we enjoyed what even then I think we knew was a final farewell to the light moments of youth.

I dreamed that night of the train—of great wheels turning, turning; hearing the clatter of their movement on the rails. The locomotive's whistle blew long, mournful echoes of sound, unleashing in me a great yearning to respond. I tossed and turned, trying not to disturb Louisa with squeaking bedsprings. I dozed and dreamed again, this time of boarding black iron steps and hurtling toward our destination, the wind whipping through my hair. Then the high-pitched screech of brakes joined the cacophony of wails and shrieks in my head, offering a first hint of a different, more fearful din. My dreams filled then, not with expectation, but vague dread.

Chapter Five

"See what I made?" I kneeled down and pulled a box out from under the bed, opened it, and held its contents aloft. "Isn't it beautiful?"

Louisa, holding her packed satchel, paused at the bedroom door. Bronson was calling from the hall—hurry, or we would miss our train.

"Oh, Susan, not another hat. We don't have time for this," she said.

"It's not just another hat," I said, twirling it proudly. I had worked hard on this one, and I was anxious for Lou to admire the trimmings of myrtle-green China crepe with an aigrette of flowers, topped with a daring silk hummingbird. "There's a hummingbird for you, too, if you'll let me sew it on that dour old black bonnet of yours," I coaxed.

Gingerly, she touched the hummingbird. "It's very nice, Susan, but you're undoing all my efforts to make you look old and plain," she said.

"What is wrong with going away in style?" I demanded.

"Please, be serious. What if they won't let you stay? If you're all fancied up, you'll draw too much attention, don't you understand? Look at me—think of me as Miss Dix." She cleared her throat, put on her best playacting face, and raised her hand to her heart. "Who is *this*? No hummingbirds are allowed here! Send this flippant young lady *away!*"

So I removed the hummingbird. But I would not leave behind

my new bonnet. "I suspect even John Brown would have allowed a few ribbons," I grumbled.

"His judgment was not always the best."

"Louisa!" I was a bit shocked.

Louisa refused to be chagrined. "Hang on to it, because if you don't, I may 'accidentally' sit on it before we get there. Better me than Dorothea Dix."

I threw a pillow at her. And on that note, we set out.

The railroad platform was windswept and cold and smelled faintly of soot. I fingered the precious commission folded in my pocket, reassuring myself of its presence, thrilled by the freedom it presented. The train was late. We huddled against the cold in our old black coats, stomping our heavy rubbers to keep warm, listening to Abba's last-minute instructions as Bronson stood still as a post, looking miserable. Every few moments Louisa would touch his arm and murmur something comforting, but it was dutiful playacting, for she could hardly hide the excitement in her eyes. Only later would we learn he was soon boasting of having sent his "son" off to war.

In hindsight, I find it difficult to recapture our moods on that exciting, liberating day, and only wonder at our exhilaration in the face of our journey toward a place of loss and death. And yet, in truth, were we so different from all the eager young men heading for the battlefields? Were we not all marching off in separate formation, delighted to be at risk, feeling immortal and protected at the same time? It is the great cheat of war. Glory beckons; glory destroys.

The train finally arrived and we were on our way, with me pulling Louisa up the steps as quickly as possible to avoid lingering good-byes. We changed to a boat at New London, then back to the train at Jersey City. A coupling iron broke when we were outside of Baltimore, bringing us to a sudden halt with lamps falling and water jars tumbling. My precious new hat was squashed by a valise that tumbled from the overhead rack. Louisa gave no smug I-told-you-so's; instead she spent half an hour trying to smooth out the creases. I gave her my share of Abba's apple cake for that.

It was dark by the time we reached Washington City. After some hesitant negotiation, we hired a carriage with a sharp-eyed driver to take us from the railroad station to the hospital, hoping he was not overcharging us as ignorant provincials. "Come aboard, ladies, I'll give you a tour of the town," he yelled. "First note of importance. Washington City had only sixty-one thousand people here two years ago, and how many do you think we have now?"

He waited. He seemed to fancy himself our host, and I realized he wanted us to guess. "Um, maybe seventy thousand?" I hazarded.

"We've got half a million people here, ladies!" he chortled. "Half a million. Now think about that!" We climbed in, and only then realized the carriage floor smelled of urine. Too late. Louisa held her nose and I leaned my head as far over the side as I could to escape the smell.

The streets boiled with people. We passed some sturdy souls bundled in wool with collars turned up, walking quickly through the streets, their breath frosty under flickering streetlamps. A shopkeeper with a huge ring of keys hanging from the belt tucked under his large belly was locking the door of his shop. Soldiers in blue jackets strolled along, gathering in clusters at the street corners, swigging from silver flasks I assumed were filled with brandy. I saw a woman with bright, red curly hair approach one group and actually grab a flask and take a drink.

"Look," I whispered, nudging Louisa. "She's all painted up. Do you suppose—"

"Pay no attention," Louisa hissed.

"There's a grand party at the President's House, shall I drive you by for a look?" the driver yelled, giving us a wink as he whipped his horses a little too vigorously for our taste.

"Yes," I said eagerly, wincing at the sound of the whip.

Louisa gave me a sharp poke in the ribs. I thought I was being reproved, but that was not the case. "Did you bring a ball gown?" she teased. "And gloves?"

I laughed, my spirits lightening. At a farewell dance the week before I had been mortified to find a ragged hole in the finger of one of my white kid gloves. Being quite good with this kind of emergency, Louisa proclaimed I should carry it in my hand, with none the wiser to note nor comment on the poverty of the family. Such small subterfuges meant nothing now. Louisa and I were to be nurses, taking care of the poor souls wounded on the battle-field, and such a noble duty was far more important than worrying about whether one's gloves were peppered with holes. I felt posi-tively buoyant.

"On to the President's House!" I shouted, and together we gig-gled as the carriage bumped over rutted roads filled with mud and water.

When we reached the President's House on Pennsylvania Avenue, we fell silent, impressed by the sight of all the lights glow-ing in the windows. Grand carriages rolled through the gates, wheels crunching through icy drifts. Dancing figures in elegant, cadenced movement moved silently behind the windows of the great veranda. It felt delicious, sitting there, watching, hugging our old coats close, listening to the faint music and bustle from within.

"It's very much like a carnival," I said.

The driver's mood changed abruptly. "I'd not call it a carnival, young lady," he muttered. "Not after Antietam. We had blood run-ning through the streets, and how they can carouse away in there baffles me. Bloody Republicans."

That silenced us. The driver took us next to the Heights above Georgetown, where we could see white tents, like tidy ghosts, lined close under the oaks for shelter. Beyond them was the dark ribbon of water that was the Potomac, and across the river, the sputtering lights of campfires. There were real soldiers huddled around those campfires on the other side of the river, men who were ready to go to battle and perhaps even die. I shivered, oddly thrilled.

The carriage driver's horse plodded slowly as we circled to the northeast corner of Bridge and Washington streets. In front of us was a dilapidated three-story building that exuded a mixed stench of evil smells that made my eyes water. Decaying food, I told myself. I recognized only rancid pork grease. Louisa put her handkerchief to her nose, and the driver took that as an invitation to extol the virtues of Union Hospital.

"Welcome to your new home, ladies," he said with great cheer. "Out of the fifty-odd hospitals in this town, you've picked a winner. No provisions for bathing, and, as you can tell with your noses, the latrines are full. All I can tell you is, they don't bring officers here. Just enlisted men. Heat don't work too well. Truly a garden spot for two pretty women playing at being nurses. Can you believe John Adams once stayed here? Back when it was a fine hotel, that is." The expression on his florid, self-satisfied face was tinged with malice. "Ain't the President's House, is it?"

We pulled our valises off the cart, boots sinking into muck, not bothering to respond. I believe I would have burst into tears and demanded a trip back to Union Station if Louisa had raised a finger in that direction, but she did not. We walked up the steps, pulling our luggage, stopping as a battered oak door swung open and a woman with gray hair curling out from under her cap filled the doorway. She was large and plump, with dimples in her cheeks that looked as if they could, under other circumstances, easily crinkle into a laugh. I never saw her laugh. Her arms looked as if they might once have held bouncing babies and hugged children; now they were crossed in front of her chest, muscular and hard, as she surveyed us coldly.

"So, the new nurses from Concord. Took you two long enough to get here. Bring those valises into the reception room where I can see you both more clearly."

That was our introduction to Hannah Ropes, the matron in charge of nurses. I pulled my bonnet off my head and stuffed it in my bag, hoping she had not yet seen it too clearly. In the reception room, a small box of a room with a desk and three chairs that smelled of mold, she turned up the gaslight and peered at us with shrewd eyes.

"How old are you?" she demanded of me.

"I'm—" my voice caught on the lie.

"She's very mature," Louisa cut in.

Mrs. Ropes just stared. I held myself up higher, wishing I was not so much shorter and slighter than Louisa. We had rubbed some cornstarch in my light brown hair to dull the shine, but I feared it wasn't enough. And I knew I should have roughened my skin more with cornmeal.

"Well, *you* may be, but she's not thirty, I can see that well enough. Do you have any idea what you'll experience here?" She didn't pause for an answer. "I've got too many of you dizzy young things giggling and tittering and vomiting when you empty a bedpan, and there's not a thing I can do about it. You come and go like silly sparrows, but you're all I get." She sounded disgusted and tired. "Come with me. I'll show you around. The steward will bring your things upstairs to the nurses' quarters."

Louisa's lips were pulled thin and tight but she held up a finger, warning me to say nothing. We followed Mrs. Ropes silently.

The place was a rabbit warren. Union Hospital had been a hotel well past its prime when pressed into its present service, and it remained a series of small rooms, one leading into another in bewildering fashion. Mrs. Ropes took us through a closet-type space filled with bottles and tins and bandages shoved onto makeshift shelves in no particular order; this, she said, was the dispensary. Next came the linen room, and then the laundry, a putrid place of stained sheets and terrible smells. Catching me wrinkling my nose at the odor, Mrs. Ropes managed a brittle smile. "Be thankful we're connected to the water supply," she said. "Not all the hospitals in this city can boast of that."

She pushed open a door and we followed her into a wide room that stretched for at least twenty-five feet: the old ballroom, where, she told us, the likes of George Washington and Francis Scott Key had once dined. Along the walls were iron beds, dozens of them, stretching to the back of the room, with billowing hammocks of mosquito netting attached to the ceiling above each one. There was little use for that in the middle of winter, I thought.

Better they add fuel to the iron stove that sat in the middle of the ward, which, given the chill in the air, was clearly inadequate for properly heating the place.

We walked slowly through the room, as Mrs. Ropes scanned her patients with a practiced eye. She spoke to one nurse, giving her an order that sent her scurrying. I was surprised to see only half the beds filled, and a bit shocked to see a raucous card game in progress at the far end of the ward. General McClellan had just been relieved of command of the Army of the Potomac, and the men were arguing over who should be his successor. One claimed Hooker was the rightful heir to the post, though vain as a peacock; another argued the army would be safer in the hands of the cautious Burnside. A wager was laid by the loudest of the group that, with Hooker in command, the Confederate army would take over Washington in less than a month. For all the yelling going on, these men in ragged robes took time to look us up and down as we passed. I blushed. The general feel was more like that of a tavern than a hospital.

"Most here are sick with flu, typhoid, or the like, and the ones getting better can be loutish. Watch out for them," Mrs. Ropes said. She suddenly stopped to study the face of a young man with a dreadful pallor. "We've only a few left from Antietam. Every bed was filled. He's one of the last," she said. She walked over, felt for his pulse, then sighed. With one hand she yanked the sheet over his head and walked on, nodding to us to follow. Louisa and I looked at each other. Not a word of mourning or ceremony? We each clutched the other's hand.

On the far side of the ward was a swinging door that led to the kitchen. She allowed us only the quickest of peeks. I saw a sweaty cook frying what looked to be meat, while another worked with a heavy wooden spoon stirring a gritty mixture in a massive bowl.

"Hardtack and cornmeal," she said. "Our usual fare. We'll go upstairs now." She turned on her heel and led us back down the central corridor to the other end of the room.

"Matron, aren't you going to show your new nurses the dead

house?" shouted a voice from the group of cardplayers. "Missed that on your tour, didn't you? And how about the black hole?"

She ignored the taunt and said nothing until we were out of the ward. "You'll see what the men are talking about soon enough," she said in answer to Louisa's puzzled query. We were just about to climb a narrow set of stairs to the second floor when I spied a brightly colored magazine with French lettering, sticking out of a trash basket. A fashion magazine? Here? Impulsively I grabbed it, tucking it within the folds of my coat, trying to ignore Louisa's warning frown. Fortunately, Mrs. Ropes seemed not to have noticed.

We climbed the stairs in silence. Mrs. Ropes took a deep breath and then started up another flight of stairs, this one steeper and narrower than the first. We were now in the attic, and had to duck our heads while she opened the door to a room the size of a closet. Two cots with a small table between were crammed together, and a single four-drawer chest took up the opposite wall. To get to the far bed meant clambering over the first one, for there was not an inch of space left unfilled. But that meant there was no central dormitory for the nurses, and I was glad of that. No one had bothered to chop out the walls up here. At least Louisa and I could whisper together without a dozen other nurses hearing every word. That promise of privacy suddenly seemed precious.

"No one has yet died on your mattresses, which is more than can be said of most," Mrs. Ropes said, watching us as we surveyed the room. "You'll be up at five for morning shift. Breakfast in the dining room at five-thirty, and those who are late go hungry. Any questions?"

"Why are there so few soldiers in the ward?" Louisa asked.

Mrs. Ropes was fiddling now with a heavy silver ring on her left hand. A wedding ring, I guessed, but I wasn't sure. "At the moment, the men we have here are mostly the victims of disease, not battle. That, of course, will soon change. Now I will leave you to your unpacking, and I will see you in the morning." She looked steadily at me. "I expect mature and knowledgeable behavior from my nurses. And I will settle for nothing less."

Of all times to hold my mouth in check, this was it. I swallowed. "Yes, ma'am, you won't be disappointed," I said.

"Good." Her expression seemed to soften. She gestured at the invisible magazine still shrouded by my coat. "A fancy lady visiting her brother left that," she said. "Filled with useless drawings of shoes and petticoats, as far as I can see. Nothing but fodder for dreams, so keep it under your pillow."

I blushed as she exited the room, not knowing what to say.

I came down the next morning fired with the determination to prove my worth. Louisa was put immediately to work sorting medicines and unpacking supplies. Not sure what duties I was supposed to fulfill or needs I was expected to discern, I decided changing the beds was a good thing to do. Moving through the ward with great energy, I stripped twenty beds and lugged the laundry to the laundry room. Then I went hastening after the steward, a slight man named Mr. Stokes. He was almost bald, and had long arms that made him look like a monkey. I asked him for fresh linens, and was taken aback when he turned surly.

"Are you crazy? We don't have enough supplies to change the beds at some student nurse's whim," he said. I pointed out that at least, surely, the bed of the man who had died the day before should be changed. He shrugged his shoulders and walked away without a word.

So I was left with no fresh linens and several soldiers looking askance at their stained, straw-stuffed mattresses. "At least in the field hospitals they use tree boughs instead of stinking straw," muttered one man. I had created a problem. I hurried to the laundress and asked when the bag of soiled linens would be ready. She hooted. "Ask the steward," she said.

By the end of the day, I was fighting tears. Twenty bare beds, and now the men would have to sleep on the uncovered mattresses. I was not popular in the ward. One man strode up and down the central aisle, banging on the stove, yelling that he couldn't stand stupid nurses who yanked the very sheets from under his head. He had a bottle of whiskey in his hand, surely a violation of hospital rules, but Mrs. Ropes was not there, and no one else saw fit to take it from him. I couldn't understand his anger. Nor could I understand the wild, hard eyes of the other men who shouted encouragement and yelled for a swig out of his bottle. I know now. Those men had seen the battlefields and knew what was to come. It was there in the way they thrashed at night and quarreled with each other during the day. A thread of unbreakable tension wound through everything in that miserable place. Louisa voiced it first as she helped me search for a few clean sheets before being ordered elsewhere.

"Do you feel it? Everyone seems to be waiting for something to happen," she whispered.

It was Liddy Kettle, a nurse who looked younger than I but had very old eyes, who finally took pity on me. She marched into the ward late that night and threw a wad of crumpled sheets on the floor. "All right, you can all quit moaning and whining!" she yelled. "Here are your sheets, malingerers! And you'll all be marching back to your units before you know it!"

I raced to help her put them on the beds. "How did you find them?" I asked as we moved from bed to bed. The sheets were actually clean.

"A little exchange under the table, as usual. You'll learn how things work if you last." She smiled, taking the sting out of her words.

I must have looked as stupid as I felt.

"Listen to me," she said. "Old Stokes sells as much stuff as he can spirit out of here, but he isn't the worst of the lot, by any means." Her eyes darted around the room before she leaned forward and whispered, "The one you've really got to watch out for is Belle Poole. She's assistant head nurse." Liddy nodded quickly in the direction of a heavyset woman with red hair rolling out the meal cart and bent to her work, saying no more. I made the mistake of sneaking another glance, wondering what Liddy meant. Nurse Poole caught me in the act and froze me with a stare. There was something odd about her face, and I couldn't look away. Then I realized she had no eyebrows.

"Are there any interesting pictures in your magazine?" Liddy whispered suddenly, her eyes lively.

I was startled. "I don't know what you're—"

"Oh bother, dearie, I saw you filch it out of the trash barrel. Got interested in you immediately! About the pictures," she giggled. "Anything, well, improper?"

"No, of course not."

"Well, it was a Frenchy magazine, I saw that," she said in a huff.

"It's just fashion. Pretty clothes," I said.

"Can I look at it sometime?"

"Yes," I said, feeling now totally uncomfortable.

With the exception of Liddy, the other nurses avoided us during that first week. No one else bothered to help or explain the routines dictated by Mrs. Ropes. A dozen people shared dinner with us in the hospital mess every night but barely spoke to us or to each other, gulping their food with spoons in their fists like farmhands. The stewards and aides were the worst. They drank and belched and grabbed food off the platters with their hands and shoved it into their mouths, expounding their opinions as if they had the brains to have any. I shuddered when one of the stewards let out a roar of laughter, showing us all a mouthful of half-masticated food. Louisa and I shared a glance after this particular display of repulsive behavior, then, together, pushed from the table and walked away.

Mrs. Ropes confronted us at the door. "Coarseness is a refuge," she said quietly. "Don't dismiss anyone who was here through Antietam." Then she turned on her heel and left.

"She's right, you know. We mustn't act like prigs," Louisa said that night as we sat whispering together on our beds.

"Well, how do we keep from vomiting when we watch them *eat?*" I replied. I had the stub of a pencil and a piece of paper in hand, and began idly tracing a French bridal gown from my magazine.

"Susan, don't waste that paper. We have to write a letter home."

"I'm sorry," I said, putting down the pencil. "What can we write that won't make them worry?"

Louisa thought for a moment. "We'll make it sprightly by creating a joint identity," she said suddenly. "We'll make our letters from . . . from Nurse Periwinkle."

"Well then, make it Nurse *Tribulation* Periwinkle."

We tried to smother our laughter. "Let's do it now," she said, a light dancing in her eye. "We'll tell them how our adventure began, and they'll love reading it aloud to each other."

And so for the next hour, tired as we were, we lifted our spirits by creating the experiences of Nurse Periwinkle from our own, making them jaunty and fun. Such a brief moment of play! I remember vividly the sentence describing our entry into the hospital with which we ended the first letter:

> . . . *Marching boldly up the steps, I found that no form was necessary, for the men fell back, the guard touched their caps, a boy opened the door, and, as it closed behind me, I felt that I was fairly started, and Nurse Periwinkle's Mission was begun.*

Indeed, it was.

I realized immediately the next morning that Belle Poole had taken an active disliking to me.

"You—" she said in a voice strong enough to silence the men clamoring for their breakfast. "You . . . the new one."

"Yes, ma'am," I said.

"Get these bedpans out of here. All of 'em. Empty 'em in back and stop staring. And when you're done, report back to me. I'll keep you busy enough today you won't have time for fancy magazines."

I bent to my task in a great hurry, thinking, with a quiver of apprehension, she may not have eyebrows, but she certainly has ears.

That night I broke down and wept on Louisa's shoulder. Too much, I told her. There had been a fistfight on the ward, with one soldier ripping off another's dressing. Belle had ordered me to rip off the bandage on the offender's arm to show him how it felt, and the lout's howls had filled the room. And I could not comprehend the filthiness of the place. The bedpans I had emptied were filled with days of excrement, but it was the place I was ordered to dump them that made me gag. Nobody had bothered to dig a latrine away from the hospital—the dumping ground was just outside the kitchen door. And how could the place be filled with so many thieves?

"Oh Susan, I'm sorry I talked you into this," Louisa said, rocking me, like the mother I needed her to be at that moment. "It's too much; you're too young. I should never have brought you here."

"It's just so awful," I sobbed, clinging to her. "I don't know what I would do without you." I was ashamed of myself for not being tougher.

"Well, I'm here, and I'm not going away," she said.

"Why can't Mrs. Ropes at least get this place cleaned up?"

"I don't think she has enough power. The man who does is Dr. Coleman, and I hear he sits behind his huge desk and never steps out of his office if he can help it. Mrs. Ropes is just doing the best she can, like the rest of us. You know what I saw tonight? One of the doctors making rounds stood in front of everybody and took a swig out of his whiskey bottle. Nobody said a thing."

I absorbed that, only barely. What sort of place was this? It wasn't just the hospital. That afternoon, after our shift had ended, we had walked down the hill together to the City Canal, hoping for fresh air, and found ourselves instead staring into brackish waters that reeked of pestilential odors.

"Look," Louisa had said, pointing to the stream.

A bloated cat was floating by, its legs splayed upward, rigid in death. A very large cat, I thought. I looked closer, then clutched Louisa's shoulder. "It's not a cat," I whispered. "It's a huge rat."

Without exchanging a word, we turned and trudged back up the hill.

I heard a quiet tapping on our bedchamber door, followed by muffled giggles. When I climbed over Louisa's bed and cautiously lifted the chain, I saw Liddy's bright eyes.

"Let us in," she whispered. "Hurry, so nobody hears."

Three nurses in nightshifts all but tumbled into the room as I pulled open the door. They climbed onto the bed and sat Indian style, chattering gaily, interrupting each other.

"We've decided to take pity on the two of you, and fill you in on the *real* rules to survive in this place," announced the oldest-looking one. A sturdy, cheerful girl, she introduced herself as Mary Cotton, and said she was from a farm in New Jersey and came to Washington City looking for adventure like everyone else, and wanted to assure us that if we learned to avoid Belle Poole and bedpan duty as much as possible, it wasn't so bad. Also there were plenty of things to see and do and fun to be had, if you knew where to find it.

"How can that be?" I asked curiously.

"Honey, look around at all the handsome young men," Liddy said. "They're not all sick, and some of them are good for a little romp now and then. You look ripe and pretty for just what I'm talking about. Wouldn't you like to snuggle up to that good-looking one who always wins at poker?"

I blushed, for I had noticed him. Was she joking?

The third nurse, heavily freckled, was busy combing her hair, having picked up Louisa's brush without a by-your-leave. "You seem like sheltered types to us," she said kindly. "So we want to help you along, and not leave the two of you in here, crying the night away."

The three of them, interrupting each other, proceeded to fill us in on how best to wheedle linens and supplies from the steward, which doctors were drunkards and therefore to be avoided, and how to recognize which medicines were to be taken internally, telling us of one man who had been given lead muriate of ammonia that had been intended for washing his feet. "That nurse is gone, as you can imagine," said the nurse with the freckles, whose name was Helen. "Nobody liked her *at all*."

I was listening eagerly to every word. I loved their insouciance, their jaunty style; the freshness that left them bouncing and giggling on the bed. They seemed more my age than Louisa's. "Are you really all over thirty?" I asked, eyes traveling from one to the other.

They cast each other quick glances. "Oh, what's the use of lying? Not a one of us is near thirty, though we try to pretend, for appearances' sake," said Mary.

"Neither am I," I confided.

"That makes me the old lady of the group," Louisa said.

"Oh, don't feel too badly about that," Mary said, giving her a comforting pat. "We can use your sobriety."

"Well, I'm happy to have something to offer," Lou replied, a bit dryly.

"What else can you tell us?" I asked, trying to suppress a giggle. Louisa and I had been floating in a vacuum, with no one to teach or talk to us, and this was a wonderful release. "Any other advice?"

Mary was clearly warming to her role as mentor to these two straitlaced Concord ladies. "Well, let's see. Oh, of course: clothes. No steel, starch, whalebones, and loosen the waists on your clothes to get comfortable. And you'd best shorten your skirts, for they'll soon be sticky and filthy. And don't even think of hoops."

Liddy nudged her.

"Oh yes, about your monthlies," said Mary. "You should filch some rags for yourselves soon as possible, but make sure you wash them by hand because if they go in with the bed linens, they turn 'em pink. A girl from New York got sacked for that."

"You know, my mother sent me a funny bandage suspender that goes over the shoulders and comes down between my legs," whispered Helen. "She found it in a catalog, with a picture and all. I've got a pair of open drawers I wear it with."

"Oh, really? Can I see it?" I asked, registering Louisa's surprised glance at me from the corner of my eye.

Helen nodded. "It's the oddest-looking thing, and I feel a bit like I'm in a horse's halter when I put it on, but I like it. I keep it tucked in one of my boots so none of the light-fingered types around here get ideas about stealing it."

"Can you imagine old Stokes hauling it out of your boot and wondering what it was for?" Liddy bent double, she was laughing so hard.

I giggled at the mental image of the rather stout Helen in a horse's halter. Louisa and I had never talked so matter-of-factly about monthly bleeding. With whispers, yes, but not with jokes.

"Are we shocking you?" Mary asked, suddenly concerned. Three sets of merry eyes were fastened on my face.

"Not at all," I said, surprised that I meant it. "We're just not used to talking about this. I've heard of women who use nothing."

"Just bleeding down their legs?" Helen asked incredulously.

I nodded.

"Messy," she sighed. "So old-fashioned."

Louisa, who had been silent through much of this, cleared her throat. "It's getting late," she suggested. "We all need our sleep for tomorrow, though you've been wonderful to come console us."

The girls realized this was a gentle good-bye and scooted across the beds in preparation for leaving. But I needed to sate my curiosity on one thing.

"Liddy, what did you trade with Stokes to get back the bed linens?" I asked.

"A few dried-up apples and a bunch of carrots. For a child at home who isn't thriving." She hesitated. "He's not such a bad sort, when you get to know him. See you in the morning."

It took me a few minutes to settle down, for even though we blew out the candle and lay quietly in the dark, I was still experiencing an odd sort of excitement. Somehow Louisa sensed it, because her last words to me before I fell asleep sounded vaguely like a warning.

"Don't believe all that they say, Susan," she said quietly. "Remember who you are."

The week moved on, and the tension grew. Nobody was laughing. No jeers, or catcalls. The card games stopped. Doctors making their rounds were ordering men to put their uniforms on and report back to their units. One after another, they heaved out of their beds, buttoned up their blue shirts, hauled duffel bags out from under their cots, and shuffled silently to the door, slapping each other on the shoulder as they left. By Friday, only five patients remained, two of whom were dying of typhoid fever.

News was leaking in, drop by drop. A carpenter building a towel cabinet told us a great battle was taking place near Fredericksburg. The *Star* claimed General Burnside had crossed the river and was headquartered in Fredericksburg, and would take Richmond in less than ten days. Two army captains dropped by to inspect the premises, and I heard them talk about a place called Marye's Heights. I had just asked the grocery deliveryman what he knew—were we winning? No, he said, spitting forcefully into the cobblestones. It was a rout. The next issue of the *Star* admitted the Rebels still occupied Fredericksburg.

The town buzzed with activity. Transports and freight boats had been unloading vast quantities of hay, potatoes, lumber, and coal on the docks every day for a week now. We heard all officers of the Army of the Potomac had been ordered to rejoin their commands. The War Department gave out no information, but the *Star* once again claimed the Union army had taken Fredericksburg. No one believed it. The sense of waiting was unbearable.

Saturday morning I walked out onto the veranda after unpacking a new shipment of bandages. Hannah Ropes was standing there, her back to me, looking out across Georgetown's rooftops to the distant Virginia shore. Her cap was off, and her gray hair clung, matted, to the nape of her neck. The morning sky was a milky blue, and the air was cool and crisp with the bite of promised snow. A peaceful morning. Fresh and young. I thought for a moment that perhaps she came out here for the same reason I did: to find respite from the smells and sounds inside. But she stood so still, making no move, I hesitated to ask.

"They're coming," she said.

Chapter Six

They began arriving that afternoon. Rickety wagons of pasted wood that looked like market carts, one after another, with drivers shouting obscenities as they maneuvered for position on the rutted street. Men in Union blue with dirty faces and vacant eyes were crammed tight in each cart. Some hung over the sides, their lolling heads wrapped in filthy bandages. Here and there a stiff arm poked out of the unholy mess of carnage. I ran with the other nurses to the first cart as the driver began pushing and heaving the men out onto the ground. Some of them rose dazedly and began to wander into the street, stumbling over their fellow soldiers lying in the dirt. Others inched their way toward the hospital on rude crutches.

"They're not garbage, you bastards, take a bit of care!" someone yelled. It was Stokes, running toward the cart with a stretcher. Mrs. Ropes was helping a bleeding man to the hospital steps. Belle Poole dragged another, but not up the steps—she pulled him around the corner to where a small pile of bodies was already accumulating. I froze. Louisa grabbed my hand and pulled me forward. We tried to haul one man out. I thought his hand was moving, but when I looked down, I saw a spiral of maggots circling frantically in the open wound in his side. The stench was as close to the fumes of hell as the living can imagine.

"Hurry up and empty that cart, we need nurses back here. Some strong ones." It was one of the doctors, the one who had swigged whiskey in the ward. Mary and Liddy ran to help him and I caught a fleeting glimpse of them hoisting an inert form out of the second cart and carrying it up the stairs with enviable ease.

The maggots were spilling out of their home, crawling over my hands. Desperate not to let go, I tried to ignore them, concentrating instead on the pleading look in the man's eyes. He held himself still, as if willing himself not to thrash around. His face was crusted with dirt.

"Put that one by the side of the building," Belle ordered.

"But he's not dead," Louisa gasped.

Belle looked him over, her eye cold but practiced. "He soon will be. Do as I tell you."

I started to cry as we obeyed, unable to look at him directly again. We took him to the side of the building and laid him down among the dead as gently as possible. By then a hazy gray film had obscured his pupils. We headed back to the chaos behind us.

The first cart pulled away and the second rolled forward. Four more stood waiting. No, five. Ten. Someone counted forty. Doctors and nurses and orderlies were lifting and lugging bodies, some on stretchers, some just swinging between two pairs of hands. By the third cartload, Louisa and I figured out how to equalize a man's weight between us and then we worked efficiently for the next hour, bringing in the living and dumping the dead outside. From that, we turned to cleaning and bandaging wounds. Time began to blur.

"You two—" It was Dr. Lyndon, the principal surgeon. A thin man with watery blue eyes who had served in the Crimean War. "Come with me."

We followed him obediently. A surgery table had been cleared at the back of the ward and a boy who looked barely old enough to shave was being hoisted on it. The boy begged for water as an aide hoisted his leg up on a box. "Give him some ether," Dr. Lyndon ordered. He handed me a cloth and I put it over the man's mouth and nose.

"That's enough; we'll run out before the day is over." An orderly pulled the cloth from my hand.

"Now hold him down."

He picked up a large knife, swore as he ran his finger over the dulled edge, and quickly sharpened it on the sole of his boot. Then he cut through the mid-thigh. I had never seen flesh cut before, and was surprised at how quickly it yielded. I saw white bone. The boy was heaving. The doctor put down the knife and reached for a hacksaw. I wanted to shut my eyes, but the boy was screaming, and it took four of us to hold him still.

The job was finished in a few minutes. The doctor picked up the severed leg and handed it to me. "Take this outside," he ordered. I put out my hands and received the still-warm limb. It had been twitching with life only moments before. In a daze, I walked outside, one hand holding the soft, bloody flesh of the thigh and the other wrapped around a muscular calf covered with downy blond hair. How could it lie so still in my hands? I looked around. Where was I supposed to put it? I turned back to ask someone and hesitated, fearful of being seen as ignorant. I should know this, shouldn't I? I stood still on a patch of dry grass, a few yards past the shallow hole where I had emptied the bedpans. I would not put it in there. The leg in my hand was turning cold. It had a faintly oily feel. I looked quickly at it and saw the toenails needed cutting.

At that moment the door banged open and an orderly came running out, holding another leg by the ankle. He looked around and saw me, shrugged, and tossed his on the ground near where I stood. He turned without a word and ran back inside.

So that was what I was supposed to do. A place had been marked. But shouldn't the legs be buried? I felt caught in a nightmare. I deposited my charge next to the other limb with both relief and reluctance.

The door banged open a second time. Mrs. Ropes stood in the doorway, staring at me. Her apron was stained with blood.

"Get out front," she ordered. "They've found another one."

I ran. I made no attempt to go back into the hospital, I simply ran around the corner of the building, stumbling once, and with full force ended up at the lamppost, breathing in short gasps. A small woman was kneeling beside what looked liked a heap of dirty laundry. She glanced up. Her hair was pulled into a knot so tight, the skin of her face looked smooth as that of a china doll. Her eyes were lined in black coal, which made them appear startlingly large. She was dressed all in black, prim enough to be heading to afternoon tea, except for the fact that caked mud had stiffened the laces of her boots.

"Well, it took you long enough!" she snapped. "Give me a hand."

I hesitated, confused.

"Are you a nurse or not?" she said. "Get your arms around his legs."

"I'm sorry," I said as I knelt quickly next to the pile of rags. Only then did I realize it was a man. His face was handsome and so still, it looked carved from stone, and I thought fleetingly of the face on the statue of David. His long legs were crumpled oddly up against his body and his right arm was wet with blood. His hands looked amazingly long and graceful.

"Heave," she ordered.

I tried. He was too heavy and I cursed my small stature.

"Put your hands under his buttocks, bend your knees and heave."

Her voice had calmed. It held such authority, I found my confidence building: If this stranger ordered it, I could do it. Together we lifted the man, who had apparently fallen off one of the carts, unnoticed, and hauled him up the steps and into the hospital. I stole glances at the fierce little woman orchestrating this maneuver and, even as I wondered who she was, I heard a quick intake of breath behind me. I glanced over my shoulder and saw Hannah Ropes watching us.

"Miss Barton? You came in on the hospital boat?" she asked.

The woman gave her a curt nod.

Mrs. Ropes turned to me. "Do anything Miss Barton tells you to do. That's an order."

By then we were lowering the unconscious soldier onto a cot

too short for his lengthy frame, leaving his legs dangling over the end. A small book fell from his coat, which I picked up and shoved into my pocket. He was moaning, turning his head from side to side. Mrs. Ropes had hurried away, and slowly I realized I had just met the woman the men were already calling the Angel of the Battlefield. They told of seeing Clara Barton on the battlefields at Bull Run and Antietam, her face blue with gunpowder, feeding the wounded, bandaging, even digging bullets out of flesh with her penknife. I was awed. I simply stood there, wondering what I was supposed to do next.

Miss Barton answered that question by shoving me in the direction of the supply room. "Get water and soap and bandages, and hurry up. If it's too much for you, get someone to help." She turned her attention back to the man, muttering something under her breath.

Mortified, I ran to the supply room. Louisa was there, digging for fresh bandages in the chaotic mess. I grabbed her by the hand. "Come help, Clara Barton is here," I whispered as I pulled her with me back to where Clara was working on the unconscious soldier.

"Get his clothes off. And be careful of his wounded arm." Miss Barton did not even look up at us.

Dutifully, Louisa and I stripped him of his grimy pants and shirt as quickly as we could. I noted his splendid body, averting my eyes as quickly as I could, and this time I tried hard not to think again of the statue of David. But his flaccid member looked like nothing I had ever seen before. I hesitated, loath to pick it up to wash beneath.

Louisa reached past me when she saw my hesitation and covered it with a rag as she scrubbed. "We mustn't let her see our ignorance," she whispered.

"But this thing has to be cleaned, too," I said. I grabbed his member and held tight—too tight.

"What the hell are you doing?" he roared. His eyes were wide open now; they were blue, a fierce, clear blue, bluer than any sky I had ever seen. He heaved himself up and tried to slap me away as I dodged the blow.

"That's enough, young man," Clara said, pushing him back down to the bed with unexpected power. "Though I'm glad to see you have some fight left in you."

We followed her lead and pushed ourselves until he fell back. Then, holding tiny, grainy slivers of soap that kept crumbling apart in our hands, we began to scrub. Such hopeless supplies we had. Louisa called to Mr. Stokes to bring fresh linens and adhesive plaster, but he simply shrugged and walked away. We had to use dirty rags, and I saw the irritation on Clara's face. I resolved to show it was not the nurses at fault here, but the hospital. So I scrubbed as hard as I could. When the soldier suddenly spoke, I dropped my rag in surprise.

"Ladies, I know you are attempting to clean me up and hopefully to make me whole, but you have not as yet had the courtesy to ask my name."

How could that dry, ironic voice be coming with such surprising strength from a wounded man? By rights, he should be moaning or speaking at least from a weakened state. Louisa and I, arms poised, were momentarily paralyzed.

"My dear boy, we would like to know your name, but we are first and foremost nurses intent on helping you, and for us, duty comes first. Now settle down," Miss Barton said firmly.

He was not intimidated.

"I choose to consider that an invitation," he replied with a mocking sweep of his good arm. "May I introduce myself? I am John Sulie, late of the army of Ambrose Burnside, one of the more crazed generals of this war. A blacksmith by trade—from Virginia." He managed a smile. "And I am not your 'dear boy.' How do you do?"

Louisa recovered first. "I am Nurse Alcott, and this is Nurse Gray," she said in the firmest of voices, nodding at me. "And you, sir, have just insulted Miss Clara Barton."

He stared at Louisa; she lifted her chin and stared back. Then he turned to Clara and said quite gravely, "I have seen you on the battlefield, and I beg your pardon, madam. How badly, may I ask, am I injured?"

She didn't answer immediately. I cast a swift glance at the festering hole in his right arm and knew there was sure to be some cutting and sawing when the surgeon came around. We were told men with this kind of wound were often dead in a few days, but some survived. "We won't know until the doctor makes rounds tomorrow," she said.

"Then there's nothing to do but wait for him to finish the job the Rebs began. If you'll excuse my bad manners, I think I'll take leave of your delightful company." His eyes closed, and he drifted off, turning his face away.

Miss Barton slowly wiped her hands on one of the rags, and faced us in a suddenly collegial mood. "This one's full of vinegar, isn't he? He'll sleep now, at least for a while." She straightened, wincing, as if her back hurt. "I need a cup of tea. Are you on surgery duty?"

I thought of my efforts to deposit the severed leg and felt instantly nauseous. "I was told to report to you, Miss Barton," I said.

"First time you've watched them hack off limbs, I imagine," she said. "You're obviously new to all this, and mighty young, if I guess correctly. Are you sisters?"

"No, but we almost are," Louisa replied. "We're cousins—and good friends."

"And I'm older than I look," I said. Conversation seemed possible now—the wagons had stopped coming; the wounded were attended to. I tried to smile.

Clara, after a pause, thrust her hand deep into a pocket of her dress and pulled out a tiny packet of tea. "I always carry my own," she said, in answer to my questioning glance. "Now let's get some cups, and then you can tell me about yourselves."

Somehow I managed to find three battered tin cups in the kitchen while Clara boiled a pot of water, working almost serenely in the midst of the chaos. But no one challenged her—not even Nurse Poole, who gave us a glare as she hauled a pot of gruel from the iron stove and put it on the serving cart.

Clara saw my nervousness. "Don't feel guilty, dear," she said kindly enough as we stood together out of the way, against a wall. "You'll work hideous hours here, and five minutes for a cup of tea won't kill your reputation."

"We do it at your invitation," Louisa said quickly.

Clara took a sip of tea with the daintiness of a queen before she spoke. "If you look to me for advice, here it is. Cleanliness matters, though some will laugh at that. Scrub the patients as often as you can and use only washed bedding. Throw those cursed rags into the wash and don't use them again. And I don't care how much you hate it, keep those slop jars emptied." She cast me a sharp look. "Where is the trench?"

"Right outside the kitchen door," I said.

"Those idiots. Tell them to put it somewhere else." She seemed cross again.

Louisa and I glanced at each other. The very idea that we could exert any control over how this house of pestilence was run was some sort of dark joke. Clara caught the glance and softened, acknowledging, I hoped, our obvious lack of authority. She began to pepper us with questions about ourselves, drawing us out with her curiosity. Soon we forgot we were in the presence of such an awesome person. I felt warmed, and eager to tell her who we were, where we were from, and why we had come. Louisa, true to her own nature, shared herself in a more reserved way. Only within the family did she reveal herself freely. Yet we both became animated, more confident; all in the space of but a few minutes.

"You seem a good combination," Clara said, casting us a shrewd glance as she drained the last tea from her cup and put it down.

"In what way?" I asked, curiosity piqued.

She shrugged, intent on removing her apron. "You have different traits, somewhat dissimilar, that's all. Opposing traits, perhaps."

"Louisa is my anchor," I promptly said.

"No, no, you are mine," Louisa said.

"Me? Nonsense," I replied.

"No need to argue, ladies, you'll figure it out eventually," Clara said, a smile flickering across her face. She prepared to leave, announcing she would stop in to see Hannah Ropes, visit with some of the men, and then head home to her apartment, which she told us was on Seventh Street. Hopefully, she added, there would be heat. One never knew. I would learn that Clara always declared what she was going to do in advance of doing it, like a general announcing strategy to his troops.

I suddenly hated to see her leave, realizing her presence had raised my level of confidence. Would I just be a frightened girl again?

But Louisa had something else on her mind. "You know the nature of the men we treat," she said to Clara as we accompanied her to the front of the hospital. "Does the man we carried in seem different from most?"

Clara glanced in the direction of the bed holding the form of the sleeping blacksmith. His legs swung over the edge, moving in a lazy arc as he slept. "He does," she said.

"How?"

"He doesn't seem to like obeying orders, now, does he? Not like an ordinary foot soldier." She chuckled. "He's going to be a handful."

"He's just a boy. I can give him the mothering he needs," Louisa said.

Clara seemed puzzled. "A boy? He's not a boy."

"Well, he needs attention, that's what I meant. Kindly attention."

"Does he bother you?"

Louisa spoke slowly. "He unsettles me."

Clara responded in sober fashion. "Then watch out for him."

It was nighttime. The surgeons were gone, their patients lying moaning in their beds. Mrs. Ropes turned down the gaslight, and the ward quieted further. Not a single bed was empty tonight, and many men lay on blankets on the cold floor. Mr. Stokes summoned me to help carry a body out to the dead house. There, I saw the bodies of dozens of men. I could not believe the sight.

"Swing him on the stack," ordered Mr. Stokes. I hesitated, but he was reasonably kind. "If we don't stack 'em, we won't have room for the ones to come tomorrow and the next day," he said. And so I swung.

When I came back in, Louisa was changing the bandage on the arm of the man called Sulie. He was awake, staring at the ceiling.

"We need to get some boards to lengthen your bed so you will be more comfortable," she said to him. "Shall I write a note to your family?"

"I don't have any, so that won't be necessary." He closed his eyes, and wrinkled his nose. "Lord, this place smells bad."

Louisa looked at me and shrugged. We could hardly argue with that. No amount of dosing the ward with lavender water worked.

"We can't get fresh air in here because the windows are nailed shut," Louisa said, as she struggled to get a hospital gown around his right shoulder.

He winced, but responded immediately. "Well, maybe you should smash a few panes. Ever consider that?"

"Don't be silly," Louisa said.

"Ah, that's a sharp response. Are you the night nurse?"

Louisa nodded, looking a little nervous. He had such a steady gaze, made all the more unnerving by the thick, dark lashes framing those unnaturally blue eyes. He had no beard, just a small mustache. His mouth and chin were strong, I thought.

"You don't know if I will live or not, of course. Not to take away from your kind efforts, but we have a saying on the battlefield: If you die in battle, you die once; if you end up in a hospital, you die twice." Then all irascibility vanished. "I'm not relishing the night. Will you stop by to talk?"

"Of course," Louisa said, casting me a slightly furtive glance, for we shared a private fascination. We liked to watch the men sleeping at night. I would stare at their faces, seeing the taut lines of manhood relax, wondering what dreams filled their heads. Their lips seemed softer, their closed eyes relieved of wary hardness or pain. It was a treat we gave ourselves, of sorts. After days of scrubbing bodies and briskly changing dressings, our every action stripping them of male power, it allowed other feelings; reflections on their mysteries. Louisa said it helped her to pretend they were children. I didn't agree with that, but wasn't sure why.

John Sulie hadn't asked me to stay and I felt a pang of disappointment. Bundling up the soiled bandages, I turned to go, but not before first stealing another glance at him. Even lying in his bed, he exuded an energy that fascinated. There were no men in Concord like this one, of that I was sure.

Hearing a thick phlegmy cough, I glanced at the next bed. A young boy no more than twelve turned toward us and pulled his skinny body up onto one elbow. We knew him as Jimmy. It broke my heart to see his pinched, vulnerable face—his eyes so frightened; a boy who should be home with his family, afraid only of the dark. I yearned to hold him close, to rock him and tell him all would be well. The other soldiers said he had been a drummer with the Union force that fell to Confederate guns as it stormed a bridge across Antietam Creek. A small, skinny boy, barely tall enough to hold a drum, that's how they remembered him. He drummed away with as much bravery as the grown men around him, they said. He never lost the beat that kept the men moving across that dreadful spot of carnage.

He was hallucinating again. I put down my bundle and went to his side.

"Bill, is it you?" His eyes squinted as he peered through the gloom, trying to see the man next to him. "Have you finally come? Are you all right?"

Louisa moved to his other side, dipped one of the dirty rags into the water bucket, and held it against his hot forehead. The boy fell back and began to cry.

John Sulie opened his eyes. "Who does he ask for?"

"The soldier who carried him off the battlefield and saved his life. He didn't survive. Some of the men here say they think he was the boy's older brother."

The sound of the door banging open made us all jump. Belle Poole. I still shake, remembering that woman. There were those who said she had suffered, something about a lost child, but whatever tribulation she had endured, she offered it back in full order to anyone helpless under her care. Those small, bright eyes sitting bare in her white face. Those thick shoulders. "So he's gone off again?" she said. "That boy will wake the entire hospital, them that ain't already screaming their heads off."

She leaned down and put a cup to the boy's lips as we watched. I remember thinking, She is coarse and rough, but what is there to do? There were few enough people who wanted to work in a hospital as grim as ours. Mrs. Ropes was a pragmatist; she took what she could get. And who was I to feel uneasy about Nurse Poole's care? I knew nothing.

Jimmy took two deep gulps and fell back. The gaslight flickering in the one lamp hanging over the ward shone down almost directly on his waxen face. The soldier was watching, too.

"Bill? Bill?" The boy's voice was faint.

With a heavy sigh, John Sulie thrust out his arm and enfolded one of the boy's clenched fists inside his own large hand. "I'm here," he said. "And I'm fine." He held tight, waiting until the boy's eyes closed in sleep before gently letting go. Belle simply snorted and left the room.

"I detest this sad need to pretend," he said to no one in particular.

Louisa looked at him in dismay. "Why would you diminish the comfort you've given this boy?"

"Because I'm not the one he wants. It's false," he said.

"No, it is not. The only falsity comes from mocking his need."

His gaze sharpened with interest. "Who are you, and where are you from?"

"I've told you my name."

"Only your surname. I'm a sick man, and I demand more."
There was actually a teasing spark in his eye.

"My name is Louisa Alcott, and I am from Concord."

"Ah, then you are probably one of those murky, vague Transcendentalists."

Louisa stiffened. "This time you mock what you don't know."

He appeared to be almost memorizing her face now. "Please pardon me. But surely you are an abolitionist, am I right?"

Louisa nodded warily.

"Then you are a lady who shares the passion of my soul. We'll have much to talk about."

My hand went to my pocket. "I think this is yours," I said, pulling out the book I had retrieved from the floor that morning.

Louisa glimpsed the title and I saw her surprise: It was a well-thumbed copy of John Milton's *Paradise Lost.* "Milton?" she said.

"It belonged to a friend who fell in battle. You're not about to make fun of his taste, I hope."

"My goodness, no. It's always been one of my favorite poems," Louisa said. "Have you read it?"

"It might surprise you, but yes, many times."

"What do you like about it?"

"Old Milton tries to account for evil in this world, hard as it is to do. And he hated tyranny—I like that, too."

They gazed at each other in silence while I stood there, staring at the shape of his powerful legs under the sheets. Louisa's voice jolted me out of this reverie.

"Go get some sleep, Susan, you're on early-morning duty."

Her words were abrupt, and I flushed. Without waiting for a response, she settled herself deep into the chair between the soldier and the young drummer, smoothing her pinafore into place with her fingers. I was struck by her calmness. She seemed . . . what is the word? Proprietary. I felt a twinge of unrest I could not identify.

I have no idea what they talked about that night. I do not know what they shared, but I know that when I came back at sunrise, they were both asleep. Louisa was slumped deep into her chair, her body awkwardly sprawled, her head almost pillowed next to his. Their fingers were intertwined. My hands shook. The men around me were beginning to stir as the sun's weak rays crept into the old ballroom, and soon someone would see what I was seeing.

John Sulie's eyes suddenly flew open. He looked directly at me, awake and clear. I saw a small mole at the side of his mouth and had an absurd desire to touch it. He smiled, almost as if he knew what I was thinking. Gently. Softly. "You wake her up," he said. "I'll pretend to be asleep. I don't like to frighten nurses."

Chapter Seven

I shook Louisa awake with more force than necessary. "Let go of his hand," I whispered.

She gave me a befuddled glance, pulled her hand away, and jumped to her feet. John's eyes remained dutifully closed.

"Somebody could see you," I said crossly.

"Susan, I fell asleep. Don't be so agitated."

"It isn't proper, it looks intimate. You know some people here would be quick to judge, and we must be careful. We can't risk our reputations." I felt oddly flustered even as I spoke. Me, scolding Louisa? This was a glove that did not fit.

"For heaven's sake, it was totally innocent," she protested, sounding as flustered as I felt.

I tried to explain myself. "It's not just the act of comforting, it's *how* you comfort, and I—"

"All right, Susan, I understand." She patted my shoulder and lowered her voice. "I need to talk to you, for this is—"

She was interrupted by a yell from the front of the hospital. We turned and ran for the door, to be greeted by the same dismal sight as the day before—more carts arriving, filled again with another wretched cargo of wounded men.

The sad caravan showed no signs of ending. The field hospitals were rapidly emptying themselves of patients. The human refuse of the battle of Fredericksburg was now our responsibility. But where were we to put them? All the hospitals were inundated now. Somehow, miraculously, Mr. Stokes procured extra beds. A pair of colored men brought them in, carrying them on their heads, and when the nurses spontaneously began to clap, they grinned. One, theatrically inclined, gave us all a sweeping bow of thanks, and I laughed for the first time in weeks.

Then, back to work. Liddy and I began stripping a man with both legs blown away. We were about to cover him with a sheet when his member popped up, hard and straight, standing like a flagpole. I had never seen such a sight. Was this what a man looked like when ready to enter a woman? How could something so obscene be happening? This stranger lying in front of me was losing blood and in delirium. He was probably going to die. What should I do?

"Move aside, Susan." Liddy reached past me and gave the fleshy, rigid thing a sharp slap with the back of her hand. It collapsed instantly, as if on command. "It's all right, we all have a first time," she said, when she saw the expression on my face. And then, with a wink: "Don't think you won't be wanting to do this in other circumstances. So whack one when you have the chance, and just remember, you got this advice from Lady Kettle."

It was a terrible day. The same scene as the day before: dozens of men in each cart, piled together. Bodies hauled onto tables; saws severing limbs; men screaming. I no longer trembled as I seized those limbs, strode to the door, and tossed them onto the growing pile outside. I thought only of moving quickly and efficiently. I was learning what I needed to do and how quickly it had to be done. The men faded as people; I concentrated on my duty. And although the ward stank of death and rot more than ever, by the end of that day, I could smell nothing.

"You did well," Mrs. Ropes said to me at sundown. I felt a weary pride at her words. She no longer saw us as the clumsy, naive recruits from Concord; we had on this terrible day earned our credentials as seasoned nurses. She turned away, and I wondered, fleetingly, how this stoic woman who had seen everything could bear the sorrow.

Louisa emerged at that moment from the storeroom with an armful of fresh bandages, the lines around her mouth carved deep with weariness. She looked up and caught my eye. Only then did I see something else, something banked behind her fatigue, something—what was it, a lively light?—that seemed impervious to the squalid scene around us. I wondered, Could something good be happening? That thought lightened my step, if but briefly.

A ripple of tension crackled across the ward. I looked up and saw Dr. Lyndon striding back into the room. We had thought him finished for the day. Lyndon sawed and hacked more efficiently than any of the other surgeons, and no one wanted him at his bed. He was a slight man with a thin neck and a large Adam's apple that bobbed up and down incessantly during surgery. Tonight, his pale eyes were rimmed in pink, perhaps from weariness. He cast a darting glance at Louisa. She had scorned his invitation to dinner shortly after our arrival, which had not increased our standing as newcomers. The story whispered about the hospital was that he was the worst drinker of the bunch, or so Mary Cotton told us. Although, she had added tartly, "How anybody could do what he does without swigging down the brandy, the good Lord alone knows."

"I hear I've got one more tonight," he said, as he strode over to the bed of John Sulie. "Let's look at that arm. Hurry up, I don't have all day."

Louisa handed me the box of bandages and moved closer to watch the rough, cursory examination. The blacksmith glanced up at her and I saw something pass between them, but he showed no emotion. Only tightened lips conveyed his pain.

"As I suspected, it has to come off," Lyndon said, which was no surprise—from what I had seen in these two days, he always said that.

"Are you sure?" Louisa asked instantly.

This time the glance he cast in her direction was shot with irritation. "Of course I'm sure. Dan"—he turned to the aide hovering next to him—"get me the saw. And some liquor for this man."

I braced myself for the inevitable. But what was there to do? If the doctor said an amputation was necessary, it was necessary. So John Sulie's response caught me by surprise.

"Not on your life," he said in that calm, strong voice that had so surprised me the night before.

Lyndon frowned. "I make the decisions on this. If you want to avoid gangrene, your arm must come off."

"Whatever kills me, I'll go out with both arms attached, thank you."

"Can't you smell it, man?" Lyndon's voice was incredulous.

Louisa resolutely stood by John's side, but her hands trembled. The sweet sickly smell of gangrenous wounds filled the ward every day. Were we so used to it that we hadn't realized how fast the wound in his arm was festering?

John nodded toward Louisa, pulling her into the confrontation. "Nurse here is keeping it clean. I don't think it's that bad. She'd raise the alarm if it were."

Lyndon raised a skeptical eyebrow, then restlessly shifted weight from one leg to the other. He licked dry lips, clearly impatient to leave. A cool drink from the brandy bottle hidden behind a dilapidated volume of Shakespeare awaited him in his office. Even I knew that. "Fine, suit yourself. You'll change your mind," he said. He turned to walk away and stopped at the bed of the sleeping drummer boy. "How much calomel is this boy getting?" he asked.

"He was given a cupful last night," Louisa replied.

"I left instructions not to give him any more. Did you give it to him?"

Louisa and I shook our heads in unison.

"Who did?"

The answer came like a growl from the blacksmith. "The fat woman they call Belle," he said.

"Damn her," muttered Lyndon as he strode away. "She'll clear the wards faster than the typhoid."

Mrs. Ropes's voice made me jump. "Go get some dinner, ladies," she said. "You'll need your energy for the work ahead."

Lou and I hurried away with all pretense of duty, headed not to the mess but to our room, which seemed now both a haven and the only sane place amid chaos.

"What were you starting to tell me this morning?" I said as we climbed the stairs.

A warning finger rose to her lips. "Wait," she whispered.

We closed the bedroom door and Louisa grabbed my hand. "Susan, it's about John Sulie. He is not a common soldier. He speaks from the mind. I'm a little frightened."

"Frightened?"

"You were quite right to warn me this morning, but you must understand, we spent most of the night talking about abolition and the war and John Milton."

"Then why are you frightened?"

"He told me I was unlike any woman he had ever met."

"How? What did he say?"

"He said I had a fine brain." She flushed, looking almost as pretty as May. "He asked to hold my hand while he slept. For comfort, he said. The way Henry did."

But only when Henry was dying. Words not to be uttered, I thought.

"I loved that," she said. "It wasn't improper, but yes, it was intimate—in the right way. I could have talked to him all night, and I'm mortified that I fell asleep. I can't believe I did something so stupid."

"No one else saw," I assured her.

"He isn't a common man, Susan. He has a noble spirit, and that's what I responded to. He listened to me. He listened to all that I said."

I had not seen Louisa simultaneously so soft and sure ever before, and it made my own heart soar in the strangest way. Perhaps she was falling in love. In a different way than with Henry; surely in a better way.

"Don't look at me with such excitement, Susan. This isn't what you are thinking."

Oh, I was sure I knew better! I could see something hopeful and wonderful in her eyes. "You don't have to be so cautious," I said. "I saw the way you two looked at each other."

"Oh Susan, such nonsense!" But a smile played on her lips.

"Well, something splendid was happening, I know it was, and there's nothing to be alarmed about." I infused my voice with certitude, thinking, Well, it *is* about time. Lou deserves it.

"I enjoy talking with him." That was the most she would offer.

"Then by all means, do so again. Do you want to take my shift tonight? That will give you the chance to . . . to share your thoughts with him—about abolition." I had a sudden inspiration. "Perhaps he is your own Ernest L'Estrange!"

She laughed. "Oh, you would remember him!"

"Why not?" I said. "It could be true."

"Susan, don't push."

"Don't pull back." I had to push her; she would never proceed on her own. She would spend her life sniffing flowers and gazing at herons, dreaming of Henry, if I didn't push. And so I coaxed her out onto the highest limb of any tree she had ever climbed. And why? Because it was the limb from which I wished to swing. I convinced myself no harm would come of this; that love would free her spirit, and if she slipped, love would allow her to sprout wings and soar. As, I was convinced, it would for me. Some day.

It grew late. Louisa took night duty. I knew how deprived she was of sleep, so I rose from my bed several times to see if she needed help. Finally I stayed up, dozing on the bench against the wall, watching as she moved among the wounded men, quietly soothing and talking to them, and always coming back to the chair next to John Sulie's bed. Each time she approached he raised himself onto his good arm to watch her progress, I could see plainly he was captivated, even though Louisa looked worn and tired, her splendid hair pulled taut under a cap, her mouth stern and jaw heavy. But she bore herself regally, almost as if she once again had the glory cloak adorning her shoulders. I could imagine her resplendent in real silk, transcending scruffy reality. If I could see her thusly, so surely could he.

"Tell me about Concord, about how you live," I heard him say. She lowered her head to his, and the intimacies of their murmurings excited me. They touched hands. I trembled, closing my eyes, imagining more.

I dozed, awaking every few moments, listening. Around midnight, I heard one of the soldiers who had fallen at Marye's Heights crying. He had been brought in that morning with his gut torn open, enduring dreadful pain. Through the day he had stared at the ceiling and not cried out once. Nor would he exchange a word with any of us as we changed his dressings. Now he cried for his mother. I moved swiftly to his side, not wanting to disturb Louisa, and did all that could be done for him at this point. I crooned an old song and stroked his head. I had tried to comfort another soldier the night before who spat epithets on my approach and weakly pushed me away, leaving me stumbling not to fall into his filled chamber pot. When was it right to intrude? I knew so little about human nature, so little about the nature of men.

A welcome glow of moonlight fell across the ward. The flame in the overhead lantern flickered even more than usual, and I prayed it would not go out. There was no more oil in the storeroom to replenish it, so we were in a race between darkness and the morning sun. I dozed again, caught in a dream of anguished murmurings.

Somewhere in the hours after midnight, the young drummer boy sat up with a grunt, his figure almost ghostly in its white linen undershirt. Jimmy's tongue, huge and purplish, was protruding from his mouth. His eyes were round and frightened, and his breathing more labored than before. Louisa moved swiftly to his side.

"Susan, help me!" she cried as she tried to pull him up straight to clear the mucus filling his throat. I ran to her side, but the flailing boy pushed us both away with surprising strength.

"Hang on," a voice said from the next bed. I looked over and saw John heaving himself up onto his good arm, pulling his body with great effort away from the covers, lurching over to the next cot. It was he who held Jimmy's head up while Louisa thrust her hand into the boy's mouth, scooping out the bubbling, awful flow of mucus. I stepped back, both helpless and riveted.

"Won't be long now. He'll be gone by daylight."

Belle Poole was standing at the end of the bed, limp coils of red hair hanging over her forehead, arms crossed against her ample chest. She might have been talking about a dog. Not a tear, not another word. Did she not see the boy's fear? One more suffering body to clear out of the ward, that was all she cared about.

"Keep your mouth shut," snapped John Sulie. "He isn't deaf."

"You keep a civil tongue in your head, Sulie. I'm the senior nurse on this ward, and don't you forget it." She turned and disappeared into the supply room.

He saw through her better than any of us, which was, I know now, his great misfortune. I was still trying mightily to understand the need to be cool under pressure, even to accept the wry humor of someone like Liddy Kettle as necessary for sanity in this work. I feared Nurse Poole, but did not yet know how to separate out her kind from others who would appear indifferent to suffering but do their jobs more efficiently than I. Yes, John saw.

The night passed slowly. John did not sleep. He balanced himself on the edge of Jimmy's cot and held his hand, watching the boy with a tenderness I was not used to seeing in a man. I moved in and out of restless dreams, but each time I looked in John's direction, I wondered, Was he a father? Next time I awoke, I saw Louisa and the soldier holding vigil at the boy's bed. John was singing a soft, unfamiliar song, the words of which I could not catch. He and Louisa murmured to each other; the boy cried and whispered to them both.

"Nurse, is the boy gone yet?" asked a burly sergeant lying near my chair who had lost his right cheekbone and an eye to a cannonball, and would live forever with a lopsided face. I started to soothe him, telling him all was well, and he snorted in derision.

"Not yet," I said, humbled.

Jimmy died at sunrise. A sleepy aide had just pulled open the curtains and let in the first rays of morning light when the boy took one deep gulp of air and let it go with a swooshing exhale. By then, I, too, was standing vigil at his bedside. We waited. His chest did not rise again.

How does one describe such a thing? You stare, expecting, waiting for the chest to heave. Movement is all. Leaves flutter, birds twitter, people inhale, cry, laugh, blink their eyes. When all is still, death has won, and it takes us to our knees. Jimmy's death was only one of so many at Union Hospital, but it is the one I will remember forever.

"How old was he?" John asked.

"Not yet twelve," Louisa answered, her voice shaky.

"God damn war. He should have been home with his folks, going to school." John's voice was thin from tiredness as he pulled himself up from the cot and returned to his own bed. He turned away as two aides arrived to wrap the body quickly and take it to the dead house. Louisa wept; I wept. He refused to weep. I saw blood oozing through the bandage on John's right arm. Louisa saw at the same time I did, but she was quicker at gathering strips of cloth from a supply basket and changing his dressing. I sat back and watched. Her hands were deft as she peeled off the soiled bandage. When he winced, she stopped and touched his shoulder. A quick motion, unmistakably a caress. For just an instant, I felt a longing.

"Why are you here?" he suddenly asked, facing her. "Why did you come to this godforsaken place?"

He wasn't the first soldier to ask. I had learned from Louisa to respond with stout declarations of duty and patriotism and then roll the questioner over for a good scrub in hopes that he might live through another day. But this time she surprised me.

"Because I feared I would reach my death without having lived," she said, as if it were the most ordinary thing.

He searched her eyes. "So, you are willing, then, to reach out for the unknown adventure."

"I hope so. I would be so ashamed if I didn't at least try."

"And what is it that you want?"

She hesitated. "I want to help humanity. But I also want to be . . . more human."

"Ah." His voice was soft. "How do we do that, Louisa?"

"I don't know."

"Perhaps war itself does the trick."

She hesitated. "I hate war."

"As do I. But we both have the taste of war in our mouths now. What it offers."

"What does it offer?"

"Intensity. The chance to be . . . how did you put it? More human."

"There are better ways."

"But it is a seductive song."

They seemed to understand each other perfectly, but what were they saying? I couldn't understand at first, but later I thought of Clara. Was not the glory of battle in part why she had marched onto the battlefields—not to leap a wall or bayonet one of the enemy but to feel more alive, to live intensely? To feel a cannonball come so close as to rip a hole in her skirt and yet to remain alive, to gloriously transcend death? Was this what Louisa understood from John's challenge? And it was a challenge. The "taste of war," indeed. It took me years to understand the deeper secret in the air, in the whisperings of the men, in the triumphal marches and rousing songs, even in the hospital where limbs were sawed off and bodies of eleven-year-olds were hauled away in mucus-soaked sheets. The "taste of war"? No, the love of war.

"Tell me again what you feel about him," I whispered at the end of that sad and dreary day.

"He is warm and kind, you saw that last night. And he is a man of valor who never complains."

"He shares your feelings about the slaves?"

"Yes. But he voices cynicism about what is possible."

"What else?"

She hesitated, choosing her words as meticulously as flowers in a spring garden. "There's a vibrancy to him—how do I describe this? Susan, he invites me in. Without effort. And I walk to where he is, without effort."

I closed my eyes, willing myself to be in such a magical place. Once there, I pushed forward. "May I make your wedding dress?" I asked.

A soft sigh reached my ears. "You are so dear, Susan. I am not going to marry, I've told you that."

"Oh, don't tell me again that you only share lofty ideals and concerns about the war, I know there's more. You don't always have to be good."

"I've tried to tell you. Good night, Susan."

"His hands look so strong. How did it feel when he held yours?" I closed my eyes, imagining the strength, the authority of those beautiful hands, imagining just for an instant how they would close over mine, commanding, drawing, holding fast.

"I said good night."

"Louisa . . ." I drew out the syllables, teasingly.

Her voice softened with approaching sleep. "Yes, I was stirred."

I drifted to sleep, lulled first by a wisp of a dream, then later awakened by emotions that set me tossing and turning throughout the night.

The days settled into a blur of caring for patients from dawn to midnight and then collapsing into bed. Legless men, armless men. Men who breathed at night and were cold and still by daybreak. Louisa and I worked together as much as we could, watching out for each other. If I saw her so fatigued she could barely stand, I would take over her tasks, and she would do the same for me. If a letter came from home—and how we loved those times—one of us would pocket it until the other was free, and then we would find a quiet place to read with all the hunger of two friends far from safety.

Only at night would we hold each other and cry over what we were seeing. Then we would wash what we could of the day's blood and grime away, and try to stay warm under Mrs. Ropes's thin blankets, reminding ourselves to lock our room so the thieves who were so active in the hospital might not take it upon themselves to steal what little we had.

I caught John watching me one morning as I hurried into the ward. I felt a sudden shyness, and then realized he was looking past me, surely for Lou. I went to his side, reaching to plump his pillows, relishing his sigh of relief as I made him more comfortable. "Louisa's on laundry duty this morning," I whispered. "She'll be by as soon as she can."

"Am I so transparent?" he said with a small grin.

"She looks for you, too," I said, spending a little more time than necessary with the pillows.

"Are you wearing a scent?" he asked, looking closer at me.

"Just an essence of gardenias," I replied, nervous that he had noticed. Liddy had drawn me aside the night before to show me a small vial she kept of crushed gardenia petals, coaxing me to use some, and, yes, I had pressed a smidgen into the warm skin of my wrists, loving the smell.

"It's very nice. Why are you wearing it here?"

His blunt question startled me, and I tried to pull back into my role as a nurse. "It's a way of refreshing the atmosphere," I said.

"I see." He nodded. "But surely you are not indifferent to the sensual pleasures of an enticing smell?"

"It . . . it makes me feel—"

"It makes you feel pretty, am I right?"

"Yes."

"Good, for you are, and you deserve to know you are."

If his eyes hadn't been so kind, I might have been more flustered. Instead I allowed myself to laugh.

"You have a nice laugh, Susan. Tell me about yourself."

"I like to draw," I offered.

"So, an artist." He spoke gravely, with no hint of mockery. "I envy someone who can render truth with the skill of their hands. What do you draw?"

"I design tangible things, such as hats and dresses." It all must sound vain and inconsequential to him, I thought. "And I love bringing my designs to reality."

"Then you see the world in a curious, creative way," he said.

"You think so? Not all do."

"Of course, you do. I'm not surprised, given your friendship with Louisa."

"She's told you about us?" I felt shy, wondering how much he knew.

"Well, I know you didn't like hiding in the oven for her plays. And that she rescued you from a bleak and lonely home."

"Then you know quite a bit," I said. "And all this time I thought the two of you talked only about abolition." I smiled, hoping my tone didn't sound too arch. I didn't want this conversation to end.

"That, also." He cast a quick, impatient glance at a cluster of the other nurses coming from breakfast. "You and Louisa are different from those giggly girls. Empty heads, all of them."

"Is there anything you want me to tell her?" I asked, finished now and with no further excuse to linger, half-hoping to hear some romantic words I could cup in my heart and deliver to Louisa.

He looked at me now, his lips twitching slightly. "Just what sort of thing do you mean?"

I flushed, and he laughed, reaching upward, touching my cheek. "Forgive me, I couldn't resist the desire to tease. You have a certain guileless charm, Susan."

I said something and went on my way, feeling both giddy and strangely exposed. I continued to feel the cool pressure of his hand on my cheek for hours. Somewhere in the middle of the afternoon, I splashed cold water on my face from one of the kitchen buckets, determined to erase the memory of his touch.

The horrors of our work continued, but Louisa seemed to float through the days in a state of suspended contentment. I snatched for understanding, wanting to be part of whatever it was, and it was like snatching for a cloud.

"You are in love with him," I pressed.

"No, no."

"You glow when you see him, and he's always following you with his eyes. I would be thrilled."

"You would?"

"Of course. It means love."

"How would you know?" she asked wonderingly.

How, indeed? It did not take examining. So I concentrated even harder on coaxing out her small confidences, trying to fashion them like blossoms into a full bouquet. I wanted them to be my gift. Don't deny something so true, I said. Don't worry about being good, embrace it. Embrace him.

She did listen. I watched her staring into the distance, her eyes dreaming; then she would nod at my words and fall silent. So I kept strutting verbally, imagining myself the authority on love, almost demanding she acknowledge my superior understanding of her heart. And I pressed a touch of Liddy's precious flower petals onto her wrists.

The rigors of work wore even this passionate commitment of mine down. Death, pain, disease, dirt, veniality. Our days were fights to get supplies, to keep men alive, to stay awake. Soon we didn't bother to talk much about anything other than bedpans and cleaning wounds. We were too tired.

Still, even grubbing through my daily chores, I was wistful. Could not, at some time, what was happening to Louisa happen to me? She was changing. I watched her at night as she unwound her beautiful hair and brushed it—not briskly as was her wont, but with long, lazy strokes. She moved differently. I imagined I was seeing my friend's sensual spirit emerge in a new and freeing way.

One night I took Louisa's brush and drew it through my own

hair in the same self-caressing fashion. I closed my eyes, trying to absorb the sensuality of the act. Finally, the tears came. Lonely, lonely. I was lonely.

After Fredericksburg, was there any well-meaning visitor in Washington City who didn't sweep through our hospital? Preachers, loyal wives who would spoon soup into their husbands' mouths while ignoring men dying next to them; noisy do-gooders with baskets of food and drink and soldiers hunting for comrades. All of them pushing and shoving and consuming space as we tried to do our jobs. I began to resent them.

One memorable morning two women resplendent in stylish clothes and full hoops presented themselves, grandly announcing they were there to dispense oranges. As they began to sweep through the ward, I rushed to warn them: hoops were dangerous in a hospital. Would they please come back later in less fashionable dress? No; they were determined to deliver their largesse now. One caught her hoop on the edge of an iron cot holding a soldier with a burst artery, whose life depended on being kept perfectly still. I ran forward—too late—to steady the cot. She tugged at her hoop, jerking it free, and sailed on. I saw the artery open. I watched the blood of the young soldier who had shown me a photograph of his wife and children drain away within the hour.

I helped carry his body in the gathering darkness to the dead house, and then climbed once again to the third floor. The Ladies Bountiful had long since disappeared, smug in their certitude that they had brought peace and comfort to the poor, suffering soldiers. If God had given me the chance, I would have booted them down the stairs and under the wheels of a hospital cart.

I found Lou sitting in bed, writing in her journal with silent concentration. She nodded as I walked in, but said nothing.

I could not bear it. Not that night. I was too haunted by the sight of that soldier's lifeblood needlessly draining away to stay silent.

"Louisa, will you put down your pen, and talk to me? How do we live with all this stupidity and selfishness? Why we are here?" I cried out.

She lifted her head, a slightly dazed look on her face. "Susan, what's wrong? I always write in my journal, why does it bother you now?"

"Because I need you. You talk mostly now to John. What about me? I'm not a writer, I can't put all this down in words and stay sane; I need you!"

Louisa put down her pen and crawled over the space between our beds and embraced me. "Don't doubt me, dear. I have more room in my heart now because of John, not less. Surely you, of all people, know that. You're the one who pointed the way. Now tell me what happened."

I returned her embrace, confused. Louisa's attachment to John was scratching away at my sense of being needed and wanted, unearthing old fears. She was filled with new life and energy from this connection, but why was she taking the contents of her heart directly to her journal, bypassing me? I was her friend, her closest friend. She should be sharing this with me, and I was jealous.

But instead of being honest and saying it plain, I poured forth my anger for arrogant ladies in hoops, welcoming her instant indignation, and we talked about stupidity and arrogance until the stub of our one candle began to gutter and had to be blown out. Soon Louisa was breathing with the deep regularity of sleep, and I was left to stare into the dark and wonder why I couldn't say the rest of it——the rest of what I was slowly beginning to suspect.

I held the precious envelope over my head, trying to catch Louisa's attention as she ladled out soup to the men. She looked up, startled.

"Lou, come quick, we've received a letter from May!"

The soldier in the next bed good-naturedly waved her away when he saw me almost hopping on one foot with excitement. There was no solace like a letter from home, and when one arrived the lucky recipient always took the first opportunity to devour its contents.

Louisa rolled down her sleeves and hurried over. We retreated to the porch, shivering in the cold.

> Dear Lou and Susan,
>
> What an exciting time you must be having! Papa reads us war news at night, and I try to imagine what it must be like to be in so exciting a place and out of stuffy old Concord. There are no people left here who are amusing. All the boys are gone, so there's no one to go skating with, and everyone else is quite long in the tooth, as you can imagine. I'm painting as much as I can, but am still forced to sew for the war effort, naturally. I truly can't stand Mrs. Hawthorne. She never has anything nice to say about anybody, and got Marmee all upset last week with whispers about the nurses in Washington. Such dreadful horror stories! She said people laugh about their loose ways, and any girl working in the hospitals there is in danger of being ruined for life. Well, this may sound ridiculous to you, but Marmee was clearly nervous, and you know how easily she gets upset these days.
>
> I'm going to a social next week, and Una is letting me wear her best lace collar. We are fast friends now!
>
> Write soon, and we all here think of you often in your crisp aprons and smart caps! Or at least, I do.
>
> > Love and kisses,
> > May

Louisa laughed, glancing down at her bedraggled apron. "What would May say if she saw us as we really are?"

I started to give a joking reply, but stopped short when we heard a sharp voice calling from the hall inside for help. Another amputation; old Lyndon was wielding his saw yet again. Lou tucked the letter away in her pocket as we both hurried back to work, saying no more.

*   *   *

"Susan, come here, I've something to tell you." It was Liddy, beckoning me into a corner of the laundry room. We were all doing laundry now, and Liddy's hands looked like boiled carrots. I thought she meant to coax me into taking over, but her normally irreverent eyes were serious.

"Your friend Louisa is having some fun, we can all see that," she whispered as I joined her. "You know, with the handsome blacksmith. The one who acts like a gentleman; now isn't that a piece of luck?"

"What are you talking about?" I said cautiously. "She has no interest in him at all, it's completely professional, he just needs extra—"

"Oh, rubbish, Susan." She waved a hand, impatient. "I don't care. I just want to give you something for her, if she needs it." She looked around quickly to make sure we were alone, and reached into her pocket, pulling out a sponge secured to a ribbon and a small bottle filled with a clear liquid.

"Now listen. What she does is soak the sponge in this. It's sulphate of iron and won't do no harm. Then"—she gestured to her private parts with her hand—"you push it up as high as it can go."

I stared at her, fascinated. "You what?"

She stared back at me. "You don't know?"

"I don't think so." Although I was beginning to understand.

Liddy hooted, then put a hand up to cover her mouth. "Are you truly such an innocent? Susan, she's sweet on him, and that can cause all sorts of trouble. Don't you know what I'm talking about? This little thing"—she dangled the sponge by the string—"keeps you from getting pregnant. It works, it really does. And nobody's going to help out except somebody who knows how to use it; that's why I fixed this up to give you for your friend."

I touched it with my hand. Thinking of where it would be, and what it would guard against. Of what it could make possible. I shivered, not with fear but a sting of pleasure. Was it really this easy to avoid shame?

"I mean, he's not up to it now, but he's not looking as if he's going to die. Anyhow, it's nice to see a true lady ready to kick up her heels."

A deep flush spread from my neck to my face. I could feel its heat. What was I thinking? Louisa was the vulnerable one, not I.

"Oh dear, I've scared the drawers off of you," Liddy murmured, hastily stuffing her offering back into her pocket.

"No, not at all," I managed. "But you don't understand. Louisa isn't that kind of woman. She's not . . . she's not loose." My voice was trembling.

"There, there, don't feel you have to protect her. We're all women here, living in a nightmare not of our making." She patted my arm, looking nervously at the door. "Now shush, dear, we don't want old Ropes catching us talking about this. Just go along now; we'll talk later. No hard feelings?"

I shook my head and she gave me a gentle shove, propelling me out of the laundry room.

In turmoil, I hurried outside and sat down on the porch steps. How could Liddy have concluded that Louisa was eager for such intimacy? Was this my fault for urging Lou to show her feelings? My brow broke into a sweat and my clasped hands felt slippery. There was nothing private about this, if Liddy knew. The whole hospital must be gossiping. What had I done? And worse, if I hadn't realized how serious this was, then Louisa, so focused on John, was truly oblivious.

Unfettered now, my imagination could not stop its roamings. What if Louisa were accused of improper behavior? What if she were banished by Mrs. Ropes? Oh, how the gossipy Mrs. Hawthorne would exult! The frustrated energy pent up inside me was finally finding a route outward, taking me from excitement to fear to indignation. I wanted to fight. But what was I fighting?

That night, in a highly anxious state, I told Louisa about my encounter with Liddy, stumbling over the words.

Louisa was silent, at first. Then she chuckled. "A sponge? Oh, my. Is that how it's done?"

"Louisa, this is serious."

"Oh nonsense, dear. It's just Liddy's fevered imagination."

"You don't want the hospital gossiping about you."

"I have done nothing wrong, and have nothing to be worried about. Good night, Susan."

I fell back onto my pillow. She would say no more.

The men in the ward were becoming raucous again. As the less seriously wounded began to heal, they drifted back and forth visiting each other, huddling for interminable card games, and ignoring us. Lou was perhaps the most admired nurse of all, for she worked long and hard and never shrank from the dirtiest work. My age and slight stature seemed to work against me in establishing authority, which was exasperating. I was not feared, like Belle Poole. And I didn't have the joking insouciant nature of Liddy Kettle and Mary Cotton, which saw them through many a confrontation of wills.

"Hey, Frenchie! Show us your drawings!" yelled a bored veteran of the ward one afternoon.

I paused in the task of making a bed, and looked around. Who was he yelling at? And then I saw him pointing at me.

"You, Frenchie! I'm calling to you! You're a cutie, you know it?"

Some of the men began to laugh. I flushed and walked as quickly as I could down the line of beds, heading for the kitchen. Someone had told them about that infernal magazine. I wished I had never picked it up. I was almost to the end of the room, just passing his bed, when he leaned forward and tugged at my apron, undoing the strings.

"Ah, now that's more friendly!" he crowed, as I stopped to retie it. He was delighted now to have an audience. "Come 'ere, Frenchie—"

"Shut your mouth, Sergeant, or I'll bash it in with my good arm. And don't think I won't."

It was a strong voice from the next bed, sharp as a needle, and

I looked to see who had spoken. A soldier, clean-shaven, with light hair and a bold chin. Lyndon had amputated his arm yesterday, so short on morphine he had simply sprinkled it over the arm before cutting. Cassidy—that was his name, Tom Cassidy. He had not cried out as his arm was hacked off. And for that alone, the men respected him. They silenced immediately.

"Thank you," I said. I stared at my tormentor in the next bed. "And you, Sergeant, am I not entitled to an apology?" I planted my feet on the floor and folded my arms. I must not back down if I wanted no repeat of that taunting scene. I had learned that much.

"Ah, hell." He flopped down on his pillow. "I was just having a little fun."

"That's not an apology."

All the men were watching. I could especially feel Cassidy's eyes on me. I wasn't quite sure what to do if I didn't get the response I was demanding.

"All right," he grunted after a long moment. "You're a good sort. I'm sorry, Nurse Gray. Can we have our lunch soon?"

I let out my breath and thought I sensed a collective sigh of relief around me. "I'm getting it now, gentlemen." And I proceeded to the kitchen, making sure my shoulders stayed squared.

"You did good," Cassidy said later as he looked with distaste at the hardtack fried in pork grease I placed before him.

"Thank you for your help," I said. "Here, try the soup, it's nourishing."

He looked at me with an expression of weary knowledge that was embarrassing. We both knew the soup was little better than brilgewater.

"No, thanks. Don't want much of anything right now."

I hesitated, not wanting to move on. "Where are you from?"

"The state of Maryland, ma'am. I'm just a country schoolteacher who's hoping to learn to write left-handed when I get out of here." He gave me the ghost of a grin, before closing his eyes and going to sleep. I tucked the blanket up around him and proceeded down the line, taking my time with each soldier.

I came to John Sulie. He was dozing; his breath moving in and out with a moist, noisy intimacy. His mouth looked sad in repose. "I have dinner," I said as gently as I could. "Are you hungry?"

His eyes opened. He waved me away after a glance at the pot I carried. "Not for that swill," he said.

"Well, you needn't be rude," I said.

"I have no time for niceties."

"You have all the time in the world, so don't waste it on rudeness." My temper was running short.

"What the devil, I'm sorry. My arm is driving me crazy. Are you satisfied?"

Not knowing what to say, I started to move on.

"Hold on a minute, you look like you've got something on your mind."

I paused, not sure of how honest I should be, and decided to speak bluntly. "The nurses are whispering about you and Louisa, and I fear her being compromised," I said in a low voice.

His gaze stayed steady, his eyes cool. "You may fear the wrong thing. We'll know soon enough," he said finally, almost indifferently.

I mumbled something and moved to the next bed with the heavy pot of rapidly cooling soup, puzzled by his words.

"He's a funny one, Nurse," the man in that bed said, nodding toward John. "Not easy to like. And different from the rest of us. You never know what he means."

I said nothing, spooning the soup to his lips, wondering how John had sensed my unease so quickly. Perhaps as I watched him, he watched me? It was true, he was hard to understand, and was indeed a man holding himself apart. In some effortless way, he kept a shield around him that the other men seemed reluctant to pierce. He didn't laugh at the same jokes or share the same reminiscences. My hand trembled, spilling some soup. Why did his countenance seem untouched by hard labor? And why was his language so different from that of the ribald collection of farmers and shop clerks filling the ward?

"Do we know enough about him?" I ventured to Louisa that evening.

"Why, Susan, how could you ask that? Of course, we do," she rejoined. Then added, her voice confident, "All that is important."

But the rosy hue I had enjoyed, my fantasies of John and Louisa, were faltering. I worried that Louisa's attraction for him was going unchecked. I grew nervous at the sight of Lou sitting on his bed when she was off-duty, and almost hostile to their long, earnest conversations. I became aware of the glances in the ward; a few winks here and there. I saw some of the men assessing him coolly. Worse, looking Louisa up and down. I lived in fear that Hannah Ropes would notice, for she was already angry over the flirtations of some of the younger nurses.

I became convinced I was right to be worried. What was Louisa thinking? We could not risk the hard-earned respect of people like Mrs. Ropes and Clara Barton. Why would she risk her reputation with such obvious behavior? She was my anchor, my moral compass. It was not like Louisa to be thoughtless of her reputation. How could she? Oh, I was whipping up quite a store of self-righteous agitation.

In the ward, John was holding forth, regaling Louisa with stories about Fredericksburg. I stood and listened. Wry, mocking, funny; his voice mesmerized me. He told about waiting, bored, for orders; about trading with the Rebs, sending them sugar and coffee and newspapers in exchange for tobacco. About knowing some of them. About the battle beginning.

"I'd wager the worst is the sound of a ball bursting a human skull. Nothing like it. Your ears can bleed from the noise. And when you hear the Rebel yell." He laughed. "What a yell it is! You've heard a sound from Hades, a yip-yipping that becomes an unearthly howl, unlike anything human. It can stop a man in his tracks. If we get a Reb in this ward, we'll get him to give us a demonstration!"

"I'd kill 'em in a minute," growled a voice from another bed.

John paid no attention. "By the time that day was over, nothing was alive on that field. Nothing. Not a man, not a chicken, not a blade of grass. But before, when we poured out on the plain and charged the wall with them firing behind it, and us rolling toward them in waves, flags thrust up to the sun, bodies undulating in a long, silver line . . ." He paused. His eyes glistened. "It was beautiful. God help me, it was beautiful."

The man in the bed across from where the drummer boy had died, a solid-jawed storekeeper from Maine, turned toward John. "Beautiful? When we were dying like dogs in a ditch? How can you say that?"

"I'm talking about the glory and the hope that comes first. You and I know the rest."

"That's crazy. You don't sound like any soldier I know." The man turned his back, hunching his shoulders and pulling up the bedding as if it were a barrier.

I looked up at that moment and saw Belle Poole. She, too, had been listening. It occurred to me that she was always listening. I shivered, overwhelmed now with the responsibility of worrying about too many things. And the person I most wanted to lean on for advice didn't seem to care.

Chapter Eight

"You won't like this," said Mrs. Ropes, her lips pulled tight.

I followed her to the front of the hospital and saw a single soldier, held up by two hospital aides. His face was puffy. There were pustules on his raw, babyish face. His hair was overly long, a dirty shade of brown. I reached to help the two aides drag him up the steps, but he shot me a hateful glance that froze my gesture. I stepped back.

"You got yourselves a Reb," grunted one of the aides.

An awful specimen. I hauled him forward with distaste, determined to do my duty. Soon the ward was abuzz over his presence, and I, assigned to wash him and change his dressings, was asked by the others repeatedly for gossip, which irritated Mrs. Ropes.

"Give them no tales to feed on," she ordered. "They busy their fingers at night stealing mutton and pies from the larder, caring nothing about starving others. Starve their gossipy tongues, at least we can do that."

In truth, I could hardly restrain my own curiosity about this man who would kill his brothers to keep colored men as slaves. Or so I thought. I am ashamed to remember I did not give him the gentlest of care, and once, when I yanked free a soiled bandage with much more force than necessary, he cried out.

"Can you not see I'm a human being?" he yelled.

Before I could answer, John spoke from two beds away, with what I felt was an odd tone of camaraderie. "Save your breath, friend," he said. "None of us are anymore. With luck, we'll be trading coffee and tobacco on the battlefield again, you and I."

"I'll never get out of here alive," the Reb replied in a petulant voice. I realized with a jolt that he was little more than a boy.

"If you get decent rations, you've got a good enough chance."

"Yeah, well that ain't happening," the Reb said. "No one's fed me yet."

John caught my eye. I flushed and hurried to Hannah, who immediately filled a bowl with the sticky morning porridge. She did not ask why the Reb had been overlooked. But I knew Belle had passed him by. Ashamed for us both, I sat next to the man and fed him, saying nothing.

There was disgust in John's voice as he loudly spoke again. "So this is what we've come to? Starving a man because he signed up on the wrong side?"

Oh, the look Belle threw at him! Her hatred for the Reb was surpassed only by her hatred for the troublemaker, as she called John. "He's no blacksmith," she declared to one and all in the laundry room. "Look at his hands! Fingertips like plump pillows. No lines, no calluses. They're too soft for a blacksmith."

I found myself studying his hands after that. They *were* soft. Ungnarled, long, almost delicate. I concentrated on them to such an extent, I hardly noticed his increasing paleness and growing listlessness. I ceased to see him through the eyes of a nurse.

Christmas Eve was as festive as we could make it. We fashioned wreaths from boughs collected along the canal and tied them with string from the door frames, leading to some grumbling by the taller stewards obliged to duck beneath them. But the men appreciated the attempt. Without snow to deter them, visitors filled the room, bringing baskets of bread and gifts of knitted mufflers and mittens to men who might never see the outdoors again, but all was in a spirit of generosity.

I breathed deeply as I listened to the laughter and chatter, feeling a momentary sense of cheer as I prepared to dispense dinner. I saw Louisa rush to John's bed. Her eyes were bright, her hands clasped in front of her; words pouring out in a girlish torrent. John, propped up weakly on one elbow, was grinning.

"What's happened?" I asked.

"I won," she said. "Susan, 'Pauline' won the hundred-dollar prize."

It took me a moment to focus, to remember the contest sponsored by *Frank Leslie's Illustrated Newspaper* she had entered months before. How long ago that seemed! *Pauline's Passion and Punishment* was Louisa at her blood-and-thunder best, with wonderful, dark undercurrents. I had marveled at her creation of a vengeful, wronged woman who unmercifully taunts her ex-lover with a new husband, leading to disaster for all. We had sent it off in the post with high hopes, and then, swept up in the realities of war, forgotten it. Or, at least, I had.

"That's wonderful," I exclaimed, delighted.

John broke in, his voice light and teasing. "See? I told you, you'd not be confined to teaching children the rest of your life. Fame and fortune await."

"Do you really think so?" Louisa said eagerly.

"Goodness, *I've* been telling you that for a long time," I said. She did not seem to hear me, and I suddenly had the awkward feeling of having walked into a private celebration. A quick glance from John told me once again he had seen into my heart, almost before I realized what was there myself.

After kissing Lou and congratulating her again, I went back to my task of ladling out one more dreary evening stew. It had never occurred to me that John might become as avid and valued a supporter of Louisa's work as I. More was going on here than I understood. I was uneasy. Who was he? Had I made Louisa vulnerable? All these years later, the turmoil of my mind at that time remains painfully fresh. How could I have failed so utterly to recognize my own yearnings?

Nothing seemed to disturb Louisa's quiet glow. She ignored the Rebel, ignored the meanness and the gossip. It was, in one sense, a delight to see her freed spirit. Never did she falter in her commitment to her duties, but she went through her days with a serenity of purpose I had not seen before.

I tried to talk to her again about my encounter with Liddy, but she brushed my concerns away more impatiently than before. "Did Liddy say anything about John's color?" she interrupted.

"His color?"

"Did she say anything about his health?"

"No, she said he didn't look like he was going to die."

"May she be right," Lou said, her voice flat.

"But Louisa—"

"She means well, Susan. Don't fret."

I soon realized why Lou was uninterested in my concerns. I watched her that morning try to coax John to eat some porridge, and saw finally what had been there to see if I had not been blind—and that was the visible decline of John Sulie.

There was no denying the evidence. Streaks of red shot down his arm, a sure sign of infection. His face had grown waxy and gray, and the night before he had suffered a spell of delirium.

"John, you must let Dr. Lyndon operate." Louisa folded her arms and stared at him, trying to be as firm as possible and not show her fear.

He glared at her with feverish eyes. "Don't be insane, I'll do no such thing."

"You must," she implored.

"Are you with me or against me? Tell me now!"

Ducking her head at the anger in his voice, Louisa hurried away. We went together to ask Hannah to intervene, but even with that good woman's best and most resolute efforts, John refused to allow Dr. Lyndon near his bed.

Indeed, Hannah was engaged in a struggle of her own. We were among her favorites now, and she confided to us her concerns about the place in the hospital cellar the patients joked about, the one called "the hole." Mr. Stokes had a habit of banishing recalcitrant patients to the cellar, incarcerating them there as a way of calming the boisterous nature of the ward. I watched her challenge him one afternoon, screaming at him, but he paid her no heed. Mr. Stokes held great power in the hospital; this was of course only because he was tolerated by Dr. Coleman, the administrator with the nervous smile who rarely popped his head out of his office. We wondered sometimes what Mr. Stokes held over Coleman. It was one of the more interesting speculative conversations tossed about, but for Mrs. Ropes, abolishing this practice of banishing patients to the cellar became a principled cause. Even to the point where, one day, Louisa and I entered her office and she showed us a letter she was about to send to the secretary of war, of all people, demanding the practice be stopped.

"What do you think of this?" she said, proudly waving the letter in front of our faces. "Now we'll get some action!"

Perhaps she saw skepticism in my face, for she stopped smiling and peered at us both.

"You have not been down there, have you," she said.

"No, ma'am," Louisa replied. "But we wholeheartedly take your word for it."

"It's not that we disbelieve you, it's that we wonder how seriously the men running this war will take your complaint," I said, blunt as always. "And we do get troublemakers here, neither wounded nor so sick they don't smuggle in liquor, making our work hard."

Mrs. Ropes slowly heaved herself up. "Come, let me introduce you to the place we are talking about," she said.

With full respect and some shameful reluctance, we followed her down a rotting set of stairs to the cellar, seeing there a cold, dank place where we could hear the scuttling of rats in the walls. On the right wall was a holding cell with iron bars about ten inches apart bolted to the ceiling. The cell was about four feet by five, with nothing in it but a frayed mattress and a stinking, filled slopbucket. Louisa pressed a hand against the damp cellar wall and shuddered.

"How can any human being be put here?" the matron demanded, establishing her squat, strong figure inside the cell and turning to face us. "May I remind you, these are our boys, trouble-makers or not, and not prisoners of war?"

I shut my eyes, trying to imagine a sick or wounded man confined in this space. But surely no one was left here more than a single night, or at least so the steward said. Was that so terrible? I can't think about this now, I told myself. I've got dying men, bleeding men, drunken men upstairs—I can't think about this, too. I wondered uneasily if my efforts to grow more professional were not also hardening me to suffering.

"This slopbucket needs cleaning," I said, picking up the ancient pail by its rusting handle. At least I could hide my thoughts behind a facade of duty.

The day was waning when I glimpsed a familiar figure just outside the ward in deep conversation with Mrs. Ropes. "Look, Louisa, it's Clara. I was hoping she would come again," I said.

We wiped our hands clean on our aprons and started toward the two women, but paused when we saw they were arguing. Clara, gesticulating, appeared to be doing the most talking. But Mrs. Ropes stood solid, arms folded, shaking her head from side to side. We tried not to stare. Because Clara loomed so large in importance to us, it was odd to see her ramrod straight, black-clad figure pitted against our Hannah and seemingly not coming off the stronger.

Their conversation ended with a a quick exchange that seemed civil enough; Mrs. Ropes gave Clara a curt nod and vanished into the ward. I was wondering if we should back away when Clara looked up and saw us.

"Well, my two young friends from Concord," she said agreeably enough as we hurried to greet her. "Mrs. Ropes says you are now a fine pair of nurses, enduring all tests with fortitude. I hoped to spot you here and say hello."

Louisa smiled faintly. She loved being referred to as "young." It didn't happen that often in this hospital, where few of the nurses were much older than I. Clara, of course, at forty years old, was an inspiration.

Yet she looked thin and worn that day, and when we invited her to sit down, I saw the soles of her shoes were patched with canvas. So, I thought, with sinking heart, the gossip might be true. Had the famous Miss Barton fallen on hard times? The whispers were that she was relying on the army for food, while friends who admired her work were providing donations to pay her rent and keep her clothed. Some said she was living on her memories of glory. But even as I felt moved to pity, I heard a hoarse shout from a soldier in a bed half a room away.

"By God, it's Clara Barton! Fellas, look who's here!"

His voice was the equivalent of a bugle call. Every man not comatose pulled himself up to crane his head.

"Let's show her what we think of her!" yelled one. And from their lips came the heartiest of cheers for this small, brave woman who had shared the battlefield with them. Clara straightened her shoulders, smiled, and with almost regal grace walked through the ward, stopping at each bed, shaking hands, touching brows, asking names. On every face I saw respect. She came to John Sulie's bed, and I heard Louisa catch her breath. Clara leaned over him, feeling his forehead and taking his pulse. We could not hear their exchange, but she lingered, talking to him for several minutes.

When she rejoined us, she seemed softer, not her usual crisp self. "I don't know what comes next in my life, but I do know no one, no conqueror or king, has heard the cheers I have. Well, ladies, let's have tea."

"How is our blacksmith?" Louisa asked, with strained casualness.

Clara studied her soberly. "Not well, dear."

"How bad?"

"Infection is rampant, as you know, and he told me of his decision to spurn amputation. Soon, it will be too late, even for that."

"What can we do?" Lou's eyes were now rimmed in red.

"A man chooses his own fate."

"I can't bear to lose him. I cannot."

No one but Clara and I heard, yet I held my breath. Clara simply put an arm around Louisa and said very quietly, "If there is anything to do, perhaps it will come from your love for him."

Louisa wiped her eyes as she spoke. "I love him for his nobility and courage, all the rest is nothing."

"Of course, dear." Clara's impatient sigh was not lost on me.

We reached the kitchen, Clara's arm still around Lou's shoulder. She began telling us about her confrontation with Mrs. Ropes, not bothering to lower her voice. "There's no use trying to keep what's happened a secret. The news will be all over the hospital in an hour or so," she said.

"What news?" I asked.

"Mrs. Ropes is booting out a nurse for moral turpitude, a very serious charge."

I stared at the old cast-iron stove, focusing on the pot of water as it began to boil, trying not to look terrified.

Clara shook her head as she picked up the pot and poured the tea. "I cannot convince her to budge from her decision, even though she knows all fifty-odd hospitals in this city are crammed to capacity with not nearly enough nurses to take care of the patients. She can be a dreadfully righteous woman."

"Who is it?" I asked, fearing.

"Nurse Kettle. A good sort, from all I hear. Losing her is a shame."

Liddy. Oh, no, not Liddy.

"What happened?"

"She was caught in the boiler room with one of the men."

"Were they kissing?" I asked.

"My dear, if only they were. Her skirts were up and her drawers down, unfortunately. No defense there."

I thought of Liddy's merry face and commonsense ways and felt sick. But full on the tail of that emotion came a resurgence of fear. If this could happen to Liddy, what might happen to Louisa? Clara Barton's comforting arm wouldn't protect her from Mrs. Ropes. I was now firmly fixated on the dangers of Louisa's love— even in the face of the blacksmith's declining state.

*   *   *

The ward grew quieter. I learned there was something worse than daily amputations in a hospital; something worse than bored patients flirting with the nurses as they healed from their wounds. Infection had taken over.

The preachers and Ladies Bountiful disappeared. We were no longer popular with the dispensers of comfort, either spiritual or material, for suddenly we were inundated with cases of typhoid, diphtheria, and pneumonia. That week snow flurries began eddying to and fro, frosting the hairs in my nose with tiny icicles each time I sought the porch for fresh air. The roofs of Georgetown were dusted in white, and the streetcars inched cautiously over ice-slickened rails. We heard that the carriage of the Russian minister was so deeply bogged down in a hole on I Street, the coachman could barely climb out. I refused to believe it even as I stood on the porch, watching passersby slog through the street in patent arctic gaiters.

We found little gaiety in the season, now. There were rumors of a raid by Jeb Stuart's cavalry that set us all on edge, but nothing happened. We needed no Confederate attack; sickness was able to vanquish us all.

When did I become aware of what else was happening? When did I first notice Louisa's cough?

It was in the week after Christmas. I lay one night in bed and listened to her as she slept. Her breathing seemed forced and labored.

"Are you all right?" I asked as we climbed, shivering, from our beds in the dark morning and began to dress for work.

"You fuss too much," she chided. "Yes, I'm fine."

The next night, her cough was worse. She tossed and turned for hours in our frigid third-floor bedchamber. I lay sleepless, worrying. New Year's Day dawned bleak and cold, and John Sulie was now barely able to speak. The atmosphere on the entire ward was gloomy. We washed faces, spooned rations into listless mouths, and tried to soothe. Louisa admitted she felt dizzy. By noontime, as she administered medicine to a soldier with diphtheria, her hand was shaking so badly, she spilled half the laudanum onto the sheets.

"It's no good if the medicine goes on the sheet instead of into the patient," I whispered. "Louisa, let's take a walk. We both need to get out of here."

We were always tired, always feeling not quite as good as we should. I thought a good, brisk walk would be the best of therapies; it was certainly our best chance in weeks to pull away from the hospital and see at least a glimmer of what else was going on in this bustling, exciting city.

There was much noise and laughter in the streets. Pennsylvania Avenue was jammed with army wagons and artillery and crowds of soldiers dressed in blue striding through the streets, singing— young men filled with strength and power and exuberance, so unlike the ones we saw every day. We passed Duff Green Row and started up the long sloping hill to the site of the Capitol building. Heavy blocks of marble and stonecutter tools were stacked under the unfinished dome, which was shrouded in scaffolding.

"Do you wonder if it will ever be done?" Louisa asked. Her thin face looked pinched and sorrowful.

I knew she asked more. But my eyes swept that swampy, fetid land stretching out toward the partially completed monument to George Washington, and I could not imagine it ever becoming the grand sweep of lawn linking the Capitol and the White House that the planners, such optimists, envisioned.

"It takes more imagination than I have," I said.

The wind grew stronger. It was cutting now through my coat, and I saw Louisa, too, was shivering. I was about to suggest walking back, when Louisa spoke up.

"John is going to die," she said.

"Perhaps not, perhaps he'll get better," I said, hearing the hollowness of my reassurance.

Louisa cast me such a look, I lowered my head. We trudged back, past the Willard Hotel, stopping for a moment, puzzled to see a large group of colored men in Union uniforms cheering and slapping each other on the back in front of the hotel entrance. These were former slaves who had joined the army, the ones they called the contrabands. Why were they celebrating? Louisa remembered first.

"Of course," she said with a faint smile. "The Emancipation Proclamation becomes law today. How could we have forgotten?"

How indeed. In Concord, we had followed every development of the war, knowing each small and large event would be a topic of animated discussion by all we knew. Here? Here we lived with the results. We had no energy for the history, for the drama, unfolding around us. It seems strange from this distance, to realize how narrow a focus we were able to muster. Can it ever be understood how much flows by those who concentrate on aching joints and fevered brows? Will history think ill of us for strolling, oblivious, past the celebration of a lifetime?

It was after three before we reached the hospital and found Belle waiting on the front porch, the sides of her mouth pinched tight with anger.

"Where have the two of you been?" she demanded. "What do you think you are doing? I've had to do double work, and I find your attitudes insolent and unprofessional. And if you think Mrs. Ropes is going to rescue the two of you with praise, you may have a surprise coming. You may—"

My feet were freezing in my thin boots. Louisa was shivering. Who needed to endure this woman's harangue? I pulled at Louisa's coat sleeve. We marched past Belle without waiting for her next complaint, a nice moment of defiance. Except for the fact I had simply given her another reason to dislike us.

The spirits of the men revived that evening. Perhaps it was the news of the proclamation or simply the new year, but for a few hours I felt an easing in the constant fight against pain and death. A false easing.

John lay still, alternately dozing and staring at the ceiling. Louisa kept glancing over to him as she did her work, periodically wringing out a wet cloth in the water bucket and holding it against her own forehead.

"What do you think?" she asked me.

I was not about to be cowardly again. "He does not look good, and I think he needs his arm amputated if he is to live."

"I won't let it happen," she said.

"Then he dies."

"No."

I was confused. "You have a plan?"

She didn't answer.

Later, when the ward was silent, she sat again by his bed. They said nothing to each other that I could hear. Louisa re-dressed the wound in his arm, and I watched, recoiling from the smell. The gangrene was out of control.

I went to bed. Louisa stayed by his side.

Dr. Lyndon arrived in the ward early the next morning. I watched him at the other end of the room as he began his day's work, bracing myself against the usual screams. John's eyes flew open. I kept my gaze on the spidery figure of Lyndon wielding his bloody saw. It was a strangely jaunty motion for a man in the process of depriving another man of a limb. Was it all necessary? Was it not just ignorance or expediency that determined these decisions, but cruelty as well? Perhaps all wars come down to that. I do wonder.

"Doctor." Louisa's voice rang through the room. "This man needs you."

I jumped, her command was so unexpected. There was clear satisfaction on Lyndon's face as he noted whose bed she was standing by.

"Of course, he does," Lyndon said, striding toward them.

"No," said the blacksmith, heaving to the side of his good arm, as if ready to fight.

Louisa pulled herself up to full height. "Cut the shell fragments out of his arm," she demanded.

"A waste of time," snapped Lyndon, starting to turn away.

"Is the operation too delicate for your skills?"

I blinked. Had I heard correctly?

Lyndon stopped in mid-stride. Only his mustache twitched. "Who do you think you are, a doctor?"

"I'm a nurse. I know my patients. This one can be saved with less than an amputation."

Men in the long line of beds were turning their heads or sitting up to watch. Lyndon's faded blue eyes darted from face to face, surveying the growing audience to this encounter. He appeared to come to a decision.

"All right, then, I'll humor you. Dan——" he shot a glance at his nervous aide and handed him the bloody saw. "Get my other tools. And hurry up, I've got more important work to do." He again addressed Louisa directly. "You understand I can't spare any chloroform for a useless operation, and there's no time for filling him up with liquor. May have to hack out some bone. Can he take it?"

"I can take it," John Sulie replied, not waiting for a response from Louisa.

Lyndon nodded and walked away to rummage through a supply box on a shelf under the window. A soldier in a yellow cotton nightcap two beds away spoke up. "Beggin' your pardon, he's not gonna be gentle, ma'am. Especially when he's been crossed."

We knew the truth of what he said. Louisa gripped the edge of John's iron bed and looked at him wordlessly, questioningly.

He shook his head. "He won't come back and do it later; he'll let me go. There's no choice, and I thank you for challenging him."

The doctor walked back with something in his hand. "Bite down on this," he said to John, shoving a slab of leather into his mouth. John bit down and closed his eyes.

Then Lyndon bent over and pushed a knife into John's upper arm, opening it with a twisting motion. He picked up a pair of pliers and began pulling out shards of an exploded shell, snipping off chunks of bone as he worked. Huge drops of sweat broke out on the blacksmith's forehead and a deep groan worked its way from his gut to his teeth as he chewed deep into the leather mouthpiece.

It was all over in two minutes. His arm looked like raw meat, but at least it was still there. His head lolled over the side of the bed. He had fainted.

"All right, Miss Alcott, let's see how good a nurse you are. Tie it up, apply plenty of styptic and we'll see how it heals. If you can't do the job, we have competent aides who can." Lyndon thrust his sharp, hairless chin forward and offered a cheerless smile.

"Of course, Doctor," Louisa said promptly. She knew better than to further anger this belligerent little man with power over life and death. But she cast me a look filled with hope, and I felt at that moment a strange, breathless certainty: If there was hope at all, it was Louisa who would save the blacksmith.

That night I came upon Louisa in the bedroom, holding up a looking glass, slowly perusing her face and naked shoulders. "I'm sorry," I stammered, "I thought you were asleep."

She put down the mirror and pulled up her wrapper, a slight flush on her cheeks.

"You were brave today," I said.

She looked distressed. "I wish that were true, but I should have acted sooner. I neglected my patient."

"No, you didn't, you were thinking of him on two levels, not just as a nurse. And he has a fierce will of his own. I'm impressed that you challenged it."

"I feared he might fight me. Yet how could I stand helpless and let him die?"

"Of course you couldn't, and you had to defy old Lyndon, too." I took a deep breath. "I think he's going to live, and if he does, it's because of you. But oh, Lou, be careful."

"Why do you worry about my reputation so much?" she said, giving me a small smile. "You've become a little terrier, pulling at me with your worries. I'm not going to throw myself away, like Liddy Kettle. Isn't that what you're asking?" She blew out the one candle illuminating the room, and we settled into our respective beds.

"Is it like it was with Henry?"

"You do press so." Her voice grew more faint. "It's nothing at all like that."

My brain and heart groped for balance. "You said you loved Henry because he taught you to be good."

I listened to her irregular, raspy breathing in the dark.

"This is different. I don't have to be good."

I had said those words to her in the first days of her attachment to John—said them gaily, teasingly. Now my thoughts were an ominous jumble of social pieties and whisperings and the mandates of well-stitched samplers and well-meaning pastors.

"Do you trust him?"

"Why do you ask?"

"Belle says his hands are too soft to be those of a blacksmith." I bit my lip. What was I doing, passing on Belle's poisonous gossip?

"I trust him."

"A blacksmith is below your station. What would your father say?"

There was a long silence. So long, I felt afraid to speak again; I had crossed a line.

"Let it be, Susan. For now, let it be."

"You don't feel wild and queer?"

She gave a long, languorous yawn as she climbed into bed and turned to the wall. Her voice when she responded was now truly muffled.

"No," she said. "Good night."

I lay there, staring so long at the ceiling, I almost imagined stars.

Chapter Nine

It took only a few days for John Sulie's fever to disappear, and soon he was sitting up. The color of health came to his face. He began making an effort to engage with the other men, ceasing to hold himself aloof from their conversations. I would not say they warmed to him, but they began to accept him.

A young carpenter from Delaware pulled out his banjo one evening and began idly picking out the notes to an old camping-meeting tune. The boy in the bed next to him started singing the new words Julia Ward Howe had penned the previous autumn while staying at the Willard Hotel. I stopped to listen, for they were quite grand. "Mine eyes have seen the glory of the coming of the Lord . . ." A few voices joined in, and then more.

"Can't miss this," Tom Cassidy murmured, pushing aside the fresh roll of bandage with which I had been about to wrap his wound. He heaved himself up on his good arm and added a baritone so strong and sad, I felt something catch in my throat.

Soon all had stopped to listen, even Nurse Poole. By the time the carpenter reached the chorus, most were singing, or trying to, even the men too sick to raise their heads from their mattresses. The voices were weak, and some trailed off, but the words gave their efforts a certain splendor. "Glory, glory hallelujah, his truth is marching on!"

The last note faded, leaving silence. No one spoke or laughed or cried out. Somehow, for just an instant, we felt ennobled, purposeful. We could lift our heads and see what part we played in a much larger endeavor; we could for an instant see beyond the stinking dead house behind the hospital that reminded us each day of where so many of our patients would finally rest. What stirring words Miss Howe had penned!

"Are you a religious man?" I asked Tom shyly.

"Why do you ask?" He had settled back, complying obediently with me as I resumed dressing his wound.

"Because you sang from the heart."

He smiled at that. "I grew up believing; no longer, I'm afraid. But music as powerful as this makes me feel I'm more than just a one-armed schoolteacher."

"And more than a soldier?"

"Pray God, I am more than that."

"Oh Tom, you are."

My euphoria disappeared as I finished and moved away, for I glanced at John and registered what my eyes had told me already—he had not sung. Nor had the Rebel. Only those two.

"Cat got your tongue, huh, blacksmith?" It was the storekeeper across the aisle. "Or maybe you don't like the song?"

"It's a fine song," John replied easily. "Just didn't feel like singing, that's all."

"Why not?" The usual buzz of voices had not yet resumed and it was easy to tell the entire ward was listening.

"Don't have much of a voice. Although, maybe a better one than a few I just heard." He wasn't backing off.

"Seems to me a good Union man would join his comrades on that one. That's what I think." The storekeeper's voice curled like a lazy snake inching through tall grass. He looked to the men around him. "Rest of you agree?"

Amid the immediate murmurs of assent, one calm voice cut through.

"Well, son, it doesn't always work that way. Sometimes people feel coerced when a group is singing. Just a human quirk, is all. Now me? I sing like a frog. But I sure enjoyed listening."

I turned and saw a man in rumpled clothes with white hair and a full white beard. His thin brown coat was shabby, and buttons were missing. He had been on the ward all day, getting in no one's way, at first inquiring about his missing brother, an officer in the Fifty-first New York. He simply sat with the men and wrote letters for them, scratching down their muttered words with his pen. I had passed this blowsy fellow several times during the day and been struck by the gentleness of his manner. When he wasn't writing letters or listening to the men talk, he was scribbling in a little homemade notebook put together with string and scraps of paper.

"Thank you, Mr. Whitman," John said. His face had relaxed. "But I suspect your voice is as splendid as your poetry."

The older man smiled. "Splendid is not the word usually used, my dear boy. Now, good night to you all." He picked up his hat, a wide-brimmed sombrero, nodded in John's direction, and strolled out of the ward.

"It certainly ain't," muttered Mary Cotton, watching him go. "I hear it's filth that he writes, that's what it is."

I made no response. Mr. Emerson had brought Walt Whitman's thin volume of strange verses to Bronson, and Louisa had smuggled the book out to the apple orchard one afternoon and read me some of the poetry. We both agreed it was shocking, but oh, the words. The power of the words.

It sank in slowly that John had been the only one to recognize Mr. Whitman. I had gone back to my duties, and was spooning mutton stew into a patient's mouth when I faced what I had wondered about since John's first night on the ward. The spoon in my hand stopped in midair.

Why would a common foot soldier, a blacksmith, be reading *Leaves of Grass?* Or *Paradise Lost,* for that matter?

I dropped the spoon and walked slowly over to his bed. He looked up at me with an expectant expression as I leaned down and poked a finger at him. His eyes were calm, with a hint of flickering amusement. That touch of play sharpened my tone.

"Where did you learn about Mr. Whitman's poetry?"

"I read a copy of his book, naturally."

"Why naturally?"

"Because I enjoy poetry. Don't you?"

I ignored the question. "Ah, and between battles, you read Milton. Clearly you are not only literate, but educated. And where do blacksmiths go to school?"

His amusement vanished. "You still have quite a bee in your bonnet, Susan. Yes, I have some education, is that such a surprise? I have even read your friends, Emerson and Thoreau. Do I know about Walden Pond? Am I familiar with transcendentalism? Yes. But more to the point, you're implying I've kept all this a secret."

"Your various identities don't quite mix, that's what I'm saying." I wanted to put my hands on his shoulders and shake the truth from him. But what was I expecting? What, indeed, had he been hiding? I knew he and Louisa talked about poetry and ideas, so why was I asking these questions now? Did I feel better, given the objections I had raised to Louisa? Or worse?

"I know you're angry. But if you don't seek unwanted attention from your patients, Nurse Gray, you shouldn't be leaning so close."

I straightened instantly, shocked at how close I had been to him. I was flustered now. Embarrassed. "But it's not common. For a blacksmith to study."

"No, it's not." His stare softened. "You can stop the interrogation, Susan. I've committed no crime." I was vaguely aware that other soldiers were listening, but then I heard the rustling of skirts behind me. I smelled a faint whiff of the heavy musk perfume that Belle seemed to pour on each day. Mary and Liddy used to joke that it was a fortunate vanity, for it meant we always knew when she was coming. I knew this time too late. For John smiled and uttered the words that would later prove so fateful; words I had precipitated with my public challenge.

"At least, not this one."

The next morning as I accompanied Mrs. Ropes on morning rounds, she suddenly clutched at my hand and stumbled.

"Are you all right?" I asked.

"Absolutely," she answered, and then fainted full across a patient's bed.

I should have known by then that all lightness and pleasure in that place of death was fleeting. Dr. Lyndon hurried over, picked her up, and carried her to the supply room, out of view of the men. I stood next to him, holding Mrs. Ropes's slack hand as he hastily made his examination. Should it have come as any surprise? Typhoid.

Mary Cotton was waiting outside the door when I emerged in a distraught state. I told her the news. "I know you like her, but I'll never forgive her for what she did to Liddy," she said soberly. "Not that I want anyone to die in this sorry place, but Susan, you'll have to shed the tears for both of us this time."

There were many to be shed, for her decline was shockingly fast. Only as I sat by Mrs. Ropes's bed did I realize how much I had come to like and respect her. Even now, sick as she was, she was valiant.

"The surgeon insists on confining me like a prisoner, which is ridiculous," she complained. What a sight, that bustling lady, now weak and weighted down with a mustard plaster on her chest! At first she refused to concede her authority, not for a minute, and we all acquiesced. Day by day, as the week progressed, she issued orders about restocking laundry and dictated instructions for the care of the patients.

But we knew what was happening. On the fifth day, she conceded her authority to the next-in-charge: Belle Poole.

Delirium set in. Still she tried. "Do not slight the Rebel," she said unexpectedly, casting me one of her famous glares. "Our job here is to take good care of everyone. Please, heed me."

That night, I slipped the boy—and yes, he was a boy—an extra sausage. Not for him, I told myself. For Hannah.

In the midst of this, the thefts began.

The first victim was a soldier from Baltimore whose leg had been amputated the day before. He called me over to his bed as I was leaving the Rebel's side. "My wife's picture is missing," he complained.

"No, it is here," I said, pulling a faded daguerreotype from off the floor by his bed.

He clutched it, looking confused. "But the frame is gone," he said in great agitation. "Where is the frame? My grandmother's silver frame. Someone has ripped out my picture and tossed it on the floor, and taken the frame. Who would do that?"

I immediately suspected the steward. Had the man become impossibly greedy? Was he confident now that Hannah would not be watching him?

"I'll find out," I promised. I almost tripped over my feet in my haste to leave the ward and collar the hapless steward. I found him skulking in the stairwell. Facing him down, hands on my hips, would have seemed impossible but yesterday. Now, it was easy.

"You have gone too far," I said. "Stealing from a crippled man? Sir, you are beneath contempt!"

His small mouth pulled tight. He went into a crouch, like an insect about to be smashed. "I ain't stolen from any patient," he whined.

I was now beside myself. "Don't lie to me. What do you call stealing their food? If you would steal a man's clothes and a man's breakfast, why would you stop at a silver frame?"

"I take only what is due me, what I by rights should have in wages, not a man's precious possessions." He cast me a defiant, yet bewildered look, one so believable, it drained all righteousness from me, leaving only confusion. Repulsed by his cringing, I turned and marched back to the ward, just in time to catch Belle Poole haranguing Dr. Lyndon at the top of her voice.

The boy from Baltimore had stayed quite vocal about his loss in my absence. Belle was by his bed, and she was the picture of indignation.

"So, we have thieves! Is anyone surprised? And does anyone besides me know who they are?"

Lyndon backed away, mute. Nurse Poole was in charge now, and he wanted no fight with her. Even as I watched, I marveled at how she relished the dramatic moment made possible by her new power. She slowly turned, lifted an accusing finger, and pointed, taking in with one thick finger both the Rebel—now gobbling his sausage as if he feared it would be snatched away—and John Sulie. "Them two! A pair, they are!"

The ward fell silent. I opened my mouth to protest, but nothing came out. Louisa had no such inhibitions. "What are you saying? Who do you think you are accusing, and with what evidence?" she demanded.

Belle seemed to grow in front of us, to swell outward and upward, and my heart sank. Malevolence, for whatever reason, when contained for too long, does not flow; it erupts. I did not know what was at stake for Belle, but I knew what was at stake for Louisa.

"I call what I see," she said. She spread her mouth in the shape of what one might normally think of as a smile. "And what I see here is a man of deceit made bold by your attention to him."

Nobody spoke. My nightmare of shameful discovery had come alive, and I stepped forward without thinking. "You have no right to talk to my friend that way," I said. I reached for Louisa's hand, thinking to guide her away from the Baltimore soldier's bed.

But John was too willing to touch flame to kerosene. Eyes flicking over Belle's soiled apron with an almost jaunty disdain, he said, "Your accusations come of course with the purpose of hiding your own deeds. As long as the entire ward is to hear us, can you tell us all how much money you stole from the coat of the soldier who died last night? Not all of us were asleep. I saw you pull the bills from his jacket and stuff them in your apron. Looked to me like you'd done it before, your hands were so deft."

Belle stared at him with eyes flat as pennies. She took a giant stride to his bed and pulled out from under it the boots we had tugged off his feet the day we brought him into the hospital. Triumphantly, she held them high for all to see.

"Look at these," she said. "Look closely! You see the leather? The cut? These aren't government-issue boots, these are Confederate boots! And why might this so-called blacksmith be wearin' 'em?"

I stared. She was right, and why had we not noticed before?

"They are Confederate-issue because I took them off a dead soldier after my own fell apart," John said evenly. "Make of that what you will."

Belle was in her element. She whirled and faced the Rebel's bed. "You know this man?" she demanded. "Confess!"

The boy stuttered, bits of sausage—how sorry I was I had given it to him!—caught in his teeth. "He's been kind to me, that's all I know," he mumbled.

The men in the ward began to grow restless, craning their heads to follow what was going on. One called out, "Hey, black-smith! Would you have sung 'Dixie' the other night? Was it just the choice of songs that kept you quiet?"

"That's enough." Louisa's voice was impressively firm. She stepped forward, looking almost unnaturally tall. The knuckles of her clenched fists were white and the sinewy cords in her throat seemed to pulsate. With a shock I realized how much weight she had lost. "Nurse Ropes would not tolerate this shameful scene," she said, glaring at them all. "And your accusations come at a par-ticularly convenient time, Mrs. Poole. Might you be making them now because your own behavior has been questioned? Might you—"

"That is quite enough, indeed."

I turned. The famously absent Dr. Coleman had entered the ward, summoned, I suspected, by a worried Mr. Stokes. I had never seen him among the patients, having only glimpsed him either behind his desk or hurrying in and out of the hospital. He was skinny, with legs like a heron, and his eyeglasses rested far down on his nose. Hannah Ropes had once scorned him in an unguarded moment as too puffed up with the gilding on his shoul-der straps.

"I'll not tolerate this kind of uproar in my hospital, and I'll thank you, Nurse Alcott, to desist from adding to the accusations. They are being flung around a little too freely here." He glared at me. "Mr. Stokes has told me about the problem, and I will get to the bottom of what's going on, I assure you. All patients in this ward should hand over their valuables, and I will keep them in the hospital safe. Now get back to work. Nurse Alcott," he beckoned Louisa, "may I speak with you privately?"

I glared at John Sulie. It was all his fault, I told myself. Louisa was being unfairly chastised by this pompous idiot of an administrator, and there was nothing I could say to defend her that wouldn't make things worse. What injustice! I wanted to rail at John, See what you have done with your intemperate words? Why did you goad Belle Poole? Reckless, totally reckless. He met my glance directly, and gave not an inch. I took a deep breath, surprised at my own ferocious feelings, and turned away. Still trying to control myself, I began straightening the blankets on Tom Cassidy's bed, yanking and smoothing, keeping my face down.

"You'll tidy me to death," he said finally in a low voice. "Don't worry about old Coleman, he's got the spine of a jellyfish."

"He's humiliated Louisa," I whispered.

"Don't stay here. When she comes out, I'll tell her you're upstairs."

I thanked him and hurried away.

Louisa looked pale and wan when she returned to our room. We had both missed dinner, and she proceeded to undress quickly, silently.

"What did he say?" I ventured finally.

"He told me not to question a member of the hospital staff in front of the men, that it wasn't loyal."

"Does he suspect the blacksmith of being a spy?"

Louisa unbuttoned her skirt and let it slip to the floor. "He said nothing of that."

"Well, that's what he would be, wouldn't he, if he were a Reb? I mean, he was in a Union uniform when we brought him in."

"He is not a spy."

"Well, I do not think he's a blacksmith, either," I said.

She turned to me with a sorrowful gaze, just as had John. "Oh, Susan, not you, too."

"He is vague about his home, tells us he has no family, and takes liberties with your reputation. I think maybe he is a spy. It isn't completely out of the question. He's too . . . challenging. Why did he not sing Mrs. Howe's hymn with us? And why—"

"Stop it! Stop it right now! You're not just a terrier anymore, you're a scavenging bear and don't think I don't know what's going on!" Louisa threw her hairbrush across the room. It hit the wall hard and bounced back with a terrible clatter. I ducked even as I realized she had not thrown it directly at me.

Hannah hovered at the edge of death. In only a few days she had gone from the mildest of symptoms to coma. A kind doctor named Rawlins attended her, and told us finally that death was inevitable. We were stunned. Indeed, the entire ward was devastated. We nurses murmured among ourselves as we dispensed breakfast, feeding the soldiers more distractedly than usual, but they made no complaint. Even Mary Cotton was distressed.

"I'll be honest with you, it's not just Ropes's passing that makes me sad, it's the fact we've got to follow Belle Poole's orders now. Have you thought about that?" she said.

Then I discovered another theft. A purse with the mustering-out money of a dying patient was missing. Only the night before the man had whispered to me, "Don't give it to those thieves, the safe is for looting. We all know that. Get it to my family."

I promised. When I checked the money belt tucked under his mattress and found it gone, the sight of his despairing eyes was overwhelming. The word spread through the room. Dr. Coleman stalked into the ward and tried to question the dying man to little avail. Men cast glances at each other; only those with amputated limbs were spared scrutiny. But few would look directly at the blacksmith.

"Somebody has taken a dying man's money. Is there anything lower than that?" I said to Louisa. She chose not to hear me. She leaned against the wall for support, her face taut, shadows deepening under her eyes. If I had looked more closely, I would have seen the fever in them.

"She'll find a way to blame John," she said back.

I was barely thinking of Belle Poole. In my mind, the villain had changed.

That afternoon the soldier died. I held his hand, shamed by the fact I had not been able to keep my promise. Without the ability to keep a promise, I thought, what was I worth?

Hannah died at twilight. Louisa collapsed at her deathbed, and when I tried to help her from the room, I realized she was burning with fever.

Mr. Stokes helped me carry her to the third floor. I will say that for him, he helped me that one night. I even saw a tear in his eye for Mrs. Ropes. Old wastrel, he already missed his principal adversary. "Here," he said, thrusting a piece of paper at me. "It was on her bedstand; one of her last letters. Mrs. Ropes said to mail it, but I dunno now."

It was to her son in the army, written a few days past:

> *My Dear Neddie,*
>
> *I have been sick, or you should have heard from me sooner. Only think how near you are to me. Why don't you get a furlough for a few days and come see me? . . . I am doing my last work now. The tax upon us women who work for the love of it is tremendous when we have a new arrival of wounded. . . .*
>
> *Miss Alcott and I worked together over four dying men and saved all but one, the finest of the four, but whether (due to) our sympathy for the poor fellows, or we took cold, I know not, but we both have pneumonia. . . . She is a splendid young woman . . . can't you come over? . . .*
>
> > *Your loving marm,*
> > *H.A.R.*

I folded the letter carefully for Mrs. Ropes's children, who were due the next day, my heart weary with grief. Stalwart, hard-working Mrs. Ropes—a mother, a warm and loving mother was indeed what she had been. And she had sensed the nature of

Louisa's cough. Was I going to lose my friend too? Was she on some terrible decline? I cooled her brow and tried to make her comfortable, then slept restlessly by her side.

Around one in the morning I heard the bedsprings creak. Louisa was rising from her bed. She seemed still half asleep, and pulled at her nightshift, trying to peel its sweaty folds from her body. I thought she needed the chamber pot, but she headed for the door.

I sat up. "Louisa? Where are you going?"

She didn't answer.

Alarmed, I rose and tried to stop her, but she shook me off.

"No one will get him water anymore," she said, still pulling at her nightshift. "I have to bring him water."

Rather than struggle with her, I followed—down the stairs, through the dank halls, all the way to the ward. She stumbled over a bucket, and would have fallen if I had not grabbed her. The noise was sharp and jarring. Men turned in their beds, restless, some moaning, but none seemed awake as Louisa made her way to the blacksmith's bed.

His eyes were open, almost as if he had been expecting her.

Caught, caught. I was caught in a dream.

Louisa knelt and leaned forward, her face reaching his. He whispered something. She put her lips to his ear and whispered something back, then he cupped her chin and guided her mouth toward his in a slow, sensual glide. I saw her start to pull away. Tentatively at first, then more firmly, they kissed. He raised his long hand with its delicate fingers and gently encircled her head, caressing her hair.

I stood in the shadows, hands covering my mouth. They were lost to their surroundings, suspended in time, sealed in a kiss, and for a long moment, I hung there, swaying, with them. Was it indeed a dream? Whose dream?

Louisa pulled away. He reached out his hand to catch her, and I heard his words: "Don't go." With gentle pressure she pushed him back, standing to full height. At that moment I saw a sudden flash of movement, something, over by the door, but when I turned, it was gone. I moved forward and tugged at Louisa, pulling, feeling the counterpull of the blacksmith's arm. "Stop this, you must let her go, she's sick," I whispered as fiercely as I could. He looked at me with such sad clarity, it robbed me of breath. Louisa allowed me to wrest her hand away from his, and I pulled her away from danger and back up the stairs to our room, only realizing halfway up that my nostrils were filled with the scent of musk.

"My feelings aren't carnal," she whispered.

I fought back tears. "I don't believe you," I said.

It was done in the space of five minutes. But it felt like a lifetime, and in fact, one might say it was.

I had morning duty. Louisa stayed asleep; Dr. Lyndon promised to look in on her. I had expected a ward saddened by the matron's passing, but that was not what I found.

Belle Poole stood by John's bed, a scowling Dr. Coleman next to her. They both turned as I entered the room.

"Nurse Gray, see what we have found," Coleman said. He held out a pillowcase that sagged under a heavy weight. I blinked as he put in his hand and pulled out a fistful of dollars. The dead soldier's money.

"Where?" I asked.

Coleman nodded at the blacksmith, who was sitting erect on the side of his bed, feet on the floor, hands laced together. "In his pillowcase."

"Doctor?"

Coleman turned. It was the storekeeper, talking in a quick, hoarse voice. "He says he fought in my unit. Came up on the right flank of Marye's Heights under Chamberlain, he says. Early in the battle. But we came up almost the last, and I never saw him until I come here. Ain't that right?" The soldier looked to another man, a pale boy with a full black beard, for confirmation.

"I reckon it is," he agreed. "And if he came with Chamberlain, how come he ain't from Maine? We're with the Twentieth Maine, and he ain't from Maine, and that's a fact."

"I was on that hill pinned by fire until your unit came up," John said.

"Nobody was alive; we was walking over Hooker's men," said the first man. "I don't believe you."

I stared at John, who said no more. I didn't like the look in his eyes; it was the same sad clarity I had seen there when I pulled Louisa's hand from his grasp.

Coleman glanced at the clock on the wall, clearly impatient. A fracas over one man was taking too much time. "This is more than just thieving," he said. "Best we move this man out of here until we get the truth."

"The military—" I began.

"What time do they have to collect a possible spy?"

"There's always the cellar until they can come get him," Belle volunteered. "A day or two."

Coleman adjusted his glasses and cleared his throat. "Is this man in danger of dying, Nurse Poole? The cellar is a damp place."

"He's out of danger. I reckon he'll live longer than the rest of us," she retorted.

I stood as if rooted to the floor, my mouth firmly shut, aware that she was waiting for me to object. I said nothing, allowing myself by my silence to flow into the stream, to bob on down this mindless course with the rest of them. All it took was to go limp.

John stared straight ahead at the wall. He was wearing his Union blue coat pulled on over his hospital nightshirt, perhaps to proclaim identity, but it proved an unreliable shield.

"Are you a blacksmith?" Belle demanded. "Tell me what a blacksmith does. Give me the details of how you shoe a horse. How do you get 'em to stand still for the job? Tell us that. Can you do it?"

Oh, he hesitated. Yes, he did. He was groping for a description, I decided. Before he could answer I blurted a question: "Are you one of us?"

His answer will haunt me all my days.

"I am not one of them, Susan Gray. And you are not either."

That shook me for a moment. Then I heard Louisa's voice. She was standing at the doorway, fully dressed for work, her skin as white as her apron.

I stopped her as she walked toward John. "No," I said in a low voice.

"I heard it all. It's wrong."

"He's not who he says he is. Louisa, be careful."

Dr. Coleman broke in, eager to end it. "This man appears not to be a Union soldier, or so the evidence tells us up to this point." He held up the lumpy pillowcase like a bounty hunter hoisting a dead fox. "And the missing money was found in this, under his bed."

Louisa's eyes widened. She turned to look at John.

"It's not true," he said directly to her. "This bogus nurse is getting worried that there might be a real investigation. So just to hurry things along, she planted her loot on me. You know I didn't do this. You know me."

"You are impugning the reputation of one of our finest nurses," huffed Coleman.

"That doesn't bother the likes of him," Belle scoffed. "Well, I'm not taking further care of him, I'll tell you that. If he's innocent, we'll find out when he's tried. Right now he needs to be put in the cellar."

"The hole?" Louisa blurted, gripping the door frame to keep from falling.

"That's melodramatic," snapped Coleman. "It's simply a holding cell."

Belle was utilizing her own melodramatic skills once again. She turned directly to Louisa. "So are you on his side or with us?" she challenged. "You, you're a gentlewoman from Concord, can you ignore the evidence of your eyes?" She paused for emphasis. "Just because he's sweet on you?"

I stepped between the two of them, determined to shelter my friend. "Louisa, we can't interfere. We have to be careful; please, please trust me, you're not well," I whispered.

Trust. I spoke of trust at that moment. And all I could think of was what I had witnessed the night before. What would Concord think if she were sent home in shame? I had encouraged this romance, taking pleasure in being the "older" one who could instruct Lou in the art of taking chances. Now it was my responsibility to pull her back.

I saw her waver. I saw it in her eyes. She was listening to me, letting me guide her. And all the while, John simply sat on the edge of his bed, as if at attention, his gaze fastened on Louisa.

"Nothing of what you are all saying is true," she said. Her voice was weak and shaky.

"He'll have a chance to prove his case. Right now he's a danger to morale in this ward," said Coleman. He turned to Belle. "Get his things together and take him to the cellar. I'll notify the authorities we have a possible spy in custody."

Neither Louisa nor I made any further protest. I was paralyzed and she was fighting to hold herself up against the ravages of fever. The uncertainty was in her eyes: Had she been drawn to someone untrustworthy? I told her later, oh, so many times, she was not to blame. I was the one who could have spoken up. Instead I chose not to defend John against what my conscience whispered was a false charge. I was a coward.

Chapter Ten

I cannot be sure how time passed after that. Days, yes. How many? I don't remember. John Sulie was confined in the cellar and Louisa to her bed. Typhoid pneumonia, said Dr. Rawlins, with great sympathy. He added that he was a great admirer of Louisa's father.

"Give her comfort, and trust in fate," he said. He had a funny little potbelly and kept checking a gold pocketwatch that rested almost horizontally on his waistcoat. I wasn't sure I liked him as much as previously.

Clara came.

"How did you know?" I asked gratefully when she appeared.

"I have my ways, dear," she said. She sat at Louisa's bed for two long hours, stroking her brow, listening to her speak as she dipped in and out of consciousness. She then guided me into the stairwell's cramped alcove and, holding my arm, half pulled me down the stairs. "Susan, I think you need to act the elder sister, at least for now," she said.

Sister. Elder sister. This time, with responsibility. "I will," I replied, and then could say nothing more.

"You can see how much she is hallucinating. The fever is affecting her brain. You and I, we've seen this before. Watch her; it can progress rapidly."

I shuddered, feeling cold and not the elder sister at all.

* * *

The shadows of evening had already darkened the stairwell to the third floor when I climbed up to our room that night to check on Louisa. The room was dark. I drew in my breath at the smell. Heavy, moist; oddly pungent. But only when I lit a candle and held it aloft to see Louisa's face did I see how her condition was worsening. It wasn't just the fever or the pale cast of her skin. She cast me a glance so dazed and wild, I almost dropped the hot tallow of the candle on her face.

"Who are you?" she demanded. "What are you doing here?"

I tried to speak, but she didn't listen, instead she grabbed at my arm, mumbling incomprehensibly. I struggled to put the candle on the table and attempted to wrestle her back down to her bed.

"Open a window," a voice behind me demanded. I was pushed aside, realizing only dimly that it was Dr. Lyndon taking my place, lifting Louisa's head, holding her shoulders firm with arms far stronger than my own. Behind him, I saw the heavy figure of Belle Poole.

"Get some calomel," he said, speaking over his shoulder to Belle. "Not a full cup this time."

"It kills people," I protested.

"We have nothing else," he snapped. Louisa's body was arching back, straining unnaturally, and the moan from her lips was heartrending.

"Help me," she gasped. "Susan, help me."

"Get me some wet rags," he said. "What the devil are you waiting for? We need to bring her fever down."

I stumbled down the stairs to the kitchen, my heart racing so fast I could hardly breathe. Again. The same run up and down the stairs, once again hoping to save a person I loved, remembering, remembering—last time, I lost two.

Louisa's weeping followed me down to the ward where I cast about for the cleanest rags I could find, soaked them in water, and then ran back upstairs. Belle was leaning over Louisa's bed, holding her head up, nudging a cup between her lips. I tried to shut down my fears. She finished the job, paid me no heed, and left.

"You know what to do now," said Dr. Lyndon. He cast me a sympathetic look as he departed, and I was grateful that he did not check his watch.

Perhaps an hour later, Louisa seemed to rally. To my great relief, she recognized me and fixed her gaze. "John," she muttered. "Is he all right?"

"Yes," I said soothingly.

"You are not a good liar. He's no better off than I am, true? I know where he is." She closed her eyes and I wondered if she was drifting into sleep. Then she spoke again. "Please, Susan. Make sure he's all right. You will?"

I nodded.

"Give me a pencil and a scrap of paper." Her voice was strengthening.

I reached up to the dresser, picked up a stub of pencil, then tore a blank leaf from her journal and handed both to her.

With great effort, she pulled herself up and scribbled a note, frowning as she wrote, faltering at first, and then writing quickly. She folded the piece of paper in two and handed it to me. "Take this to him, and take the pencil," she said. "Ask him to answer; I am desperate for something from him."

I hesitated, wondering if she was lucid. Did she know what she was doing?

"You must understand." She spoke more urgently, her breathing laborious. "I am going to take a chance. I must . . . offer more."

"Louisa, this isn't—"

"You used to think I was so brave when I climbed trees, but I was pretending. To be truly brave is to let go. . . ." Her voice faltered.

Her eyes were impossibly wide and dark. Was she raving?

"I know what you're thinking. I'm not crazed, Susan. Remember the day you found the boy in the oven? You promised to obey me if I promised to be your friend. Do this for me, please."

"I'll do it," I whispered.

"Thank you," she said. For a brief instant, she looked at peace.

Back down the stairs I went, holding up my skirts, praying for I knew not what. The bewildered night nurse unlocked the door to the basement stairs at my request, and I descended into that dank space as quickly as I could, wanting no second thoughts. Skitterings and slitherings across the floor . . . did I imagine them? I lifted my skirts higher. I could not believe that John was down here. There was a full moon that night and a small window outside his cell; otherwise I would have seen nothing.

"John?" I saw a seated form stir behind the iron bars. I had not before called him by his Christian name.

"Susan?" His voice was strained, devoid of fight. He stood and moved to the bars, leaning against them heavily, reminding me that he was not yet a well man. His hair had touches of gray; had I noticed that before? Had it only now turned? His eyes looked darker than usual; searching; knowing. I moved closer, twining the fingers of one hand around a bar near the one where his rested. I tried to find my voice, almost overpowered by the intimacy of this lonely, shrouded place.

"Louisa is sick," I said.

"I was afraid of that," he muttered. "She has typhoid, doesn't she?"

"Yes, John." I wanted to keep repeating his name, to take it down to a whisper. "I'm sorry."

"What for? Letting them put me in here or for Louisa?"

The intimacy shattered. "For having to bring you this news," I said, pulling back slightly. "And for not protesting when they took you away. But don't impugn my feelings for Louisa, you know I love her and will protect her."

"I do know that. Pardon me for not being as grateful as I should be."

"She is worried about you. And she wants me to—"

"Do something about this sorry mess? That's not possible. Don't say more, Susan. Just listen to me. There isn't much time."

"If you're innocent, nothing's going to happen to you."

"Events will take over, I can't say more. I won't be able to get to Louisa, I know that now." He sounded weary, sorrowing. "How sick is she? Will she get well?"

"She's strong, I think she will," I said, trying to hide my doubts.

"I've never known a woman like her."

"Nor have I."

"Forgive my roughness." His voice grew thinner, tighter. "She lifts everything above this squalor, do you understand? Everything. None of it matters—the thievery, pain, stupidity—when she's here."

These weren't the words of the mocking, cynical man who enjoyed challenging the likes of Belle Poole, this was the man Louisa loved. She had found what was true in him.

"You shouldn't be in here, you're no thief," I whispered. My wariness of him was evaporating like smoke into the sky.

"On that you are correct." The mocking tone was back.

I cast about in my mind for a course of action. "I'll talk to Dr. Coleman—"

"Don't bother, that won't be necessary."

Our hands now were almost touching, each of us gripping the bars. "John, I need to know. Are you truly a blacksmith?"

He actually chuckled. "Susan, I would not know how to shoe a horse if my life depended on it. But I am no one who could embarrass you, I promise you that."

"What do you want from me?"

He pressed his face close to the bars, still in shadow. "A lifeline. Someone to assure her I'm to be trusted. I want a connection, so I can find her again. I need to know if I am free to seek her out when all is over."

"She wants that, too." I was a messenger, I had a duty.

"I want to believe that, but I'm not much of one for wishful thinking. Susan, I know you're afraid to trust me. I don't know how to change your mind. This may come as a surprise, but my feelings for Louisa are deeper than carnal. I need you to believe that."

I shivered, remembering the sight of him drawing Louisa's mouth to his. "But I saw how you kissed her," I said.

His eyes searched mine and when he finally spoke, his voice was quiet. "You were watching. Why were you watching?"

My heart began to pound and I felt my face burn with heat. I felt dizzy, unable to think. I tried to find my voice, not knowing what to say.

Only then did I remember the piece of paper in my left hand. Louisa's note. How could I have forgotten it? I thrust my hand through the bars, touching his. "Here, this is—" I began.

Somehow his fingers were encircling my wrist. Did he pull me forward or did I press close?

"Oh God," he whispered. I blindly reached for his other hand, pulling it through the bars. Did I really cup it over my breast? Yes. I could not have pulled away if the Almighty had walked into the room. The cold metal of the bars pressed deeply now into my face and his lips were so close . . . I found them. I sensed his surprise—was it surprise? I held fast to his hand as we kissed. The taste—oh, so salty and yet sweet. So soft. I wanted to drink, inhale; never move, and vaguely, somewhere, I realized he didn't pull away.

Something scrambled over my foot, shocking me back to awareness.

I turned and ran. Up the stairs, through the dark hall, and to the porch. I stood there, shaking, waiting for the unimaginable fire inside me to cool. I waited, breathing in deeply and then exhaling into the frosty, winter air. A cloud of dread descended. I ran back inside and up the stairs, pushing my way into our tiny room.

Belle was leaning over Louisa. I squinted in the poorly lit room and saw her cradling Louisa's head, pulling it up toward the cup she held in her hand. "Stop!" I screamed.

Belle jumped and twisted toward me. Liquid from the cup in her hand slopped onto the bedsheet. "It's only water," she said, backing away.

"It's only water? Why should I trust you? Give me that." I grabbed the cup, took a sip, and spat it out. It was indeed water.

Dr. Coleman stepped forward from the shadows. "Control yourself, Nurse Gray. You are not helping. Please leave."

But I was rooted to the spot, for Louisa was again in delirium. She tossed from side to side, heaving her body up, and then down, up again, and down. Her long dark hair sprawled out onto the pillow like a blot of ink. She looked possessed. "He's coming at me from the closet," she muttered. "I'm going to be burned as a witch and sent to hell. I've sinned; I've sinned."

"I can't leave," I whispered.

"You know what's happening. You've seen it before," Coleman said.

The nurse in me struggled to surface. Typhoid loosened the tongue and unleashed nightmares of the darkest kind in many of its victims, and indeed I did know what was happening. Louisa was delusional, and what she said meant nothing. Or did it? Only slowly did I become aware of something crunching into my palm. Only slowly did I think to open my hand, observing first the chapped, bleeding creases on my newly released fingers. A piece of paper, crunched tight, congealed with sweat, rested in my palm like a tiny ball. Louisa's note.

I had not delivered it? How could that be?

I tried to open it up without tearing it, but the paper began to crumble. I ran from the room. I had to give him her note. This time I slipped and fell on the basement steps even as I heard the scuttling sound again of unseen rats. By the time I righted myself and made my way to John Sulie's cell, I was crying. I whispered his name once, then more urgently. There was no answer. I peered through the bars, trying to see him. How do I describe the eerie sense of searching through nothing for everything? The door creaked as I leaned against it. And then, as if it were the most natural thing in the world, the door swung open wide.

With the fear of someone plunging into the void, I stepped into the cell. John was gone. Vanished.

"You left," I whispered, hearing my own voice echo through the damp, empty space, wondering why it sounded so angry. "Why did you leave?" I stepped out of the cell and back into a pool of moonlight coming from what I now saw was the broken cellar window. And only then did I gaze down at the paper in my hand, staring at what was left of Louisa's shaky scrawl. All lost. Not a word was legible.

Louisa had few moments of lucidity during the following dreadful days. I stayed by her side for long hours as she battled the fever. At one point I felt a gentle hand on my shoulder, and looked around to see Clara. She held vigil with me through the entire afternoon as we took turns sponging Louisa's forehead and holding her hand. We spoke comforting words to a woman who heard nothing. We did for Lou what we did for all the sick, and it meant nothing. Even Clara could not heal my friend.

"I hear he's gone," she said quietly.

"Yes."

"Tell me."

As I recounted his request and the blundered venture that ended with me staring into an empty cell, she listened intently— and I had the strangest feeling that she had heard it all before.

"I betrayed her; how can that be?" I whispered. "How could I do that?"

"You were overwhelmed by your emotions, Susan. Don't flagellate yourself. It's done."

"But what happened to him? He isn't a thief, and I don't think he's a Rebel spy. Why is he gone? Did he escape or was he taken away?"

She sighed. "It's best to let it be, dear. You must put him out of your mind for now. You need to concentrate on getting Louisa well."

The men in the ward asked for Louisa in hushed tones. They were used to waking up to empty beds around them, used to seeing each other die. But finding that typhoid could fell the women who cared for them was a different thing. I walked my rounds as if in a dream, answering their questions with as few words as possible, for Louisa's illness wasn't the only topic of conversation.

"We hear Sulie's disappeared," the storekeeper said, not bothering to contain a grin, which showed at least two rotted teeth. "Got himself out of here finally, didn't he? How do you think he managed that, Nurse?"

I shrugged my shoulders and looked past him as I moved on. The others were not so blatant, although their snickers and whispers followed me through the ward. By thunder, he was a dirty spy, all right, the soldiers said. Why else would he disappear? Who helped him escape? The steward, the nurses, all denied responsibility. Were there more spies about? The voices grew louder.

Finally the Rebel chimed in. "Why are you all so convinced he escaped?" he demanded from his bed. "You dullards don't think for a minute he could have been dragged away and killed? If he was one of us, I suspect he's dead. I wouldn't put it past your kind. How many of you waitin' to see me die?"

That silenced the chatterers. I felt desperate to leave, but stopped at the bed of Tom Cassidy to check the dressing on his arm.

"Can I offer some advice?" he asked in a low tone.

I noticed he now had the stubble of a beard that matched his light hair. It made him look older, somehow. "Of course," I said.

"Don't let these louts pull you down. They're scared, all of 'em. Remember, they count on you to stay strong. Just do your job."

Touched, I thanked him and did what I could to make him comfortable before leaving to resume my vigil over Louisa. The useless fragment of paper on which she had written her note remained in the pocket of my apron. I had some vague thought that if John came back, I would at least put the corporeal remains in his hand and be spared some portion of the burden of guilt now in my heart.

In the meantime, I concentrated on fighting off Belle's attempts to dose Louisa with calomel, at one point taking both hands and, with the strength of fury, shoving her out of the room. I could not save my friend from the typhoid, but could I not at least save her from this heartless nurse? Belle in high dudgeon summoned the fusty little Dr. Coleman, who seemed to enjoy stomping in and overruling me.

"But her tongue is swelling and her hair is falling out on the pillow," I protested, trying not to cry. "She is not getting better. Can't you see that?"

"Are you a doctor? No, you are not, of course. You are just a hysterical girl who doesn't know anything! Calomel cleans a body out. The less inside her, the less chance disease has to feed," he sputtered.

I stared at him, knowing I wasted my time. A man like Coleman always followed the rules, blind to what his own senses surely told him. How ironic now to remember that, fewer than four months later, the army would order its doctors to stop using that dreadful mercury compound. Somebody in the surgeon general's office would finally summon the courage to face what so many of the nurses knew: Calomel was poison.

I retreated to Mary Cotton's room, and with her soothing me as much as she could, I shoved my face deep into the mattress and sobbed uncontrollably. I knew what I had to do. Mrs. Ropes had declined so rapidly, no one had thought to summon her family, and the grief they experienced at not having been at her side when she died was haunting. I sat up then, asked Mary to bring me some paper and a pencil, and then scratched out an urgent note to Bronson. She is growing sicker by the day, I said. Please hurry. She needs to go home.

The very act of sending that note off to Concord calmed me. It was, I was convinced, the only thing I could do that might save Louisa's life. And still I kept her crumpled message in my pocket. I fancied it as the last possible link between Louisa and John. If in some way, at some time, he surfaced, I could thrust it at him and he would write on it his own words of love. I would have something to give her. As it was, she had nothing.

This memory will always pull me down to a lonely place. It is not just the note never delivered, but all the human words of comfort and love not written or spoken, the promises unfulfilled, hopes unrealized, the acts of connection that get lost, diverted, never made. I do take myself into the abyss with these thoughts, but I am determined to follow their path and remember my friend and what truly shaped her before Mrs. Cheney and the powers of Concord create their own icon for history. If I weave something pretty and sanitized now, I will not come back to the truth again.

Louisa appeared to rally briefly on Thursday. I sat beside her on a gray afternoon, half-dozing, my dreams filled with restless shadows flitting back and forth. Bronson had sent word he would arrive on the evening train. A great weariness had taken over my body, and I could do little now but wait for him by Louisa's side.

"Susan."

My eyes flew open. She was looking at me, her face pale and sallow, yet resolute.

"Did you give him my note?"

I took her hand and stroked it helplessly, saying nothing. She lifted her head partway off the pillow and searched my face, her eyes widening.

"Is he dead? Is that why you don't speak?"

"He escaped. He fled his cell and escaped."

Her stare was uncomprehending.

"Louisa, did you hear? He escaped. He's not dead. I'm giving you good news, not bad news."

"But . . . did you give him my note?" She began to cry, a small, harsh sound broken by choppy coughs.

I reached for her, trying to envelop her with my arms, searching for what to say. I should confess. Yet how could I deal such a blow? I was woefully unprepared for dealing with this moral choice. Was there one clearly less evil than the other?

"Yes," I said.

"Thank God," she murmured.

It was done. In my heart, I knew I could not undo it. And I vowed at that moment to stand by her always, to throw myself into the flames, if need be, to never let her down again.

The heavy oak door of our bedroom creaked open, and I turned and saw Bronson. His head grazed the top of the door frame, and his long gray hair hung in strings onto his collar. Draped over his bony shoulders was one of his old black jackets and in his gnarled hand he carried a silver-tipped cane. He looked, thin as he was, almost immense.

"May the good Lord help us," he muttered as he strode forward and bent over Louisa's bed. She was still sobbing, seemingly unaware of his presence. His eyes flickered at the sight of strands of hair glued by sweat to her pillow. It was my habit to scoop up what fell out each day and throw it away so Louisa would not see, but I had not yet done so that afternoon. Surely the sight shocked him. He straightened, crossed his hands in front of him, and stared gravely at his daughter.

Oh, I heard the sadness in his voice. The concern. And yet still contained, as always, still steady and cool. Something inside me wanted him to cry out. I wanted to hear fear or anguish.

"You were right to notify me," Bronson said. "Have you packed her things?"

I nodded.

"Then I will bundle her against the cold and take her to the carriage. The train leaves in three hours. Are you coming with us?"

"I came with Louisa, and I shall leave with Louisa." My voice quavered, but he scarcely noticed.

"Then say your good-byes and pack your trunk. And ask the head doctor to come in here, please."

I had already packed most of my things, so I wandered downstairs, looking for Dr. Coleman. I tried to absorb the fact that it had been only a few months since Louisa and I had arrived in this city, all blithe and purposeful. And now it was over.

The ward looked as it always did in the late afternoon. Two nurses cast pitying glances in my direction as they rushed through their usual routines of bandaging, washing, writing letters for the wounded men. Oh, they had been whispering for days that Louisa was soon to die. And I had heard snatches of giggling from some of the younger ones when the gossiping included speculation about Louisa's closeness to the blacksmith. Even as I nodded in their direction, I had an unwelcome thought. Surely no one would take this tale to Bronson.

And the thefts had stopped. Not a single item had been stolen since John was banished to the cellar, which was taken by many as proof positive that he was the culprit.

I watched Belle make her lumbering way among the beds. Her legs were laced with swollen veins, her shoulders chunky and hunched. I still trusted her not a whit, but I feared her no more. I saw her for what she was: a crafty survivor feathering her nest in her own way, not unlike so many in this evil place. Dr. Coleman said Belle's daughter had run away with a tinker who beat her and left her to die on a Virginia highway. That had hardened her soul. And left her free of moral obligation to any other.

I felt old that day, so very old.

The steward came up to me and thrust forward an awkward hand. "Sorry about Nurse Alcott," he said.

And so I shook hands with a known thief and thanked him for his concern.

"Din't you notice? The Reb kicked the bucket."

I looked over at the bed where the Confederate soldier had lain and saw only a bare, filthy mattress. It must have happened that very day.

"Where did you take him?" I asked.

The steward shrugged. "Anywhere, we find places, don't you worry."

"But what about his family?"

"Who knows? He never did give us a name we believed." He chuckled. "Just like that damn spy. Nothing unusual about that, a lot of men disappear in this war. That gentleman who comes in to write letters? The poet? A bit daft, I'd say. He told me he wants to rescue these men from obscurity. Obscurity? We're all obscure."

Mary Cotton rushed forward to give me a hug good-bye, so I didn't have to answer. I promised her I would write, although we both knew Mary was almost illiterate, and unable to read cursive letters. But it helped to promise, all the same. As I turned to go, I thought of Tom. How could I leave without bidding *him* farewell? I turned back into the ward and saw him watching me, a curious smile on his face.

"Thought you'd forgotten me," he said as I came to his side.

"You've been one of the few bright spots here, Tom, and I'll miss our chats." I was relieved to know his wound was healing, and I felt reasonably confident this sturdy-bodied man with his sandy hair would survive Union Hospital. Something good could happen, even here.

"Don't forget my advice," he said. "Don't let anybody pull you down. Holds for Concord, too."

"I won't," I promised. I hesitated, feeling awkward, then reached out and touched his shoulder. "You take care of yourself."

"I'll do that," he said with a wave of his hand.

I felt his eyes follow me as I exited the room.

Just beyond the door, I spotted Clara standing on the veranda, looking as weary as the night I first came upon her leaning over the still form of John Sulie. She seemed bent, somehow. Sorrowing. Almost old. I felt shaken with this heretical thought.

"Susan." She approached and took my hands in hers. "Don't despair. She may recover in the safety of her own home with her family."

"Everybody here with typhoid dies," I replied.

"Not everyone. Be brave. And be a good friend."

I had no tears left to shed. "I haven't been either. I have nothing to give her. I told her he lives, and she doesn't believe me."

"That may be just as well."

"Why do you say that?"

"We're at war, that's why. He may have been alive when he left here and dead, now."

"That's what the Reb said."

"A pity he lasted as long as he did," Clara muttered.

That startled me. Clara was not one to wish any man into his grave, not even a Rebel. "I don't understand," I began.

Clara made an impatient clucking noise with her lips and pulled herself straight, putting a bit of distance between us. "There is much you don't know. Nor do I, for that matter. The black-smith—"

"He is not a blacksmith. He told me so."

"Whoever he was, his feelings for Louisa were real."

"How do you know?"

Clara let out a small whistle of a sigh from her straight and formidable nose. "He spoke to it the night I talked to him."

Another surprise. I found myself remembering the night Clara had walked through the ward, stopping for conversation with John. He had cared enough to speak up to Clara. What had he said? I had much to ask but at that moment, from the corner of my eye, I saw movement on the stairs. Two of the steward's men were carrying down our trunks, with Bronson following close behind. In his arms he carried Louisa, her tall form shrouded in blankets.

"Will he come find her?" I asked quickly. "Will he do that?"

Clara relented somewhat, putting her hand on my shoulder. "I don't know," she said. She studied my face thoughtfully and then leaned forward, planting a dry kiss on my cheek. "Go, Susan. Remember your duty. Take care of Louisa, and perhaps we will see one another again."

"What are you going to do?" I asked.

"The same, until the war is ended, if the Sanitary Commission doesn't monopolize all the medical supplies." She frowned; the government was no longer taking kindly to her brand of independence. "They want to control everything and make it impersonal. Turn the men into fodder. I can't bear the thought of so many of them vanishing into death, with no one to know who they are."

"That's what Mr. Whitman was saying. Something about saving them from obscurity," I replied.

She smiled. "Each in one's own fashion," she said. And then she turned and walked away, not looking back.

How can people take their leave in this manner? How can there be not a tinge of desire for another glance? I, for one, am incapable of not looking back. But Clara could live without the need for one final peek over the shoulder, one extra gesture of farewell, one smile of connection. Head held high, exhibiting a strength of will I admire but cannot emulate, she could march away.

I grabbed my coat from the wooden hook in the hall and hurried after Bronson, wanting desperately to be both out of this place and to remain in it, pausing only to flick the remains of Louisa's note into the hospital stove. I felt overwhelmed with the sense of destinies and stories left suspended. But there was no time; all was finished.

And of course, nothing was finished.

Chapter Eleven

We rode in silence to the depot, Louisa wrapped in warm clothes next to me. She seemed to know where she was, but kept complaining of the cold. "Susan, have you dipped me into the river?" she whispered, trying to smile. I wrapped my arm around her to add as much human warmth as possible.

The depot was grimy and cold as ice, the floor slick with saliva from overflowing spittoons. Boxes and bundles were piled high everywhere as porters jostled each other, shouting as they vied for the job of hauling passenger gear to the trains. The clusters of soldiers lounging about were winking at pretty females and joking with each other, exuding a restless energy that made me want to shrink away. They were healthy, almost obscenely so, with high color and strong limbs, and I shrank away because such vigor was foreign to me.

Bronson said little, intent on getting us on the correct train. We took our seats at the end of the carriage and settled Louisa as comfortably as we could on the wood seat facing ours. "I'm fine, just let me sleep," she kept saying. Seeing her pale face, people around us pulled back. One little fellow in a red cap kept peeking over the seat, waving to me, until his mother yanked him down with a scolding after catching Louisa giving him a wink. All feared the typhoid.

Bronson turned to me, looking befuddled. "I brought no food for the journey," he said. He tugged at his waistcoat, looking around

the carriage as if he thought a tasty lunch might suddenly material-
ize from the air.

I had the eerie sensation of being Abba as I leaned forward and
handed him a small bundle of apples and three sponge cakes I had
bought from a vendor at the station. In my pocket, guiltily, I held
on to a cache of nuts and raisins. His face brightened, and he gave
me an approving nod.

I pressed my face against the glass as the train began to move,
straining to catch one last glimpse of the Capitol as the station disappeared from sight. But I could see only wagons and roads and
half-finished wooden structures sprinkled across the landscape.
Then, nothing but barren fields, matching the emptiness in my
heart. A deep physical exhaustion flooded my body; all the sleepless nights and grinding days seemed to exact their toll in one
overwhelming moment.

It was over. Union Hospital had been my entire world for many
weeks now, and it was gone. Finished. I slumped back, pulling the
thin linsey-woolsey of my skirt tight around my legs for protection
against the piercing drafts already finding their way into the carriage.

I stole a glance at Bronson, who had begun to pare an apple.
We had never talked alone.

"I'm deeply grateful to you for coming," I said with some
shyness.

"Why would you say that? Of course, I would come," he said,
giving me a startled glance. "I could not abide the anxiety of leaving my child here."

"Oh, I know that," I said with haste, adding, "I think she will
revive when she is home and surrounded by her family."

"If the fates so ordain." He looked as miserable as I felt.

What common ground did we share? Should I tell him about
our lives at Union Hospital? Haltingly, I started to talk about the
ward, and the soldiers we had nursed. About Mrs. Ropes, and
about Mr. Whitman. I chatted on as he sat silent, telling him about

the drummer boy and the Rebel. About missing laundry and the card games. Little details, watching his face, testing, waiting for a response. I began to hear the tension in my voice as it rattled on. I did not talk about John Sulie.

"This is a setback, but the Alcotts are no strangers to setbacks," he broke in.

"You are a strong breed," I said obligingly.

"Our happiest times were at Fruitlands."

I hesitated. Fruitlands? Bronson's grand communal experiment in utopian living?

I glanced at my friend, grateful that she slept so deeply. Fruitlands. Every time Louisa had mentioned that disastrous time, it was with a certain mordant wit. How awful it must have been! Grinding work, meager harvests, little food, impossible rules set by Bronson. Up at five in the morning to help her mother with the cooking and washing, to bed at dusk, no chance to read books or mend clothes, for Bronson would not allow the use of whale oil lamps—they exploited whales. And no team to help till the land—that would exploit oxen. Then the final blow that left Abba in despair: Bronson began to mull over the virtues of free love against the institution of marriage, as she and the children struggled to tend their crops. A defiant Abba lit her lamp from that point on until Bronson admitted Fruitlands was a failure.

What strange spirit possessed him to call that the "happiest time"?

It was as if he heard my thoughts. "We were searching for new ways of perfecting the human spirit. There was a purity to such a life many would not understand, I fear," he said almost timidly.

"I fear I am among them, sir," I said.

"You were not there."

"Louisa has talked about it."

"She found the life too severe, and I acknowledge it was much too hard a place for children. But there were fine moments, too. Henry understood." He leaned forward, eager now to talk.

"We used to go to his cabin at Walden Pond—Emerson, Ellery

Channing, and I. We would push our chairs back against the walls and shoot ideas at each other—the glory of it all!" His eyes shone. "At times I would go alone and sit there whittling on a piece of pumpkin pine, talking with Henry, listening to the sound of the wind in the trees outside. Nothing but nature—and thought. If anything comes close to heaven on earth, that is it. It is what I had hoped for, at Fruitlands."

"People need to eat," I said stubbornly.

"You overlook the useful tools of self-control and discipline."

"They still need food. And money. Louisa says it was dreadful."

He sat back, the light fading from his eyes. "Her spirit was quite dark as a child. Goodness did not come easily to her."

"Perhaps goodness did not suffice," I said.

He did not respond. His eyes strayed back to Louisa, his gaze lingering on her face. There was a fatherly softness to his expression I rarely saw, and I was suddenly ashamed. Why was I challenging this old man? "I'm sorry," I said. "That was rude."

And then he surprised me again.

"You are like her."

Could that be true? "I'm not sure I agree," I said.

"Your anger bursts forth, followed by contrition. This is Louisa's way." He stared at me over the rim of his round glasses. "You believe you know her spirit, Susan. But I know her better. You will not want to accept that, but I tell you now, it is true."

I could think of nothing to say. At this confusing juncture, Louisa turned, raised herself on one elbow, and looked at me beseechingly.

"Where is John?" she said. "Is he all right? Does he know I'm here?"

I leaned forward and pulled the blanket I had tucked around her closer to her chin, murmuring vague words of comfort. She stared at me, then closed her eyes and drifted back to sleep.

"Who is John?" Bronson asked.

"A soldier, one of many we nursed," I said. "They were all important to us."

"Was this man a particular friend of my daughter's?"

"No, no, just a blacksmith."

Bronson pulled out a handkerchief and proceeded to wipe a film of soot from his forehead. He asked no more.

We rode all night. Louisa would from time to time raise her head and scan her surroundings in puzzlement, settling back only when I whispered to her.

"Why are we on a train?" she asked at one point.

"We're going home. You've been sick, and you need to heal," I replied.

"Not everything heals," she muttered.

Bronson dozed most of the way in a rigid, upright position, and I kept busy visiting the water jug at the back of the carriage to rewet a flannel cloth for placing on Louisa's forehead. Each time I lifted it to be remoistened, it burned hot.

I fell into a doze, waking only when morning dawned. We were approaching Boston, and I saw Lou was awake. I fed her an orange, wishing I had more. The nuts and raisins in my pocket were gone, as were the apples and sponge cakes. A kindly porter helped us disembark, and found us a place to rest in the station while we waited for the four o'clock train to Concord.

"My goodness, is it Louisa? Susan Gray? And Mr. Alcott?"

I looked up into the surprised face of Una Hawthorne. She looked quite beautiful. Her long dark hair was parted in the middle and hanging free, and she wore a very fashionable brown coat. When Louisa attempted a smile through her dreadful pallor, Una's eyes widened in shock. She did not cringe or draw away as I expected, and my liking for her deepened immediately. She was returning from a quilting bee in Brookline, she told us as she stroked Louisa's hand, and had not heard of her illness.

"I've thought about the two of you so many times, and everyone in town wanted to know how you were doing. I can see the terrible cost, but was it as exciting as you expected?" she asked timidly.

Exciting? The word meant nothing now, no more than a hollow sound, an empty collection of syllables.

"It was unlike anything I've ever experienced," I said.

Perhaps it was my monotone, bleached of feeling, but Una began chattering about other things as we boarded the local train and settled ourselves once again onto two long facing benches. Bronson promptly folded his arms and went to sleep. And once again, all others shunned us. Una clutched her rich, warm coat close and sat resolutely across from me, two pink circles prominent on her cheeks. "Did Louisa give away all those copies of Dickens she packed?" she asked.

"There was little reading going on in the hospital," I said with a sigh. "Most of the books disappeared by the second week. Thieves, you know?"

Her eyes filled with tears. "That's terrible," she said.

"Tell me how everyone is," I urged, eager to change the subject.

"Well, we're still sewing away at Orchard House, pricking our fingers and gossiping about all sorts of things. Did you hear Mrs. Lincoln is supposed to be very strange? A little daft, we hear. Mother's nerves seem to get worse all the time, and Father just sits writing and smoking cigars." She giggled. "Julian is still sweet on May, but she told him she was going to marry the first man who took her to Europe to study art. *That* pricked a hole in my brother's pride! And, oh, Sophia Thoreau? Of all things, she's taken on running the family business making plumbago. That little shop of Henry's has been in back of the house for so many years, but now her brother's dead, she says she can run it better than anyone."

"She'll grind the graphite and clay herself?"

"In a mill, a few miles out of town. She's very independent. Can you imagine? Sophia will be keeping us all in pencils now!" Una's eyes fluttered heavenward, and for just a moment, I was able to be amused with her.

"Water," whispered Louisa, half-opening her eyes.

I jumped up, cradling her head and holding to her lips the cup I had ready. Una fell silent. Louisa tossed back and forth fretfully, then settled down and dozed off once again. I looked at Una. Her eyes were frightened.

"Susan, is she going to die?" she whispered.

"Not if good nursing can pull her through," I replied.

As we approached Concord, moving through the woods and lavish thickets surrounding the village, I began to feel anchored again, less afloat in a nightmare. I could see a few farmers trudging out in their black boots to feed their livestock, leaving tracks across the gently curved snowy meadows. The train moved steadily northwest, its whistle screaming—how did Henry once put it?—like a hawk sailing over a farmyard. And now we were skirting the icy, dark blue waters of Walden Pond. Bronson smiled as he spied a cluster of figures at the edge of the lake. Pilgrims, of course. "They come like robins to this hallowed ground," he murmured. "And well they should."

We were approaching the depot at Milldam, and I searched hungrily for familiar sights. There, yes—a curl of smoke from Mr. Emerson's chimney. The light was waning fast, but I could see the First Church and the Middlesex Hotel just past the village center. Beyond, the Sudbury and Assabet rivers flowed into one, forming our own Concord River, moving splendidly out from the Old North Bridge in a great rush of sound and purpose. I closed my eyes and remembered days spent picking blackberries with Louisa along that river and wondered if we would ever again fight our way through brambles, pulling our skirts free as we laughed and talked.

The train gave one last, long, gasping wheeze and grew silent. And there on the platform, looking like blackbirds in their heavy cloaks and bonnets, were Abba and May.

We were home.

Louisa's recovery took many weeks. I expected May to flee the house, given her fidgety spirit, her dislike of illness, and the extent of the work involved. But she found in herself the resolve to stay by her sister's side, spending long hours there, performing all tasks, from holding her hand to emptying her bedpan.

"You would make a good nurse," I said to her after one particularly harrowing day. She lifted her chin in pride and gave me a smile.

At one point Abba brought in a mesmerist who promised to magnetize the pain out of Louisa by holding her hands over her body and drawing it out. It didn't work, and Bronson was irritated at his wife's futile efforts. Louisa's illness, indeed, kept everyone's nerves frayed. I saw the cost it was exacting, and decided my job was to take charge of nursing Louisa and hold the rest of the family steady. I owed everything to them.

I have since wondered what holds a family together through terrible events, and am quite sure heroic sacrifice is not enough. It is more the daily effort to lay aside petty squabbles and resentments, if but temporarily, which takes its own heroism. In the dark days while Louisa was ill, we held together, struggling to transcend minor concerns—who prepares tea, who cleans the sickroom, who pays the tradesmen—at a time when such ordinary tasks were fraught with tension and fear. May refrained from complaining; Bronson rolled up his sleeves and hammered away, building a sun porch for Louisa; Anna cooked vats of food and walked with them through bleak winter days to Orchard House to ease the burden for her mother; Abba and I took turns sitting up through long nights by Louisa's side. I tasted the deepest fear of loss of my life. I loved Louisa, beyond all. I watched her still face in sleep and vowed to never waver in loyalty again.

Memories of those many weeks wash into a haze of endless, weary care. Abba would allow few visitors. Not only did Louisa recognize no one, she hallucinated constantly. Where, buried in Louisa's fevered brain, was John? I did not know. I moved through my days, searching for ways to break what had happened into digestible pieces, to make it better, to be worthy of Louisa again. I made a bargain with God—let John be alive, and I would force him from my heart and from my dreams. I would do that for Louisa.

*   *   *

"The doctor said it must go."

"Why?"

"To help release the fever." I tried to sound matter-of-fact, but my hand trembled as I picked up a lock of Louisa's hair. May was staring at me with large round eyes, the kitchen shears in her hands. I reached out silently and took them from her, then sat as gently as I could on the edge of Louisa's bed. She saw what I was about to do.

"Chop away, dear," Louisa whispered. "It will grow back."

Steadying my hand as much as possible, I cut away the last remnants of the beautiful dark hair that had hung to her waist, snipping at the doctor's directions as close to the scalp as I could, fearful of cutting her. I could barely see as I made the final snips.

Before our eyes, she changed. Softness disappeared. Her strong chin seemed suddenly masculine and her nose too heavy for her face. I cast my eyes about the room, determined to remove any looking glass before Louisa could see herself.

"Hurry, before Marmee comes up," May urged.

I hurried as quickly as I could. "Now," I said, laying down the shears.

May thrust into my hands a cap of limp strands of hair gathered from Louisa's pillow that I had sewn onto a piece of webbing, doing the best I could to fashion something presentable. We settled her back onto the pillow, tucking the strands around her ears.

"It doesn't look too queer," May said, giving us both a glimmer of hope.

"She's right, it'll grow back," I said with more certainty than I felt.

A sudden sharp knock on the front door cut through the silence, making us both jump. May moved to the window and peeked out. "It's Mr. Emerson," she said. "He'll want to see her. Oh, I'm glad you had the cap ready!"

I hurried down and ushered him inside, noting as we stood in the vestibule that his shoulders seemed more stooped than usual.

The great man was aging. He seemed vague, a bit confused. In his hands, he clutched a bouquet of hothouse posies. Abba came from the kitchen and took him by the hand, up the stairs and to the side of Louisa's bed.

Tears rolled from his eyes when he saw her. "My dear girl, you used to lay flowers on my doorstep when you were a child," he said. "Now these are for you." Carefully he laid his bouquet on her coverlet. Louisa opened her eyes at that moment and gave him so luminous a smile, I felt a surge of hope that she would recover.

Yes, the worst had passed. And yet, in truth, Louisa emerged from that time a different person. Wan and wasted, yes, but more than that, her spirit seemed extinguished. She didn't talk about the hospital. And she didn't mention John. She simply rose from her bed and began to move once more through her days in the old way, as if nothing had happened.

One early spring day I walked into the room and saw her bent over her desk, scribbling away. She lifted her head, with something of the old fire in her eyes. "It's high time we try to find him, Susan. I dream of nothing else, and I cannot bear the thought that he is lost to me."

"John?" I sat heavily on the bed, savoring the chance to once again speak his name.

She nodded, unsmiling. "I'm writing the secretary of war to find out what I can. They must have his records. They must know where he is."

"Surely, they will," I said. It thrilled me to hear the energy and focus in her voice. Finally, a plan.

We wrote letters to everybody—Lou dictating, me scribbling away. We would find him, I told myself. We would find him for Louisa.

Each day we watched for the post. Each day I felt more distanced from my betrayal, more able to argue it was an aberration. Without saying it aloud, we agreed to speak of John to no one else. He was our secret, in more ways, I vowed, than Louisa would have to know.

Finally the answer came from the secretary of war. Louisa opened it with the care she would use cleaning a fireplace of hot embers and then read, eyes darting back and forth across the page. Without a word, she handed it to me.

> *Dear Miss Alcott:*
>
> *We have received your inquiry as to the whereabouts of a certain John Sulie of Virginia who served under General Burnside at the battle of Fredericksburg. We regret to inform you that, due to an administrative problem, we cannot locate his records at this time. He is undoubtedly recovered from his wounds and serving his country on the battlefield.*
>
> *Thank you for your inquiry.*
>
> *Sincerely,*
> *Edwin M. Stanton, Secretary of War*

"They can't find him," I blurted. And instantly wanted to bite my tongue. "No, it's that he escaped; he must be hiding."

We stared at each other for a long moment.

"Hiding from his own army?"

"No . . . maybe he's injured."

"We don't even know how he escaped. If he got out on his own or someone helped him."

I didn't want to tell her about the speculation on the ward. "Either way, he was unjustly accused and had to get out of there," I said.

Louisa rubbed her eyes and spoke with a tremor in her voice. "We have to face this, truly. Susan, it means one of two things. Either he is dead, or he really was a spy."

"He was *not* a spy."

"How can you be so sure? You thought so at first."

"Yes, but—" I stopped. "He said—"

"What did he say?"

"When I went down to his cell, I asked him if he was a blacksmith. He said . . . he said he would not be able to shoe a horse if his life depended on it. But then he said—and Louisa, I can't tell you how convincing he was—he said he was not someone who would embarrass us."

Louisa put a hand to her forehead. "What does that mean? Could I have loved a spy, a traitor?"

"Absolutely not," I declared. "Please, I feel it." How could I convey my visceral trust in John? What *did* make me so sure, so ready to believe him totally? I had a sudden inspiration. "Isn't that what your father and Mr. Emerson say is missing from intellectual discourse? Trust in the intuitive?"

"Ah, spoken like a true Transcendentalist," she said with the ghost of a smile. "I do draw strength from knowing I wrote him. Whatever happens, he knew I loved him. I found the words to say it, finally." She looked at me shyly. "How did he respond? What did he say when you gave him my note?"

I heard the clock in the parlor begin to strike the hour. One, two, three, four, five. The mellow sound of the chimes made their cadenced way up the stairs and into the room. Six. It would be dinnertime soon. Abba was baking gingerbread. My fingers curled tight around an invisible ball of paper in the palm of my hand.

"Susan?"

The clock ticked too loudly. She was looking at me now with naked expectation. Perhaps I should confess. But could I go back on what I had already said? I would deprive her of the one comfort to which she clung. If Louisa became ill again, I could not bear it.

The words tumbled from my mouth with a mix of despair and embarrassment. "He said he was thrilled. That . . . that now he knew you truly loved him."

"Why didn't he write me back?"

"He couldn't bear to part with your note. And . . . I had no more paper."

She closed her eyes, and tears trickled through her lashes. "At least I have that," she whispered.

We stood in silence for a long moment before Louisa spoke again. "I should have fought harder and stopped them from dragging him to the cellar; you are right, he's no spy. I know it, I need to keep my faith in him. Oh, this needn't have happened. If only—"

"You did nothing to be ashamed of, I did," I said stoutly, feeling sick. Was the trap I had made for myself so impenetrable? "Louisa . . ." My voice broke. Nothing I could say would be the full truth. Everything was tainted by the reality of my kiss. For I knew there had been nothing hasty about it. I had lingered, savored, and in my heart I believed that kiss had been returned. This was what I must forget.

"What more, Susan?" She looked frighteningly fragile.

"I pushed you into this in the first place," I began.

"What are you saying? Do you think I regret falling in love with him? Your support gave me the courage to allow it."

"I should have stopped Belle Poole from forcing him down to the hole."

"You didn't confine him down there. You were confused, too." She spoke soothingly, as if to comfort me. "Here is what I know: If John were alive, he would have contacted me. He knew the full-ness of my heart, and now I know the fullness of his."

"What did you say to him in your note?" I asked hesitantly.

"Very straightforward, dear." She smiled. "I wrote, 'Come for me. Let nothing stand in our way.' I wanted no ambivalence. You're sure he was happy when he read it?"

"Oh, yes," I said, trying to hold back tears.

"You see? It's been many weeks. He would have found a way, no matter what, to send word to me." She sank back down at her desk, looking suddenly depleted. "I need to think, dear friend. Would you leave me alone for a little while?"

I left the room and sat on the top step of the stairs. The min-utes ticked by. At one point, May appeared at the bottom of the stairs and looked at me questioningly. I shook my head warningly. She nodded and whispered, "Dinner, soon." Half an hour later, Louisa opened the bedroom door.

She tried to smile. "I knew you would be nearby. What would I do without you? Susan, I can bear it now. I can finally face the truth."

Truth? I would not hear the word again without experiencing a twist of pain. And at that moment, I did not want to know what "truth" she had accepted.

"Dinner is ready," I announced helplessly.

She hardly seemed to hear. Her expression turned vague and dreamy, the look she often had when she lifted her head after a long day of writing. Silently she took the government letter back from me and held it in her hand, staring at it for a moment, and then dropping it gently into the wicker wastebasket next to the door. "I have a great deal of work ahead of me," she murmured. She turned to go back to her desk and suddenly stopped. "I'm sorry, Susan—did I tell you the *Boston Commonwealth* wants me to write up some of my hospital stories? Now I know what I will write, and I'm starting tonight. Tell Marmee I won't be down to dinner," she said. And then floated back into the room, clicking the door lock shut.

I moved in with May that night, so as not to be forced to knock at that door. Louisa did not appear at breakfast, nor anytime that next day. In fact, Louisa was to barely emerge from her room for weeks. This was her usual pattern when she was in full writing mode; she would go into a trance, stopping for nothing, not for food or drink or sleep. Abba would tiptoe about, concerned for Louisa's health, but no one could break her concentration. We were all in awe of it.

I brought her tea one afternoon and ventured a question. "Are you writing about John?" I asked.

"Yes," she said.

"What are you saying?"

"I'm telling his story in my own way. It feels real again. I've never dealt more with reality than in this book, and I can feel the difference. John was so humane a man, so compassionate when the drummer boy died. He was a wonderful man and I want people to know that."

"Was?"

"He didn't live. In war, the good die."

"He escaped," I corrected, not sure I had heard right. "We don't know if he's dead or not."

"I do." Louisa tapped her pencil softly against the side of her desk. "I'm writing about the essence of John. He was a brave man who suffered terribly, and I believe his story is inspiring. You'll see."

I began to speak and thought better of it. What was there to say? I had offered what barren comfort I could at the cost of my own integrity. I turned and went back down the stairs, slowly coming to terms with what I saw happening. Writing was Louisa's protection, her blessing, and although ultimately her burden, it served her well at that point. She could not tolerate the loss of the man she loved. She could not deal with the possibility.

And so she created the story she *could* tolerate. Do we all not, in some way, do that with our lives? And I, of course, kept writing in my brain another story. What if I had not kissed him, and had instead handed him the note that held all of what was in Louisa's heart? Would he have stayed, or found a way to reach her? Slowly, I convinced myself that everything would have turned out differently. I wrote my own inner story, creating the fantasy that it was up to me to bring them together again. Only then could I atone for my betrayal. I could not bear the thought of living with the deception necessitated now by my actions. I had to purge him from my thoughts, forcing any unbidden erotic dreams back into a deep place. I turned each night in my bed, back and forth, always in restless sleep. Trustworthy. I had not been trustworthy. And I would live a lie the rest of my life.

And so Louisa and I, each haunted in complicated ways, proceeded.

Chapter Twelve

Louisa handed me the manuscript of *Hospital Sketches* with an uncertain smile.

"Well, here it is, and I believe it is the best thing I have written. If I am wrong, I apologize, but I feel so much better about this than any of my stories." In a gesture becoming common now, one hand went to the provoking wig, which was always slipping, pulling it back into place.

"You don't have to wear that thing anymore," I said with a sigh, glancing at the wig as I took the manuscript.

"I refuse to part with it until there's something more than a scruffy cap of hair on my head. I know I'm vain, but I can't help it."

"You aren't vain, you just miss your glorious hair."

"I love your literal spirit, Susan," she said, looking amused.

I quickly retreated to my favorite chair in the parlor. Within moments I was transfixed. At first I struggled with the combination of reality and fancy, my own memories bumping self-consciously into Louisa's. It took several pages before I could relax into the fact that Nurse Periwinkle had been taken far beyond our first sprightly letters home. I was reliving our daunting introduction to Washington, reliving the overwhelming horrors of the amputations and the responsibility of tending sick men, reliving the fights against incompetent aides to hang on to our meager supplies. Louisa had re-created it all, pulled it out of my nightmares, made the smells and the pain and the fear real again. My hands trembled as I turned the pages. And yet in a curious way I was also detached, reading about events and people in another world. I almost felt guilty sitting there, safe, pushing deep into my chair as I read into the fading evening light. Louisa's words allowed distance.

I turned a page and there was John Sulie. Louisa's written voice grew loving, lingering over his struggle to live. Her pen crafted a soldier of almost saintly courage, molding him to his fate with a tenderness I had never seen before in her work. My detachment evaporated as I mourned the fictional man, my heart beating faster as I followed Louisa to his bedside where he breathed his last.

> *"For God's sake, give me air!"*
>
> *It was the only cry pain or death had wrung from him, the only boon he had asked; and none of us could grant it, for all the airs that blew were useless now. . . . The first red streak of dawn was warming the gray east, herald of the coming sun; John saw it, and with the love of light which lingers in us to the end, seemed to read in it a sign of hope or help, for over his whole face there broke that mysterious expression, brighter than any smile, which comes to eyes that look their last. . . . He never spoke again, but to the end held my hand close, so close that when he was asleep at last, I could not draw it away. Dan helped me, warning me as he did so that it was unsafe for dead and living flesh to lie so long together; but though my hand was strangely cold and stiff, and four white marks remained across its back, even when warmth and color had returned elsewhere, I could not but be glad that, through its touch, the presence of human sympathy, perhaps, had lightened that dark hour. . . . I kissed this good son. . . . Then I left him, glad to have known so genuine a man, and carrying with me an enduring memory of the brave Virginia blacksmith, as he lay serenely waiting for the dawn of that long day that knows no night.*

I wept. I do not believe anyone could have read her story and not wept. Even knowing the truth under the fiction, I believed. And I knew why in the early years, in this very parlor, Louisa had been able to enthrall with her dramas. They had transported us because they were real to her, and she was still able to work her magic. I was seeing what a writer can do with the tatters of truth, the unfinished stories that give us no rest.

"So do you like it?" Louisa asked as I returned the manuscript to her hands. Her strong, stubborn chin was raised, as if to ward off a blow.

"It's wonderful," I said truly.

"Do you really mean that?"

"Oh, yes, Louisa. It's your best work. I'm so proud of you. You've re-created it as it happened in the most gripping way." My eyes filled with tears. "I feel honored to be part of what you've written."

She seemed to collapse in relief, literally falling into a chair. "Your opinion on this matters more than anyone's. But I know you have more to say."

I groped for the right response. "I find myself shedding tears for a man I cannot believe is dead, Lou. I'm trying to reconcile truth and fiction."

"I so want this story to have a happy ending, but it isn't there— it will never happen." She straightened, wrapping her shawl tighter around her shoulders, as if to ward off the chill of heart- break.

"I mourn the John Sulie you created, but we mustn't give up the real person. Not yet," I said, pleading.

Lou stared past me, her eyes focused on a wrapped bundle Abba had left on her desk. She stood and reached for it, slowly unwinding the twine around it, talking as if to herself. "We can't always have what we want," she said.

"Just don't make this your true ending."

She paused before answering. "But it is a satisfying one, isn't it?"

I stopped and tried to think along her path. If John died, what would I want? Would I want his deathbed scene filled with love and hallowed by bravery? Would I choose to believe a story like Louisa's over the anguish of uncertainty? Was she indeed giving us both a chance to mourn a man who *was* most likely dead—was this not one way to rescue one man from the obscurity Mr. Whitman had deplored?

"In its own way, yes." Still I struggled.

"It is solace, Susan. Solace."

I nodded slowly, accepting her words. Yet was it solace? Or simply a safe way to give up hope? Certainly I felt no solace in my heart.

"Look what Marmee brought," she said, holding up the contents of the package. "I had forgotten about this. It comes from another time, doesn't it? I wonder why she brings it out to me now?"

The old glory cloak, neatly folded, its vivid colors somewhat faded, rested in her hands. I reached out and smoothed the silk between my fingers.

"Perhaps to remind you that dreams do come true, and are not always fated to die," I said.

"Would that it were true of people," Lou said softly.

The bound book was delivered on the very day the first morning glory in Abba's garden burst into bloom. Abba immediately hailed this fortuitous connection as an omen of good luck. Certainly, the fact of possible fortune was there—an edition of one thousand copies, and Louisa was to get five cents on the sale of each and every one. What excitement! One man in Concord bought eight copies. How grand it felt!

The books sold quickly, for Nurse Periwinkle gave readers their first account of what happened *after* the heroism of the battlefield. There was no glory, no heroic battles in that book. People could hear their sons crying in pain from her pages, even as war news engulfed us all with each passing day.

Hospital Sketches did not paint death and suffering over with glorious words, nor did it shrink from the craven truths of human behavior. How honest Lou was, how clear-eyed! No one else yet had given such open glimpses into a military hospital. Letters poured in; people came to call, especially soldiers, to pay their respects to this woman who knew and had so eloquently rendered the realities of their suffering. Bronson puffed up with pride. He found excuses to go to the post office or to saunter up to the Old North Bridge through town, nodding to his friends, basking in their praise, making a point of his modest contribution when asked. Louisa was dazzled. How could it not be a thrilling experience when people in the village, in the stores, at the market, spoke of nothing else?

Soon she was churning out more stories and sending them to eager publishers. The money began to trickle in, and then, for a while, to come in a steady flow. Not lavish sums, but a heartening amount. Louisa was finally fulfilling her pledge to herself: She was rescuing her family from the humiliations of genteel poverty, and paying off many of the family debts. It was a fine time for the Alcotts, even as we kept an eye on the progress of the war.

"Well? What do you think? Is it time to send this one out into the world?" she asked me gaily one morning. In her hands was a somewhat tattered manuscript she had pulled from the bottom of her cupboard.

"What is it?" I peered closer.

"*Moods,* of course, silly."

Well, of course. What made me think this novel of her heart would have been forgotten? In *Moods,* Louisa had dared to envision and explore the struggles of an unhappily married woman. Was it safe to send it out into the world now? Surely, it was.

"James Redpath said he'll publish it. I have to revise, of course; shorten it, especially. But isn't that wonderful? He's afraid I'll go somewhere else and he'll lose me! Things have changed, Susan. I don't have to write rubbish anymore."

"You certainly don't. You must feel glorious—just think, *he* needs *you.* Isn't that a splendid switch?"

Her hand went up warningly, as if to ward off too much good news. "If indeed that's true. Regardless, the inspiration of necessity is what has brought me to this point, nothing more."

"Oh, Lou, that's not so." I hated to hear her wring joy out of accomplishment. "Mr. Redpath was fortunate to get *Hospital Sketches,* and its quality was not produced by financial need. And the same is true for *Moods.* Who else has written so honestly about a woman's passions? *Moods* has brave ideas, and you mustn't diminish your talent."

She smiled, her demeanor lightening. "I need you to scold me sometimes. I wish my nature didn't pull me down."

"It isn't your nature, it's the aftermath of illness."

Even if Louisa did deny herself pleasures she deserved, at least her work was always fired with energy. I only wished she was not so constantly grave and purposeful, her goals always defined by duty.

Yet where was I after our wartime adventures? Restless, aimless, not sure of my own direction. I loved the fact that Louisa's career was blossoming, but that meant she did not need my support as much anymore. I would take long walks after my household chores and visit with Anna and make clothes for her baby, but at the end of each day I still felt in need of something more vigorous and satisfying. It was too easy to grumble over petty problems, too tempting to let small things loom too large. Sometimes I reverted to childlike ways, once again falling into squabbles with May. I had no idea how dissatisfied I had become until the day May was due to leave for a month's vacation at Clark's Island, courtesy of her sister's generosity.

I spied her on her knees in her bedroom, wrestling closed a valise stuffed with clothes. Her face was flushed, with curls tumbling over her cheeks. "You certainly are a lucky girl," I said.

"Yes, I am, of course—to get a whole month away! I can't wait," she bubbled. "Will you be a dear and help me get this thing closed?"

I bent to the task in a sour mood. Louisa had once again denied herself a new frock while outfitting May at the dressmaker's last week. And she was taking every extra penny she had to pay for May's art lessons. A vacation, too? With nothing for herself? My friend was too duty-bound, too determined to be good and self-sacrificing. She did nothing but write, the financial demands of the entire family resting on her frail shoulders. By the time I had May's valise latched, I was in a high state of dudgeon.

So with great cloddishness I stomped into Louisa's room where she sat bent across her desk and blurted out my thoughts. "You're sending May off on a long holiday? Why do you continue to deny yourself for that selfish girl?"

She raised her head, shoulders stiffening. This wasn't my first complaint about May. "I'm doing what gives me pleasure," she said. "Now do you mind, Susan? I'm working."

"That's all you ever do anymore, and it's all to make enough money to keep her in fancy duds and vacations. You're trying to make up for being jealous of her. I cannot—"

"For *what?*"

I scrambled for safe terrain. "Well, she's always been everybody's pet, the prettiest, the most gay—"

"I am *not* jealous of May! How dare you suggest that! It is my money and May is my little sister. I will do for her what I want to do, and you have no say. Now, *will* you leave me alone?"

I retreated, stunned and humiliated. Louisa had never spoken to me in that way. I had no say? What did she mean? Was it that I remained a guest in this house, and not on an equal footing with her sisters?

Downstairs, May was spooning out a bowl of soup and did not look up as I entered the kitchen. I knew from the rigid set of her shoulders that she had overheard. And Abba, looking dour and nervous, was too busy making cinnamon cake to even cast me a glance.

"Susan, would you like some tea?" said Anna.

Anna, placid Anna, was better than anyone at calming the waters at Orchard House. She visited often these days, bringing along her little boy, which calmed Abba. I wondered sometimes why it was that Anna was the only one in this family who fulfilled her duty without being consumed by it. She charted a middle course with her emotions, quite a remarkable achievement in the face of May's volatility and Louisa's swings from despair to elation. Anna floated above us all.

But I was too busy nursing my hurt feelings that day to respond with grace. "No, I'm going to town," I replied. Already ashamed of my abruptness, I left the house and trudged alone into the village, intent on an errand. I would pick up the coat Mrs. Sanderson, the village seamstress, was relining. And scold myself along the way.

The day was hot and the road dusty. How many times had I walked this road with Louisa or Abba! On the left, at the intersection of the turnpike and Lexington Road, was the old Emerson house. Louisa used to enthrall me with wonderful stories about the crazy Mrs. Emerson, who would not allow a wood-burning stove in the house for years, and would indeed plunge her children into icy-cold tub water every morning as a health measure. We had doubled over with giggles, shivering at the very idea.

There was no activity at the Unitarian Church. The building stood solid in the heat, cool interiors empty. Across the road, a small cluster of men in work caps and women clutching bags of apples and fish stood conversing animatedly in front of the Town Hall. Undoubtedly about Gettysburg. With the Confederacy split in two, could victory be far behind? Bloody Gettysburg. I closed my eyes, imagining the dead men lying behind fences, in crevices, scattered over fields; horses and humans putrefying. . . . I knew something of the costs of victory. I had seen the results. I will say this for Bronson, he was not one of those who took this victory as a reason for celebrating. Not after the riots in New York a few days later, with the Irish smashing windows and stoning Negroes, and the corruption of a terrible draft law fanning the flames. It all seemed far from sleepy Concord.

My steps took me onto Main Street, past the Concord Gun Manufactory and Mr. Walcott's store filled with fragrant coffee and tea. The shop next door that sold rosewood chairs and heavy carpets was shuttered against the sun. Everything looked the same here, day in and day out. I could walk this street blindfolded.

Somehow that put a new bounce in my step and, at that moment, I heard a voice call my name.

"Susan!" It was Una, her pretty face glistening with sweat even though it was shielded by a large, straw bonnet. Her eyes darted back and forth from me to different passersby. Her voice lowered. "Have you heard what happened?"

I braced for the latest gossip. Una loved to pass on the stories that gave our small town its preferred release from boredom; stories of fights and drunken sprees and marital discord. What now? I raised my eyebrow questioningly and waited.

"I'm sorry," she said, clasping her hands to her bosom. "It's such a shame, and I do so want us to remain friends. Can we? Oh, Susan, can we?"

"What are you talking about?" I said in alarm.

"Mama and Mrs. Alcott. They met this morning at the market and Mrs. Alcott was, well, she was hysterical. She confronted Mama and cried that the Rebels were marching on Concord, right then, at that very minute!" She paused, waiting for my reaction.

"She's been very agitated and fearful lately," I murmured. I had been afraid of just such an event.

"Well, Mama is so nervous, you know—she said her heart began to palpitate, even though she knew Mrs. Alcott was becoming a bit . . . I mean, you know, a bit—"

"She isn't crazy," I interrupted. "It's the change, that's what it is. And it's hard on older women."

"Well, no, but she does this kind of thing all the time now. Worrying about attacks and terrible ruination—well, most of us have become used to it, but this morning Mama was dreadfully upset and she pushed her away and said loudly, for all to hear, that she couldn't stand the woman, and wanted never to see her again." Una's eyes were filling with tears. "Everybody heard."

"Oh, no, Una." That meant the split between Sophia Hawthorne and Abba was now the gossip of the day. I felt saddened, although not completely surprised. Mrs. Hawthorne was a difficult woman in the first place, and not very likable. But she and Abba, indeed all of the Hawthornes and Alcotts, had been friends for many years. Now what?

"I think Mama means it," Una said.

"I don't know, maybe Bronson can intervene."

"Oh dear, please don't tell him, don't even try—at least not now. Father hardly talks to anyone anymore and Mama is too enraged."

Una looked so unhappy, I took her hands in mine. "Whatever happens, we will remain friends," I said. At that moment I saw Sophia Thoreau walking toward us, her step brisk.

"Have you heard my news?" she asked happily. "I'm expanding the mill, and having the grandest time!"

"How wonderful," I said, a touch of envy in my voice. Everyone knew Sophia was flourishing in her new capacity as head of the family business. How startling it was to realize she was running the entire operation on her own. The three of us chatted for a few moments, and I was glad to see Una wipe away her tears and gave her a hug before I said good-bye to them both and moved on.

I stopped briefly to stare in the window of the Cheap Cash Dry Goods Store. An idea was forming in my mind, one that served to lift my spirits as I made my way to Mrs. Sanderson's tailoring shop north of the Courthouse.

Mrs. Sanderson, the granddaughter of the original founder of the shop, was a cheerful, rotund woman who never overcharged and who kept bits of licorice for the children who came with their mothers for fittings. Her hair was the color of rust, and always pulled back into a cap. I liked her. I liked looking at the bolts of bright calico and soft challis stacked along the walls of her store and sorting through the lovely snippets of leftover fabric she kept in a bin and gave to the children for their dolls. I especially liked her stories of the old days.

"What's that?" I asked, pointing to an odd-looking cylinder of faded wool.

"An old hat, of the kind boys in the country wore when my

mother was little," she said, glancing at the object. "They were heavy with glue and fell into the shape of a saucer when soaked with rain. My uncle used his for a drinking cup."

"Did it regain shape?"

"When the glue dried again, but not through too many drenchings, I'll wager."

"That's interesting," I said.

She laughed. "Susan Gray, only you would find an old hat interesting." She held up my coat, showing me the fresh lining.

"Do you enjoy sewing and having your own shop?" I asked timidly as she tried the coat on me, then knelt to snip a few spare threads with huge shears.

"Of course I do, it puts bread on the table," she said matter-of-factly.

"I'm good at making hats," I said.

I saw her eyes widen. We were no longer seen as poor, not with Louisa's new celebrity, and we had always been seen as gentry. Not shopkeepers. To this point, I had made and trimmed hats for neighbors and friends for my own amusement.

I took a deep breath. "Could you use some help in that regard?" I asked.

Mrs. Sanderson sat back on formidable haunches and regarded me with a steady eye. "I doubt if it's what you truly should be doing," she said, not unkindly.

But now my resolve was set. I would not be Bronson, living in his head while his daughter supported the family, nor would I be May, living off her sister. Would Louisa disapprove? I wasn't sure. Bronson would probably be mortified. But who was I? Not a daughter. Not a sister. Perhaps not always even a friend. "Please let me try," I said.

Mrs. Sanderson kept her gaze on my face. And then slowly nodded. "Can you do silk flowers?" she asked. "I'm making two wedding gowns, and I'll wager we could sell some bonnets to match."

*   *   *

"Selling hats?" Louisa's hands tensed. I had rushed home to convey my news.

"It is my skill, as writing is yours. And I can't bear to be doing nothing of importance any longer." I saw a glimmer of something in her eyes that looked like sadness.

"I'm perfectly capable of taking care of you," she said. "You don't need to go outside this family for money, if that's why you're doing it."

"Oh no, it's much more than that. I want to have something all my own, something that makes me feel accomplished, the way writing makes you feel accomplished. I need to be sturdy, too."

"But you already are, Susan. You are sturdy for me." She paused and said nothing for a long moment. Then, "I'm sorry I was so cross."

"No, I was quite wretched. I'm sorry, too."

"Will you still read my stories and tell me where I go wrong?" she asked after a pause.

"Of course I will."

And so we were able to move past our argument, but it had altered the balance of our relationship. I was about to turn twenty-one. I could not live forever in Louisa's shadow, and, frightening though it would be, it was time to fashion my own life. I only wished Louisa had agreed more enthusiastically.

Nathaniel Hawthorne died unexpectedly a short while later, and we discovered Sophia Hawthorne was a woman of her word. She had not even a glance for the Alcotts at her husband's funeral. Louisa was outraged when she heard Sophia had tucked Nathaniel's unfinished novel into his casket, but that was but a minor development—when friends are ignored at death, it is as if friendship never existed. Not for the first time, I thought that the prime families of Concord were too inbred, too close to be forgiving, too wound into their own intellectual lives to understand or forgive any other reality. There is no one I knew not truly mourned, but the petty hurts and misunderstandings were exhaustingly akin to those of a family. Hawthorne was a strange bird, a distant man, but he had his friends. And Sophia was in truth a queer, narrow-minded woman, who strove too hard for perfection and control at all levels. But that of course was common among our Concord friends. I think now, to be our best selves is to see others kindly; to blend the two, ah, there's a challenge.

The year moved on in quiet fashion, even as the war continued—a strange alignment of events. Some days it was too easy to be self-ishly content. I would go each morning to Mrs. Sanderson's shop and shape straw and felt into bonnets, loving the feel of the mate-rial as I turned it into what I wanted it to be. Customers began to notice, some even stopping to watch me work. I enjoyed their praise while trying to be modest. It was not, after all, my shop.

"Susan, you have an artful eye," Mrs. Sanderson said one after-noon as she held up a finished hat, turning it slowly in the light. "You can do more."

"But my skills are nowhere near as good as yours," I protested.

She gave me an impatient toss of her head. "Don't be so mod-est. I've seen your sketchbook of designs, and you should be able to make them all. Come here and help me."

Soon she was showing me tricks I had never known for draping and tucking fabric, letting me experiment on old bolts of muslin. My sewing had always been simple before. Now I took chances. After a few weeks she even trusted me with fittings, which meant a more generous income. I had not been so happy in a long time.

War news was never long off anyone's lips. The Confederate army ran short of supplies and food, and the hope was that they would soon lose their thirst for battle. Their men were deserting. We even heard of Southern women rampaging through the streets of Richmond, smashing windows and grabbing food and clothing for their families. "Old Jefferson Davis himself couldn't stop 'em," reported a train engineer up from New York to buy a hat for his wife. "He gave them five minutes to disperse, or he'd have them shot down."

"Did they go?" I asked, amazed.

"You bet they did." He laughed. "Those simpery Southern belles hiked their skirts and skedaddled fast."

Mrs. Sanderson and I cast each other a glance. We took no pleasure in the thought of hungry wives and mothers being dispersed at gunpoint by their own kind. But triumphalism was rampant. With the dreadful General Hooker gone, the Union was enjoying a string of victories. General Grant was on the march. First came his triumphs at Vicksburg and Chattanooga, then the Battle of the Wilderness, fought midst the skulls and bones of the dead from the year before. We heard of men at Cold Harbor pinning pieces of paper with their names and addresses to the backs of their coats, knowing they were likely to be killed in the upcoming battle. We lost some Concord men that day—and might not have known it but for those pieces of paper. After hearing the latest dispatches in the shop, I would come home and toss and turn and dream of the dead. It all blurs now. For the young, war is just a series of battles to be memorized in school. How quickly the blood shed by one generation is forgotten by the next!

Moods was published in December of 1864. It hurts me even now to remember how poorly it was received. I had thought Louisa was surely protected by her glory cloak, but quickly learned even past success is not a secure frame from which to reach for the future.

So many things went wrong. The publisher insisted, against Louisa's better judgment, that she cut the story almost in half. Even then, the sales were modest. Worse, the reviews were poor. Young Henry James scoffed in *The North American* that she knew nothing of human nature. There was no avoiding humiliation, for Louisa was no longer hiding behind "A.M. Barnard," her favorite pseudonym. Now, after proudly presenting a work of her heart under her true name, she was enduring an almost unbearable scorching. She took to walking around the house in her wrapper, not even bathing or dressing. At meals she would pick at her food, then lay down her fork and silently leave the table. I would find her in her room, staring out the window.

"Many people liked it, don't forget that," I said one day as she sat at the dining room table slowly reading a batch of reviews sent from Boston.

"Not the people who matter," she said, crumpling one in her fist. "Why did I think I had the talent for this? The fault is mine entirely."

"You dismiss yourself too quickly," I protested.

"I don't mean to. I just know my limits now, that's all."

No amount of support changed the fact that the failure of this particular offering was a bitter blow. I half suspected a door was closing, and indeed there would be no similar baring of Louisa's heart again. She was giving up the exploration of human moods that had so distinguished her tale of Sylvia Yule.

By February of 1865, the Confederates were deserting in vast numbers, fleeing as far as Texas, as Sherman laid waste to the South. This did not soothe Abba. Each day she would announce an imminent invasion that we had to convince her was not happening. Bronson would sit her down and read to her the news from the paper. No, Abba, don't worry, he would say. Every day, he would do this. His solicitousness was touching.

Which, of course, made it quite an event the day we heard drums and the still-distant piping of fifes coming down the road. Anna was feeding her baby and Louisa had her arms around Abba, assuring her the Rebels were not on the march, when May came running up the front steps and burst through the door.

"The Concord men are coming home!" she announced. "Can you hear them? They're marching up the Lexington Road right now!"

We rushed to the door, and saw neighbors running to the road, pulling on jackets and waving flags. A few held up hastily scribbled signs of welcome. May ran upstairs and came running down with the red rigolettes I had tucked away at the back of a drawer and thrust them toward me and Louisa.

"Here, put them on," she urged. "You earned them, wear them."

"Oh, that's nonsense," I said, pushing her off.

"Why?" she demanded. "Who gives medals to women? Flaunt the emblems you are allowed!"

Her ferocity stirred me. Louisa took one and placed it carefully on top of her new crop of hair, smiling as I donned my own. We shared the same thought. Why not? We *had* earned them.

May hoisted the baby and we all hurried to the road. What a sight it was! Those young, fresh-faced boys who such a short time before had left their fields and headed off to war were marching home, no longer farmers and tradesmen, but soldiers. We watched them come, sunlight dancing off their polished gun barrels. They looked older and harder, but not that hard. When they reached us, the captain, a carpenter who had helped Bronson build our front porch, drew his sword from its scabbard and shouted a command to halt. He gave us a grin and led the men in a cheer. All sixty thrust their caps into the sky in salute.

"What are they doing?" I asked.

May grinned. "They're saluting you and Louisa, silly," she said. "You fought in the war, too."

Louisa and I laughed and gave graceful bows as the cheer faded into the air. On impulse, I did a quick little jig in the road, which brought applause from all. How delighted we felt as the company moved on up the road, taking the bend past Moore's barn! Even Abba relaxed enough to laugh. There would be celebrating tonight in the village—much talk and mingling, much news of the men still at war. And I had a sudden, hopeful thought: Perhaps someone might have news of John Sulie.

My queries that night brought only puzzled responses and kindly shrugs. People were always searching for someone who would never appear. Anyone coming from the front was used to questions like mine, and I finally stopped asking, feeling oddly like a cliché.

But we heard much of Clara. Amazing woman, we were told as we threaded through the crowd in the village center that evening.

"You worked with her in Washington City?" the thick-waisted son of the town baker said, pumping Louisa's hand with great solemnity. "Many a soldier in the field has thanked God she chose nursing. And we thank you, too."

A less adulatory assessment came from the youngest of the seven children of the bootmaker, a thin boy not yet eighteen with a black, scraggly beard. "She's driving the army brass crazy," he said in an offhand way.

"Why?" I shouted, over the sound of beating drums and exploding firecrackers.

"With her resolve for finding missing soldiers now."

"What do you mean?" I pressed.

Another man standing nearby broke in. "You don't know?" he said. "She wants President Lincoln to put her in charge of locating the missing men of the war. Thousands and thousands of them ain't been found yet! And then there are the ones coming out of Rebel prisons. She wants to be in charge of identifying them and linking them up with their families. Lord, we hear they're in terrible shape, some of 'em starved most to death and others with their brains gone, they've been treated so bad. A lot of 'em are being dumped on the wharves at Annapolis."

"Ever hear of Andersonville, ma'am?" the son of the boot-maker said, arching an eyebrow.

I nodded—a prison in the South. I knew not much more.

"It's the worst of the lot. A nightmare place that's killed thousands of men. Good place to start. She's out to identify as many soldiers as she can, both living and dead. People all over the country are writing her for help."

I pressed him eagerly for more details, fascinated with this news. Soon I was pushing my way through the crowd, craning my head, looking for Louisa. This was perfect. Clara would have not only the resources for the search but also the concern, the knowledge of having known John Sulie. She was the person who could find him. Who else?

I found Louisa trying to talk above the music with some soldiers as she sipped a cup of celebratory cider. She smiled as I tugged at her arm, holding her hand up to keep the cider from spilling.

"For goodness sakes, Susan, what is making you bounce up and down so?"

I told her, my words tumbling out. "It *is* a good idea," she said slowly. "What do you want to do?"

"We write her a letter immediately," I said. "Why should we settle for that vague response from the War Department? Maybe he was captured and thrown into a prison like Andersonville. The government doesn't know what's happening, that's easy to see. They've lost track of thousands of men, that's why Clara is taking on this job."

The cup of cider moved to its destination, leaving a slight froth of liquid on Louisa's upper lip. I watched the muscles of her throat contract as she swallowed. Slowly, everything slowly.

"Will you write it?" she asked.

"Of course," I said.

"Then I know we will find out whatever there is to be known." She turned away, coaxed back into conversation by the admiring soldiers, and I thought little of the detached nature of her response. Instead I felt the strangest jubilation, the most unfamiliar jump of hope.

Chapter Thirteen

At last. I slipped the letter so eagerly awaited from the stack of mail on the front hall table and ran to the apple orchard to find Louisa. My step slowed when I saw her—once again, pale and listless, wrapped in her heavy coat, staring at nothing. She was leaning against a tree.

Should I wait? Sometimes I despaired of lifting her mood. She had good days and bad ones, the effect of the calomel shoved into her by Belle Poole. The doctors had no treatments other than advising her to eat and rest. The wretched aftermath of mercury poisoning continued to stalk her, although we hoped the effects would not be permanent. All I hoped *that* day was to lift her spirits.

"You can't guess what I have in my hand," I started, in a teasing voice, and waved the letter.

"I can take anything but another rejection," she retorted.

I winced, for Louisa's dreams of sustained glory in the aftermath of *Hospital Sketches* had been dashed after the lackluster reception for *Moods*. Editors were not clamoring as much now for her work, and her early uncertainty had crept back, especially on days when she was low.

"It's a letter from Clara," I chided gently. "You know I wouldn't skip out here holding some awful rejection."

Louisa did look up then, a flicker of interest in her eyes. "What does it say?" she asked.

I slit the envelope with my fingernail and began to read.

10 March 1865

Dear Susan,

I write this note in haste. It is welcome news that Louisa has recovered, and that the two of you prosper and are well. I read her recounting of your experiences in Hospital Sketches and was much impressed. What a talent she has! I envy her ability to put all of what happened into words.

Now, my news. President Lincoln has officially put me in charge of finding the countless missing men of this war. All I can say is, finally! Mothers clamor to know what happened to their sons, and no one seems to know—certainly not the government. Only last week one poor soul appeared at my doorstep, weeping, relating a tale of a vanished father. How could I tell her it was an all-too-familiar story? Unfortunately, I have yet to convince Mr. Lincoln's subordinates that such an honor involves money to do the job. I will prevail. As you know, I can be persistent.

You ask about John Sulie. His fate is a mystery. But I have added his name to my list, and I am well aware that you have a personal interest in bringing that particular story to conclusion.

And now I ask something of you both with great hope that you will respond. I need people with commitment to work with me. I am setting up an office and there is so much to be done. I will tell you, as my nursing colleagues, I can at this time think of no better way for a woman to be part of the sad and necessary job of making sure the fates of the men who fought for the Union are not lost to their families and to history.

Would you consider coming back to Washington? Your assistance would so facilitate the work, that I find myself searching for the right words to elicit a positive reply. The ones you read are but poor substitutes for the fervent plea in my heart I send to you.

> *Yours,*
> *Clara*

I plopped back against the tree, the letter falling to my lap, and took in a sharp breath. Clara had knocked at a door closed for too long.

"My goodness, what an interesting idea," I said.

Lou reached for the letter and read it again, this time silently. She finished and folded it into small squares, cradling it in her hand before giving it back to me. She said nothing.

"Lou, we could do this, we really could. What do you think?" An excitement was building in me, and I held my breath, waiting for what I was sure would be her similar reaction.

"She knows how to make our hearts beat fast, doesn't she?" Louisa said finally. "But it seems so impractical. Your work and mine . . . how do we do such a thing without being irresponsible?"

Her point was reasonable. At the same time, wasn't this also a call to duty? I thought of all that had been left undone, incomplete. That was my virtuous argument. I also admitted to myself that I was both curious and restless. We had left Washington prematurely, because we had to. But what if we had been able to stay? What would have happened? The story was unfinished, the commitment unfulfilled. I did not admit to myself a single thought about John Sulie.

"It would mean completing our service," I argued. "Why did we go? We went to be part of something larger than ourselves, to do something to help win the war besides sewing uniforms—and we *did* do more."

"Yes, we did."

"Then Clara is giving us a chance to finish what we started," I said triumphantly.

Louisa fingered the folds of her skirt. I waited impatiently for her to look at me, but instead she said, "I need to tell you something." Her voice took on a soft, almost pleading tone. "Remember how we've dreamed about going to Europe someday? Seeing the cathedrals and splendid palaces, and walking along the canal in Venice. We're going to do it, Susan, and we'll do it together. But not yet. Not together."

"What makes you think of Europe?" I asked, genuinely puzzled.

"Because I am going there."

"You are?" I said stupidly.

"I've made a commitment, and I can't get out of it. I'm going to Europe as a companion to Emma Weld. I've been trying to find the right time to tell you this, but Clara's letter forces my hand."

"What?" I was incredulous. Surely I had heard wrong. Emma was an invalid, a petulant young woman with a wizened leg, the spoiled daughter of rich parents who lived in the big house with the iron gates on the other side of the town. She complained about everything.

"I don't *want* to go with her, I wish you and I were going together, but she is willing to pay me very well. We need the money, Susan. How could I turn down such an opportunity?"

"I don't believe this, I can't believe it," I said. "Emma Weld? She just wants a nursemaid. You don't even *like* her! Why would you do something so silly?"

"It isn't silly. And it is unkind of you to say so. I am ten years older than you, and I have to live my own life."

Now it was I turning my head away, cut to the quick.

"I've hurt you, and I'm sorry," she said, reaching for me. "Let me try to explain. No one knows more than you how frustrated I am in my work. I feel trapped, and I don't know what to do. All my dreams, Susan . . . nothing is going to come true. All my publisher wants is sensational rubbish I can finish in my sleep. Surely you understand. Even some of my better work is being turned down if some stick of an editor sniffs out antislavery sentiments. Oh, I can hear what they are really saying when they ask for something— how do they put it?—something 'less heated.' 'No abolitionist prose, Miss Alcott!—that's what they're saying."

"But you can keep writing," I protested. "In Washington or right here, at home."

She hardly seemed to hear. "I keep asking myself, why didn't *Moods* do better? If it had, I would have been able to make much more money. I put my heart in that book. Have I no talent at all? I hate my stories! I need to break from here, to find a way to start again."

"Why do you always berate yourself so? *Moods* was brave and excellent and——"

"Well, I can't feed this family on your praise," she retorted.

We sat silently, mutually cowed by her harsh words.

"I'm sorry. But don't you see, I have to do something to get out of here?" she said.

I balked at the plea for understanding in her tone. "I know we have different lives, but we've shared our adventures from childhood on," I said. "It doesn't seem right for us to be split apart."

"I'm not such good company these days, you know that," she said, not unkindly.

"What about John? I know you still love him and want to find him. Neither of us believes he was a Confederate spy. Don't pretend."

"Susan, he's dead, please accept that. I can't bear——" She stopped, flustered, then continued. "If you want to search, I understand. I believe it is useless."

"We can search together," I said. "I know you're not one to give up! What are you saying?"

"I'm not giving up. But we can't face everything together."

I felt a surge of frustration, and threw myself on my sword. "This is my fault. I ruined everything for you. I lost him. I didn't speak up and stop them from taking him away."

A fleeting expression of pain crossed her face, and I instantly chastised myself for a hasty tongue. Louisa would only begin blaming herself again. She reached out her arms and hugged me with the fervor of our closest times. "You did no such thing," she said. "You were a dear and loyal friend. You gave me at least the knowledge that, at the end, he knew my heart. You burden yourself with responsibility—that's what you tell me I do, and if it's wrong for me, it's wrong for you."

Her effort at graceful absolution made me ashamed of myself and silenced my arguments. What right did I have to feel hurt? But I wished she had told me earlier. Oh, I forced myself through the paces of understanding soon enough. When might she ever again have the chance to go to Europe? And her blood-and-thunder stories weren't producing much money. She churned them out, tossing pages of manuscript on the floor, hardly caring to look at them a second time. At times, when I bent to pick them up and sort them into some semblance of order, I wondered why she hated them so. I understand better now. They were the cheap residue of her dreams.

Yet even as we both laughed and cried, I felt a pang of abandonment. I knew my hurt was false, but lonely fears do not answer to reason. And indeed, Louisa was right. We both had to live our lives separately, as well as together.

And so I made the decision to go to Washington alone. Surely if Louisa could leave me, then I could also leave her. But deeper in my soul was the conviction that it was indeed time for me to find my own way. I wanted to see action again, to be part of helping on a scale larger than any that sleepy old Concord had to offer. I lay in bed, staring at the ceiling, feeling my excitement grow. I would be fine.

Louisa caught the growing bounce in my step as I began my preparations. "You are thrilled, I can see that," she said one morning, somewhat wistfully.

I threw my arms around her, wishing I could will some of my excitement into her bones. "It's the perfect thing for me," I said. "I know that now, and couldn't be happier."

"You have not lost your capacity for adventure," she said in that same wistful tone. "I cannot find it inside myself anymore."

I clutched her tighter. "You will have it again," I promised, hoping it would be true.

No one tried to hold me back; all were kind and supportive. In some ways, it was hardest to say good-bye to Mrs. Sanderson. She was genuinely sad to see me go, and told me I would have a job with her when I came home. The day before I left she presented me with a new brown faille gown, trimmed in beige lace.

"This is beautiful, the most beautiful dress I've ever owned," I gasped as I held it up and peered into the long glass at the shop. I blinked back tears. So this is what she had been working on into the late hours after I had gone home each day.

Mrs. Sanderson beamed, then turned serious. "I will miss you dreadfully, dear. You are a creative force, and indeed you have rejuvenated me."

"It is you who have provided guidance," I said. "You've given me confidence to try new things."

"Susan, I have a proposal," she said slowly, folding her plump hands in her lap. "When you come home, would you be interested in becoming my partner?"

Interested? I could hardly believe my ears. In fact, I almost dropped my new dress. To be a partner in this shop? To have a hand in shaping its future? For a brief instant, I wished I wasn't leaving.

"Oh my, yes—I would be honored," I managed.

Mrs. Sanderson smiled again, somewhat forlornly. "I will be lonely without you, dear."

"I will be back, I promise." I kissed her good-bye, struggling to swallow a lump in my throat. This dear woman had opened up my life, and I felt a deep, abiding affection for her.

It was April of 1865. On an early spring day that veered between rain and sunshine, Louisa and I climbed into the old wagon with the heavy wooden wheels and headed to the railroad station. We moved slowly, leaving deep ruts in the sodden road. Once again, we stood together on the platform, waiting for the train. We said little.

"How *can* you go back there?" Louisa asked unexpectedly.

"I'm not afraid of Washington," I said.

"Whatever you do, keep an eye out for Belle Poole." Louisa puckered her brow and gave me a petulant scowl, a good imitation of Belle.

I tried to match her mood. "She's probably hunkered down under a bridge somewhere, counting her gold and silver," I said.

"That's good. Perhaps she's really a troll. I could believe that, can't you?" We kept tossing lighthearted nonsense back and forth, trying to keep up each other's spirits. It filled the time and eased the tension of parting.

The train pulled into the station, and I prepared to board. My heart raced uncomfortably as I turned to go, realizing fully now that Louisa and I were separating for the first time in seven years.

"Wait, dear." Louisa handed me a small wrapped box she had been carrying in her muff. There were tears in her eyes. "You never know, you may be invited to dance at the President's House. If you are, here's something to wear on your new dress. I love you, Susan. Don't forget me, I promise I will not forget you."

"I love you, too, and I promise," I said, trying not to cry. I pulled myself up the stairs, turned to wave good-bye, and felt the train coming to life under my feet.

The tears flowed later, long after Concord had receded from view. Moving very slowly, smoothing each piece of tissue paper, I opened the little box. Inside, folded neatly, was a strip of green silk—the sash to Louisa's glory cloak. And with it a note:

And why should the glory be for me alone?

Your loving friend,

Lou

The Washington railroad station seemed transformed. The noise and activity was overwhelming, and the tone so different from when I had left in 1862. Chaos, yes, but this time a sense of victory pulsated through the station. I could see it in the faces of the people, in their shouts and laughter, and in the sense of purposeful movement. I stood motionless for long moments after disembarking, trying to get my bearings. It was one thing to hear in Concord of the war's progress. It was another to stand here at its crossroads. I tried to snatch news from the air.

Lee was trying to keep his men from deserting as his army crumbled away. No, old news. General Grant was tearing Lee apart at a place called Five Forks. That, too, was yesterday. Lee had lost a fourth of his men—had I heard that right? I strained to listen as I picked up my valise and boxes—there were no porters available, we were all on our own—and struggled to the street. Can you believe it? They're burning government documents in Richmond. Women and children are fleeing. The South is done for; it's in shambles. We'll hang those secessionists now.

The road swarmed with wagons and teamsters and soldiers shouting and rumors swirling, and I, desperately holding on to a fragment of paper with Clara's address, threw myself into the battle to find a driver. Finally a wizened little man with a face like a raisin offered me a ride.

"Look there!" he shouted, pointing with his whip to a hazy sky. "They blew up their own arsenal and now they're burning their own town! Chopping up their own fire hoses, the crazy bastards! I'll be damned if you can't almost see it from here!"

I sat straight, peering into the smoky sky, ready to believe all that I heard, thrilled to be back. The huge gray horse pulling the wagon plodded slowly through the crowds, moving up past the wharves along the Potomac River, past a huge market swarming with vendors and buyers and covered wagons filled with goods. It took an hour to reach the commercial district where Clara lived. Seventh Street was filled with stores selling shoes, wallpaper, and furniture. People elbowing past each other under faded red awnings that reached to the street shouted bits of news back and forth, but the din was so great now I could hardly make out a word.

"It's here!" I shouted, glancing quickly at the address on the piece of paper to be sure: *488 1/2 Seventh Street.* The driver had the courtesy to help me down and then he was off, whip aloft, his old horse stumbling around the inescapable potholes with greater patience than his master.

I looked up at the shabby building, feeling a bit daunted. Was this really where she lived? Lugging my suitcase, I climbed the steep, narrow stairs, increasingly breathless as I neared the top. The sound of shouting voices swirled through the hallway, guiding me to a thick oak door stenciled with the number 9.

I knocked as loudly as I could. The door flung open and facing me, a wide smile on her face, was Clara. Her eyebrows were now laced with gray, giving her something of a forbidding appearance, but her hair was as black and shining as ever and her eyes still carefully lined in coal.

"Welcome, Susan!" she said. She radiated energy, so much so, she seemed almost poised on her toes as she greeted me, reaching out her arm and pulling me in with surprising force.

The room was long and narrow, lit by gas lamps shaped as gargoyles with apricot shades. I stumbled slightly; the floor was covered by painted canvas that rippled under my feet. There was gold- and-silver striped wallpaper on the walls that glittered in the reflected gaslight, giving everything an almost holiday appearance. Perhaps a half-dozen people lounged against the walls or sat with their legs hunched up on wooden packing boxes, of which there were dozens scattered across all available space.

Once inside, under the light, she relaxed her grip, turned and scrutinized me. All I cared about at that moment was how I appeared to her. Did I seem calm and competent? I wanted nothing of the flustered girl-woman reputation that had dogged me at the hospital. I held myself as erect as possible.

"So you really meant it when you said you would come," Clara said with a tone of astonishment. "Forgive me, dear, but I had my doubts."

"Well, so did I," I replied.

"You won't be sorry," she said. She turned, taking in a clutter of boxes stacked in the hall with a dramatic sweep of her hand. "See these, Susan? Do you know what they hold?"

"No," I said, a bit taken aback, my attention distracted by the sight of a small goldfish darting back and forth inside a bowl sitting precariously on one box.

"Oh, pay no attention to my little prisoner, whom I sometimes most heartily wish was in the bottom of the Potomac," Clara said impatiently. "He is such a bother. Letters! I am inundated with letters from the families of soldiers. They implore me, beg me, to find their missing men. Look at these——" She pulled open one box, shoved her hand inside and hoisted a fistful of envelopes. "I can barely open them all, let alone answer them. It frightens me sometimes to think of how much trust these people are putting in me." She lowered her hand and tucked the letters back inside with the tenderness of a mother tucking in a child. "We're getting more space across the hall in a few months; until then these boxes make fine chairs."

By now, people were watching us curiously. She pulled me to the center of the room and began introducing me to her friends. I tried to absorb their names——Edward Shaw, a thin, nervous clerk in the U.S. Patent Office, whose bones seemed to jut out at odd angles through his homespun jacket; Samuel Lamb, a captain in the army, mustached, dressed in a black frock coat and wearing a black silk vest; and a young man with hair the color of a sand dune smoking a cigar, blowing cheerful halos into the air, who looked oddly familiar.

"Tom Cassidy," he said, putting down the cigar and reaching out his left hand. "Ward One, Union Hotel Hospital. Just one more of the men under your care." I saw then the empty right sleeve sewn neatly just below his shoulder and reached out to clasp his hand with both of mine.

"Why . . . Tom! How good to see you!" I felt my spirits rise.

"Wasn't sure you would remember me," he said with a grin. "You took care of a lot of us back then. Stood up pretty well to that tough bunch, I'd say. Not many did. You've come here at a mighty exciting time. Did you see the smoke from Richmond?"

"I did indeed, or at least so the driver said."

"It's over. God bless America, it's over. I think the South is crumbling."

"Don't speak like that, it's bad luck," Clara warned.

Tom laughed. "Clara, it isn't going to be bad news forever. I hear Mr. Lincoln is planning a visit to Richmond once the Union troops move in. What do you think of that? It's a matter of days."

"I'll believe it when it happens," Clara said.

"And when it does, when the war's over, it will be because of men like you, Tom," I said quickly.

His cheeks reddened. He picked up the cigar and blew a hasty cloud of smoke as Clara hustled me on to meet her other guests. Next came two teachers from Ohio, Frances Gage and her daughter, pleasant and plainspoken, also here to help set up the Missing Soldiers Office. We shook hands. I turned around and saw another familiar face. I could hardly believe my eyes. It was Liddy Kettle.

"Not a face you were expecting, right?" she said, her words followed by the throaty giggle I remembered well. She sat atop a box, swinging her sturdy legs in their button-top boots, looking immensely happy with herself.

"Liddy has been invaluable in Annapolis," Clara said firmly. "I couldn't have put this together so fast without her help." She began passing a platter of thick brown bread and salt fish around the room. I realized I was hungry, but refrained from taking a slab of the bread, afraid there might not be enough.

"You'd be fast, too, if it was that or be sent home in shame," Liddy said directly to me.

"You've been in Washington all this time?" I asked. I was awed by her resilience. The scandal had been so talked about. The whispers and the frowns. The ruin of her reputation.

"Went to another hospital and got myself sacked again," she said brightly. "Miss Barton took me under her wing; told me I wasn't the dregs of society after all. May God rest her soul, and I'm sure he's doing just that, but Mrs. Ropes was a prig."

"What's your work?" I was fascinated with the idea that the wages of sin could be happiness.

"I meet the hospital boats. I minister to the men and give mothers and wives a shoulder to cry on when they see no one they know coming off. It's happening more every day, and I'm doing a bit of crying myself."

Mrs. Gage spoke up. "Almost two hundred thousand unmarked

graves from this war," she said with a nod to me. "Can you imagine? All these men have died and no one can identify them."

"Ah, but now we have the magic words to open the door! I intend to frame this." Clara picked up a piece of paper from her desk and thrust it into my hand.

"Read," she demanded.

I read, haltingly at first, then with wonderment.

> *To the Friends of Missing Persons:*
> *Miss Clara Barton has kindly offered to search for the missing prisoners of war. Please address her at Annapolis, giving her the name, regiment, and company of any missing prisoner.*
>
> *Signed*
> *A. Lincoln*

"Oh, my," I said, fully impressed. Everyone began talking at once, telling me what was happening, giving me my first inkling of the task ahead. Wives and parents and children from everywhere were coming to Annapolis for advice, begging for news, gathering at the dock to watch wraithlike prisoners with pale skin and rotting teeth staggering off the boats and then mostly dying within a few days of their arrival. Chaos in Washington? I was assured it was nothing compared to what was happening in Annapolis.

Soon we were all eating Clara's fare, chattering about the bewildering rapidity of events across the Potomac, speculating on whether General Lee would make a last, bloody stand, and if so, where? How would that affect the influx of wounded? It fascinated me to watch Clara order and instruct, to see the others listen and nod and make notes. Her energy was contagious. Tired as I was, I felt my excitement and sense of purpose grow.

Through the entire evening I sensed Tom Cassidy's eyes on me. It was not an unpleasant feeling, for he had welcomed me warmly, but I wondered if I was being assessed. I hoped he would conclude I was up to the job ahead.

Later, after everyone had left, Clara unrolled a mat wedged against the wall, plumped the pillows, and spread out a thin blanket. "You'll sleep for now in this corner. It's not the fanciest, but it's better than Union Hospital, don't you think?"

She grinned at me and I smiled back through my weariness. Anything was better than Union Hospital. I wanted now only to shed my clothes and wash up. I looked for a basin and pitcher.

"I use a bathhouse down the block for washing," she said, catching my glance. "The cost is reasonable. Quite a luxury, really. And I take many of my meals out at Mrs. Springer's on Ninth Street. We'll go there for breakfast. It's a cozy enough place. But I cannot offer you the same comfort level you have at home, Susan."

"I'm happy to be here," I protested, wondering if she had seen a shadow cross my face. "I want to help."

"Good," she replied, standing straight. She reached one hand behind her back and pressed in on her spine, grimacing. "I must confess I've wondered about your motives for coming."

My cheeks grew warm. "Why do you say that?"

"I've hoped you're not on some romantic quest to find John Sulie. There's plenty else to do."

It had taken me long enough to work this through in my own mind, and I hastened to share it. "I would not have left my job to come here only for that," I said. "But I won't deny I want to find him. Louisa loved him, and the sadness in her since he disappeared has been a weight on us both."

"We've had two and a half years of war since then, dear. Anything could have happened."

"He survived Union Hotel Hospital. Surely there's a chance."

"I can help you find his records through the War Department."

"We did that. Louisa wrote them."

"And they had no idea where he was now?"

I nodded. "But they also seemed to have no idea *who* he was."

"Susan"—she chose her words carefully—"don't rule out the possibility that you were right in the first place. Perhaps he was a spy."

And I said, not knowing until the words were out of my mouth how much I believed them, "I wouldn't care."

Her eyes seemed to be testing me. She started to say something, hesitated, then said, "I think you have surprised yourself in that regard before. Good night, dear." With a quick nod she retreated to her room.

I began unbuttoning my shirtwaist, plagued with unsettling thoughts. What did she mean, I had surprised myself in that regard?

"Richmond's half-destroyed," Tom announced the next morning, breathless from running up the stairs to deliver his news. "They're setting the fires themselves and killing their own—can you believe it?"

"Surely not," I said, horrified.

But that was just the beginning. Next we heard that Union troops were marching into the city and slaves were meeting them, crying in the streets, overjoyed; waving rag banners, singing and celebrating "the day of jubilo," freedom at last! And then Lincoln, in a silk hat and long black coat, was stepping off a boat and walking up the hill to Richmond's Capitol Square, with the slaves shouting "Glory to God! Glory! Glory! Glory!"

"Don't get diverted," Clara warned each time I came running in from the street with the latest news, so excited I could barely talk. "We have to stay focused on preparing for our work in Annapolis; the news will reach us soon enough." But she smiled at her own words, for none of us could resist the excitement of feeling caught up in a glorious moment of history.

On Saturday night, Clara plunked a leg of mutton on the table for dinner and made an announcement. "Tomorrow is Palm Sunday, Susan. After breakfast, I am taking you somewhere important."

"Where?" I asked, my fork suspended in midair.

"It's a special surprise, so don't ask any more."

The next day I wore my gingham dress, leaving the jacket behind, for the day promised to be hot. Clara and I ate breakfast and then rode a carriage, heading at Clara's directions toward the Potomac. When we reached the bridge and began crossing into Virginia, I was struck with the beauty of the rolling hills of green. Rising at the crest of the highest one was what appeared to be a grand mansion, its pillars gleaming in the sun.

"Do you know where we are?" Clara asked.

A memory was stirring. "Is that the house I think it is?" I asked, pointing. We had reached the other side and were now moving up a wide, winding trail into the hills.

Clara nodded. "General Lee's home, and this is his front yard," she said with satisfaction. "He didn't invite us, of course, but here we are. Now it would be unneighborly of us not to pay a visit. Shall we drop in on him, Susan?"

I laughed, though still wondering what we were doing here. I didn't wonder for long. As we wound our way up the trail, I saw lines of white rectangular stones with black markings. We were in a cemetery.

"Can you think of a more fitting resting place for our soldiers?" Clara was almost gleeful. "We ran out of grave sites last year, and it was General Meigs's excellent idea to take over Robert E. Lee's front yard. No Southerner will be able to live again in a house sur-rounded by the graves of the Union dead—brilliant, don't you think? Now we'll pay a visit to Mrs. Lee's rose garden."

The horse was straining by the time we reached the crest and Clara ordered the driver to stop. We climbed out in front of a silent, moldering home graced with thick marble pillars set on a grand portico. As we walked to the back, I noticed the wooden steps were rotting away.

So this was the home of Robert E. Lee. Deserted now, keeping silent watch over thousands of men sent to their graves because of its owner's traitorous acts. Indeed, I could think of no more fitting a resting place for them.

Clara took my hand. "Look," she said.

Before us on this silent hill were the ruins of a garden, untended, with flowers here and there still attempting to bloom. And around the garden was a wide ring of carefully tended grass. I counted twenty-six raised mounds of earth.

"All of them, unknown! Can you think of a worse description? What if it were someone you yearned for and grieved for?" She waved a hand to take in the entire sweep of property. "We'll give them identity—they'll be the men who laid claim to Mrs. Lee's garden. We're collecting bones from the battlefields and bringing them here. You know what this is, Susan? It is our national cemetery." Her eyes were shining. "And all these unknown men, for whom wives and children and mothers and fathers grieve each day, will have the honor they deserve. Do you see why finding and identifying the fallen means so much to me? Oh God, to save as many as possible from anonymous death—" She stopped talking. There were tears dampening her cheeks.

Moved, I blinked back my own tears. We turned to walk back to the carriage, and suddenly I spied a Union soldier standing on the portico of Lee's house. He was jumping up and down, waving his cap, and shouting something unintelligible.

"Didja hear?" he yelled as we came into range.

"Hear what?" I called back.

"The traitor surrendered to Grant this morning! Old Robert E. Lee has given up!"

"Oh my goodness," I said, elated.

Clara reached into a small felt bag she carried on her arm and pulled out a small linen hankerchief. She dabbed at her eyes with vigor. She then straightened her shoulders and walked briskly forward, giving the happy soldier a cool nod as we passed by.

"Well, that's the first step."

"What do you mean? Surely the war is over, Lee has surrendered!" I said.

"One general, one army? That's all?"

She sounded so cross, I quickly muted my delight. And waited for a cue. We climbed into the carriage and settled ourselves into our seats, pulling our bonnets close against the unseasonably hot sun. Seeing my uncertainty, she relented and patted my arm. "I tend to bite, I know. You'll get used to it, dear. It's very good news, of course. But we would do well to hold our celebration."

"Why?" I asked, mystified.

"Because a war this terrible doesn't end so cleanly."

Chapter Fourteen

꧁꧂

"Look, look, oh my goodness, I don't believe it," I gasped.

Clara and I clung to the edges of the carriage as our driver tried to maneuver his way through the tidal wave of movement in town. Shopkeepers in stained, flapping aprons stood in the streets cheering and women who wouldn't dream of improper behavior were dancing jigs and flinging their bonnets into the air. A newsboy ran up to us, shouting, shoving a grimy paper into our hands. "Read the great news, ladies! War's over!" Soldiers, drivers, children—all were cheering and clapping, grabbing hands and hugging total strangers. The crowds grew so thick we abandoned our carriage at the President's House and descended into the celebrating crowd. Strong arms pulled us forward, with much laughing, joking, even hearty slaps on the back. Church bells tolling, soldiers shooting pistols into the air—what a grand day it was!

Dear Louisa,

Surely this has been one of the most exciting days of my life. I wish I could describe the joy that filled the city when we all heard of Lee's surrender. The excitement! A soldier filled to the gills with liquor grabbed Clara by the waist and twirled her aloft and another grabbed me for a quick hop and a skip down the street, all of us laughing, bereft of dignity and caring not a whit. Brass bands went tootling down the streets and joy was everywhere. I saw a child waving a flag from a window of the President's House, and someone shouted, "There's young Tad Lincoln! Three cheers for him!" At that moment there was the most awful sound; I thought I was deafened for life. I learned later a 500-gun salute had been set off, a salute so powerful, it actually blew out windows on Lafayette Square! Oh, my friend, our world surely grows stronger now. This terrible war is over. It grows late, and I bid you good night, wishing only that you had been here to experience it all with me.

I sealed the envelope, listening to the shouts and singing of celebrating crowds outside, imagining the reaction in Concord. Everyone would be pulling on their coats and caps and hurrying into the village. Shops would be closed, sewing put aside, the farmers coming in early from the fields. Friends and neighbors would gather at Orchard House. And Abba . . . would Abba be baking pies?

For one long lonely moment I missed them all. I missed the rhythms of daily life, my walks with Louisa, helping Abba in the kitchen, my work at Mrs. Sanderson's shop. I forgot my restlessness, my spats with May. I missed home.

Don't wallow in melancholy, I scolded myself. You are in the midst of historic times, not watching from afar. This is a splendid opportunity to do good. I closed my eyes and went to sleep, my dreams a jumble of delights and yearnings.

Clara swept apart the curtains the next morning, bringing me bolt upright to blink at the morning sun.

"Time to get up, Susan. Others may celebrate, but we have work to do."

Once enlisted in Clara's army, I realized, there was no malingering. One leap into the air, one huzzah—and then it was back to work. So it was that a few hours later I found myself squeezed into a carriage with Clara, Mrs. Gage, and Tom Cassidy for a trip to Annapolis.

"We can't miss any of the hospital ships," Clara said. "If we do, men vanish forever. That's the way I see it, and that's what drives me." She talked incessantly the length of the journey, wringing her hands together and then smoothing down her hair; one gesture following the other with never a moment of stillness.

"She's getting ready to fight," Tom said in a low voice when he saw me watching her in some puzzlement.

"Fight what?"

"You'll understand soon enough."

The horse pulling our carriage slowed to a walk as we moved through a surge of people heading in a great hurry to the docks. A hospital boat had just pulled to shore.

"Just in time. Another cargo from Belle Isle and Andersonville," muttered Tom.

Soldiers began unloading dozens of stretchers carrying wounded men, lining them up in tidy rows along the wharf. They moved efficiently. Soon I counted over sixty men lying there, their faces pointed to the sky. Their work done, the soldiers stepped back. I wasn't prepared for what came next: The crowd of people surged forward with shouts and cries and began hurrying up and down the rows. There were a few happy cries of recognition. I fixed my attention on a haggard woman wrapped in a green wool shawl moving from one stretcher to the next, holding up her skirt to keep from brushing the still forms on the ground, peering into each face with an expression of fear mixed with hopefulness. Finally, despairing, she fell to her knees and cried to the skies: "Who are these men? Where is *my son*?"

Tom turned and spat a large dollop of tobacco onto a dry patch of grass by the side of the road. He jumped from the carriage and reached up a hand to help me down. "Here we go again," he said. "One more sad mama whose son is rotting in some godforsaken field."

"That's cruel," I protested, surprised.

"No, it isn't," he said. "It's just true."

"Don't be dismayed by Tom," Mrs. Gage said as he moved away through the crowd. "He's as sad about this as you are, that's all. He has two brothers out there somewhere, and the ones coming in are dying so fast, no one is recording their deaths."

I followed his thin form, noting the length of his legs, his fluid, swinging gait. Mrs. Gage broke my concentration, gesturing in the direction of a cluster of men in dark vests working to push the crowd away.

"Watch them. Those are government men. Most of them are rogues who see their job to be hiding the disorganization. Oh dear, Clara never gives up. She's trying again."

Clara approached one of the men, stepping in front of him so he had to face her square. I could not hear her, but she was talking rapidly as she pushed a piece of paper in front of his face. The man stared at her with a blank expression and turned away.

"See? They pay no attention." Mrs. Gage tugged at her gloves, clearly exasperated. "They don't give a fig for President Lincoln's letter. They laugh at her behind her back, and no one will take on the responsibility of helping her set up an office or even give her the records with which to work. I'm afraid Clara's dream is becoming a charade."

Clara strode back to where we stood, her face stubbornly set. "Let's do the work we're here to do," she said.

Following her lead, our little band fanned out with pads of paper and pencils—kneeling by the men to scribble down their names and hometowns and as much other information as they could give us. Many were desperately sick. Several were dying, their eyes turning opaque as I leaned close, trying to hear what they were able to tell me. I felt a fire in my heart: I vowed not to let them slip away without finding out who they were. I scribbled down scraps of haltingly whispered information: first names; a state; even notes on what a man looked like as he lay staring at the sky. Would it help for someone to know that James, whose last name might have been Anderson, or maybe his first name was Anderson and James his last, had a scar stitched across his left cheek? It might, I told myself. Write it down!

"I admire your fresh energy, Susan. You're looking as resolute as Clara," Tom said as together we bundled one poor man into a cart collecting the dead. "You know, though, we're trying to empty a mighty ocean with spoons."

"Perhaps so," I answered. "But Tom, look at them. They need us."

Another hospital boat docked as I spoke; more soldiers jumped out and began unloading more stretchers filled with more groaning and silent men. Tom gazed out at this almost overwhelming scene and spat once more. "I'll have to watch out," he said. "You'll deprive me of my cynicism." He tipped his cap and hurried off to the newest crop of stretchers.

Clara took me for a brisk-paced walk through the town later that afternoon, railing away about the slovenly government officials who refused to give her the authority she demanded. I said little, listening and taking in my surroundings. Annapolis fascinated me. With tidy streets that flowed into elegantly laid-out circles and then meandered up the hill to the state capitol, it was definitely not a rough seaport town, and far more charming than Washington City. Or must have been once, I thought. Now this graceful place that yearned to be beautiful was covered with tents and sodden grass turned to mud by so many tramping feet.

"Well, there's only one thing to do," Clara said suddenly, breaking into my musings.

"I'm sorry?"

"I must get President Lincoln's ear directly. He knows who I am, and I trust him to be a reasonable man. Who else can prod these miserable people into giving me my proper authority? They're afraid, that's the problem. They don't want people to know they can't keep track of their soldiers." She frowned, mulling her own words, and brightened with new resolve. "Susan, we're heading back. Do you have a good dress?"

I thought of my elegant brown faille, the carefully stitched bodice, the soft hand of the ribbed silk. "Oh, yes," I replied.

"Good. We're going to a victory celebration."

The next morning we traveled back to Washington in such great haste, my back ached from bouncing over rutted roads. Clara seemed far less agitated than she had been on the journey up. "Watch me," she said with glee. "I'll show you today how things get done."

The sun was high when we reached Washington. Two days after Appomattox, and the festivities had not abated. We could hear drinkers bellowing out songs from saloons, and on every street corner flags fluttered in the wind. On Pennsylvania Avenue, a large crowd was preparing for an evening torchlight parade.

"President Lincoln is giving a victory speech tonight and going to a victory party, so we have two opportunities to catch his ear," she explained as we arrived at Seventh Street. "All I have to do is find a way to get close to him."

I looked quickly through the mail the postman had slipped under the door and was thrilled to find a letter from Louisa.

"Don't go anywhere," Clara warned as I ripped it open. "You must be dressed and ready to go when I come back." She fished in her pocketbook, a frown on her face. "I have to find Tom. Wait here."

Obediently, I set my letter aside and donned my beautiful silk gown, at first relishing the feel of the fabric on my skin. I peered into a small looking glass on Clara's dresser. I looked elegant. How fortunate I was to own this lovely creation! I traced the delicate stitches on the sleeves and noted how smooth and unpuckered they were, much in awe of Mrs. Sanderson's skill. With none to see, I swirled around the room, imagining myself dancing at a ball with all eyes on me. I was going to a victory party, and perhaps I would meet Mr. Lincoln.

Only then did I arrange myself in a chair and begin Louisa's letter, wishing there had been enough time for her to respond to the news of Lee's surrender. But the excitement of the past week had not missed Concord.

> *Dearest Susan,*
> *We hear amazing tales of the fall of Richmond and of the freed slaves dancing in the streets—never again will they be chained together and forced to bend their heads to slave collars! How I*

missed sharing the joy with you when the news came. Our little town danced a happy jig, and many of us have been haunting the telegraph office, eager for every morsel of news. How long ago it seems now, those grubby days at Union Hospital. Were we really there or have we simply imagined them?

I am finishing off my latest pot-boiler, rubbishy stuff, but already sold, to pocket as much money for the family as possible before I sail. And that date, my friend, will be in early July. Much remains to be done. In truth, young Emma Weld is something of a chore to be around, as you so correctly predicted. She does fuss so. But we are promised a good view of Europe and its treasures, and all proceeds as expected.

The one subject I do not raise is the one you have not spoken of yourself. Do not worry for me, dear Susan. I have accepted that John is now a part of my past, although I dream of him frequently. I know he is dead, and I also know how fervently you wish other-wise. You have a splendid, optimistic spirit, and I love you for it, but I feel the truth in my bones. How deeply his poor mother will suffer when she learns the truth! Life is not always what we wish it to be, and I am learning to accept the constraints on my heart.

Puzzled, I rose, rereading her words. John's mother? We knew nothing about John's mother. Louisa had created her for the fictional John Sulie.

"Susan? Is that you?"

Tom Cassidy stood in the doorway, staring at me.

"I'm waiting for Clara. We're going to Lincoln's speech and then a party," I said, flustered.

"I'm quite taken by those fancy duds you've got on."

His tone was so bluntly admiring, I felt uncomfortable. "Do you need something?" I asked, trying to hurry him along. "We'll be leaving as soon as Clara gets back."

"No, just thought I'd check in and see if you recovered from the scene in the harbor yesterday. Clara loses a few recruits a week after they see how grim a job she's taken on."

"Tom, you know I'm no stranger to dying soldiers."

"True, but you're a sensitive soul. I see you going on grit and fervor and don't want you getting overwhelmed."

"I am *not* overwhelmed." It was the dress, I was sure of it.

He shrugged, ignoring my snapping response. "Then I beg your pardon. That certainly is a handsome gown."

I reminded myself that he was a country teacher, not sophisticated, and no older than I. "Yes," I said. "Well, if you don't mind, I was reading a letter—"

"Then I'll be on my way. I actually stopped by to give this to Clara." He tossed an envelope onto the table, flashed an unreadable grin, and left with no further comment. Not even a goodbye.

I had no time to think about him or my rudeness. I sat down again and reread Louisa's letter to confirm what she had said and, indeed, she had blended her two John Sulies. An absentminded sadness was surely to blame, but I was startled. Should I point out that John had no family at all? No, that would be making too much of her slip.

The hours were ticking by. As dusk descended, I felt uncertain and even foolish, sitting there in my fancy clothes. Where was Clara? She came in the door at half past seven, her step heavy and her manner dispirited. Tickets for the victory party were sold out. And even hours spent trudging from office to office trying to cajole someone to perform alchemy had not produced results.

"We'll go to the President's House for his speech anyway," she said. "We'll stand outside like ordinary supplicants and I will attempt to engage the president when he enters his carriage. It's the best we can do, and my cause is just. Now we must make haste."

"Tom Cassidy dropped this envelope by for you," I said.

Clara ripped it open and let out an exclamation of delight. "Good old Tom," she said. "He found tickets! What a bully boy he is. He knew my plan and did what he could to help without telling me. Hurry!"

I threw my heavy cloak over my good dress and hurried after her, discomfited by the fact that Tom had not seen fit to tell me what was in the envelope. I had hurt his feelings, that was clear. We ran down the stairs, and out into the damp air. The fog was so dense, I feared losing sight of Clara. All sound was muffled in the streets, even that of the horses' hooves on the cobblestones. It was almost as if my ears were stuffed with cotton.

As we rushed down Seventh Street and onto Pennsylvania Avenue, looking for a carriage, I gasped and stopped. What a sight lay before me! Everywhere, buildings were illuminated—mansions, storefronts, the meanest of hovels. Thousands of candles filled every window of the post office, and the newly completed dome of the Capitol glowed with the flickering movement of thousands more. The city seemed to be dancing with light. I could hear rockets exploding in the distance.

"Clara, look, isn't it beautiful?"

"Hurry, hurry. Lord, we can't miss our opportunity," Clara said, her breath coming in short gasps.

We picked up our skirts and ran nearly a mile to the President's House, pushing our way through the crowds and onto the back lawn. I felt the dampness soak through my boots and prayed my skirt had made it through the muddied grass unscathed.

"There he is!" Clara pointed upward. I saw a tall figure step out onto the second-floor balcony. An aide stood next to him, holding a single flickering candle aloft for light. The effect was to cause the shadows around them to dance, producing an almost ghostly apparition. I pressed forward, trying to see better, disappointed that Mr. Lincoln's features were obscured by the fog. He raised his hand to quell the cheers of the crowd, and then, with no fanfare, he began reading from a text.

"We meet this evening not in sorrow but in gladness of heart," he began. "The evacuation of Petersburg and Richmond and the surrender of the principal insurgent army give hope of a righteous and speedy peace."

He read in a steady voice that seemed oddly out of tune with the exuberance of the evening. Although there was hope now for peace, he warned the war was not over. The difficult job of reconstruction lay ahead, fraught with the perils of disagreement on how to go about it.

"I missed his words," I said, straining to hear.

Tom had silently walked up and stood beside us. "He says we face 'a small additional embarrassment,'" he whispered.

"Embarrassment?" I whispered back, confused.

"Shush. Listen."

Lincoln's voice continued; somber, almost flat.

"We, the loyal people, differ among ourselves as to the mode, manner, and means of reconstruction. . . . Unlike the case of a war between independent nations, there is no authorized organ for us to treat with. No one man has authority to give up the rebellion for any other man. We simply must begin with, and mold from, disorganized and discordant elements." He hesitated a moment, fumbling with the pages.

"He's mulling over this devil of a war!" roared a bystander. "We don't need that!" Indeed his ruminative words were now sending puzzled murmurs rippling through the crowd. What was he proposing? Negro suffrage? Amnesty for the Rebels?

"Come on, Mr. Lincoln, give us somethin' to glory in," a man with his collar pulled up to his nose muttered. "Don't talk to us about making things good again for them damn Rebels."

"Let's kill the bastards!" shouted a man. "Do to them what they did to us!"

"Shut up, you louts, he's thinking out loud," Tom muttered. "Can you imagine what's ahead for him?"

I felt uneasy, listening to the voices around me shouting for vindictive action. Clearly it was not what Mr. Lincoln had in mind. Would he prevail? If the South was to be tromped down under the heel of the Union, the fighting would never end. Never.

There was polite clapping when Lincoln finished, although much of the crowd had already drifted off to the saloons, the parties, and the torchlight parades.

Clara grabbed my hand as the president disappeared inside. "Run," she demanded. We sprinted around the side of the mansion, rushing toward the Portico where I saw a large well-polished carriage. "Oh my, we are in luck, they haven't got in yet!" She picked up her skirts and rushed over to the carriage.

At that moment, a man and a woman emerged at the top of the steps and slowly began to descend. I stopped and stared as they moved closer, for they looked quite elegant. The man was tall with a deeply lined face and hollow eyes, wearing white gloves and a high black silk hat, and the woman at his side was plump and pretty, shivering in a low-cut pearl-gray silk dress. Fog swirled around them in wispy spirals.

Clara stepped forward, her voice cutting through the night air, clear as a bell. "Mr. President, may I have a word with you? It's Clara Barton, surely you know me."

Her boldness took my breath away.

Lincoln nodded vaguely in her direction as he prepared to enter the carriage, turning away even as Clara stood there with her hand outstretched.

Suddenly Mrs. Lincoln turned around. "Miss Barton?" she said, peering through the fog. "How good to see you. We are such admirers of yours."

"Thank you. Then surely you will do what you can to help me get funding for finding our missing soldiers. I've not been given the means to do the job President Lincoln has assigned to me. I assure you, the mothers and wives of this country will thank you for your intervention."

Mrs. Lincoln startled, but immediately the ghost of a smile played over her face. She said nothing, nodded, and took her husband's arm. He helped her into the carriage and followed her inside.

"Done," Clara whispered, elated, as the carriage clattered away. Her cheeks were flushed, as a cluster of people in the driveway stared at her curiously. I was puzzled. The president had not said a word to her, so how could she be so pleased?

"That was perfect," she said, squeezing my hand. "She'll talk to him, I'm absolutely positive. How fortunate we were to be here at precisely the right moment! I must follow immediately with a note to her. Let's go home."

"But aren't we going to the party?" I asked in dismay.

Clara looked at me incredulously. "We don't need to, now," she said, as if it were the most obvious thing in the world. With a grand sweep of her hand, she offered the tickets to a pair of bystanders who grabbed them eagerly. "Let's go," she said, tugging my arm.

Surprised by my own disappointment, I followed after her. Tom, striding beside us now, chuckled when he saw the expression on my face. "There's not much you can do with her," he said. "She gets in her mind what she wants done and is blind to anything else."

"I had some image of play and pleasure in my head that made little sense in this topsy-turvy time," I said with a sigh.

"Definitely not with Clara. But if she weren't so resolute, the generals wouldn't be shaking in their boots when she comes marching in. And anyhow, I still think you looked splendid standing on the president's lawn."

I smiled, my mood lightening. "Well now, Mr. Cassidy, I thank you for the compliment. And I must say, Mrs. Lincoln *did* seem encouraging."

Clara sent off her note the next morning. With great cheer, we headed back to Annapolis for two days of more exhausting, sad work, not returning until April 11. The weather was again damp and foggy, and our spirits were down.

"If I haven't had a message, I'm going to write Mrs. Lincoln again," Clara said.

"It's only been two days. Shouldn't you wait a little longer? Otherwise she'll see you as just one more anxious supplicant."

"There are too many of us; it's easy to forget."

We rode the rest of the way in silence. It was past dark when we reached Seventh Street, and we both trudged up the stairs with more weariness than usual.

I had just settled down to my writing desk, thinking the night seemed quiet, when I heard shouting and the sound of running feet outside. Clara and I exchanged glances. This wasn't the celebratory shouting of the past week—something was different. I hurried to the window, lifted the sash and peered out. To my amazement, I saw people on their knees on the cobblestones, weeping. Others ran by, shouting hoarse, despairing cries.

"What happened?" I shouted.

A burly carriage driver heard me and stared upward, not really seeing me. "He's been shot, you hear me? Shot! Lord have mercy, they say he's going to die!"

"Who? What? What are you saying?"

He gestured with his hand, sobbing. "Over on Tenth Street, at Ford's Theatre. Some bastard shot 'im."

"Shot *who?*" Clara screamed.

"The president!"

And then he ran down the street as Clara and I clutched each other for comfort.

A military patrol came thundering up the street, guns drawn. We could hear the rolling of drums. People running by shouted up fevered rumors: the secretary of state had been knifed; his daughter knocked unconscious; assassination of the vice president narrowly averted. Who else was targeted? What was happening? They're after General Sherman. They're out to kill Grant!

And then the only news that mattered. President Lincoln was dead.

I wrote Louisa that night, tears falling on the paper, blurring the ink, trying to clear the page with my fingers. I was not a religious person then, nor am I now. But that one night I prayed to God, challenging him. If he had any authority at all, he should wipe the grief of this night away, put Mr. Lincoln back in the box at Ford's Theatre unscathed and send him back in his handsome carriage to the President's House, where we so urgently needed him to be.

Only later, as I took off my dress, did I see the results of my distraught efforts. Smears of ink from my fingers had stained the skirt, stains that would not wash out. I had few clothes. And so it is, I thought. Each time I wear this dress, it will forever remind me of the night President Lincoln was shot.

Even great grief succumbs finally to the distractions of everyday life. Everything in our world had changed irrevocably, but our work went on. If anything, it felt more important than ever.

"Miss Barton, Miss Barton!" A young woman clutching a daguerreotype pushed toward us at the market one morning. "See? This is my Edwin. Edwin Martin. Can you find him? Please, have you seen him? Gettysburg, they say he was at Gettysburg, but nobody can tell me for sure." I ducked to avoid having the picture thrust in my face, but Clara never flinched. "He's a farmer," the woman pleaded. "We have a farm. Southern Maryland. See? He's got brown hair, a small beard. Mole on his right cheek, and another on his left arm, below the elbow." She was crying now, standing in front of us, holding the picture aloft. Clara simply put her arms around the woman and held her in a long embrace. "I'll do my best," she said. Incidents like this increased our resolve.

Weeks passed; April turned to May and then to June. Through that strange time, Liddy Kettle and I spent each day opening box after box of letters—repeatedly moving Clara's goldfish to safety—sorting them by state as we sat together on the floor of Clara's apartment. My legs would ache, but that was nothing compared to my heart as I read those pleading missives.

"Oh, Liddy, read this one," I would say about once every hour. "We must find this woman's son!"

"And this one's, and this one's, and—" Liddy clutched a pile in her hand and held it aloft. "It's a good thing we're obstinate types."

Each night Clara recorded every name on a master list, sitting bent and small over the table, her hand pushing so hard on the pen it would sometimes cut through the paper. She wanted the names published in local newspapers, hoping veterans would read the lists and provide clues to locate the missing soldiers. To some the scheme seemed hopeless, but I found myself absorbing Clara's intensity and passion, finding a perseverance of purpose unlike any in my life before. At the same time, new concerns were rising, for I was running out of money and Clara had none to spare.

When I raised the issue of funds one afternoon, she brushed me away.

"We'll get the money, I'm sure of it," she told Liddy and me as we handed her pile after pile of letters through the long weary hours. "We'll soon have thousands of names published. I won't be thwarted."

Liddy and I glanced at each other. Was Clara deluding herself? So far she had been unsuccessful in getting the War Department even to pay for stationery and supplies, let alone answer her pleas for an official list of the missing. The government declared itself swamped with demands for everything from overdue pay to payment for confiscated property, and no one seemed in a mood to help.

When I shared my concerns with Louisa, she immediately urged me to come home. "There's much to be said for pulling back to safety," she wrote. "And Mrs. Sanderson is forlorn without you. She asks about you every day." I folded Lou's letter and tucked it away with the others from Concord in my copy of *Pilgrim's Progress,* realizing how little she understood of the depth of my commitment. The thought of returning home had not occurred to me. I was not going to give up. I believed in Clara. She was opening my eyes to ways of doing and seeing things that made me feel confident and strong.

"Clara's done more good than half the people in this city, and it's unjust, it is. People are forgetting all that she did in the war," Liddy complained. "Nobody has the grit she has. If truth be told, she doesn't like being out of the limelight, and some might call her vain. I see nothing wrong with that. She's meant to shine."

"Absolutely." I had grown fond of Liddy. There was always a touch of the outrageous about her, which for me was part of her charm. "And how could anyone ever think all of this effort is useless?" I asked, surveying the growing number of boxes filled with imploring letters.

"Not us. Otherwise we wouldn't be here," she replied. She slit open an envelope and began scanning its contents. Her eyes widened and she broke into an explosive giggle.

"Look at this!" she said, tossing me the letter. I read quickly.

> Dear Miss Barton,
> I have had the sorry experience of seeing my name printed in the newspapers and I understand this is your doing. I would like to know what I have done, so that I am worthy to have my name Blazoned all over the Country. I have no desire to be found. If my family in New York wishes to know where I am let them wait until I see fit to write them. Kindly take my name off your rolls.

Liddy let loose with a laugh from the belly. "Oh, wait until Clara reads this. She'll scorch him with her reply!"

I checked the signature and went to Clara's master list, scrolling carefully until I found it. An army gunner from Rhode Island. Both his wife and his mother had written to Clara, pleading for help in finding him.

"Shall I take his name off?" I asked.

"No, no," Liddy replied. "Clara will write him back. It'll be blistering."

I stared at the roll. "Are there many people who write and say they don't want to be found?" I asked.

"No, thank goodness. We don't need many as indignant as that one."

"I'm wondering about the various ways people are lost."

"You're thinking about the one who called himself a blacksmith and escaped from the hospital, aren't you?"

I nodded.

Liddy shot me an exasperated look. "Susan, you're a hard worker and I like you, but where is your curiosity? Why haven't you gone to the hospital to see what you can find out?"

"I don't want to see that place again," I said, taken aback.

Liddy heaved herself up from the floor, brushing dust from her skirt. "Seems to me, if you're serious about finding him, you'd go there and piece together what happened. You and your friend, begging your pardon, seemed too high-bred for the rough-and-tumble of that place. Personally I never thought the two of you would outlast me. You didn't pick up on all that was going on."

I put down the letters I was sorting and stared at her. "What do you know, Liddy?"

"I know he was a prince of a man. Wonderful shoulders. A great, manly chest. Didn't get to bathe the rest of him, but I wanted to. Liked him myself."

"Don't evade my question, please."

"You were sweet on him. Be honest." Her eyes challenged me.

"Yes, I was." It was a relief to say it plain.

"God, I'm glad you admit it; wouldn't respect you half as much if you hadn't." She beamed me an almost beatific smile.

"What do you know?"

"I know there must be a few answers at Union Hospital."

"Will you go there with me?" I asked.

She nodded, the smile spreading across her face. "Why not? Anything to get away from these letters for a brief while."

The building seemed dark and, if anything, more dilapidated than I remembered. I braced for the familiar smell of sweat and blood and filth, and was astonished to breathe in only the faintest of the familiar odors. We walked up the front steps to the porch. A large hole yawned in front of us where some floorboards were missing. We hopped over it, catching the brief attention of a couple of workmen digging a ditch nearby.

"Looks like nobody's here. Guess they've pretty much closed this wreck down," Liddy said as we stepped inside. She picked her

way with great fastidiousness to the central stairwell. "No surprise. It never was a hospital that did the Union proud. Not that
any nurse would be shocked by that." She giggled without humor.

Walking slowly, I rounded a corner and pushed open a door.
Once again, I was staring at the beds of Ward One. But there were
no suffering patients. If I closed my eyes—and I had no intention
of doing so—I feared I would conjure a vision of the young drummer boy crying through his last night on earth and the ones we
called "men," scarcely much older, moaning through long nights as
they tried to accomplish the difficult business of dying. The enormity of what they had endured! I shivered, half-expecting to see
old Lyndon stalking the aisles with his bloody saw.

"You'd think they'd burn the mattresses, wouldn't you?" Liddy
said with a sniff. "I'm surprised the place is even open. Who wants
to admit it ever existed?"

"What do you think happened to Belle Poole?"

Liddy leaned down to pick up an unwound bandage from
under a cot, wrapping it absently around her hand as she straightened. "Probably disappeared somewhere, hoping no one would
snatch her loot. Especially after your soldier showed up."

I could hear our footsteps echoing on the stained floor. "What
do you mean?"

"Susan, haven't you guessed yet?"

"Guessed what?"

She studied me with the exasperation of a teacher faced with a
dull child unable to learn its alphabet. "John Sulie was a spy."

"I don't believe it."

"Well, it's true. Some of us who had been around for a while
knew. But that's because we were sharp on what to look for."

I was feeling annoyed, now. "Liddy, don't play with me."

"If it makes you feel better, he was a Union spy. Although
they're all cut from the same cloth."

My expression must have amused her.

"Oh, you babes from Concord! He was a *Union* spy, do you
understand? He spied *for us*. But he had to lay low, even here. We

had at least one Rebel in the ward, remember? I had my suspicions about a couple of others. Who knew if they'd get well enough to sneak back to enemy lines? John Sulie would have been killed if the Rebs got their hands on him."

"How did you know he was a spy?"

"Guessed it. Watched him. So did Belle, but she guessed the wrong side."

Could it be? I ran through my mind every scene, every conversation, every suspicion. Of course, that explained so much, including the vague response from the War Department when Louisa and I tried to find him. They were not about to admit to knowing the whereabouts of someone like John Sulie, let alone confirm his very existence.

We were standing facing each other now at the head of the stairs I had clambered down that dreadful night, fearing rats and death and loss.

"I want to know who set him free—and why," I said.

"That I don't know."

I took a deep breath, every muscle resisting this decision. "Well, let's go down there and see what we can find out."

We began to descend the stairs. The place was as dank and evil as ever, but the cell where John had been imprisoned pulled me forward. In my imagination, I could almost see the shape of his body standing behind the iron bars, almost feel the magnetic attraction that had taken me so close. I could once again inhale his breath, feel his urgency.

I stopped and stared at the lock on his cell, remembering more. Remembering one thing he had said that had puzzled me.

"Now if you weren't locked in, that could be a handy exit," said Liddy, pointing to a small window, a rectangular glow of light cut in the stone foundation, halfway up the wall opposite the door. "Easy for a man to fit through, don't you think? And you might notice, there are no bars."

I felt curiously calm. "After someone let him free."

"And who would do that?"

"Someone who feared army officials would be enraged if they found they had locked up a valuable spy. Someone who would be mighty relieved to have him out of here, with none the wiser. Someone, how did Mrs. Ropes describe him, someone 'puffed up with the gilding on his shoulder straps' who feared a blotch on his record."

Liddy snapped her fingers with a quick, rakish gesture. "Dr. Coleman."

"The very one."

"Oh, my goodness." Liddy thought about that, both of us remembering the pompous, detached doctor who ran the hospital yet never showed his face in the ward but once. Then she performed an awkward pirouette, laughing all the while. "Isn't war grand?"

I was sure it was true. After Coleman allowed Belle Poole to put John in the cellar, he must have found out from the War Department he was mistreating a valuable spy. It was he with the keys and the authority to go down to the cellar and unlock John's cell. And John knew he would—that's why, when I wanted to go to Coleman, he said it wouldn't be necessary. Of course not.

I laughed back, tossed my head, acknowledging the joke on us all. Then I led the way back up the stairs, desperate to get away from the cauldron of emotions in that cellar, keeping my shoulders straight so Liddy would not sense my inner turmoil.

John had known he was about to be released—that had been his urgency. Had he returned my kiss knowing I would be horrified at myself and run away? Why had he never contacted Louisa? Had she and I been victims of a cynical charade?

Yes, he was a spy. Like Belle Poole, I had simply guessed wrong as to which side he served.

Clara was pacing the room, hands clasped behind her, her eyes bright with joy when we arrived back at her apartment. Tom was sitting in a chair, laughing.

"Where have you been? I've been waiting for hours, why did you leave?"

I began to explain, but she cut me off.

"You'll never guess what has happened, the most wonderful stroke of luck," she began. "I can hardly believe it. This will change everything!"

"What is it?" I asked. And then listened, growing increasingly excited. A soldier once imprisoned at Andersonville had contacted her with no advance warning, offering a store of priceless information. A list. A list recording the name, rank, and cause of death of every Union soldier who had died in that terrible prison.

"Where did he get it?" I asked. "How did he come by something so important?"

"He could read and write, so the lazy brutes put him in charge of recording deaths, until they became too nervous over the horrendous death toll. So can you guess what he did?" She spread her arms out in a triumphant gesture, her gaze going from me to Liddy and back again. She was hugely enjoying our attention.

"He secretly copied the master list," she announced. "And he is bringing it to me."

I was immensely impressed. "Clara, that's wonderful!" I said.

"What's his name? How do you know he's telling the truth?" Liddy asked.

"I've checked his records and I'm sure he is genuine. His name is Dorrance Atwater, and he was indeed at Andersonville." She was pacing again. "I am going immediately to the War Department and demand those graves be properly marked," she said. "Think of how many letters we will now be able to answer with certitude! Think of—"

"When is he bringing the list?" Liddy interrupted.

"I sent a note back and asked him to come as soon as possible," she declared. "I told him not to tarry, I wanted no chance of anything to go wrong."

Three days inched by. Clara was beside herself, waiting. We worried, not for the first time, that her enthusiasm had stretched beyond the facts. But if the information was true? What a coup this could be for Clara! Nothing mattered more than knowledge, and the list offered to her would be worth more than mere money. It would alleviate so much pain and worry—and get the necessary attention that had been lacking.

My sense of high anticipation had dulled by the third day. Where was this man promising such precious records? Probably just another charlatan. There were many out there, hoping to prey on the gullibility of earnest do-gooders.

So when we all heard the sound of heavy footsteps climbing the stairs on the third night, we barely paid attention. It was Clara who ran to the door and threw it open.

"Mr. Atwater?" she called.

"Yes," a male voice responded.

"It's about time, sir," she said.

"Whose? Yours, or mine?"

"Don't be so—" and then Clara's voice went still.

"So, we meet again," I heard a man say. "And you start it with a scolding."

Clara stepped aside, allowing him to enter the room. I registered first what I had already come to recognize as a prisoner look: youngish, prematurely stooped, with graying hair and dark half-moons of weathered skin beneath his eyes. And yet handsome, a man of considerable presence and hauntingly familiar. He wore a shabby black frock coat.

I stared. He stared back. His questioning eyes roamed the room, searching each corner, then came back to me. A moment of time, as long as the existence of the world, passed.

"Hello, Susan," he said.

I reached for a table to steady myself. "Hello, John," I replied.

Chapter Fifteen

"For heaven's sake, why didn't you tell us who you were?" Clara demanded.

"Who I *am?*" He looked genuinely baffled. "I'm just one of hundreds of wounded soldiers you saw in the war, am I not? What makes me special?"

"You know we nursed you at Union Hospital. You are toying with me." Clara did not like surprises.

"If you feel affronted, I can only pretend to be sorry. I'm here because I survived Andersonville. Isn't that what you're interested in? I don't have the patience for or care about anything else. So, what more do you need to know?"

"You needn't set this up as a hostile encounter," Clara said, taken aback.

"I don't mean to, sorry. Let's get to business and be done with it." He pulled a handkerchief from his pocket and wiped his brow, his breathing still wheezy from the climb. With a quick, almost careless flick of his wrist, he tossed a thick manila package on the table. "Here's the death register. I've listed the names of almost thirteen thousand men. Do you understand? Thirteen thousand. And it's the only complete list anyone will ever find. Now may I sit down?"

Clara snatched up the package, pulling at the string like a child ripping Christmas paper off a gift. After the first shock of recognizing John Sulie, I realized I was looking at a vastly changed man. Eyes hollowed, rimmed in red; his body curved forward as

if warding off pain. The sight was far worse than that of his collapsed frame in a hospital bed.

"So you went from Union Hospital to Andersonville," Tom said
in a faintly mocking tone. "I guess that proves you weren't a Rebel
spy."

I glanced at him, surprised, watching him pace the room. That
hardened voice wasn't from the Tom I knew.

"Does it?" John's voice answered. "Not to anyone who wants to
believe otherwise."

"Oh, you were a spy, all right, just a Union one," Liddy said,
with a toss of her hair. "Me and my friends figured that out right
away. You were lucky you weren't hung by the Rebs. All spies get
hung, sooner or later."

"You really think so, Liddy?" His eyes glittered with something
that made me want to cry.

"Would you like a glass of water?" I asked.

The glitter diminished as he glanced in my direction. "In the
absence of beer, that will do fine," he said.

I hurried to the next room. Pulling a tin cup from the shelf and
filling it from Clara's water pitcher gave me time to straighten my
thoughts. John Sulie was alive. The man I had dreamed about for
three years was in the next room. Physically changed, yes. But the
same man. I walked back to the room he inhabited, so unexpectedly and so fully, wild with questions and an almost crazed hope.

He took the cup from me with awkward, gnarled fingers and
caught me staring at them. "A little trick of the guards," he said.
"They liked crippling men. They broke my fingers with a hammer."

Clara ignored him. With that singular ability she had of shut-
ting out everything but what most immediately absorbed her, she
sat at the table, reading, the gaslight above casting flickering shadows over the death register. "How do I know these records are
complete?" she asked.

"You know they're complete if you believe me, simple as that.
I wrote every name down myself. And I know where each man is
buried. Never figured I'd be alive to bring the list back."

Tom had stopped his pacing. I moved to Clara's side and stared at the list: name after name, in cramped, careful handwriting, the handwriting of someone who wanted not a single letter misread.

John pushed himself back in his chair, teetering on the back legs in a casually reckless pose. "You might also want to know that nobody in the War Department wants it published. I know——I've tried."

"Why not?" asked Clara.

"Because there's no glory in it for them." His harsh laugh was like a bark. "That's what it's all about. The men we'll be honoring won't be the best ones, just the ones who feed what we want to believe. People like General McClellan. He'll have a grand statue, for sure."

"That fool?" scoffed Tom. "I doubt it."

John wheeled in his chair to face him. "Just watch," he said.

Tom seemed taken aback. "I'm a cynical man, but not *that* cynical."

"Why not? Doesn't seem like an inappropriate response to me. We heaped men up in dead houses or left them to rot on the battlefield because we had to, but there's no excuse for what's happening now. Who cares about all the missing men? Only their families. The cowards running the government don't want the country to get a true bead on the slaughter. They'd prefer nobody ever counted those bodies——certainly not the ones lying in the dirt down at Andersonville."

"I believe you," Clara said, shaking her head in vigorous assent. "Nobody wants to face it. They ignore my efforts, I know that."

Liddy seemed oblivious to his anger. "So what'd you do when you scooted out of old Union Hospital?" she asked in a carelessly coquettish tone. "Where'd you go?"

"Back to my regiment," he said.

"A glutton for punishment," she said with a grin.

Finally I found my voice. "Were you really a Union spy?"

He smiled faintly. "I fought for the Union, Susan. Let's leave it at that."

Twice he had spoken my name. I wanted to say more, but Clara, focused only on the treasure in her hands, waved me quiet. "You've brought me the best gift I could ever receive, and with this in hand, the army can't ignore me anymore. I'll push it in their faces and you'll see—we'll get clearance to mount an expedition!"

"To do what?" I asked.

"To travel to Andersonville and mark those graves, every last one of them." She shot a hard glance at John. "How do you propose matching the names on this list with the unmarked graves?"

John reached into the pocket of his jacket, pulled out a wide sheet of paper, and spread it flat on the table. I leaned forward.

"This is a map of the Andersonville graveyard, and these," he said, pointing to hundreds of carefully drawn rectangles, "mark the burial spots. Each is marked with a numbered stick. I keyed my list to those numbered sticks."

"Why did the Rebs let you do that? Took a lot of walking around on your own, seems to me. Why would they give you so much freedom?" demanded Tom. He stood slumped against a wall, the picture of scowling skepticism in his baggy, dirty pants. I resented his posture, his tone, his words. Later, when I challenged his meanness, he told me I made John too noble a figure, that he was just one more haunted, hunted man. I turned on him in a huff for that.

"That's easy. I could read and write, and they were too ignorant to keep their own records," John said. "Why don't you ask *why* I did it?"

"All right, I ask that."

"Because I wanted to survive. If they needed me, I had a chance. They finally realized I knew too much and broke my fingers so the pain would keep me from scribbling for a while. But"—he raised his hand in mock triumph—"they didn't know I'd already copied their list. Name for name, word for word. Does that answer your question?"

In the ensuing silence, Clara rose to her feet. "I can't tell you how much your list means," she said. "I don't know yet how, but I assure you, I promise you, we are going to Andersonville. And we are going to give recognition to every man who died there."

Her conviction was instantly contagious, straightening Tom's shoulders, wiping the smirk off Liddy's face, bringing me back in from the shadows. We had a new task. If anyone could find a way to save the dead of Andersonville from anonymity it would be Clara. I glanced at John, hoping he was as thrilled as I by her fire— and saw him watching me. I could not look away, caught and held by his gaze as he sat at the table in front of me, so close I could reach forward and touch his cheek.

"Is John your real name?" I asked.

He shrugged, as if the question was of no importance. "I never fancied Dorrance. Think of John as my middle name, that will do fine."

Could one shrug off identity so easily? A spark of anger broke through my enthrallment. "Some of us would like to know what is true," I said.

His look gentled. "Susan, my name isn't important. I am the person you believe me to be, and I have never been untrue to those who mattered to me."

Did he mean Louisa? Of course he did. He must.

"Louisa will be thrilled to know you are safe," I said.

His face softened even more; oh, now I saw. Yes, he loved her.

"And I would be thrilled to know she is well and happy."

I nodded, afraid my wistfulness might creep out if I spoke. My duty here was plain to see.

The next hour was filled with Clara making plans, assigning each of us a specific role in her new campaign. She had yet even to apply for the army's permission to travel to Andersonville, but I knew it was a matter of hammering on doors and shouldering her way into offices, raising her voice higher than the guttural males who remained, thank goodness, flummoxed by the likes of Clara Barton. John and I would accompany her to Andersonville, she directed. Liddy and Tom would handle the work in Annapolis. Tom looked not at all happy with the plan, but he made no objection. Clara was our general.

"Do you have family here?" she asked John.

"No. None anywhere, as a matter of fact."

"Then you are to move in with Tom." She cast a quick glance at the almost skeletal John. "And Tom, feed the man," she ordered.

Later that night, I bent over the same table, alone, my brain still filled with questions, writing to Louisa. This should be the most joyous note of my life, I thought. And yet my hand moved sluggishly.

> *Dearest friend,*
> *I have found him. He lives, after having suffered as a prisoner in Andersonville. He wants you. Come, come to Washington, quickly. Oh, do not tarry!*

My pen flew now over the page, almost urgently.

> *Remember your advice to me to always reach for the highest apples in the tree? Jumping, stretching, not ever settling for those on the ground, the ones pocked with wormholes and pecked by birds? Louisa, here he is—Ernest L'Estrange. Come, come!*

And then, worn out, I dropped my pen, put my head on the table and burst into tears.

Tom outfitted John in fresh clothes and brought him over the next morning, handing me half a ham and a large loaf of bread as I opened the door. "Here, you can feed him," he said ungraciously. "I've got work to do."

"Cranky sort, your friend," John said, with a glance at Tom's departing back. He slumped into the same chair he had occupied the night before, and I proceeded to cut large slices of ham, placing them on a tin plate with a large chunk of buttered bread. He ate greedily as I watched, drinking in his every move. I could see him better now, under that prison pallor. The John I knew, the man I loved, was still there. I could see him. But I couldn't reach for him.

"I'm posting a letter to Louisa," I said.

He paused between bites, studying me. "I thank you," he said simply.

"Finish up, finish up," Clara declared as she strode into the room. "We have work to do."

We spoke no more that day, nor for several more. There was little time to reflect as I busied myself preparing for the operation Clara was so sure would soon come to pass. She positioned herself in the front office of the commissary general for prisoners, demanding an audience. General Hoffman, who liked and admired Clara, finally put her proposal before Secretary of War Stanton. He summoned her to his presence.

Clara dressed carefully that morning, asking me a dozen times if her clothing looked properly severe or too severe, turning anxiously in front of me, rehearsing her words. "I will not leave his office until the secretary of war grants my wish," she vowed as she tied on her best bonnet, clutched her purse to her breast with both hands, and walked from the room. What a marvelous picture of determination she made! I was learning from her that when you believed in something, when you wanted it, you fought for it. Timidity went hand in hand with defeat. There was no virtue in lowering one's eyes and accepting mindless authority.

Still, I was astonished when Stanton caught Clara's fervor and declared yes, the government would sponsor an expedition. Andersonville, he announced, would become an important national cemetery. A symbol of the nation's sacrifice. All this, decided in a matter of days.

"Why did they suddenly listen to Clara?" I asked Tom. "Why does it matter to them now, when it didn't before?"

As usual, he took his time answering. Although this trait made me impatient, Tom almost always had something worthwhile to say.

"Because they are becoming nervous," he said. "Stanton and the rest are afraid of what happens when people finally realize the extent of our losses. Most of a generation gone, on both sides, Susan. How do we come back from that? How do the generals and the politicians explain when the scope of it all comes clear? You have to be ready. You have to be able to say those deaths meant something." He laughed shortly. "Listen to me, on my soap box."

"So you build memorials," I said.

He nodded. "Something for memory and mourning."

"Tom, just think of it: This will be nothing less than a cathedral, that's what this cemetery can be. And *we're* going to build it."

He smiled, a flicker of sadness in his eyes. "Yes. *You* are."

I tried to ignore his dissatisfaction, knowing how disappointed he was to be left behind. Instead I floated through the day on euphoria. Until I opened the letter to me that was propped on Clara's mantel.

> *Dear Susan,*
>
> *It is with regret that I inform you Louisa set sail for Europe Tuesday last, the day your letter arrived. She professes herself heartened by the survival of the patient you describe as John, and regrets her inability to come to Washington. Duty, she asked me to tell you, comes first. She knows you will understand and conveys her best wishes. As do I and Abba, to you.*
>
> > *Cordially,*
> > *Bronson Alcott*

I stared at this note for a very long time, filled with confusion. Was this truly Louisa's response? How could it be? She loved John, had never stopped loving him. Her constancy of feeling for those she cherished never wavered. She would have flown to him, ready to nurse him through the unseen wounds of war. She would have grabbed her cloak and bonnet and rushed from the house to the rail station, oh yes, surely she would have done that. And if she had not? Perhaps it meant she no longer cared for him. Was that possible?

What nonsense. I ground the letter into a hard ball and threw it into the fireplace. Bronson had intercepted my letter, that was the explanation. Louisa would not have responded so coolly. Never. All my anxieties and worries about Bronson's power over Louisa were once again unleashed. I remembered the trip back from Washington with him, reviewing again in my mind Louisa's moaning plea for John. His quick frown. His question: "Who is John?" The thought of his reading my words about reaching for the highest fruit on the tree made me flush. And as I watched the tiny wad of paper ignite and burst into flames, I was convinced. This was a fraud. Louisa could never have seen my note. I sat down to write her immediately, with more urgency even than before.

> Dear Louisa,
>
> I send this ahead, knowing you have long since reached Liverpool, but I am hoping you will check for your mail in Brussels before you move on—if not, I pray you will think to write me. Somehow you were not informed of the great news. John has appeared, safe and sound, though much depleted from two years in prison. Louisa, he waits eagerly for you. . . . We go with Clara on an expedition to Andersonville to mark the many graves of the war dead. We leave soon, and our task will take several weeks. Please, please write. Better yet, please come.
>
> Your loving friend,
> Susan

Under orders from Clara, John and I traveled together the next week to the Center Market on Pennsylvania Avenue to buy supplies for the trip. There was much activity, and we had to leave the wagon some distance away. It felt strange to walk beside him, sharing quiet companionship. I could relish that without disloyalty, surely. We walked quickly, with much to be done, and at one point he turned to me and said, "You've developed quite a stride, Susan. Very authoritative. Much like a man's, I would say."

I flushed, uncertain if this was a compliment. "To walk with you at any pace is a remarkable thing," I said.

He laughed. "True. You've mostly seen me prone."

"Mostly."

He said nothing at first, letting that reminder go by. How could I be so bold, I asked myself.

"Well, you've changed in a number of ways, I'd wager. Can see it in your eyes. Don't take it ill; it's a good thing."

I realized he was dragging his foot and breathing heavily, and slowed my pace. "I had to grow up, John. I hope I have," I said.

We walked on in silence, soon reaching the clutter of fruit and vegetable stalls that lined the avenue. The Center Market was a teeming place, filled with the shouts of shopkeepers cajoling buyers to sample their wares—vast quantities of string beans, tomatoes, small gnarled apples, and pears all heaped together—the abundance of summer that made this one of my favorite spots in the city. But that day I ignored most of the fresh produce. We collected provisions more suitable for a sea voyage, and I bargained hard with one warty old shopkeeper for a large quantity of tinned meat. He finally threw up his hands, took the cash I offered, and turned away.

"Impressive," John said with a smile as he stooped to pick up the heavy box of meat and carry it to the wagon, wincing at the effort. "You stood your ground and got a good price."

"Oh, I've bargained with that one before. I always win." I followed him with our other purchases, saddened to see the weakness of his body.

"John, I need to talk to you," I ventured as we loaded the wagon.

"I don't like your tone. Bad news, right?" He leaned against the cart and closed his eyes.

Hesitatingly, I told him about Bronson's letter. His face stiffened, and I rushed to stave off his reaction. "Louisa would never have sent such a message," I said. "I know my friend quite well, and you have never left her thoughts."

He had his back to me now, one hand braced against the slats of the cart. He said nothing.

"Please, don't be upset. I know Louisa, truly," I pleaded.

He turned to me, a hint of the old mocking smile on his face. "Can you imagine, Susan? We forgot the bloody potatoes." He turned to stride back to the market, whistling mirthlessly.

"Wait," I said, touching his jacket. "Walk with me, I beg you. I need to make you understand."

He yielded. We walked together away from the wagon, into the scrubby field of dried brush beyond that was withering under the hot July sun. I began to speak, to repeat what I had said before, but he stopped me.

"You're trying too hard to play Cupid, Susan. Don't be anxious; I understand this."

"What do you mean?"

"She's gone to Europe, that's all. I can wish she had not, but there it is. A part of Louisa wants to hide, I believe. And I'm a reading man. I read *Hospital Sketches*. Do you want me to say more?"

I bent my head to dodge a low-hanging branch and half stumbled over a deep rut hidden in the brush, trying to think of an answer. "All I'm telling you is this message is fraudulent. There is a love in her that wants expression, and not just through her writing."

John stopped and turned to face me, his face inscrutable. "Let's say something plainly, Susan. I can't say I'm surprised. The man she fictionalized is better than me."

"No, just different."

He barely heard me. "A much better package—a saintly, noble soldier able to endure a terrible death without cracking. Who wouldn't admire her John Sulie? She took a fantasy and pressed him into her book like some orchid after a blasted dance. That man isn't me, Susan. She never met Dorrance Atwater. And I suspect she loves the man she created more than the one who is real."

My thoughts flew back to Louisa's memory lapse in her letter. No, it was ridiculous. "Louisa would come in a moment if she knew you were found," I argued. "She cannot be the author of the message Bronson relays. You must understand. Her passionate spirit is real."

"I certainly can hear yours coming through," he said lightly. "Don't fret, Susan. There are more important things that need doing right now." He turned away, ending the conversation, closing me out.

"Wait." I was suddenly angry. "I went back to Union Hospital and figured out how you escaped. You knew when I came down there you were getting out, didn't you? But you told me nothing. I want to know, why did you leave before I came back?"

"You were coming back?" he said, startled.

"Of course. I hadn't given you Louisa's note." I stopped.

"*What* note?"

Now it was my turn to pause, struggling painfully for a steady voice. "John, I beg your forgiveness. Louisa sent me to you with a note and I forgot to give it to you."

"'*Forgot*'? What happened to it?"

"I tried to make amends, I tried to bring it to you." My voice cracked.

"Did you tell her? Does she know I didn't read it?"

"No."

"Damnation!"

I winced at the tone of his voice. "She was sick, and I couldn't hurt her more. Please, understand, she is everything to me—mother, sister, friend—and I did not have the courage to tell the truth."

"So she wrote me, after all," he said slowly.

"Yes. She wanted you to know she loved you."

"So it was true," he said.

"Yes."

We stood there for a long moment in time, one of those where all assumptions and expectations are readjusted. With a painfully slow movement, he turned and faced me, his eyes unreadable.

"You were a terrible messenger, Susan," he finally said. "We both know why."

My voice failed me for a moment. "Yes," I said. "But it doesn't change the fact that she loves you. Do you understand?"

"No."

"Why not?"

"She consigned me in her book too quickly to the grave." He paused before speaking again. "She chose not to come in response to your letter. Do *you* understand *that?*"

"She never saw it."

"Well, you can believe that if you want to, but I doubt it."

"You are giving up too easily!"

"Don't talk to me about giving up," he retorted.

"Then why didn't you contact Louisa after you escaped?"

"There was no bloody time, don't you understand?"

"Maybe you never intended to."

"Would I have gone to her if I hadn't been sent to Anderson-ville? Yes. Does that surprise you?"

"Then why . . ."

"Go ahead. I knew we'd get to our unfinished business."

"Then why did you let me kiss you?"

I held my breath, watching his face darken.

"You want to force it out of me? By heaven, you'll get it, then." He stared away from me as he continued. "I smelled your lust. How do you like that, Susan? And it matched mine. I wanted to touch your skin, to see if it was as soft as it looked. And, God help me, I enjoyed the taste of your lips. Are you satisfied? Will you stop now?"

I covered my eyes. "Oh John, I'm sorry," I said.

"Fine, then we both can be ashamed."

He strode past me without a glance, and headed back to the wagon. I noticed his shoulder bones, still deprived of sufficient flesh, jutted out sharply from the back of his shirt. I wanted to touch them. How could I be thinking so wantonly? My head pounded as I hurried after him.

The letter on the mantel this time was addressed in Louisa's handwriting and had been posted in Liverpool. I opened it slowly.

Dear Susan,

I cannot come; I can never come. Please understand how painful this decision was for me, and forgive my cowardice for not telling you immediately and directly. Oh, Susan, it's been such torment, I don't know why I cannot, but I know the truth of it. Don't misunderstand, I am elated that John is alive, but I have my own commitments of duty that must be maintained. Please, please understand and don't fault me. It is so painful to face certain truths, but Life cannot be lived over again. As my ship took me farther and farther away, knowing an ocean couldn't hold my tears, I knew I had to say to you, dear Susan, Ernest L'Estrange lived only in my mind. I do love your memory of him, but it is more vivid than my own and offers nothing solid and safe.

With much love,
Your Lou

With a cry, I threw her letter across the room. A cry of anguish, anger. I envisioned Louisa damping down her emotions, holding them in abeyance as she packed her dark and dreary clothes for her dark and dreary trip of duty, squeezing out any hope of reunion, and why, why, why? How could she cheat herself so? "An ocean" couldn't hold her tears? Yes, but only after she was safely deposited on the ship and couldn't change her mind! How could she not come to John? *How could she not?*

I grabbed my pen and pad and began furiously to write.

I cannot believe you would give up, turn your back on love; I cannot believe it! You've been hoping for this all your life. Henry could not offer it, but it is offered to you now. What truth do you speak of, Louisa? You want me to understand your torment, but have you thought of mine? Oh, this pain! What have you become and what

No this was useless. Throwing down my pen, I shoved the paper into the desk drawer. There were no words for this.

I flung myself on the bed and wept into my pillow. For what? For everything. For Lou: for joyous runs through the woods and grand, brave plays; for Ernest L'Estrange: denied now the breath of life forever; for John: for love lost, for love not claimed; for me: for guilty passion, frustration, and remorse. And when I had wept myself out I lifted my head and felt a sudden, startling release, a sensation of being freed.

Whatever else had happened, I was about to make a journey, too.

The day we were to leave was evilly hot, and I hurried to help move our provisions to the dock for the trip to Savannah. As we pulled our belongings from the wagon, I gazed at the boat that was to take us on the first leg of this five-hundred-mile journey. The *Virginia* was a shabby excuse of a ship. It seemed too small to hold both us and the forty-odd workmen assigned to the expedition. I thought with trepidation of how cramped our quarters must be.

"Damn it, madam!" a tough little spit-and-polish man, gnarled as a walnut, standing on the upper deck, roared down at Clara. "You and your crew are late! Some people don't deserve to go anywhere, and what in hell do you want to go for?"

This had to be Captain James Moore, the assistant quartermaster in charge of military burials in Washington. Stanton had named him head of the expedition, and he was in an ugly mood.

Clara wheeled and stared up at him, her hand shielding her eyes from the sun. For a moment, no one dared speak. "Well, good day, Captain Moore," she sang out. "I apologize for our tardiness. May we come aboard now?"

Without the grace of a response, Moore turned his back and walked away.

Quickly, we loaded our things. "How can he treat me as an intruder?" Clara said with lips pressed so thin, they drained of color. "There would be no expedition if it weren't for me. He's a small-minded, vain man who hates to see a woman usurp his space."

"But you were right not to cross him," I said quickly. Indeed I had admired her restraint. This was unlike Clara, and I feared there would be a collision ahead between the two of them. None of us could afford that.

Restraint was not easy on that difficult journey. The five days to Savannah were hot and terrible, and we had not a moment of relief from the obvious animosity of Captain Moore. Clara grew violently ill and was unable to leave her berth next to the boiler room. Twice I saw John wringing out cold cloths and laying them about Clara's head—a gentle gesture that added a small grace note to a worrisome adventure.

"You've been very kind, taking care of her," I said on our second day out.

"Small payment to a woman who took care of many of us," he said, turning away.

"Wait, John. Please don't ignore me. I did the same."

"We've gone far beyond that, I would say. I'll never think of you first again as a nurse."

"Nor I you as only a wounded soldier. Ever again."

He turned back at that bold statement and matched his questioning gaze with mine.

"She's confirmed her father's letter, am I right?"

My gaze faltered, but there was no recourse but to nod assent.

"So. It is as I expected. Ah, Susan, don't look anguished. You are so at war with yourself." Unexpectedly he stepped forward and kissed my forehead; the brush of a feather.

And so I dreamed, relishing small moments from each grueling day. From Savannah we took a riverboat to Augusta, then a train west to Atlanta, southeast to Macon, and finally, southwest to Andersonville. We endured heat, delays, roiling waters, everything. I thought we would never arrive. The entire trip, with delays and ruined rail lines to circumvent, took us seventeen days.

Andersonville. The name still strikes a hollow chord in my heart. What could have prepared us for what we found?

The first thing that struck me as I stepped onto the railroad platform was the vast emptiness of this forlorn outpost. Before me was a rickety structure of rotting wood that passed for a station, built indifferently to shelter travelers; beyond that, a lonely, heavily wooded stretch of land that promised frightening isolation. Oh, there was activity and noise, to be sure—shouting voices and grunting workers unloading supplies and the clatter of horse hooves—but underneath it all was the unsettling stillness of a brooding land.

I glanced at John. His face had grown pale, and he seemed to be steadying himself. He turned to Clara.

"The cemetery, first," he said quietly.

She nodded.

"Miss Barton?"

We turned to see an earnest man with a sallow, worn face approaching us. He thrust out his hand.

"William Griffin, ma'am, superintendent of Andersonville. At your service."

"How do you do, sir. Can you take us to the cemetery before we set up camp?" she asked, ignoring Captain Moore as he strode the platform, bellowing out orders to the workers.

"Hoped that's what you'd ask," he said. The three of us climbed into his waiting cart and headed off, traveling up a dirt road past a huge, square structure of pine logs—the Stockade, I learned later—and onto a wide plain surrounded by spindly, anemic pine trees.

I looked out upon long columns of ragged, molded earth, each marked with a series of fragile wooden sticks. "The graves," I whispered.

Griffin nodded. "A barren, forsaken place," he said apologetically, "and I thank God you all are here to change that."

Only later did I discover that shortly before our arrival, Griffin and his crew had found pigs and dogs rooting out the shallowly buried bodies, chewing on the hands and feet of the dead.

I followed slowly behind John as he strode silently into the graveyard, shoulders hunched forward, looking only to the ground. Sons, husbands, brothers—all lay buried in trenches, no caskets; one hundred to one hundred and fifty bodies in each hole. To find anyone? To identify what was once a living man? Hopeless. The enormity of what John had set out to do struck me full for the first time.

"I'm told you're the one who recorded the dead lying here," Griffin said to John when we walked back to the cart. "My hat is off to you, sir."

John smiled at the man, a smile of such sadness I could hardly bear the sight. "This graveyard holds more men than died in some of our worst battles," he said.

"I know, sir." Griffin said quietly.

"Such tragic waste," blurted Clara.

Griffin said nothing, he simply removed his hat and bowed his head.

"Nobody quite believes it, ma'am," he finally said.

Moore's men were hard at work establishing our camp when we arrived back at the Stockade, and interested in little more than mocking our presence. The workmen made a few jokes as we approached, sniggering behind their hands at the prospect of two women sleeping on the ground under flimsy canvas. It all seemed so mundane and stupid after what we had just experienced.

"Don't you worry, Susan," Clara muttered. "I'm good at this. We'll do fine."

The work was brutal. Captain Moore's dislike of us all deepened, even as white headboards were nailed together and lettered with the identifications from John's death register, then placed in the ground. He and John exchanged sharp words a few times, and John took to standing by each grave as the men worked, checking and rechecking the markings for accuracy.

"So you don't think I know my business?" Moore snapped at him.

"There's no room for mistakes, Captain. That's why I'm here."

Moore let him alone, then.

I waited several days before exploring the Stockade, unsure of how much I wanted to see. I knew the bare statistics of its terror—at one point, thirty-five thousand men had been crammed without shelter or adequate food into its sixteen acres. That was enough for the imagination.

I made my solitary pilgrimage late one afternoon, walking into the Stockade, staring up at walls built of thick pine logs fifteen feet high. I spied the sentry boxes, trying to imagine the Georgia soldiers up there training their guns on the broken, emaciated prisoners below, many of them clad only in shreds and tortured by vermin. Walking farther in, I saw a small, sluggish creek cutting through the structure.

"I've got some good stories about that creek."

I started at the sound of John's voice behind me. I turned and saw him watching me, his face haggard, his shabby jacket hanging ever more loosely from his body.

"I'm trying to envision what you suffered," I said.

"Well, welcome to my old home," he said, in the tone of a master of the house greeting a guest. "Would you like a little run-through on our exciting lives in this place? The Rebs up there"—he pointed to the sentry boxes at the top of the wall—"used to get bored with guarding us. We could tell when they were getting restless for supper or tiring of scratching mosquito bites. First they'd complain. Then we'd hear them joking with each other and we'd try to press back against the walls, but there were too many of us. They'd start taking bets on who was the better shot, and they'd choose which one of us to aim for. They won more money if they got us in the legs, but nobody minded too much when they exploded a head here and there."

John stepped to the very center of the stockade and turned slowly, taking in every inch of this space he knew too well. The mock welcoming tone was gone.

"Strange to be the only man standing here," he said. He seemed in some strange reverie. "Captain Wirz liked putting men in the stocks. You'd stand there with your feet manacled and your head locked between the boards and then be turned around—your face to the sun or the rain or the wind—for days at a time. Men came back to their cells with skin peeled from their faces. I did my time in them."

"Who was Captain Wirz?" I asked.

"A sadistic sonofabitch. Ran the stockade."

"How did you survive?" I whispered.

His footsteps echoed in the empty space, and he seemed to be thinking about my question. He picked up a small rock and, with a lazy looping motion of his arm, threw it with dead accuracy at the nearest sentry box. I heard the ping of the rock echo through the stockade. He smiled with satisfaction.

"Well now. I'm not sure I did."

I moved closer to him. "John, how were you captured?"

"We were facing a Rebel division that surprised us and almost wiped us out. The few of us who survived took to the mountainside as they plundered our tents. After three days with no food, we surrendered. I wonder still if it would have been better to stay free and die in the woods."

I took his hand, holding it to my face, in a gesture that seemed so natural, neither of us spoke. He did not pull away.

"I mentioned the creek," he said, nodding toward the listless thread of brown water I had noticed before. "We drank from it, we bathed in it, and we got sick from it. See that spot?" He pointed to a patch of ground. "That was the Dead Line. Orders were, anybody who reached beyond it was shot on sight. But right over there"—he pointed toward the Stockade wall—"was where the creek came in. The only chance to get any reasonably clean water was to reach past the Dead Line and try to fill a cup while the guards weren't looking. At least one man a day was shot trying to sneak a tinful. You had to be desperate. And most of us were."

My voice shook. "It must have been terrible."

"I survived. Susan . . . I can't talk about it anymore. First time I ever have. You do have a kind ear." He smiled, took my hand and kissed it lightly. Together we walked out of the stockade, silently surveying the surrounding countryside. It felt less oppressive to me now.

"The colors are beautiful, aren't they? They remind me of a quilt." I scooped up a handful of earth. "See? It's brown, but so many shades of brown."

"I still see a battlefield," John replied. "Those red flowers? Blood. The yellow ones? Faces of men about to die."

I groped for words. "There is beauty, John. We need it, and it is here; we need to see it to survive."

"That's your job, Susan," he said gently. "Thank God you have the soul and the eye for it." He put his arm around my shoulder, and I allowed myself to rest within the curve of his elbow, calm, and no longer unsure.

Typhoid hit our camp in August. Clara and I were pressed into duty as nurses, once more packing wet rags around the faces of fevered men and doing what we could to hasten healing. Moore needed us now, and grudgingly gave us more respect, which helped calm the tension in the air. But nothing improved the tension between Moore and John, for John made no effort to hide his contempt for that strutting bully of a man.

Within days the outbreak subsided, with only one worker lost. Immersed in work, I had not visited the cemetery for over a week. I pulled off my grimy apron one afternoon and tramped out to see the progress, gasping with amazement at how much had been done. The white headboards, not all up yet, stretched across the field in orderly lines. Where before there had been barren anonymity, now there was recognition. Identity. Distinction. Along the periphery, Moore's men were laying out streets and walkways. Most impressive of all was a newly constructed wooden arch above the entrance to the once-faceless field of death. It read: *National Cemetery, Andersonville, Georgia.* The sight of it was thrilling. John made this possible, I told myself. John and Clara.

By August 17 the cemetery was completed. We dressed hurriedly for the official flag-raising ceremony, trying to look respectable after so long a time of living in a tent. Clara was cross; she had two buttons missing off her best bodice and it was too hot to cover up with a shawl. I hunted for a needle and thread and tore two buttons off a nightshift and quickly sewed them on. They didn't match, which caused more fuss. By now I was irritated, too. I began throwing our garments into Clara's trunk for the voyage home.

But when we reached the cemetery, we fell silent. The sight was magnificent. Finished. Complete. Before our eyes were row upon row of white tablets, stretched across the entire site, all marked with the names of men finally honored in death. A stillness hung soft above us, and I heard but a lone bird sing.

"We *are* in a cathedral," I whispered to Clara.

She nodded. "Look," she said, pointing.

Coming in under the proud new arch were clusters of people. As we walked closer, we saw government officials, people from neighboring towns, and even a cluster of reporters carrying note-books and cameras.

"I recognize some of them," Clara said, her eyes lighting up. "They've come all the way from Washington."

Captain Moore strutted through the crowd, stopping here and there to answer eager questions, clearly considering himself the man of the hour. Standing off to one side was John, hands in his pockets, as obscure as a common workman but for the sardonic smile on his face. We were not done with Moore, I sensed. That feeling grew as he strode up to Clara, his smile fixed in full view of the waiting crowd.

"Miss Barton," Moore said, with a deep bow. "Will you do us the honor of raising the colors?"

Clara's hand flew to her breast in astonishment, but she quickly recovered. Whatever Moore's motives, this was an honor she could not refuse. "Certainly, Captain Moore," she said. Taking a deep breath, she walked slowly to the flagpole where a soldier stood poised to hand her the flag.

A breeze lifted from the earth, a breeze filled with whispers. Clara attached the flag and raised it high. As it unfurled gloriously over that sacred place, we all—townspeople, reporters, soldiers, the men who had planted the grave markers and built the paths—sang "The Star-Spangled Banner."

The horrors of Andersonville had been quelled at last. No, not quelled, contained. I wished Tom could be here. He had so wanted to be.

Clara walked back to stand next to me as the last words of the song were caught by the breeze and taken into the surrounding pine groves.

"I raised it with my own hands," she said, her voice trembling. "I ought to be satisfied. I believe I am."

Late that night, unable to sleep, I pulled on my cloak and walked out to view the cemetery in the moonlight. We were breaking camp in the morning, packing up for the long voyage home. How hard it was to leave, I thought, as I gazed out onto the silent rows of white markers. Did the dead rest easier now? Did they need us anymore?

A voice broke my reverie. "So you can't pull away either."

It was John. He sat on a rock by the cemetery arch, jacketless, his face both softened and illuminated by the moon, his eyes in shadow.

"I had to see it one more time, in the moonlight," I said.

"In the moonlight?" He smiled. "Moonlight softens and deceives."

"It's honest light, sunshine at secondhand. Anyhow, you're here, too."

"That's because I don't know if I can leave at all. They were my friends. Share this with me?" He held up a bottle of Mr. Tufft's Blackberry Brandy and grinned. "Or is that too wicked a temptation?"

"Not at all, for I'm not a teetotaler." I sat down next to him, comforted by the intimacy of the night. He passed me the bottle, and I took a long gulp before passing it back. The liquid was sweet and soothing. It made me brave. "Why do you say you're not sure you can leave?"

"Nowhere else feels real. I thought coming here might help put memories of the war behind me, but it doesn't." He pushed at a rock with his foot, and a tiny lizard darted away from the ground beneath.

"They may never go away, John. Mine haven't."

"Do you have nightmares?"

"Yes."

"Tell me one."

I hesitated for a moment. "I dream I'm running through a field carrying a severed leg and I'm desperate to throw it away, but I can't. I can't let it go."

"I dream of being underground with those fellows," John said, nodding toward the graves. "With dirt in my eyes and mouth, trying to breathe."

"You're here, not there. And I'm here, not running through a field with a severed leg."

He took my hand with great gentleness. "You have a sturdy spirit, Susan. Do you know that? And I owe you something."

"What do you mean?" I thrilled to the pressure of his fingers cradling my hand.

"Sulie was my mother's maiden name, so, you see, there is an authentic John Sulie. He was not made up."

"I know that. I know my John Sulie."

He drew his hand back. "I must tell you, you shouldn't waste time on me. I'm not worth it."

"It's too late for that." I tried to laugh.

"My dear." He sighed with such force, his body seemed to deflate. "Susan, Susan, I am a chameleon. I've lived in the skin of too many fabrications to know myself what is real anymore."

"You cannot be both real and false, John. And the man who held the drummer boy in his arms during his last night on earth was not a fabrication. He was real."

He sat still for so long, the lizard, encouraged, moved slowly back to the rock and tucked himself underneath.

"I've worn too many guises," he said, finally. "There's no more blending into the landscape. This place"—with a sweep of his hand he took in the cemetery—"is home."

"Not the cemetery," I protested.

"All of it. Can't separate it out." He slapped his foot down in the dirt, scaring the lizard once again. "I've decided to move on west as soon as the death register is published. I'll have done one noble thing, and one is all any man can hope for in times like these."

"No, no." I sat up straight. "You can't do that. I won't let you go."

He smiled. "You have a fine way of hurling yourself into your emotions; I wish I could match it."

"You do, I can feel it coming from you," I implored. "John, don't leave me."

He seemed to consider my words, not answering immediately. "I've thought about this, Susan," he finally said. "I want to match your feelings, but I'm not much of a man anymore. You've found yourself a pale ghost, dear. You're living a fantasy."

"That's absurd!" I cried. "How can you leave? I've just found you! And Louisa . . . she never stopped loving you through all your time in this terrible place, do you understand? And now you want to turn your back on both of us?" I raised my hand in a sudden fury, wanting to grab him, shake him, make him understand.

He caught my hand and jerked it down, hard enough to make me wince. "Don't mention Louisa to me, ever again. Do you understand, Susan?" His face was now almost touching mine. "Keep it where it truly is. Can we agree on that?"

"Yes," I whispered.

"Good girl." I felt his breath on my forehead as he kissed the tears on my cheeks. I knew I should draw away, but my body would not move.

Instead I cupped his face with my hands and kissed him on the lips. It was a shameless kiss, without subterfuge or excuse. I knew what I wanted. There would be no giggles or fluttery fans or courtship dances for me. When he pulled my head to his chest, raising his arm to encircle my shoulders, I spied under his rolled-up shirtsleeve the scar left by Lyndon's knife—still vivid, still angry. A mottled mass of red, ugly skin. It was warm to the touch and, without thought, I kissed it, too. Lyndon's knife was the reason John still lived. My conscience told me otherwise: No, Louisa's courage was responsible for purging that wound. No thoughts now, no. She could have been here; she chose not to be. My willful spirit would not be denied, though I felt myself hurtling into the deepest and darkest of pits. Exhilarated.

His hands reached under my skirt and moved up my legs, pulling at my ribbon garters; tugging urgently at my drawers. What took me over? All shame was gone. I exulted.

"Susan," he groaned. "Let me hold you."

When he pulled me to his lap, I lifted my hips, moved my left leg across his body and pressed close. I heard his sharp exclamation of surprise as I straddled him full, and then, moving in unison with him, only seconds later—was there time involved at all?— rejoicing in a wet, slippery hardness that instantly, smoothly satisfied the deepest hunger I had ever known.

"Susan—"

"Don't talk," I whispered. For this brief moment, I owned him. I could not pull away. I could not have been dragged away.

"I'm sorry," he said again, stroking my hair.

I lifted my face to his and slowly kissed him one last time, holding back the fears and contradictions of my soul for as long as I could. "Well, I'm not," I said.

I pulled away then and ran back to the tent, my demons in full pursuit.

Chapter Sixteen

The weather on the water journey home was most foul. I could think of nothing but John, even as I clutched the rail and tried to focus on the horizon to quiet my stomach. All order and discipline in my brain had evaporated. I found it almost impossible to tear myself from my memories of that last night at Andersonville, even while Clara was analyzing our trip and planning future strategy.

"Susan, you are not paying attention," she said the second day out, as the ship reeled and pitched, leaving us both grabbing for balance in her cabin.

"I'm sorry," I said.

"I can't tolerate any daydreaming, we have too much at stake." Clara huddled deeper into her berth, legs pulled to her chest, moaning as the ship heaved and pitched. I grabbed a pan I had taken from the ship's mess and put it by her head as she began to retch.

She waved me away when she was finished. "Go, go out on deck and get some fresh air, and while you're there, ask John Sulie if Captain Moore has given him back the death register. It is his property, not Moore's. I don't trust him."

I was only too happy to leave the sour, stagnant air of her cabin and came up on deck, breathing deeply, clutching whatever stable form presented itself, holding on finally to the ship's railing as the sea boiled beneath me, splashing salt spray up onto my hands and face. I shut my eyes against the sting.

"You look like someone dipped you into the sea," I heard a voice say.

I squinted upward at John.

"Are you all right?" he asked.

"Yes," I said, blinking away the salt and looking him square in the eye.

His eyebrows drew together in a worried frown. He started to speak, but the ship took a sudden, pitching lurch downward. He caught me around the waist and we clung together for a moment, drenched in seawater. If the ship sinks at this moment, I told myself, coughing, I will have died content.

"I love you," I said, clinging to his arms.

"Ah, Susan——" He pulled me close as two sailors walking by glanced at us with more than ordinary curiosity. One of them whispered something to the other, and the two of them broke into ribald laughter.

John stepped back from me. "No use in giving our esteemed captain more ammunition," he muttered.

"Why would he care about us?" I demanded.

"It's not us, it's me. He's still got my death register."

"Clara is worried about it."

"Tell her not to worry, I know what is at stake." He glanced around. "I'm more concerned right now about you. I lost control. Please forgive me."

"I told you, I am not sorry." Brave words, harder to repeat in the light of day.

He gave me a quick, amused smile. "Amazing what is inside that proper Concord soul of yours, Susan. But I doubt you will continue to feel that way."

"I love you, I've told you that."

He did not immediately respond. For a long moment I concentrated on the sound of the ship's flag snapping back and forth in the wind, growing increasingly nervous. I felt a hot flush spreading up my throat.

"I'm not sure I'm capable of love anymore. I've tried to tell you that. You are a passionate, stalwart woman, and I wish I were worthy of you," he finally said.

"You are telling me you can't love me."

"Susan . . ."

I felt the sting of tears and backed away. "I need no placating words from you. Just go away. Go."

"I didn't say——" He sighed. "Never mind, I will do as you ask, for now. It's best we not be seen together again on this ship, any-way. Stay watchful." Bending down, he laid a gentle kiss on my ear and was gone. I listened for his footsteps, but all I could hear were waves lapping up against the side of the boat.

"Has he got it back yet?" Clara demanded as I made my way back into her fetid chamber.

"No, not yet."

"For heaven's sake, it's John's property. Establishing the ceme-tery is all well and good, but it is the publication of the names that matters—that's the missing link, the necessary thing to make the nature of our work understood. John must demand it! Oh, how I hate this wretched trip!"

I soothed her as I emptied the contents of her slop basin yet again. "He says all will be well," I answered.

"He doesn't worry enough," she snorted. "Moore doesn't want to give the list of the dead back to him; I can sense it. You know it, too. Why do men think everything is all right until it is too late? I'm going to talk to John myself."

I felt a tremor, worried now. "He said to be watchful. Moore stays hostile."

"Except, of course, when he tried to mollify me by giving me the honor of raising the flag," Clara said. "What flattery comes next? Nothing they try is going to dissuade me. Go, Susan, get some rest. How fortunate you are not to be plagued with this con-stant sickness." She moaned, her voice fading. "The names have such power. Just the names. There is no greater memorial than that. Moore, Stanton—they're all afraid of what publication might unleash."

I tiptoed out, pulling the door shut, and leaned against the wall, closing my eyes. In the days that followed, it was hard to keep my mind on the death register. Hurt by his reticence, I had pushed John away with my usual impulsiveness. Had I reacted too hastily? The next moment I would be scolding myself for my wanton behavior, and immediately after, aching to straddle him again. Then, whispering thoughts: Why had it not hurt? It was supposed to hurt, that's what other women said. It had been my first time, and I yearned for more. Was I a loose woman? And then with a lurch of the stomach worse than any Clara was enduring, my thoughts would turn to Louisa. Even though she had given him up, had I betrayed her again? I would think of our days together, our confidences, our loyalty to each other. She didn't want to take this risk of love, I told myself. Did that make it any more acceptable that I had snatched it instead? Round and round my thoughts would go, giving me little rest.

What can I say of that terrible voyage? The sea calmed during the last few days, and I paced daily, fretful, searching for John. Hope refused to be quelled. I kept repeating to myself his words "for now."

But when I did see him, I shrank back. He stood on the deck in a scornful stance, hair flying in the wind, hands jammed into his pockets. Facing him was that banty rooster, Captain Moore, huge veins bulging from his forehead.

"You're a thief, Moore," he shouted. "And you won't get away with it."

"A thief, eh? You think so? You're a sniveling excuse of a soldier, Atwater, and nothing you've got to say will matter! I've got it, and I'm keeping it!" Moore turned and stomped away.

John didn't see me as he, too, turned and strode in the opposite direction. But I caught a clear glimpse of the anger in his face, and it was frightening, for I was seeing a part of John I had not seen before.

The day we steamed into port was sticky hot. I dressed in a hurry, hardly able to bear either the smell of my clothes or Clara's complaining, and carried our bags up to the deck for unloading.

There was much shouting and running about as we inched into our waiting slip. I watched as some of the crew jumped out with tethering ropes and swiftly looped them over the iron hooks on the dock. The boat shuddered to a halt.

John materialized at my side, standing so close I felt my legs weaken. He spoke quickly in a strained voice. "Susan, there really isn't much time now to answer your questions—some of them, anyhow. I was a contraband merchant, selling gun caps, ammunition, and quinine to the Rebels. Working as a spy for Allan Pinkerton when I wasn't on the battlefield. Good man; did a lot for the Union. I owe you that information. In another life——" He stopped, then went on. "I owe you more, but there's no time." I felt his breath on my hair. "Susan, I won't compromise you."

I turned to speak. But at that moment Captain Moore appeared on the upper deck, dressed in full uniform, thick medals catching the glint of the sun. He saw us. A slow, lazy smile spread across his face. I marveled at his shiny teeth, which caught almost as much sparkle from the sun as his medals.

"Ah, here it comes," John said, quite calmly. Puzzled, I opened my mouth to ask what he meant.

What will I remember? The wind catching his hair, curling it forward over his eyes, almost giving him the appearance of a boy. The quick, tender look he cast me. Was he conveying love? Or pity? Most of all, I remember his closeness. I will go to my grave knowing I was fully capable at that moment of wrapping my arms around him with no concern for compromising my integrity. I was capable of flinging away all.

Captain Moore glanced away from us to the dock. I saw a small band of soldiers in Union blue preparing to board our ship. "That's the man, gentlemen," Moore shouted out in his best thundering tone, pointing directly at John. "Now goddamn it, do your duty."

"What do you think you are doing?" Clara's shrill, astonished voice pierced the air as she burst onto the deck from the boiler room stairs, spied the soldiers, and lifted her face to address Captain Moore.

"It's none of your concern, Miss Barton," said Moore. "Ladies, kindly step aside."

The soldiers clambered onto the deck. I reached for John's hand, but touched only his fingers before feeling them slide away. A soldier with pistol drawn grabbed him by the shoulder and shoved him toward the others.

"This is absurd! What is the charge?" Clara demanded.

"Theft," spat Moore. "This man has stolen government property."

"What are you talking about?" she yelled back.

Captain Moore gazed on her with the wonderment of the sane for the daft. "The list of the dead, of course," he said. "He stole it from my cabin, and that constitutes larceny. And nobody on my watch gets away with that."

My glance went swiftly from John to Clara. And what did I see? Stony resignation on John's face. On Clara's? Something else besides anger. For a moment I was puzzled. But when I realized I saw guilt, I clutched the rail tightly for balance, and then stood there helplessly, watching them take John away.

"I'm sorry." Clara whispered the words in the dark. It was nightfall, and we were climbing the stairs to her apartment on Seventh Street. "I should have dissuaded him, but he was determined to get it back."

I waited.

"Nothing would have changed his mind, Susan. Remember, it *was* his property."

I did not trust myself to speak. I wasn't going to accept her righteous indignation.

"You are angry with me," she said.

"Of course I am. You could have urged caution. I cannot believe you were so, so——"

"Arrogant."

"Yes."

Clara sighed. "Susan, I promise you, I will get him freed. I've got good friends at the War Department. Moore is jealous of me and doesn't want to share credit for establishing the cemetery, that's why this is happening. It's all political, do you understand? There's no way they can keep John on such trumped-up charges."

"He told me he was a Union spy, selling contraband goods to the Rebels. Did you know that?"

She averted her eyes. "Yes. He told me at Union Hospital."

"Why didn't you tell *me?*"

"Because he felt he had enemies on the ward. He wanted one person to know the truth. Susan, I couldn't tell you. I promised him I would tell no one. He didn't want to compromise you or Louisa. I thought when he reappeared, he would tell you himself."

"So now you've compromised *him.*"

"He made the decision to get it himself, all I did was agree. Can we put this behind us and concentrate on making things right?" We were on the landing now. She reached into her pocketbook and pulled out a key, shoved it into the lock and pushed the door open, brushing ahead of me without another word.

I followed her inside, determined not to be made apologetic for my anger. I knew John had done it on his own, but I wanted to believe she could have stopped him. I cared about the death list, but I cared more about what now might happen to John. She knew this. As I stepped over the threshold I spied a letter on the floor and stooped to pick it up. The handwriting jolted me back to the life I had left behind. Louisa.

> *Dearest Susan,*
> *I have been a fool. I am afraid, but I want to come. You were right, how can I hold back? Tell me when to come, I am poised to try.*
> *Love,*
> *Louisa*

I clutched the letter, tears squeezing through my shut eyelids. Oh, Lou, you changed your mind, too late, too late. What had I done? I had robbed her, as surely as if I had snatched her most precious possession. My dearest friend.

"For heaven's sake——" Clara rushed to where I sat in a heap and put her arms around me. I handed her the letter without a word. And Clara, that dear, cranky, energetic, bossy, wise woman, knew all. She held me in her arms, crooning, saying nothing. Only later, after she had forced me to drink some tea, did I tell her the whole story. She nodded slowly, then took my hand. "Louisa had her moment and she let it pass her by," she said.

Would that it were so clear, I thought. I remembered again the look of hope in John's eyes and how it faded when Louisa didn't come. In my heart I believed he would welcome the reversal of her choice. Or would he?

> Dear Louisa,
> John has been arrested and will be tried for theft. We are not allowed to see or communicate with him, which is dreadful. It is a shocking act by deceitful men and we will get him freed. There is more to tell, but we are just now back from Andersonville. I will write again, soon.
>
> > Susan

John was taken to the guardhouse near the War Department, and was transferred to Old Capitol Prison two days later.

"My God," exploded Tom, when he heard that news. "That's where Henry Wirz is. I can't believe it. Captain Wirz is being tried for the murders of thirteen thousand men at Andersonville, and John is being court-martialed for wanting to publish their names. The government is insane."

The trial lasted two days. Colonel Samuel Breck, to whom John had originally brought the death roll, testified the government had the right to seize the document without compensation. Captain Moore declared on the stand that he, as head of the Andersonville expedition, had been entitled to full control over all documents relating to the marking of the graves. The man known as Dorrance Atwater had stolen those documents, probably influenced by "unwise advisers." Heads nodded; no one challenged his assertion.

When the final witness was called, we were in the hallway outside and close enough to hear the name shouted out in the reedy tones of the court bailiff.

"Mrs. Belle Poole, please come forward."

My eyes began to blur. "No," I whispered.

Her testimony galvanized the courtroom, stifling the ordinary hum of whispers and gossip. A terrible man, one who stole from the dying, she declared on the stand. More than that, there was good reason to suspect he had served as a spy for the Confederacy. Gasps greeted this accusation. How fitting that he would be accused once again of stealing. How fitting that he—although it could not be proved, but then that wasn't what he was on trial for, but everyone in the hospital suspected—would be capable of betraying his country.

John refused to call any witnesses on his own behalf. He presented the court with a statement declaring the death rolls belonged to him, and he would do no more.

"Why not?" I demanded when Clara, who found out through a friend of hers at the courthouse, gave me that news.

"He says his doom is sealed, and he knows it. He's very calm, but my friend said he will tell them nothing else."

No one came forward to defend John. Only those government officials who knew his true work in the war could have saved him, but this was no ordinary trial. We tried to be heard, but our attempts to speak up were diverted quickly. With increasing horror, we realized John was right: This was not a trial, it was a choreographed farce. The government had no intention of admitting it traded contraband goods with the Confederacy for intelligence. That raised too many questions.

"He's a lost man," Clara said.

I could do nothing but nod.

John was convicted with stunning speed. He was dishonorably

discharged and sentenced to eighteen months in prison. Clara and I stood outside the courthouse as he was led away in irons through the streets of Washington to the train station, to be taken to Auburn Prison in New York. We were not allowed to talk to him.

"This is terrible, terrible," Clara moaned, wringing her hands.

"He can't survive prison again, it's not possible," I mumbled to myself. I caught a glimpse at that moment of a haggard-looking woman mincing down the courthouse steps, attempting to control an unfamiliar hoop under her faded gray muslin skirt. It was my first unobstructed view of Belle Poole. She looked much older, and chewed nervously on her thin lower lip as she descended to the street. It came as no surprise when we found out later that she had struck a bargain with the prosecutor—her early release from prison on theft charges in exchange for testifying against John. But at the moment I saw her, she saw me. I froze at the triumph in her eyes. She had won, and was savoring her moment.

I tried to stand upright, but faces were blurring and I felt sweat break out on my forehead. I swayed. The rumbling wheels of the cart carrying John and his guards had barely faded away when I slumped against Clara, unable to stand. I was only vaguely aware of her staggering to hold me up.

I lay in bed, a wet towel over my eyes. Clara had hailed a carriage for the trip home and enlisted Liddy to help me up the stairs. Now all I wanted was to lie there and drift; thinking nothing. Feeling nothing. I felt a desire to die.

Clara's voice seemed to emerge from fog. "Have you been having your monthlies?" she said quietly.

"No."

Her breathing remained regular. No cry of repulsion or alarm.

"I'll fix you some hot tea, dear."

I felt a rush of gratitude, finally venturing a response: "I'm frightened."

She didn't respond immediately, and when she did, her voice sounded very tired. "Your sin was one of the flesh, Susan, and mine was of pride. I'm the one who could have moved John from harm's way. My sin is worse."

"I don't know what to do." I couldn't straighten out my thoughts. Who was I, inured now to the weeping of barren women, virtuous in marriage, hoping to conceive? I tossed and raged. Unfair. Why to me? Why not to one of those proper ladies of Concord sniffing into their handkerchiefs about their private deprivation?

"You could try to expel it. I know someone who works with wire and salts. But many women die, I must tell you, and I do not advise you to try."

"I know."

"Perhaps this is your ultimate test of fortitude. Perhaps good will come of it."

This time it was I who reached out to comfort her. With a touch, no words.

Only later did I learn that Clara had been struck from the registers of the Patent Office that very day, and now had no income at all. The new secretary of the interior was trying to purge as many women as possible from government positions, and Clara's absence had made her an easy target. I learned this finally from Tom Cassidy, a week later, as he sat next to me on a bench in Lafayette Park. He had coaxed me to the park to share some country peaches and nuts at noontime. The leaves of the trees surrounding us rustled in the wind, cooling the pretty space that had become one of my favorite spots in Washington. Nursemaids pushing perambulators chattered away together, craning their heads to see if they could get a glimpse of President Andrew Johnson's wife walking the grounds of the White House across the street. She was wont to do so, in those first chaotic months of her husband's presidency. Wringing her hands constantly, whispered some. And yet the park was a peaceful spot, and I soon realized Tom had chosen it as our destination with deliberate intention.

"Susan Gray, you are a fine woman," he began, with a certain sturdy formality. He looked suddenly very young. His left hand rose in what was a habitual nervous movement, plucking at the coarse cloth of the jacket covering the stump of his right arm. "This may sound abrupt. But you would do me a great honor if you would become my wife."

My eyes opened wide with astonishment. "Tom, what are you saying?" I asked. "We are not . . . not . . ."

"Not romantically attached, I know." His eyes searched mine. "But you are my friend, and your friends will not abandon you."

I flushed. "You know?"

"Yes. Liddy and I guessed pretty quick what was going on. And Clara is very concerned. She's selling some of her assets, you know."

"Why?"

"She lost her job. Didn't she tell you?"

My eyes filled with tears. "No, she's kept that secret."

"Well, I've got employment, and I can offer you steadfast friendship. And legitimacy for your child." His gaze never wavered.

What a good and kind man he was, I thought. As plain and straightforward as a Quaker, with no pretense or sham. I reached for his hand, once again clasping it with both of mine. "I thank you, Tom Cassidy. I know you've thought this little speech through. I can hear the rehearsing in your voice. But I can't marry you, it wouldn't be fair."

"You're waiting for John, aren't you." It was a flat statement, not a question.

Was I? I didn't know myself. I saw no clear route. I had no idea what to do. One thing only was clear to me. With more urgency than ever before, I had to make a decision that was truly mine. What did I want? To kill my baby? No. Would I ever be able to go back to Concord with a child? My lips went dry at the thought of the shock and reproach in the eyes of the Alcotts and all my friends. Tom was offering me a way out, an honorable way. But I could not take it. Underneath everything, the hope remained: If John was released, perhaps we would be together . . . with our child.

"Tom, I can't marry you. Thank you, I'm honored and grateful. I don't know what I'm going to do, but I cannot marry you."

He drew back, his face falling. His obvious disappointment wrenched my heart.

I went to the bank the next day and sent for a good portion of the small inheritance my parents had left me and gave it to Clara when it arrived. She was very surprised. "Why are you giving this to me?" she asked. "I'm supposed to be paying you for your work, and will again when I get some money coming in." I sensed her assessing me, searching my face as if she were searching for the green, nervous girl I had been the first night we had met.

"I want to strike a bargain. You use my money if I can stay with you here," I began.

"My goodness, you could stay with me if you were a pauper!" she said, sniffing her indignation. "Did you doubt that?"

I smiled, the first smile I had been able to muster in weeks, and shook my head. "No," I said.

My modest funds helped us regain our momentum. Some thirty-five hundred letters had piled up in sacks and boxes that filled the front hall and cried out for answering. With Liddy's help, we fell to work, spurred by Clara's declaration that here, in this hall, was "the coinage of aching hearts." She herself moved about town with a frenzied pace, buttonholing officials and presenting petitions in her effort not only to win John's release but to get the government funds she needed to continue her work. We tried to get access to John, but he was allowed no further visitors. The government seemed determined to erase his very existence.

Clara sat very still at the other side of the room, studying me as I sewed for the baby, my habit now when the day's work was done. I bent close to the soft cloth, wanting each stitch to be perfect. If I could give my child nothing else, I vowed, it would be a fine christening robe. And I would trim it with the lace snipped from the bodice of my brown silk gown.

"Susan, you have to make some decisions," she began.

"I know."

"You aren't going to marry Tom, I can see that."

"It's not right. We don't love each other."

"That's either brave or foolhardy, dear. I don't know which to call it. Do you want me to look into finding a family to take the baby?"

I folded my hands across my bulging stomach, feeling surprisingly calm. I had thought about this for weeks. And I knew what I wanted to do, right or wrong. "No, I can't bear the thought of giving it away. And I will find a way to support us both."

"Ah, my dear, perhaps I've taught you independence too well," Clara said with a sigh. She did not begin to lay out all the problems my decision implied. She made no arguments. She simply stood, smoothed down her dress, and prepared to fix dinner.

Later, as we prepared for bed, she stood at the door of my room in her muslin nightgown, holding a sputtering candle. "Susan?"

"Yes?"

"You'll always have a home here."

"Thank you," I said, feeling a deep rush of affection for this woman I had grown to love.

She blew out the candle and padded away in her bare feet in the darkness.

On December 1, Clara came stomping up the stairs and threw down in front of me a copy of the *Washington Chronicle*. "Take a look at this," she said. Her hand was shaking as she pointed to the announcement.

I quickly read.

Major J. M. Moore, Chief of the United States Burial Bureau, has prepared a report of the number of deaths and burials of the soldiers of the Union which he will soon release to a grateful public.

"MAJOR Moore, do you see that?" sputtered Clara. "He's been promoted! This wily, mean, jealous man would deprive John of the honor he has due him and——"

"And deprive you of the government money you've been promised," I finished.

"Yes. Do you see, Susan? I was right. Moore was plotting all along to take all the credit. He is depriving our work of all meaning. I am done, ruined." Her head sank into her hands. Liddy and I embraced her, but Clara was not to be consoled.

The weeks passed, with no good news. The list was not released, which surprised us not a whit. Moore and the government would stall as long as they could, and most likely would never release the death register. The details of actual names were too specific. The truth was so clear: Moore was to be given full acclaim for the grand duty of establishing the Andersonville Cemetery, making it easier for the government to avoid blame for the hideous delay in releasing to the country an honest accounting of the dead. There was no desire to count. The country was comforted by the government's hazy act of closure, although not the mothers and wives of the men who died. It wasn't the count they cared about, it was one boy or one man.

Moore might have succeeded. So much was hidden and passed over in those scrambled days following the end of the war. But one event changed everything.

I try many times to close my eyes and will myself into the scene as it unfolded, as if by so doing I could change the outcome. On one bitter cold night in January, John fashioned a noose from the bedding in his cell, slipped his head through it, and stepped off the iron cot he had positioned under a lantern ceiling hook. How long he hung there I do not know, but when he was found by a guard, life was gone.

Found in his cell was a painstakingly prepared copy of his death register, complete to the final name. John had added an account of his harrowing experience at Andersonville, his struggle to convince the War Department the graves of the dead should be marked and their names published, his court-martial and his imprisonment. It was a meticulous, devastating chronicle. The sympathetic guard, who knew what John was doing, delivered it quickly to Clara before it could be found by prison officials. We learned from him that John had managed on the boat to copy the original he had taken from Captain Moore. But his gnarled fingers must have made the task more laborious than he expected, for he had run out of time for slipping the original back in Moore's trunk.

John had never given up, I realized. He had made a plan and almost carried it off. It was prison that defeated him, not Belle Poole or Captain Moore. The black, deep pain of what he had seen and experienced at Andersonville could not be held back. I tried to visualize his final night. He must have finished his explanation of what he had chosen to do, put down his pen, and wondered what indeed could come next. He had accomplished the "one noble thing" he spoke of so yearningly to me that last night in Andersonville. And then he had let go.

10 January 1866

Dearest Louisa,

I bring you news so sad, I can hardly pull the words from my pen. John was found yesterday hanging in his cell. You know from my prior letters what a fraud his trial was, and how resigned to his fate he had become. Clara had all but wrung a promise from the War Department to release him, but the hope came too late. This brave man we both loved survived the cruelties of the enemy, but he could not take the cruelties of his own government, so shamefully aligned with the likes of Belle Poole. My heart is heavy. The sorrow is too much to bear, truly beyond endurance. He is gone.

I posted the letter to yet another address in Europe, changing not a word, not caring what it might reveal.

4 February 1866
Nice

Dear Susan,

I took myself to an old monastery near the ruins of a temple to Diana to read your letter, sensing something terrible had happened. Diana, the goddess of the moon and of love. What irony. I walked then for hours, thinking of all that might have been. I weep for John, for decisions made and not made. Your words tell me your anguish matches my own, indeed, I suspect it holds it's own unique features.

I will try and depart for home this spring. My time is too valuable to be spent in fussing over cushions & carrying shawls, and always was. I see too late what you knew. Susan, how have we distanced from each other? You must go home, too. Leave that place, go to safety.

There was no safety. My belly was quite swollen now.

Clara, Tom, Liddy, and I stood on a small knoll below General Lee's old home, watching silently as John was laid to rest. The day was dull, with heavy, sullen clouds covering the sun. There were no other mourners, only a military chaplain who said but a few hurried prayers before rushing off, as if afraid of being seen. I closed my eyes, concentrating as hard as I could on the baby moving inside me, thinking, At least something of John will survive. Something that might, truly, ease my sense of loss. Perhaps. Please, yes.

The following day Clara took the death register to Horace Greeley, that bombastic man, then publisher of the *New York Tribune*. He pored through the pages, amazed, with Clara eagerly awaiting his decision. Would he publish it? she pressed.

"My dear Miss Barton, of course I will. This is a national document of utmost importance," he said.

Clara came home in happy tears, repeating his words to us over and over. "I have done what little I can to make up for my fool-hardy advice to John," she said.

And so, on February 14, John's list rolled off the presses of the *Tribune* in the form of a seventy-four-page pamphlet. It was headed simply *A List of the Union Soldiers Buried at Andersonville* and included as an introduction the summary John wrote in prison. I wept when I read it. I could hear in his written words the anger and irony that had so marked his life. John had wanted to do something good, and this he had done. He had illuminated the breathtaking cruelty of war: When men who fight become nothing, only pack-ages of bones and blood deposited in the earth with no clarion call to memory, those they love are left without a way to make such devastating loss hold meaning.

What a sensation the pamphlet caused! Huge numbers sold for twenty-five cents each. A letter from a weeping woman was pressed into my hand the day after copies were distributed in Washington. "The pain of knowing what happened to my son is far preferable to the pain of knowing nothing at all," it said in a shaky scrawl. "Dor-rance Atwater is a hero."

Not only was his name heaped with honor, but Clara's, too. Her report on the Andersonville expedition was included in the pamphlet, and Clara was delighted at reports of Moore's bluster-ing anger when he realized he had been outmaneuvered.

"We won," she crowed the night friends came pounding on her door with an armful of copies of the *Tribune*. Her face was flushed with triumph.

How could I not share her fierce delight? We *had* won, and I was thrilled. "This is a tribute to John!" I cried, clapping my hands. And for that one exhilarating moment, I felt cleansed.

During the first week of March, I fancied my baby had quieted to grieve for its father. At night I rubbed my belly with my hands, crooning, feeling for the small thrusts of movement that had come to signify the life inside, life I had begun to love, coaxing it to respond. Gently at first. Then more urgently.

On the third day I asked Clara why the baby wasn't moving. She held her hand to my stomach for a long time, eyes troubled. She had me stay in bed on the fourth day. I slept and dreamed, and awoke every few hours to see Clara sitting by my bed, watching me.

I was only in my seventh month. But my labor began on the fifth day and lasted many terrible hours. Liddy and Clara were the midwives, their faces sweaty and grim as they worked to pull the infant from my body. Somewhere in the midst of that nightmare of pain, Clara called in a doctor, and I heard them arguing as he bled me and gave me opium. Nothing could alleviate this pain. I screamed for my mother, my long-gone, sweet, helpless mother; dreaming of her holding my hand and then coming from delirium to see this strange, bushy-whiskered man coming at me with a hideous instrument of steel that he thrust into my body. I heard the words "a footling presentation," and then the sound of Liddy crying.

At the end, they all but tore the child from me, and there he was, a boy, perfectly formed. Feverishly, I counted his fingers and toes and scanned his little face, memorizing all that I could as quickly as possible. But the only thing that mattered was the bloody cord wound tight around his neck, leaving a line of puffy blue skin on each side of its insidious grasp.

"Clara, please, I want to see him look at me," I begged as she bundled the small form in a waiting shroud.

Such sorrow in her face! "No, Susan," she said quietly. "He's gone."

At that moment, I experienced the most piercing grief of all. I would never see him open his eyes. I would never see John's eyes again.

Chapter Seventeen

We buried my son in a small metal box under a tree in George-town's Oak Hill Cemetery. A steady rain was falling. Tom scooped out a grave with his one hand, allowing no one to help him, water dripping from his hat as he bent doggedly to the task. I wrapped the baby in the skirt of my splendid silk gown, which seemed an appropriate shroud of sorrow. Liddy held me as Clara put his body in the grave. Tom and Clara filled it in and we stood on the sodden ground in silence. I tried to pray, but thought surely God would not be listening. Not now. And not to me.

The days that followed barely registered as I floated through time, until the afternoon Clara, breathless from running up the stairs, stood by my bed, peeling off her shawl, throwing it to the floor.

"Susan, I have amazing news. Oh, they thought they could get away with burying him fast and forgetting him, and they have failed!"

I rubbed my eyes. A week since burying my child, and I found myself sleeping so much, I frequently lost track of the hours. With great effort, I responded. "What are you talking about?"

"I've just come from the War Department," she said tri-umphantly. "I told Secretary of War Stanton that John *must* have a second funeral ceremony, one complete with full military honors and a twenty-one-gun salute!"

"No," I groaned, turning back to the wall.

"Don't turn away, Susan. We must fight for what John deserves. Stanton knows he will be scorned by the newspapers if this maligned man isn't honored properly. He has agreed!"

She saw it as a high honor; I did not. But I trudged reluctantly back to Arlington. My son and his father were already buried, and I felt little appetite for this glorification of death, when it was so clearly a substitute for justice in life. My body still ached from childbirth, and I wondered if I was fated to spend my life walking through cemeteries.

Still, the simple splendor of the ceremony for John lifted my heart. I heard for the first time the haunting notes of a melody played by the bugler that brought tears to my eyes. I straightened my spine as the cadenced music lifted to the sky, somehow stronger for it. What was this?

Tom leaned close to me, as if sensing my question. "A soldier's bugle call," he whispered. "They began using it for funerals in the Peninsular Campaign instead of a military volley for fear of drawing fire from the enemy. They call it 'Taps.' Much like a hymn, don't you think? Like Mrs. Howe's?"

"Oh, Tom, it's more like a lullaby," I whispered.

In truth, this ceremony was for Clara. She stood as if hewn from stone, without fire and determination, simply an observer to an injustice that should never have happened. I respected her strength and still drew from it. Yet I wondered how she managed to transcend the personal in this political homage to fate.

And I? No complexity. I mourned John and had wanted to bury my child with his father, but knew such a request would only horrify the military. My child was fated to lie alone in the Georgetown cemetery, deprived even of his father's name. Once I accepted that fact, I knew I could live with anything. Nothing would touch me so deeply again. Or so I thought at the time.

All I could do as we turned away and walked once more down the hill to the waiting carriage was wish for Concord.

"Don't go back yet, Susan, if that's what you're thinking of doing," Tom said. He had drawn alongside me, matching my pace. "You aren't ready. Stay until you're stronger."

"I agree." Liddy's sharp face had a hopeful look as she warily eyed the uniformed honor guard accompanying us down the hill. "I know small towns, I come from one," she said. "They're all crows, those people, ready to pick you apart like carrion. I know what happens."

The very next day Clara, now a national celebrity because of John's list, was summoned to give testimony about Andersonville to the Joint Committee on Reconstruction. She was the first woman ever to testify before Congress, and she impressed them mightily. Within a few weeks, the splendid news came: Clara was now officially recognized as head of a government department set up to locate missing soldiers. That meant sneak attacks from the military—most obviously the former Captain Moore—could not take away the job that was rightfully hers. Clara felt vindicated because money was finally allocated for her work, although only a meager sum of $15,000.

"Should've been more," mumbled Liddy when Clara came flying upstairs with the news. But she brightened in the face of Clara's great joy, as did I. How could we not?

"Come with me downstairs!" Clara shouted, her voice hoarse. "I've had a sign made and we are going to hang it!"

We followed her down the narrow stairs to the first floor. I walked sideways, supporting my stomach, still holding back pain. On the ground floor, Clara had a package that she immediately ripped open, holding aloft its contents. I saw a sturdy square of black tin, and had no need to squint to read the bold lettering:

Missing Soldiers Office

3rd Story, Room 9

Miss Clara Barton

"Very impressive," I said.

"Absolutely grand," added Liddy, as she licked her fingers, having just finished a goodly portion of sausage sent up to Clara by the grocer on Sixth Street. With great fanfare, Tom pulled out a stool and as Clara stepped onto it, he handed her two nails and a ham-mer. With all of us clapping and cheering, Clara hammered in the nails and hung the sign, her eyes as bright as I had ever seen them.

And so I stayed. I made no firm decision to do so, I simply made no decision to leave.

> *10 April 1866*
>
> *Dear Louisa,*
>
> *I wake up each day to the demands of thousands of poor souls still searching for loved ones, and Liddy, Tom, and I strive mightily to bring as many queries as possible to conclusion. It is both a sad job and an enthralling one. Clara is always in need of money, so she has begun to make speeches and is gaining much recognition, which helps our cause. The actual day-to-day work, therefore, is mostly done by the three of us. I have no complaints, for it is deeply satisfying to be needed. When do you sail for home? Will you come here first?*
>
> *Much love,*
> *Susan*

I knew Louisa would not come. I knew it in my bones, and thought it just as well. There would have been no hiding the extent of my suffering. When she wrote to say Abba was feeling poorly, and she would travel straight home to Concord, I was not sur-prised. Lonely, yes. Yearning again for home, yes. But Abba grew better, and I stayed.

Our letters became less frequent as the months passed, devel-oping a predictability that caused me to write hastily and skim Louisa's responses. Oh, I wrote about the work we were doing, identifying and notifying the families of the dead, and she kept me well abreast of what was happening with the family, but I could not share my deeper thoughts anymore. And somewhere, at a certain point, I believe Louisa stopped sharing hers. We were in a time of superficiality. A winter came and went; and then another. And then on one cool spring day, I received this letter:

May 1868

Dearest Susan,

Mr. Niles wants a girls' story, can you imagine? So I begin "Lit-tle Women." Marmee, Anna, and May all approve my plan. So I plod away, though I don't enjoy this sort of thing. Never liked girls or knew many, except you and my sisters, but our queer plays and experiences may prove interesting, though I doubt it.

Engrossed as I now am in re-creating our world, I think of you often. I'm not the only one to do so. Marmee wants to read every letter, as does Anna, and Mrs. Sanderson asks for you each time I go to town. She is not well these days, and is thinking of retiring.

I do not fully comprehend why you stay on. When is the work of identifying the war dead completed?

With eager hope you will soon abandon Washington and come home,

Louisa

"Are you going to tell her the truth about what happened?" Clara asked, when I handed her the letter to read.

I shook my head, lacing my fingers together in my lap. "Nothing I can tell her now will do anything but give her pain. I don't want that."

"Well, of course, I grant you, there is something self-indulgent about confession." Clara picked at a piece of cake on the table in front of her as we finished our lunch. "But Susan, you lost the man you loved and your baby. Are you absolutely sure that means you must lose Louisa, too?"

"I'm not sure you understand," I began.

"I understand you have been walking around here with a great weight of sadness. Your shoulders are stooped, do you know that?" She waved her fork, growing agitated. "There's too much guilt in this world. Why do women allow it to engulf them? You are not the only woman who gave yourself to a man for whom you had no legitimate claim. Haven't you suffered enough? The hold of that provincial backwater of yours! Women are crippled by guilt, caught at every—"

"Please, Clara." I loved this fierce, fragile woman, but she frequently wore me out now with her causes and orations. "Concord is not *that* provincial."

"High thinking and lofty morals do not compensate for the juice of life," she retorted. "And from what you've told me, you worried about the same thing when you were there. Wasn't that why you came to Washington?"

I hesitated. "That's only partly true. But Clara, what comes next? I fear no matter what I do, my relationship with Louisa will never be the same again. I did take what was hers, for he did love her." It hurt to say it.

She sat back with a long sigh. I noticed how dry and wrinkled her neck had become, and the paleness of her skin. As usual, Clara was working too hard, but no one could persuade her to do less. "My dear," she began, much more slowly and kindly, "why do you not see that Louisa had a role in this, too? I don't recall her rushing here for a reunion with John. And may I point out, she was not on our doorstep when we came back?"

"She would have been if—"

"She waited too long. Life moved on."

I smiled. I wished I could view the world with Clara's obstinate clarity. "I know that. But the Lou I have loved all my life finally surfaced."

"Too late. And perhaps you were brave to risk all."

"Oh, my goodness, no."

"And perhaps you truly lose your friend, whom you love, by not addressing what separates you. Perhaps you need to risk your friendship to keep it. Will you think about that?"

I was silent. "I fear the test," I said finally. "But I will."

> *Dear Louisa,*
> *This will be the hardest letter I have ever had to write. I will not ask you to forgive or understand. I ask you only to hear the sequence of events, for if I do not share my heart with you, flaws and all, I fear I drain our friendship of all value. I also know what*

I write you now may alter that friendship forever, but I must take that chance. . . .

My letter went on for six pages. I told her everything. I mailed it, resigned to whatever outcome was ordained. There was no other course of action open to me, I was convinced. Clara watched me silently as I walked through my days, drained of all expectation. I faulted her not at all for urging me to lay out the truth. It had to be done; I was relieved to have done it, no matter the outcome. The weeks went by. Months. Letters came from Abba, even May . . . but no answer from Louisa.

Or, shall I say, no answer delivered directly. That awaited me the day I wandered through a small bookshop off Lafayette Square and spied Louisa's new novel. It was only October, and I was shocked to see the volume already out in print. It was crisply bound, with a frontispiece of four young girls gathered lovingly around their mother. My heart quickened: Why, that looked like May's work! Why hadn't Louisa written and told me? I shoved money forward to the bookseller, seized my copy, and rushed to a park bench to read. I opened to the first page and read the initial words that children everywhere would soon know by heart.

> *"Christmas won't be Christmas without any presents," grum-bled Jo, lying on the rug.*
>
> *"It's so dreadful to be poor!" sighed Meg, looking down at her old dress.*
>
> *"I don't think it's fair for some girls to have plenty of pretty things, and other girls nothing at all," added little Amy, with an injured sniff.*
>
> *"We've got father and mother and each other," said Beth con-tentedly, from her corner.*

I read quickly, enthralled by these four young girls who, with their mother, endure the deprivations of war with sacrifice, humor, and love. It was wonderful. Soon I was pounding my hand up and down in my lap, alternately laughing and crying. Passersby, I dimly realized, were walking a wide arc around the crazy lady talking out loud to herself.

How even now to assess my dear friend's accomplishment? *Little Women*—oh, so true and so false! From Louisa's pen flowed the story she had always yearned to believe, richly imagined, filled with true events, mostly the comic and happy ones. How had she remembered the burnt dress before the dance? I felt caught once again in her imagination, but this time, it was different. This time, it was with the breath of truth and reality, and her story danced from the pages. There it was, the story of the Alcott girls, with all the wonderful moments and none of the angers and resentments. I loved them all—Meg, Jo, Beth, and Amy. I *knew* them all. Especially one.

> *Fifteen-year-old Jo was very tall, thin, and brown, and reminded one of a colt; for she never seemed to know what to do with her long limbs, which were very much in her way. She had a decided mouth, a comical nose, and sharp, gray eyes, which appeared to see everything, and were by turns fierce, funny, or thoughtful. Her long, thick hair was her one beauty; but it was usually bundled into a net, to be out of her way. Round shoulders had Jo, big hands and feet, a fly-away look to her clothes, and the uncomfortable appearance of a girl who was rapidly shooting up into a woman, and didn't like it.*

Lou, oh Lou, I thought, everyone will love you. Her spirit, her yearnings, her taste for adventure, her clumsy efforts as a young girl to be what others wanted her to be—it was all there! And Bronson? I rifled through the pages. Bronson, the principal dilemma in Louisa's life, was the father off to war, conveniently excised. *Little Women* had come to life without his sorrowing disapproval.

I had lived this, so much of it, even though her fictional "little women" were younger than the real ones had been when I shared their events and adventures. On every page I found something that thrilled me with the power of Louisa's imagination, and I exulted inside. Oh, the crisp cleanness of the story! People hurried past my bench, and it was all I could do to keep from shouting out, Read this wonderful book! Louisa had finally found her ticket to fortune; of that I was convinced. It read so true, transcending the mundane difficulties of real life, and if it was a highly scrubbed, glossy view of the Alcott family, what did it matter? It was, it really was, the first golden egg of the sister who saw herself as the ugly duckling.

There was but one thing wrong. I was not in *Little Women*. Nowhere was there the glimmer of my presence. I flipped pages futilely, hoping I had missed just one vignette, one anecdote, that would acknowledge our friendship. None was to be found. Oh, Louisa. Had my existence as the "fifth sister" depended on my being who you wanted me to be?

I closed the book and sat very still, my shawl held tight around my shoulders. The wind sweeping the park was turning chilly. Louisa had once again told a story, writing out of the deepest pain. This time she excised the person who caused the sadness. That was her answer to my letter.

That night I lay in bed, dry-eyed, assessing reality. Now that Louisa knew all, she would never forgive me. How strange to be deprived in this manner of meaning! I turned on my side, lifted myself up on one elbow, and stared out the window at a luminous full moon. No, I thought. Only I can strip myself of meaning, and I must not let it happen.

A letter in a stiff, official-looking envelope arrived from Concord at the end of October. Nervously, I scanned the return address: a solicitor's office, one I vaguely remembered. I opened the envelope and scanned its contents quickly. Mrs. Sanderson had passed away and bequeathed her flourishing business to me. Was this real? She was dead? I would never see her again? My hands shook as I read, and my legs began to tremble. I wept as Clara tried to comfort me.

"Is this what you want?" she finally asked in her direct way. "To go back?"

"I can't imagine wanting anything more," I said slowly. "I loved working in that shop. Mrs. Sanderson talked to me before I left about joining her as a partner. I can hardly believe her generosity."

Clara took both my hands in hers. "And you can go back there with your head high and your shoulders straight?"

I nodded. "I believe I can," I said.

"Well, then, you've picked a good time."

I laughed. We were all but done with our work, and Clara was soon to make her final report to Congress. There were no longer piles of boxes filled with letters stacked in the halls of 488 1/2 Seventh Street. One by one, we had emptied them, checked their pleas for information against our lists, added names to circulars listing the missing, and written back to almost forty-two thousand letter-writers. All in all, we had identified twenty-two thousand men. But twenty thousand soldiers had vanished into history. Clara's last effort for them was to demand Congress declare them dead so their families could collect survivor benefits.

"You've been a wonderful help, Susan."

"It's been proud work," I said.

"What will you do?"

Clara had a slightly faraway look in her eyes. "I want to go to Europe. France, I think. I see many opportunities ahead." She cast a quick look around her apartment. "I love my little rookery," she said with a certain wistfulness. "But it's time to move on. I wonder what I should do with everything here?"

I knew Clara well enough to know that once she had her sights firmly set on her next venture, there would be little sorting and sifting. She would simply toss everything in a pile somewhere in the attic and probably never come back to it. I felt a rush of affection. Her enthusiasm would carry her far from her rookery very soon, of that I was sure.

"I know one thing we should do."

"And what is that?"

"Let's take down the sign. We put it up together, now we need to take it down."

Clara brightened. "A full ceremony! Call Liddy and Tom."

It was a bittersweet task, with Liddy wiping tears on her sleeve. She planned to go back to nursing, she announced, as I stood on the stool this time and did the honors. Carefully, I removed the nails, not wanting to bend the tin, and handed the sign to Clara. She sighed, looking at the proud lettering of her design. "Nothing will ever match the last few years here on Seventh Street," she said. How unlike Clara; she was not an outward sentimentalist. She will really miss us, I thought. And I will miss her.

Tom was exceptionally quiet over the next several days. He, too, had his plans set—he would enter into business with Frances Gage who, it turns out, was quite a businesswoman. She had purchased a small tavern in Georgetown and asked Tom to run it for her. She might also, I suspected, have plans for Tom and her dutiful, spinster daughter.

The time came finally for my departure. Kissing Liddy goodbye was like hugging a sweet, fat pillow, for she had put on a few pounds, which we laughed about as I promised many letters. "Don't forget me," she begged.

"Come see me in Concord, and I'll make you a splendid hat," I said. And we hugged again, both knowing that journey most likely would never be made.

I hesitated to embrace Clara, feeling suddenly shy. But she stepped forward and enveloped me with her thin, strong arms. "Don't let your mistakes defeat you, dear," she whispered. "And remember, I've made more of them than you have."

I thank her for that.

I bounded into the wagon, not waiting for Tom's helping hand, and saw the quick amusement in his eyes as he took his seat next to me. He had insisted on driving me to the train station, an offer I gratefully accepted. I turned to wave once more as we rounded the corner, anxious for one last glimpse of what had been my entire world for over three years. I was captivated by the sight of Clara standing on the dusty street, hands clasped firmly across her rigidly corseted middle: a tiny steel rod of a woman, with determination and ambition, and no apologies to anyone. Her black hair shone in the sun. She raised one hand slowly and waved.

"I suspect you'll want to pay a last visit to Arlington, so I left enough time to go by the grave," Tom said. He held one rein while skillfully manipulating the other, which was looped around a wooden horn, as we clattered along the road. "Both of them, if you want." He didn't look at me. "Oak Hill, first?"

"Thank you, Tom," I said, touched. I would miss him, too.

We arrived at Oak Hill Cemetery while dew still freshened the leaves of the trees. It was a narrow, rocky path on a steep decline to my child's grave, and Tom held my hand as we all but clambered down, slipping and sliding, to a small patch of earth next to a creek. My eyes widened. A small white headstone had been erected, replacing an unmarked block of wood. On it were the words:

Baby Gray

1866

"Seeing as how this was the business we were in, it seemed unnatural not to have the baby's grave marked," Tom said a bit diffidently. "I hope you don't take it as an affront that I did it on my own. I'll take it away, if you choose."

My eyes filled with tears. "Oh no, Tom. You were right, and I thank you."

"I know you wanted him with his father." Tom was staring

down at the ground, his mouth drawn tight. "But Susan, it's all right that he's here. He's yours, too."

I said nothing, simply turned and put my arms around him. And for a long moment, we clung to each other. Finally we separated and began our way back up the hill to the carriage. By the time we reached the street, I was confident of my decision.

"There's no need to stop at Arlington," I said.

Tom cast me a startled look.

"It's all right, Tom. I've said my good-byes."

Chapter Eighteen

I stepped from the train, putting foot to ground, testing for sta-
bility. I looked around. All was changed—busier, quicker; unfamiliar faces . . . and yet all was the same. Would I fit back in?

I spied a potbellied little man at the end of the platform hurrying toward me, and assumed he was the solicitor. His greeting
was effusive. Mr. Boyleton, at your service. Edmund Boyleton;
call me Edmund. Everything was readied for my arrival, he
assured me. A comfortable apartment above the store, part of the
inheritance, awaited. Sans furniture, of course, except for a fine
iron bed and a chest, but furnishings involved personal choices,
the trustees of Mrs. Sanderson's estate had advised, best made by
the recipient of the property. He arched an eyebrow at this statement, and I nodded, if only to bring down that eyebrow.

My concentration faltered. I had seen at the end of the platform
the fleeting sight of a black bonnet. Or had I? An illusion? Had I simply seen what I hoped to see? It wouldn't be the first time.

"Miss Gray? Did you hear me? I have a carriage waiting." His
politeness bordered on the obsequious, which I found bewilder-
ingly strange.

"No, thank you. I want to walk."

I strained to catch another glimpse of that black bonnet.
Although I had written Abba, I had not told Louisa directly that I
was coming back. Each time I tried to fashion a letter, no words
came. I could not forget turning the pages of *Little Women* and
realizing how thoroughly she had banished me from her life.

It was a familiar, short distance to Main Street. Mr. Boyleton hustled annoyingly close, chattering away, as I marveled at what I saw. Fewer fields, more people. Main Street seemed almost crowded. What was the most significant difference? Pace. I could sense, inhale, the quickened step of everyone I passed, and it was unsettling to see many unfamiliar faces.

"Susan? Susan Gray? It really is you! Welcome!" There was Jonas Bitterwill, rushing from his pastry shop, pumping my hand with effusive goodwill. And twenty yards farther down the road, Mrs. Rollings emerged from her shoe store with a similar greeting. I realized I was one of them now, the heir to an anchored shop, and therefore part of the town in a different way than before.

When we reached Mrs. Sanderson's, Mr. Boyleton had difficulty getting the key to work, and I told him to be patient, it had always been a bit balky. Finally the lock turned, and we stepped inside. I looked around. Thick bolts of fabric still rested on the shelves that lined the walls, all arranged as tidily as ever. I missed Mrs. Sanderson acutely, half-expecting to see her cheerful face pop up as she emerged from the back room.

"You'll find the books in order," said Mr. Boyleton. "It is your good fortune that Mrs. Sanderson was a meticulous business-woman." He tipped his hat, clearly in haste. "I'll have your trunk brought in and taken up to your quarters, which I hope you will find satisfactory. Anything I can do to help, just call on me. My offices are across the street, on the second floor above the hardware store. Oh, I almost forgot—" he turned at the door and nodded toward the far counter. "Miss Alcott sent over that bouquet of posies."

"Miss Louisa Alcott?"

"No, no. Miss May Alcott. Good day, Miss Gray. And welcome back to Concord."

He was gone. I tiptoed over to the vase filled with flowers from Abba's garden, and gently removed the note tucked in between the roses and lilacs.

Dearest Susan,
Welcome home. It's high time. Look out the window.

I peered through the glass and saw May standing with Anna, both of them laughing and waving. It took me but a second to throw open the door and embrace them both. I was crying and laughing at the same time. What a relief to be welcomed!

"You wrote so seldom," scolded Anna, bussing me soundly on both cheeks. "Have you forgotten us? Mother wants you to supper tonight, and you cannot say no. The Emersons are coming, and we'll have a jolly evening—that is, if Father and Mr. Emerson don't start again discussing the meaning of life. Remember what Louisa said about Father? 'He's a man up in a balloon with his family and friends holding the ropes which confine him to earth— trying to haul him down.' Well, it is still true, and when he has Mr. Emerson in there with him it's all but impossible." I laughed again, this time without tears. Anna looked hearty and happy; marriage and motherhood must be agreeing with her, I said. "John is a lovely man and my boys are well," she replied. "We are prospering," she added, with a blush. A new thing indeed, for the Pratt family.

May nodded, her blue eyes dancing. "We're all prospering because of Louisa, isn't that the truth? Oh, Susan, I'll never wear a hand-me-down again! Look—" She danced away a few steps and did a quick pirouette, skirts swirling. "China silk, the best, and my drawers are of the finest combed cotton you can buy," she announced. She made a funny face, squinching up the nose she had always complained about, clearly enjoying her small comic turn.

"Where is Louisa?" I ventured as casually as possible.

There was a hesitation as the two sisters looked at each other, obviously surprised that I didn't know. Anna spoke first. "She's in Boston, working away on a sequel to *Little Women,* although I think she's getting homesick. Plus, her health, you know."

"What about her health?"

"She's always feeling poorly," May chimed in. "And so depressed!

Sometimes I cannot figure her out—here she is, famous and on her way to being rich, and so crabby."

"She holds a lens before every fault and folly these days, and values only what is intrinsically noble and true," Anna volunteered loyally. "Which is not a fault, mind you."

May tossed her hair back, a familiar gesture of impatience. "I think it is, so there. Lou is a queer one, if you ask me. Always has been, though I love her dearly. The doctors say it is part of her general ailment."

"Is this a new one?" I asked.

Anna's eyes widened. "You mean you don't know? She hasn't told you? The mercury has never left her body. From the calomel they dosed her with at Union Hospital."

Was I truly surprised? No. Memories rose instantly of trying to keep Belle Poole from pushing that dreadful medicine through Louisa's lips. "Of course," I whispered.

Anna, true to her nature, adopted a comforting tone, almost that of mother to child. "It's not life-threatening, Susan. The doctors are trying different medicines and she has good days and bad days. But surely she would have told you all about this."

I made some remark about possible missed letters and hoped she would press me no further. Fortunately May had begun to explore the fabric bolts with squeals of delight, holding up a shimmering blue silk.

"Susan, will you make me a dress? Look at this! Oh, with you here now, I'll have the fanciest duds in town!"

And so I started my new life as the owner of Mrs. Sanderson's shop draping May, pinning and stitching, listening to her chatter away about her art classes, her plans to get out of Concord, everything under the sun this golden-haired perennial child could think of. Anna offered suggestions as she sat placidly by the window. They both were fully diverted from my distress. Thank goodness, for I could not trust myself under Anna's sharp eyes to talk anymore about Louisa.

Anna sensed something amiss. I'm sure that's why she came

straight to me a week later and, with a sweet smile, handed me the
letter that had just arrived from Boston.

> *Dear family,*
> *People are remarking on how familiar my best black silk has*
> *become. I shall either have to get another or go home to Concord. I*
> *am going home to Concord.*
>
>   *Louisa*

"Why don't you meet her?" Anna suggested kindly.

I met Louisa's train five days later, catching my breath as I spied her
descending from the steps to the platform. Had I really not seen
her in over three years? She trudged slowly in my direction, a tall,
oddly hulking figure, for all her thinness. Her face had a pallor of
illness, and her clothes covered her like dark, drifting smoke:
heavy, formless, engulfing. She seemed consumed by serge and
boiled wool. I thought fleetingly, achingly, of the Louisa who used
to twirl around the room wearing the magic glory cloak in all its
bright splendor. It was hard to imagine her now in that jaunty
swirl of green and red silk. Her face seemed lengthened, thinner.
Her eyes appeared dulled.

She had not yet seen me. Her attention was distracted by a man
with legs like a grasshopper who suddenly jumped in front of her.
"Miss Alcott, I'm with the *Herald,* can I have a moment? You've
been asked this a hundred times, but your fans beg to know. Tell
us, please, will Jo marry Laurie? Can you really mean to keep
them apart?"

"Go away, no interviews." She tried to dodge him, but he would
not be discouraged.

"Then it's true you won't let them marry? Why? Little girls
everywhere will be devastated! They want a romance, and shouldn't
you give it to them?" He hopped, he grinned. I could not help but be
fascinated with his extraordinary ballet.

Louisa's expression had changed to one of weary resignation.

Before she could answer, I heard behind me a clamor of young voices. "Miss Alcott! Miss Alcott!" I turned to see a group of young girls elbowing each other as they ran toward her on the platform. They, too, began to hop like grasshoppers.

"Watch yourselves, girls," Louisa warned. "Don't get so near the tracks, please."

"Miss Alcott! Miss Alcott!" They barely heeded her.

I heard the long, lazy whistle of another train approaching. All now was pandemonium. The train rumbled toward the station; the children, tumbling and tripping dangerously close to the edge of the platform, were shouting, holding out copies of *Little Women* in hopes of coaxing Louisa to sign her name.

"Move back!" Louisa shouted, waving her arms, her black bonnet askew. "This isn't a time for signing! Do you hear me? Please, children, move away from the edge! Go!"

The girls shrank back. "Oh," wailed one, a starched-pinafore child with a yellow ribbon in her hair. "She doesn't like us, how can she be so mean?"

They turned and ran. The reporter? He watched it all and scribbled into a notebook before he, too, hustled off the platform. Louisa collapsed onto a bench and buried her head in her hands.

"Louisa." I could barely catch my breath. By now I was close enough to put out my hand to touch her. "Are you all right?"

She looked up, and I could have sworn she shrank back. I hoped it was my imagination.

"Susan." Said so flatly.

"Yes." I was at a loss for words beyond that single one.

"I wondered how we would meet again." She cast a glance after the fleeing children and raised her hands to straighten her bonnet, visibly trying to rally herself. "Did you think you would get so quick a view of the rewards of fame? There go my loyal fans. Poor things, all they find now is a witch who scares them away."

"You were only trying to keep them from falling in front of the train. Why would they think you a witch? There's no nastiness in what you did."

She cast me a glance that seemed to question my sanity. "It won't appear that way in the *Herald* tomorrow. That reporter knew what he was looking for, and he found it."

I felt clumsy, unsure how to proceed. On what level? On Louisa's concerns, or mine? I had not envisioned how life had changed for my friend, and I no longer knew her emotional landscape.

We stood facing each other, frozen in awkwardness.

"How do we start?" I asked simply.

"I don't know. Have you read *Little Women?*"

"Of course. It's wonderful. More than that, it is magical."

She jammed her hands deep inside her muff and looked away. "I've trapped myself, you know. The children want Jo. And Jo is who I was, not who I am. Now all anyone wants from me is more of the same fantasies. I can write nothing else."

"The Alcott family is not a fantasy. There is much love and truth. You simply imagined it as you wanted it to be."

"Why is it that you remain the only one who understands? Everyone else is eager to believe only the fantasy. But then, you've always been the memory."

"You are a marvelous storyteller."

"For what that means. You are the truth-teller. I'm famous for goodness, isn't that a marvelous joke?"

I paused to think of what to say next, but she spared me the effort.

"I want to make one thing clear, first. Father isn't in my book either," she said.

"I did see that." I shifted my feet.

And then she said something curious. "I was Jo, wasn't I?"

"Of course you were," I said, surprised.

"I am no longer."

"You couldn't have created her so splendidly without the truth of it. You *are* Jo, whether you think so or not."

Louisa fingered the strings of her bonnet, looking past me with the distant gaze I had always excused and now ached to challenge.

"I often think of Anna and her children. She is a happy woman. My children? I sell them, and though they feed me, they don't love me as hers do."

Such sadness in those words. I pushed my gloved fingers deeper into my muff and glanced around. We had been standing too long on this platform; curious gawkers were craning their heads for a look at Louisa.

"Come, walk with me to my shop. I'll fix us some tea," I said.

For a moment I feared she might decline, but she nodded. We made our way, walking briskly, to Main Street, saying little. I'm not the only one who is afraid, I thought, as I turned the key and ushered her into the shop.

Louisa took off her cloak and looked around with interest. "You've fixed things up quite nicely, Susan." Her gaze rested on a strip of cloth tied around one of the gas sconces and I heard her audibly catch her breath.

"Is that what I think it is?" she asked.

"Yes." I felt warmed by her recognition.

"The sash I gave you from the glory cloak," she said.

I looked up at the fragment of silk and my voice trembled. "I hung it there for memory . . . and for good luck," I said.

She seemed to go still. Then, "I'm sure you'll have lots of business. But isn't life in Concord going to be a bit tame after the excitement of Washington?"

"You mean 'the town of reflected history and transplanted geniuses' can't match the nation's capital?"

She smiled.

Encouraged, I went on. "I've always wanted to come back. This is home; it has been since the days I spent here as a child with you and your family." The teapot trembled in my hands. "Louisa, I can't make small talk. I have to ask you again, forgive me."

"You want me to forgive you." It was a statement, not a question.

"I know it's expecting a great deal. But it is the hope of my life."

And then, in a move so unexpected I almost dropped the pot, Louisa began to cry.

"Louisa, I'm sorry——" I put the pot down and sank to a chair in front of her.

"Stop being sorry, I can't bear it." She fumbled for a handkerchief and dabbed at her eyes.

"Is it totally unforgivable? Just say it, and I'll stop. I'll walk away and give up hope, if that is the way it has to be."

"Unforgivable? Why? Because you took what I didn't have the courage to grasp? I have no right to fault you for that. I was afraid. Can you accept that? I was mortally afraid."

Oh, I wanted to hold her. "When your first letter came, I saw that, and I was sad for you," I said.

She brushed aside my words and began to pace. "What unknown situation were you drawing me into? You wanted me to drop everything and run toward this dream. It was impossible, truly impossible. Can you understand that? All I would be was the old Lou again, hurling herself into the pit. Running off to Washington would have been inexcusably irresponsible. Do you understand?"

"Yes, I do," I said, reaching out my hand to grab hers.

She wheeled and faced me. "Not enough to honor my true feelings. You knew what they were."

I blinked, my hand stilled in midair. "Are you saying I should have denied mine after you relinquished yours?"

"I think your feelings always came first, which is why my note never reached John."

There was nothing to say to that. No words to convey how passion had taken hold of me that night in the cellar—body, brain, and soul. I would live with my regrets to the grave, but there was no way to explain to my wounded friend what the moment had been like.

"Against that, I have no defense, only guilt and sorrow," I said.

"Ah, I see. Why aren't you saying your letter imploring me to come *absolved* you? You challenged me, pushing me forward, knowing I could not deny my duty. You laid a trap."

I stared at this tall, gaunt stranger in front of me whose eyes blazed with fury. No, not fury, something else. A sad desperation,

perhaps. Was there no way to reach her? Where was my Lou? I
thought with sudden pain of her daring stories filled with head-
strong heroines and passionate, dangerous lovers taking breathtaking chances, risking all.

"Help me understand. You actually knew he was found and you
sailed anyway. Why? How could you detach yourself?"

"Don't use that word, I'm not detached."

I spoke as carefully as possible. "You needed time to accept the
fact that he was alive and waiting for you?"

"Yes, I think so." Her voice broke.

"How was I to know that?"

"It doesn't matter." Her jaw locked as firmly as it had the day
she scolded me for peeking in the oven at the little colored boy.
"*Your* duty was clear. You should not have been ruled by your passions. That was not right."

Something was floating in the air, something not to be denied.

"Louisa, could it be that you never intended to come?"

"No, of course not. I did. If I could." Her eyes darkened with
pain and she turned away.

Was that true? Would I ever know? More important, would
she? I sensed John's instinct had been right—she *had* loved the creation more. Had she indeed expected me to obediently play my
role as loyal friend and enthusiast after she relinquished her claim?
And should I have?

Louisa was pacing now with giant strides the narrow corridor
between the front door and the shop counter. "I thought I could go
for a while and then leave, going straight to Washington. I counted
on you to keep me well apprised of what was happening, but I had
to absorb it before I could act. When I finally wrote—"

"He was headed for jail."

"And you were already with child." Her tone was not accusa-
tory, but the words made me shiver. "Even after all of what happened, after your letter telling of the baby's death, I struggled with
one terrible feeling."

I waited.

"Jealousy."

We stared at each other in silence. Two friends, staring across a terrible gulf that now separated us.

"I doubt if I can ever overcome that," she said.

I was again unable to respond.

"Susan," her voice caught. "What did it feel like?"

I could hear the footsteps of shoppers outside. Laughter from the shop next door. The hint of a bawdy song from an eating place down the street.

"At first, as if I were being split apart. As if a cleaver cut through me. And then I felt filled up, all the empty spaces filled up, flowing with warmth."

"Was it pleasure?" Her voice now was very small.

"Yes." The skin on the palms of my hands began to itch, a prickly fire that spread up my arms to my neck, to my scalp. One word. One honest word.

She sat in silence.

"If you had come to Washington, nothing would have happened. I wish you had come and claimed what was yours, with all my heart. My love for you would have won out. I did not want to betray you," I said.

"I believe you think you mean that."

"You doubt?"

"You don't know how I have suffered since your letter confessing all. You are a more impulsive person than I am, and perhaps your impulses would have won out in the end. Or perhaps not."

Could I not have been kinder? If I had not been suddenly engulfed with memories of John's hand slipping away from mine for the last time on the boat and my reaching to hold, just once, the lifeless hand of my child, would I have had more sympathy? Might I not have forgiven her such a stiff, guarded endorsement?

"I am *not* more impulsive than you, Louisa. But I'm not as afraid. Thank God, I am not as afraid." Even as I saw her pull away, saw her face close up, I could not stop. "All this time I've considered myself a sinner against all decency. I've been sure God punished me for this by taking my baby. Wasn't that a grievous loss? And you . . . you were being careful, shielding yourself. You were too happy with your sanitized blacksmith to take a chance on the real person."

"Stop. Don't continue this."

"No. You want me to grieve *for* you, but you are remote from my suffering. I don't think you understand what I lost. It's too messy. Too, how can I say this, too real."

"I know you never delivered the one note of love I have written in my life—and I wrote it to a 'real' person, Susan, not a fictional character. I have admitted my jealousy. Why don't you admit yours?"

Silence fell between us. Yes, I had been jealous of her, and I had held back my feelings at Union Hospital, never allowing Louisa to sense the confusion in my heart. There had been no words I could wrap around my yearning. It was a form of lying to myself, wasn't it? My head began to ache.

Yet how could Louisa have hesitated? How could she have convinced herself she was only delaying a reunion with him? Because she had forced herself to settle for emotion dripped slowly from an eyedropper, that's why. What made her think others could do the same? Stop, stop, I told myself. It is futile to argue over which of us is more at fault, for I wove my own fiction by fantasizing a perfect love, imbuing the two of them with a passion for each other that went beyond what either truly wanted. Was that so? Would I ever know? I had made it what I wanted it to be; most truly, what I wanted it to be for myself.

"Yes, I was jealous."

"So, here we are." Louisa's eyes stayed steady. "We mutually betrayed each other. If that is what we are destined to call it."

I waited a long moment before answering. My lips parted to offer a bridge of words that might heal us, somehow, but then the memory of my baby's grave in the trough of land just above Rock Creek took away my voice. And once again I heard the mournful bugle salute and the sound of the honor guard's guns firing into the sky over John's grave. And I remembered Clara's wise words pointing out to me that Louisa had a role in all of this heartache, too. Yes. Indeed she did. And it had been all over for her, long ago. Put aside, distanced. While I had agonized, she had moved on.

"I can think of nothing else to say," I whispered.

Louisa stood. I saw her wince in pain, and wondered fleetingly if mercury was causing more problems than her sisters knew. "Nor can I," she said.

I rose, too. We stood there for a moment, staring at each other. How could such distance exist between us? In the silence, I heard in my mind our shouts as children running through the grove of apple trees behind Orchard House, the sound of our footsteps as we leapt through piles of autumn leaves and threw ourselves on our backs to stare at the sky and talk about our dreams.

"Good-bye, Louisa," I said.

"Good-bye, Susan," she replied. She put on her coat and walked a bit unsteadily toward the door, opened it, and was gone.

Chapter Nineteen

How did the years pass so quickly? I cannot quite pluck one from my memory and set it free—the result, I suspect, of the fact that they flowed, one into another, with no one clearly differentiated.

Certainly business flourished. I expanded my shop and grew deeply contented with my place in Concord. At times I would see Louisa in town, and we would nod politely to each other and say a few words, but nothing more. To the casual observer, all would have seemed pleasant, though each time I turned away with a lonely heart. We had lost our way toward each other, and the troubling truth was, it became easier as time went on. I vowed not to hope, and tried to squeeze my feelings dry.

Community life absorbed me, which helped. When the very rich William Munroe funded and built our splendid library, it was a delight to become part of the endeavor. I couldn't believe it when we managed to open with a collection of 220,000 volumes, which was very respectable for our intellectually proud town. The day it opened I ascended the newly completed steps, eager to tour. A small girl in a white pinafore sat hunched in a small ball on the top step, hair falling into her face, still as a mouse, absorbed in a book. I started to walk around her. I stopped when I saw that the green leather-bound book holding her rapt attention was a worn copy of *Little Women*.

"Are you enjoying your story?" I asked.

She looked up, her eyes not quite focused. I had interrupted her reading. "Oh yes," she said politely.

"Who do you like best?"

She looked at me with amazement. "Jo, of course."

"Ah, of course. And why is that?"

She folded her hands protectively over her book. "Because I like to climb trees and be a tomboy, too. And I want to be a writer. Oh, she's just like me."

"So you think you know her?"

"I know how she feels. She tries really hard to be good, even when she wants to be bad. And sometimes she's not bad at all, she just thinks she is."

I continued up the stairs, this time on wings, suspecting for the first time that Louisa's book might outlive us all.

The library was immensely popular. There was that small, embarrassing flurry over a silly rule that decreed no borrower could take out more than two books at a time, only one of which could be fiction. When Sophia Thoreau stood up at a town meeting and said, "What do you people think, we're going to be morally tainted by a story? In Concord, of all places?" the rule vanished almost overnight.

Sophia and I became comfortable friends, perhaps bonded by the fact that we supported ourselves as merchants—a fact that gave us both great pleasure. There was at least as much demand for her product of soft lead as for my bonnets and dresses, and only with each other could we talk about shipping supplies and accounting needs, as well as the usual town gossip. Yet it was never a sharing of hearts; never what friendship had been with Louisa.

The big news of 1872 was the terrible fire at Mr. Emerson's place. He told us later he awoke to what he thought was the sound of rain, and instead found crackling fire spreading through the walls. There was nothing to be done but grab the manuscript he was working on and the hand of a frightened Mrs. Emerson and run for his life. Dozens of us arrived to battle the blaze and try to save their possessions. I glimpsed at one point a grim-looking Louisa running from the house, her arms loaded with books and papers. May, her arms equally burdened, followed right behind. I saw sparks on the sash of May's gown and ran past Louisa to pull it off her. I had the wild hope then that Louisa would stop, but she did not.

What else do I remember? Ah, the sad decline of Mr. Bull, our esteemed creator of the Concord grape. After a career honored with gold medals for his horticulture, he was deserted by his wife. I used to feel sorry for him, watching this once splendidly attired man wandering among his cherished vines in an old bathrobe, mumbling to himself, turning dottier with each day. Was this in store for me? I wondered.

Louisa's writing fame grew rapidly. So many books, so quickly! All of them following the fortunes of the March family; all chapters in a splendid saga of life at home. Children everywhere adored her work. *An Old-Fashioned Girl, Little Men, Eight Cousins*—I tick them off in my brain with pleasure. Louisa would never again have to churn out a "rubbishy" potboiler. Her literary footprint was firm. But she spent much of her time away from Concord during those years. And May, determined to succeed as a painter, renounced Concord and all things American, moving to Paris, finally to lead a life she chose on her own.

May broke the news one evening, falling into step with me as I strolled toward the Old North Bridge, one of my favorite destinations for a solitary walk. I wasn't surprised. I knew as she told me it had been only a matter of time.

"Do you think I'm terrible?" she asked. She was no longer a saucy child; there was a gravity in her eyes. "I know I'm spoiled, and I owe so much to my family. But I also know that if I don't get out of here, if I don't break free, I'll end up like Lou. Oh, she's rich and famous, now. But—" She looked at me helplessly. "Do you understand? I don't want to be trapped."

What an odd position to be in, I thought. It was up to me now to encourage May to do something solely for herself, when in all the years before, I had decried her easy willingness to do precisely that.

"I do understand," I said. "You should go."

"Thank you, Susan," she said, squeezing my hand. "You know, don't you, that I love Lou dearly? It is she who has made my career possible. Without her help, how could I go to Europe to study?" She sighed. "I'm not an introspective person, I fear. But I do wonder at times, why is it that Lou has always been best at giving, and I am so good at receiving?"

"Oh, my dear, I have no answer for that."

"I don't know my sister very well," she continued slowly. "I know her more from her writings than from all the years spent living with her."

"I have sometimes thought the same." The words were difficult to say.

And so she left.

Abba and I began to share tea once a week, and I saw how she sorrowed for May, but I could not help but feel admiration—May had broken the bonds to home at last. Such a different need, hers from mine! Perhaps someday, I thought, we might laugh about it together, not knowing those chances were gone.

Abba often spoke of the mercury poisoning still draining Louisa's strength, convinced it had changed her daughter's nature. "Why else would she care only for duty, taking no pleasure from her success?" she fretted. I saw one day a sudden glint in her eyes and was startled with what came next. "Too much is made of the virtue of duty. My husband should have made more effort to show her love."

But it was Anna who became my steadiest connection to the Alcotts—practical Anna, who baked and cooked and cleaned with all the same bustle and industry as ever, running after her two boys and taking care of the rather vapid John Pratt, whom she never ceased to adore. He died in 1870, leaving her at first bereft. But Anna wiped her tears and carried on, living for her sons.

"You started me on my work, you know," I said to her one day when she stopped by my shop to have a bonnet retrimmed. I cut as I talked, piecing sashes of red, white, and blue. "Remember when you had me pull apart the stitching on the dress and put it back together?"

Anna smiled, her soft chin doubling. "I never told you it wasn't an old frock at all, it was the only one I had besides the one on my back. But I could see your restlessness and how well you could sew so I crossed my fingers and let you do it." She glanced at the long bolts of goods I was busily cutting. "What are you making now?"

"Sashes and hats for the women's rights rally next Saturday," I said. I could not hold back a flush of pleasure. Susan B. Anthony herself was coming to speak, and I had been given the honor of outfitting all the participants. Nothing had galvanized me more since returning home than the suffrage movement. Something grand was stirring among women. The first time I heard Susan Anthony speak, I was ready to march in any army she would choose to muster.

"Louisa is one of the speakers, did you know that?" Anna said, smoothing her hand over a bolt of woolen goods with excessive interest.

"No, I didn't."

There was a pause; a hesitation. "I don't know the nature of your estrangement, for neither you nor Louisa has seen fit to speak of it. And I will not ask now. But if it is in part due to her growing celebrity and her . . . her changing nature, can we talk about it?" she said gently.

I kept my face down as I continued cutting through the fabric, hoping she did not notice a slight wavering in the trajectory of my scissors. "It is deeper than that, Anna, but I thank you for your concern," I said.

"Nothing between the two of you should cut so deep. May I speak to my own feelings?"

I looked up, startled. "Please do."

Anna smiled. "You know, there is many a time when my distinguished sister is roaring about among the other lions when I feel like a poor Cinderella, knowing I cannot leave my children for such grand times. And I have on occasion resented that." She was blushing, and I loved her for her honesty.

"It isn't jealousy, Anna, at least not that kind. I'm very happy with my own work."

"She has increasing dark moods, and sad health."

"I have heard that, and I am sorry."

"Is there nothing to be done? You two were as close as sisters, so close, I was jealous of you at one time." Anna's eyes filled with tears, and I rushed to embrace her.

"Maybe someday," I said, wondering when and how such a "someday" could come about.

The rally was noisy and exciting. More women came than I had expected, and it was thrilling to look around and see determination in their faces that matched my own. Our sense of sharing an idea arched over our separate lives in a way I hadn't known could happen. We sang, we listened to speeches, and I stood rooted to the ground, enthralled, as Susan B. Anthony opened her vision of the future to Concord's women. Her voice, filled with passion, reached to the outer bounds of the hall, reverberating back, galvanizing us all.

Outside I could hear jeers, faint catcalls. The gauntlet of angry men who had lined the walk as we entered the hall had shocked me. Why should they be so rudely opposed to female enfranchisement? It was so clearly right. Of what were they afraid?

I spied Louisa on the platform, and saw to my satisfaction that she wore the identifying hat and sash of my design. I wondered, did she know they were from me? And even as I mulled that over, I heard a brisk, familiar voice at my elbow:

"Well, Susan, I hoped to see you here."

I turned. It was Clara. A different Clara, somehow more honed for soaring flight and yet fragile. "How wonderful to see you!" I cried, embracing her, scrambling to remember her age. Well into her fifties, I surmised. I was struck immediately by the delicacy of her bones, fearing my clumsy grasp could collapse them inward. I pulled back and looked at her face, which was sallow and gaunt.

She was dressed as I had always known her—all in black. "How are you?" I asked.

Clara shrugged. "Don't get duly concerned by my yellow skin; I'm much better than I was, dear. And don't make the mistake of dismissing me because of my age. Not that any doctor ever seems to know what's wrong with me. They told me I had 'heated blood,' so I gave up on all of them. Come——" She wanted no more talk of health, I could see that. She tugged me to some empty chairs against the back wall of the hall. "I'm here as much to see you as to witness the strength of the movement. Let us catch up. Wonderful expression, isn't it?"

I had missed Clara, more than I knew, and amid the songs and speeches, we did indeed "catch up." She was in Concord at Susan B. Anthony's request, she told me. Miss Anthony wanted her to make women's rights her new cause, pleading that she should not commit herself to any other new interest before completing the fight for enfranchisement; come see what we are doing and how much the women of America support us. "And so I am here," she finished. "I support her work, but I must tell you, I don't intend to take a leadership role."

"Why not?" I asked, aghast.

Her answer was the declarative Clara at her best. "There's too much focus on getting the vote to the detriment of other goals. We need marital reform, legal reform—and what about the Negroes? Their enfranchisement should come first."

"But surely they can come together!" The words burst from me. My single-minded friend had always been a fierce supporter of rights for women; surely she wasn't backing away.

"Don't look at me as if I hit you across the face," she said crossly. "Of course, I'm for suffrage. I suppose the real thing is I'm afraid it will divert my energies away from something else." She looked at me with an unlikely hint of shyness, searching my face to see if I was willing to listen. She must have decided I was, because she continued, "Susan, I know now what my life's work will be."

Pacing, gesticulating, corseted body ramrod straight, she told me of her new venture, a commitment to start a disaster-aid group in America similar to the International Red Cross. I felt myself swept along by her enthusiasm, experiencing vicariously her fights with officialdom and victories over small-minded adversaries. She was very good at self-dramatizing, but that had always been true. It was part of what made her leadership enthralling, as Tom and Liddy and I had many times agreed. I realized how lucky I had been to work by her side.

And then she brought me to ground with a thump.

"How is it between you and Louisa?" she asked. "I talked to her backstage, but even I did not have the audacity to ask."

And so I told her. Behind us, the final speech had just ended, greeted with a roar of applause and cheers. Women jumped to their feet and the band began to play, producing a cacophony of scraping chairs and tootling horns. The crowd began to disperse, a blur of animated women talking with each other about more, now, than the price of eggs and fruit at the market.

I looked up, seeing for the first time the final speaker, standing solemn and straight at the podium. I realized the one speech I had missed was Louisa's. She was sitting on a chair behind the podium, a grave and weighty presence. Did I just imagine her looking at us? I could not tell for sure.

Clara's glance followed mine. She turned back to me.

"Don't give up, Susan. I saw what existed between the two of you and I don't think it dies in this way." She took my hand in hers. "I must go now, dear. I have to rejoin Miss Anthony, for we are traveling together back to Boston. You are not ready to believe this, but life will change, and the opportunity for reconciliation will come." She bussed me quickly, briskly, on the cheek and disappeared into the crowd. I have not seen her since. But after Louisa's death, I received from my stalwart old friend a poem she had written entitled "The Women Who Went to the Field."

The women who went to the field, you say . . .
A few names were writ, and by chance live to-day;
But's a perishing record fast fading away.
Of those we recall, there are scarcely a score. . . .
And what would they do if war came again? . . .
They would stand with you now, as they stood with you then,
The nurses, consolers, and saviors of men.

It came in a crumpled, handwritten note. I smoothed out the paper and tucked it inside Louisa's coffin, finding it not only a gift of great comfort but a proud declaration of all that we had shared and done.

I speed ahead too fast.

One late night in November of '87, I awoke to a hammering on my front door. I pulled it open and saw a young boy standing on the step. Silently, with a quick tip of his cap, he handed me a message from Anna. I opened it, bracing for the contents.

"Please come," the not unexpected message read. "Marmee is dying."

I dressed quickly, pulling on my stoutest shoes, and made my way to Orchard House, walking as quickly as I could through the darkened town. The night was moonless and I stumbled a few times as I listened to the sighing and whispering of the oaks above me. Abba had been ill now for weeks, and I had dreaded this call. All thought was suspended, only sensation remained, the sensation of knowing an era was about to end.

The house was dark but for the flickering light in Abba's bedroom. Anna met me at the door with a resigned, sad look on her face.

"She cries for May," she said. "She reaches out her hand to the picture at her bedside and asks 'Where is my youngest child?' and I have nothing to tell her."

I threw off my cloak, shivering. I still couldn't believe that May had made no effort to come home from Paris, even with repeated warnings of what was coming. "Has she written?" I asked.

"Oh, she chose, Susan. She chose not to come back."

Never had I heard such cold words from Anna.

The sickroom was filled with sorrow. Bronson stood by the mantel, head bowed. Louisa wept by the side of her mother's bed. I walked into the room as quietly as I could, but Abba heard my footsteps.

"May? My baby? You've come home, after all!" she cried. She reached out her arms with such desire and aching love, I couldn't hold back my tears. What should I do? I glanced at Louisa, whose stare was impenetrable. Bronson's head stayed bowed.

"May? Oh, please be May!" Abba was delirious now, thrashing as she struggled for breath.

The image of young Jimmy crying for his brother from his hospital cot flashed through my mind. So many years ago. "Yes, it's May," I said. "I'm here, Mother." I sat on her bed, waiting for no one's permission, and put my arms around her. I soothed her and hummed an old lullaby I knew she loved. And within minutes, her painful gasps for air ended.

Abba, you became my mother, and I love you. That is what I thought, even as I heard the final expulsion of air from her lungs. I rose from the bed in tears, not knowing whether I had transgressed.

The family gathered close, and I drew back. I found it difficult to breathe. I had crossed a line never articulated, and if I knew it, surely the others did, too. For I was neither of this family nor apart from it; my ambiguous status with them was part of my journey of life, always moving on, never with a fully acceptable place to rest. I turned to go, thinking only to reach the stairs to grieve alone. I sank onto the top step and buried my head in my hands.

Downstairs the clock struck the hour. The house stayed still. Then the quarter-hour. At half-past, I heard the soft rustling of skirts as someone sat next to me on the stairs. I looked over to see Louisa.

"Thank you, Susan," she whispered.

I tried to speak, but words wouldn't come.

"That was a great act of kindness."

"I loved your mother very much."

"You gave a lesson in loyalty, as well as love." She put her arm around me and hugged me close.

We made no attempt to speak, no attempt to find the right words; words weren't necessary yet. I cried on my friend's shoulder, but now with more than sadness for what was gone, with hope for healing yet to come.

The next day Louisa struggled with the letter she would send to her absent sister. It took hours to drain from it the anger she felt. Louisa wrote of how Abba had pointed up at May's picture on the wall, whispering "Good-bye, little May, good-bye." I would not allow her to write of my act of loving pretense, feeling this was too much to put on May's conscience. The letter in its final form was a struggle between Louisa's hurt and her love for May, and that struggle ended with no advantage for either side.

> *I wish I was with you, my darling, for I know how hard it will be to bear alone this sorrow—but don't think of it much 'til time makes it easier & never mourn that you didn't come. All is well, & your work was a joy to Momma. We will write often & tell you all that goes on.*
>
> > *God bless you dear,*
> > *Your sister*

"Is it all right?" she asked, before sealing the letter.

"It's honest and loving at the same time. It's fine."

And so we began again. Bruised, sorrowed, perhaps wiser. What is love about if it does not at least seek to endure against disappointment and betrayal? Neither of us embraced vindication, and certainly not innocence. And I for the first time was able to accept the elusive nature of my friend's personality without attempting to breach it. We were who we were, and we came together again as friends out of a sense of unbreakable bonds.

"Susan, do you think we've mellowed?" Louisa asked one afternoon as she helped me pack up a wedding gown to be shipped to Boston.

My mouth was half-full of pins at the time, but I managed to say, "Indeed, I believe we have."

Louisa's eyes suddenly sparkled. "Feel like climbing a tree?"

I dropped the dress into the box. "I can think of nothing better."

And we did. We hiked up our skirts and tied them with rope, chose a splendid oak hidden from the curious eyes of those in town, and climbed high above the ground to a point where we could survey all of Concord. We sat there and watched the sun go down in full glory, united again in a way we both cherished. And it was there that Lou suggested the two of us go back together to Washington.

"I owe it to you," she said.

"And perhaps to yourself."

She smiled. "That, too."

We managed three days for the trip in the month that followed. I feared Lou would find it too hard revisiting so many painful memories, but her spirit was resolute. We retraced our steps, from that first night peering into the windows of the President's House to visiting our tiny room on the third floor of the abandoned hospital, staring at where we had slept as two novices overwhelmed by the horrors of war. Louisa asked about my life with Clara. I told her many things, showing her Clara's old building, pointing to the third-floor window from which we had shouted down our questions the night Lincoln died.

"Can we go in?" she asked, staring up at the window.

We tried.

"Offices of Clara Barton?" The shopkeeper on the first floor peered at us, scratching his head. "Dunno, ladies. That place got closed up years ago. Boards over the door; never been up there, myself."

It was disappointing, an indication of the flow of time.

Without ever discussing it, we went next to Arlington. The day was very cold. We trudged up the hill to John's grave in silence and stood there listening to the wind move lazily through bare trees, each with our own memories, knowing we finally had a hard-won peace.

"One more stop?" Louisa pressed gently.

I nodded. The day's light was waning when we reached Oak Hill Cemetery and I gazed once again on my baby's grave.

She stared in silence before whispering, "Dear Susan, I'm so sorry."

I took her hand. "We've shared it all now," I said. "Let's go home."

The day after we returned to Concord, Louisa took me into the library and pulled several thick notebooks from a desk drawer. The weather was raw, and a brisk fire warmed the room. "Marmee's diaries," she said in a hesitant voice.

"Oh my, what a treasure," I exclaimed. "I didn't know she kept journals."

"Yes, and I used to dream of someday publishing them. Mother was a valiant woman who did much to help the poor, and she deserves recognition. But they're not . . . they're not what I expected. I've been reading them. I need to show you some of this before I destroy it all."

"*What?*" I couldn't believe my ears. Destroy Abba's diaries? Why?

"They aren't meant to be public, they were meant only for her. It's what she would have wanted, I'm sure of it."

"Then why did she not destroy them herself?"

Louisa held one notebook out to me. "I want you to read some of the entries. This is the book she kept from 1841 to 1844."

Stunned, I sat down and silently took the book she handed me. I hardly recognized the wild scrawl of Abba's most personal writing or the sheer—what was it?—physical energy of what I saw.

The book was filled with scribbles in the margins and news articles and pictures pasted on the pages, slapped on in any direction, surrounded by more scribbling. I glanced at the entries, slowing turning the pages. Years of entries exhorting herself to greater character and discipline, followed by great outbursts of feelings. Abba—anxious, self-sacrificing, devoted Abba—had lived an inner life filled with storms.

What was happening in those years? Of course, Fruitlands. Bronson's experiment in utopian living.

> *Mr. Alcott cannot bring himself to work for gain, but we have not yet learned to live without money or means. . . . I'd like to see my husband a little more interested in support, I love his faith and his reliance on Divine Providence. But a little more activity and industry would place us beyond most of these disagreeable dependencies on friends. For tho they aid, they censure. . . .*

And at another place, her scrawl ever more agitated:

> *. . . he meanders to and fro on the face of the earth . . . I willingly forgo his presence here—tho I sometimes feel as it were robbing my dear children of their birthright. . . . He's wrapped up, not in himself but in the principles of which he considers himself the embodiment. A perplexing character—one of much beauty, purity, ideality.*

There was no question of whom she spoke. I read on, slowly, for an hour, remembering how Abba would, on occasion, give a hint of her deeper nature. I had seen glimpses of the fire under her determined domesticity and paid little attention to what I, along with the others, had been able to take for granted. Abba was the first who served as heart and backbone of this family. Who else was there to keep it together when the girls were little? Abba had done it all.

Wherever I turn I see the yoke on woman in some form or other . . .
they are but beasts of burden . . . she may die daily in the cause of
truth and righteousness, the lives neglected, cries forgotten—but a
man, who never performed in his whole life one self-denying act but
who had accidental gifts of genius, is celebrated by his contempo-
raries, while his name and his works live on . . . he is crowned w/lau-
rels while scarce a stone may tell where SHE lies . . . a woman may live
a whole life of sacrifice and at her death meekly says, I die a woman.
A man spends a few years in experiments or self-denial & simple life
& he says, "behold a God." . . .

I closed the book with that entry, and said to Louisa, "Don't
burn this. It is your mother's honest voice, her passions. I think it's
wonderful."

She looked away from me, into the fire. "I can't keep them,"
she said. "I don't want them to be around, for someone will try to
publish them after I die."

"Don't burn them, Lou. Don't do it." Why, I thought, must
Abba be remembered only as the saintly mother in *Little Women*?
Her true voice excited me, made me wonder about the mysteries
of those we love intimately and yet never completely know. Why
were her revelations to be feared?

She looked at me then, the flickering light of the fire catching
the deep lines that curved around her set lips. "I suppose I've created the family I wanted, just as I created the world I wanted," she
said softly. "I suppose it's always been something of a dream. But I
can't stop now."

I could think of nothing to say. Had I not created my own
dream world? For so many years, Lou had been my hero, my mentor, my friend who could do no wrong. And how long it had taken
for me to realize finding my own way meant leaving this safe harbor. For Lou, the dreams that had trapped her were at least as
painful as reality. She had escaped nothing by retreating. Looking
at my friend's face, I felt a surge of compassion and love.

"Don't do it, please."

"I must, Susan." A tear dribbled down her cheek.

"You will regret it all your life."

"Oh, my dear friend, no, I won't."

Shivering, I held the book in my hand aloft. "At least save this one. Don't take away your mother's voice."

"It matters that much to you?"

"Yes. I want to read it and know her more fully."

There was a long silence. "It is easier to read than many of the others," she said quietly.

"Then keep it."

She smiled. "Then I shall. But only if you will stand by me while I do what I need to do."

"If I must," I said, clutching the one notebook close.

Picking up the other books, she knelt by the fire and slowly began feeding them to the flames. I watched those pages filled with Abba's thoughts and hopes and angers curling tight at the edges, turning black, and crumbling into the coals. Page after page; book after book. Tears ran down my cheeks as Louisa continued her sad, methodical task. How quickly it was done! Years of writing, gone within an hour into smoke. All gone.

We sat in silence, staring at the lapping flames.

"Susan, I want my journals and letters burned when I die," she said.

"I'm not surprised."

"But watching you clutch that notebook makes me think you aren't the person to whom I should entrust that duty."

"No, I am not," I said with great conviction. "For the rest of my life, I will do anything for you, but not that."

"Then I will do it myself."

And so she did. Only weeks before her death. For all of what I will do to protect the privacy of my friend now, I wish with all my heart she had not burned so much of the truth of her life. Louisa chose to defer to the image she was expected to maintain. I believe she worried too much about the children looking only for Jo.

*   *   *

May announced her engagement to a young Swiss named Ernest Nieriker but three months later. Now we knew why she had resisted the trip home, which made it no easier to greet her news with the joy we wanted to feel. She was married in London in March of 1878, only a few weeks after her engagement, writing gaily that doing so kept her from "working myself sick beforehand over clothes." No family member attended. Many good wishes were sent, but the letters that traversed the ocean went with tears and hidden bitterness—I knew what was hidden in those written words of congratulations, at least for Louisa.

"Read this!" Louisa stormed, throwing a letter down on my desk. "And this!" Another was plunked down beside the first. Her hand trembled; it was another one of her bad days. Louisa's health continued to deteriorate steadily, and no cure or medicine seemed to help her. Each time she rallied, but never all the way back. My friend was going downward, I could see that, and each time I thought of those doses of calomel thrust down her throat by Belle Poole, I was angered.

I read the letters; they were so like May. She wrote happily of her new home in Mendan, where she could see the buildings of Paris from the balcony; of her nervousness meeting her new in-laws, blithely and obliviously writing that she was sure "they are far finer people than my own of whom I am always bragging." Then telling us triumphantly that she wore a new peacock blue robe that Ernest claimed made her look "slender and girlish" and "entirely captivated" her in-laws at their first meeting. "And with my curls in picturesque disorder and a little nosegay among my laces, I felt quite ready for inspection by my new Mama."

That bothered Louisa the most. "Her 'new Mama'? What is she talking about? She doesn't have a 'new' Mama! There is only one, and she is in her grave."

I ached for my friend. This sister she had both envied and adored seemed too happy, too far away. I could not say it, but it was clear May was enjoying life in a way Louisa would never understand. Yet how could she not know what it meant for Lou to read such lines as these?

A woman does not know what happiness is till she has a good man to love. I feel as if I am living in somebody else's romance, and I cannot believe it is mine.

I looked at Louisa, slumped now in a chair, and felt a great loving pity. I remembered how abandoned I had felt when she left for Europe without me. She had correctly pointed out to me then that she needed to live her own life, as did I, as did May. And yet how it hurt to be left behind!

I am still walking through my part in this interesting novel, and see less and less of my old self, the floating blue gown being the only trace of May Alcott.

"You know what I'm thinking, don't you?" she said finally. "You've always had a way of seeing inside my brain."

"Hardly that," I retorted. "But I know what alarms you here."

"Why is she trying to kill off May Alcott? What is wrong with who she is?"

Oh, Louisa. You could not see that May, in her own way, was writing a new story of life. She was re-creating herself, differently from how you had with your tales, but with the same purpose: escape. And with the same imperfect outcome. What do I believe you really feared? Not that she was killing May, but killing you.

For a while, it must have been splendid. May reported she had seven studies on exhibit in Paris, and even a panel in the Manchester Gallery in London. None of this, she wrote, would have been possible in America. She urged Louisa to come visit, to share her ideal life, promising she would never want to live "in stupid America" again. Louisa smiled at that, and I sensed she was beginning to soften, to hear again the blithe voice of her beloved younger sister.

"I will go soon," she said.

"Write and tell her so," I urged.

"I will. Soon."

What did May think through this time? One letter she wrote we chose not to show to Louisa, for it was May's response to her sister's distance.

> She must not think my own happiness has made me unmindful of her, for it only draws us nearer. But I have laid out my future life and hope not to swerve from my purpose. I do not mean to be hindered by envious people or anything to drive me from accomplishing my dream. For myself this simple artistic life is so charming that America seems death to all aspirations or hope of work. . . . With Ernest and pictures I should not care if I never saw a friend or acquaintance again. It is the perfection of living. . . . Nothing could ever seduce me to live in Concord again, burdened with cares.

I felt sympathy for May. Her defiance provided the energy she needed to seek her own transformation, to resist the tugs back to earth from her older sister. Would that she could have had more time, for I believe the two of them would have soon reached each other again, as Louisa and I had done. But time, of course, is a fickle component, and frequently runs out when we need it the most. Louisa began to make plans for the long-postponed journey when news came of May's pregnancy. Sometimes I feared she did not have the strength for the voyage, but the idea of a baby coming seemed to bolster her spirits.

May's child was born November 8, 1879. She named the baby Louisa May Alcott Nieriker. The letter received from Ernest, scribbled so happily, came quickly:

> About 11, LMAN lay in innocent astonishment before me. The doctor says he never had an easier case. . . . May had a slight shiver soon after birth, but toward morning was most comfortable again.

May pulled herself up in her bed to add a small postscript to her family:

> *Dear girls,*
> *All right. Baby a dear. And I a wonderfully good case. I write this the 7th day. Now good-bye.*
>
> 　　　　　　　　　　　　　　　　　　　　*May*

It was her last letter. That "slight shiver" became three weeks of fever and stupor that killed our May on December 29. On the last day of the year, that night of celebratory hope for the future, Mr. Emerson made the cold, lonely trek from his home to Orchard House, carrying the news in the form of a telegram sent by Ernest. I saw him approach, walking slowly, and feared the worst. Louisa came down the stairs quickly and clutched my hand as I opened the door.

"My child, I wish I could prepare you, but alas, alas!" The old man handed the telegram to Louisa.

I have never heard the likes of the wail that emerged from Louisa. The little sister, once described by Abba as the family's "cricket on the hearth," was gone. It was as if Lou's soul had been run through with a blade. She sank against me in despair.

"Oh, why wasn't I there to help?" she cried. "I should have gone sooner, I should have been there with her!" I held her fast. The room swirled around us, and Anna folded herself into a chair, quietly weeping as Bronson, in his helpless, vague way, tried to console.

"This would have happened whether you had been there or not," I said, hating the finality of my words. "But you loved her, and she loved you."

I knew true consolation was not possible, for indeed, so much died that day at Orchard House. The blithe spirit that had been May, the saucy girl whose behavior for years had let us all roll our eyes and complain, will she never grow up? Gone, gone. And all that was young and carefree in the family had evaporated. Was there no way to find joy again?

Yes, there was. Her name was Lulu.

May's last wish was that her baby be sent to Louisa. Ernest had promised his wife he would follow her desires, and, after ten months, he put his child on a ship and sent her to her American family. It was a sharp, windy day when Louisa and I traveled together to Boston to meet the steamer. We stood, staring as the ship approached, facing a future under no one's control.

"I must do this right, for it is my last chance," she said.

"You shall."

"I don't want to retreat. I don't want to hesitate." Her breathing was fast and painful.

"You won't. This is May's child."

"Stay by me, Susan. You've pointed the way, and this time I will follow."

Never will I forget the moment I first saw that pug-nosed little girl with downy-soft yellow hair come down the gangplank in the arms of the ship's captain, with the nursemaid close behind. He put her gently to ground and she hesitantly hobbled forward.

"Lulu?" Louisa held out her arms, her voice wavering.

The child stared at her, uncertain. She was a tiny replica of May. All was suspended for a long moment as she assessed the scene with the keenest eyes I've ever seen on a small one.

"Marmar?" she said. And then, reassured I believe by the love and hope in Louisa's face, she took a shaky step into her new mother's arms. My joy was tempered by a sudden tide of loneliness as I remembered the baby I had never been able to hold. Louisa turned to me, holding Lulu. I felt a fog lifting, and an unexpected lightness of heart, even before she spoke to the child, pointing at me.

"Lulu," she said, "I want you to meet your Aunt Susan."

Epilogue

The wind is picking up; I draw my cloak closer and shiver. It's time to leave this hill and travel home. But my communion with the dead is not yet over.

Louisa, you are gone too soon. But oh, what happiness little Lulu brought to us in those final eight years! She will flourish and grow, and yes, it was in the end all worthwhile.

Tears sting my eyes as I gaze on your coffin. Thirty-eight years since I peeked in the oven and saw the little colored boy; thirty-eight years since our mutual pledge of friendship. We walked a long road, sometimes together; sometimes separately. We shared things so far beyond our own unimportant lives. If you were here now, we would be reminiscing again about that splendid night in 1880 when we marched into Town Hall and voted for the first time. We thought the entire city of women would show up for the school committee election, but there were only eighteen besides ourselves. That didn't spoil it for us, did it? "Susan, we lived to see this!" you cried and the two of us, grown women, danced an impromptu jig on Main Street and then ran home, laughing.

I can accept now that your defiant spirit, the spirit that took me jumping into piles of leaves with you and from there, tagging along, made strong by your bravery, to participate truly in the war that changed all of our lives, was only a part of you. I followed your courage. And for so long, you defined my life.

But I see now that through all these years I have been in search of myself, that I was not by my nature destined to live in your shadow. Only with that fully realized am I freed of sadness. I know what Mrs. Cheney will have to say, for all the praise she will give and rosy scenes she will paint in her book. She will say, such a diligent biographer, that duty held you back from a greater literary flowering. Success without pleasure was your compromise. She will only be able to speculate as to why, but those who loved you know that it was in your nature to be more comfortable with the people you created than with those of flesh and blood. John saw it almost immediately, and loved you still, even as he knew the truth of why you hesitated to come to him.

What were your words as you lay dying? "We had no choice," you said to me. I understand, now. Each of us was bound by nature to different destinies, and our healing came from accepting that.

Perhaps my effort to think all this through is just a way of fashioning an image of my life as carefully constructed as yours, even though I have no written story to feed to the flames.

Perhaps; perhaps.

Betrayal? I would like to take that word, crumple it as tight in my hand as the note from your heart I never delivered, and say yes, but more than that. We found each other again—weighted with loss, but real all the same. We no longer romped in the woods, but we marched together to the voting booth. In part because of your immersion in your imagination, you were the person, the flame, most real to me, of all. Such wonderful irony! It took us a lifetime to build the framework for our friendship. But we managed, finally, to endure.

When all is said and done, these last eight years thrilling to the miraculous exuberance of little Lulu were the best. I can hear you laughing now as Lulu pedaled furiously away on her tricycle, the tattered remnants of your glory cloak tied around her shoulders, daring the two of us to once again hitch up our skirts and chase her down the path. I can hear you yelling: "Wait up, little grasshopper, wait up!" as she laughed merrily and pedaled faster. What fun we had with that bonny child! Ah, me. She goes home now to her father, who aches for his daughter, but Anna and I will miss her sorely. Dear Louisa, she leaves Concord at an earlier age than you or I. All things change.

It is peaceful here. The unrest and confusion within me is dissipating, and I wonder now why I feared making the journey back through time I knew was inevitable. You are with your father, your mother, Beth, and May. I am left to honor our pact, and I will follow your wishes. I promise you, the private sorrow of your life will die with me. I have no doubts anymore. The letter to Mrs. Cheney will be easy to complete.

"Susan?"

The sudden voice makes me start. I peer through the gloom down the path and see a figure walking toward me. Tom? Of course. And he is laboring. A bad leg, the result of a fall last year from a wagon. Right on Main Street, into the path of a pair of horses who couldn't stop. Older now; his gray eyes not nearly as bright and clear as they once were. But I am still able to see again the solemn look on his face, the stalwart set of his shoulders, on that long-ago day in Lafayette Square when he first proposed marriage and I turned him down. It is my good fortune that he persisted. That he waited until his tavern prospered, then showed up at my shop and presented himself to me one sunny afternoon and asked if I might have second thoughts. Has it been ten years already since we became man and wife?

His brow is furrowed as he approaches. "Thought I'd find you up here. Why didn't you tell me where you were going? I've been looking everywhere for over an hour."

"Even though you thought I'd be up here?" I tease.

He smiles. "Well, I wanted to leave you alone for a while."

"But get in a little bit of a scold at the same time?"

"Of course." He bends down and kisses my brow. "So, have you accomplished what you wanted?"

"Yes."

He nods, and I see a smile flicker across his face. "You went farther, I suspect, than simply up this hill to visit Louisa."

I pull myself up, rubbing my aching back. "You know me, Tom. All the way to the beginning."

"Without getting stuck, I hope," he says gently. He touches my chin, lifting it to look me straight in the eye. "And are you with me now?"

"Yes."

"Good. I've been waiting."

I tuck my hand into his and, together, we work our way back down the hill, away from Sleepy Hollow, back to the place we call home.

Afterword

For me, part of the pleasure of reading historical fiction is discovering how truth threads through the story. Many of the settings and details of *The Glory Cloak* are historically accurate. But Susan Gray—the woman at the heart of this tale—is fictional. In my search for Jo, I found Louisa elusive, a woman who hid herself too well. Creating Susan was a way to get closer to Louisa. I found in her a narrator who could provide a window into the lives of the Alcott family as well as into the mind and heart of a woman living through that tumultuous era.

So, to the true facts: Clara and Louisa were indeed in Washington after the battle of Fredericksburg in 1862. Louisa worked at Union Hotel Hospital in Georgetown—although I have lengthened the actual span of time she spent there for the sake of the story—and some of the detail of the grim nature of the place comes from her memoir, *Hospital Sketches*. Could they have met? Quite possibly, although I have no evidence they did.

Louisa did indeed harbor a long-term unrequited infatuation for Henry David Thoreau. And—as an active suffragist—she knew Susan B. Anthony, although their appearance together in Concord is imaginary.

John Sulie and Dorrance Atwater were both real Union soldiers. John, a blacksmith, was wounded at Fredericksburg and treated at Union Hospital, while Dorrance was confined at Andersonville. Both men played significant roles in the lives of Louisa and Clara: Louisa's emotional account in *Hospital Sketches* of her attachment to John has led some biographers to speculate she was in love with him. The description of his death is Louisa's. And Dorrance Atwater did bring to Clara the list of the dead buried at Andersonville; the details of their expedition to that notorious prison are essentially accurate. And yes, Atwater was imprisoned and charged with "stealing" his own list, but he did not die in prison. He survived to work with Clara in her quest to identify the missing soldiers of the Civil War. Belle Poole, his accuser, is totally imaginary. Merging these two men into a single person gave me a fictional bridge between Louisa and Clara.

The discovery in 1997 of Clara's apartment on Seventh Street in Washington, D.C.—in a building about to fall to the wrecking ball—astonished some historians. The third floor of this decrepit building had been closed off since the late nineteenth century. It was only when a curious government employee reached into the boarded-up area and pulled out Clara's tin sign announcing her presence on the third floor that history was gifted with a veritable time capsule, left by Clara and forgotten for 130 years.

Hannah Ropes was a real person, the stalwart chief nurse at Union Hospital. She worked with Louisa and died of typhoid pneumonia.

Many of the excerpts from letters and diary entries in this book are taken from the original sources at Harvard's Houghton Library, including May and Abba Alcott's diaries. Some are intertwined with fiction to accommodate the story, but I tried to retain the true voices in the documents. Reading through the agitated scribbles of Abba's surviving diaries, for example (Louisa did indeed destroy most of them), gave me a sense of the contained anguish of her life in a way nothing else could have. I have also recreated certain scenes as Louisa described them—for example, her description of little Lulu's arrival in Boston.

I started this book looking for Jo. Like so many women of many generations, I dreamed from the day I closed the last pages of *Little Women* at the age of ten that I would be a writer. I imagined myself in a garret eating "russets" (it took me a while to understand they were apples) and writing down everything swirling in my head.

Did I find Jo? Yes, and Abba helped, for the "glory cloak" was a real garment. Abba fashioned it and presented it to Louisa when she was struggling to be recognized as a writer. Louisa wore this cloak of red and green silk, understanding her mother's message: Sit straight and proud; work hard; believe in yourself, and you will succeed. It was a remarkable message for a mother to send to her daughter in the nineteenth century, and one that those of us who grew up enthralled with *Little Women* can both understand and appreciate.

All this said, it is important to remember which word is the noun and which is the adjective in the phrase "historical novel." *The Glory Cloak* is entirely a work of fiction. With Eudora Welty's memoir, *One Writer's Beginnings*, by my bedside for the past two years, I tried to follow her advice to write as a listener. She reassured me at various points that "emotions do not grow old," a compelling invitation to try to capture some fragments of Louisa's life, including her connection to her family, in the context of a hometown and a time, all caught up in a period of breathtaking change.

Bibliography
&
Acknowledgments

I am indebted to several fine biographies for help along the way, especially Madeleine B. Stern's *Louisa May Alcott: A Biography* and Martha Saxton's *Louisa May Alcott: A Modern Biography*. Both were sources of insight into Louisa's complicated personality. Elizabeth Brown Pryor's *Clara Barton, Professional Angel* and Stephen B. Oates's *A Woman of Valor: Clara Barton and the Civil War* provided rich factual material on Clara's efforts to identify the missing and the dead after the war. Oates's account of Clara's connection to Dorrance Atwater and their trip to Andersonville to mark the graves of the dead was particularly helpful. For some sense of what the chaotic atmosphere of Washington was after the war, I turned to Jay Winik's *April 1865*.

A number of other books were also helpful, especially *Civil War Nurse: The Diary and Letters of Hannah Ropes*, edited by John Brumgardt, and *This Was Andersonville* (the memoir of Andersonville survivor John McElroy), edited by Roy Meredith. Also, "The Alcott Family Arrives," by Ann Struthers. And, of course, *The Selected Letters of Louisa May Alcott* and *The Journals of Louisa May Alcott*, edited by Joel Myerson and Daniel Shealy, and Madeleine B. Stern, associate editor.

I am especially grateful to Harvard University's Houghton Library and to the literary heirs of Louisa May Alcott for permission to quote from the original Alcott documents. Valuable research advice and material was also provided by Margaret Power and Zsuzsa Berend.

Gary Scott, a historian with the National Park Service, was the person who put me in touch with Richard Lyons, the man who first discovered Clara Barton's apartment. It was Lyons who actually climbed the ladder and pulled out the ancient sign that opened up this previously unknown chapter of Civil War history. Mr. Lyons took me on an enthralling tour of Clara's Seventh Street apartment, and I thank him for that. The apartment is slated to become a museum.

Much thanks and gratitude to Irene Wurtzel, Judith Viorst, Ellen Goodman, and Mary Thaler Dillon for their suggestions and critiques; to my editor, Trish Todd, whose ideas and energy were invaluable; and to my agent, Esther Newberg, for being such a staunch friend as well as a great agent. A big hug to my friend Laurel Laidlaw for many favors. Finally, a special thank-you to my daughter, Margaret Koval, who first began ruminating about "looking for Jo."

Most important, special love and gratitude to my husband, Frank Mankiewicz. He is my glory cloak.

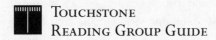

TOUCHSTONE
READING GROUP GUIDE

THE GLORY CLOAK

1. In *The Glory Cloak*, historical fact and fiction blend seamlessly. How did you feel about rediscovering Louisa May Alcott through the eyes of a fictional character? Did reading this novel enhance your understanding of Louisa May Alcott?

2. Describe Susan's role in the Alcott family. How can she be considered both an integral member of the family and an outsider?

3. How would you characterize the early friendship between Louisa and Susan? How does it change over time? Was it realistic for them to think that the form of their friendship would last forever?

4. Quoting Emerson, Louisa says, "It is impossible to extricate ourselves from the times in which we live" (67). How is the novel as a whole guided by that statement? What famous Americans make appearances in the novel, and what does their presence add to the story?

5. At what point does Louisa cease to be the carefree, courageous girl of Susan's memory? Why? What unique burdens does she bear, and why won't she allow herself to enjoy the fruits of her labor?

6. What does Louisa's youthful enthusiasm—even passion—for Henry David Thoreau reveal about her? How does it foreshadow her eventual relationship with John Sulie?

7. How would you describe Louisa's vision of the ideal family, and how does this vision shape her writing of *Little Women*? Why is Louisa so unreasonably upset about Anna's marriage? Also, what makes her relationship with her father unique?

8. How do Susan and Louisa's experiences as nurses mature them in ways that life in Concord never could have? Like Louisa, Clara Barton is a guiding influence in Susan's life. What does Susan learn from Clara that she cannot learn from Louisa?

9. After the war, Louisa refuses to believe that John Sulie is still alive, writing his death firmly into her book and into her mind. Why is it so crucial to Louisa that he die in her fictional account?

10. Discuss how John Sulie could be viewed as both a typical soldier and a singular hero. How does his experience of war change him? Why is he unable to return Susan's love, and why do you think he ultimately chooses to take his own life?

11. When Louisa decides not to return from Europe to be with John, even he suspects that she preferred his fictional self. Do you agree? Had the two been reunited, how do you think they would have changed, if at all?

12. Was Susan right to confess all to Louisa? Do you think Susan was in the wrong—or had Louisa truly given up her claim to John?

13. Reflecting on her life with Louisa, Susan asks herself (9), "Did I lose or find myself through Louisa? Did she consume me or set me free?" Having now heard her full tale, how would you answer her?

14. Susan is critical of the way that Louisa occasionally bends her reality into a more palatable fiction. In Susan's telling of their shared story, however, is it possible that she's guilty of the same? Are we ever fully knowable, even to ourselves? Don't we all fashion our lives to fit a story?

Discover more reading group guides and download them free at www.bookclubreader.com.

An Interview with Patricia O'Brien

1. *What drew you to the story of Louisa May Alcott? What kind of research did you do to immerse yourself in the Alcotts' world?*

As a child I was enthralled with Jo March in *Little Women*. Louisa and Jo were always blended in my mind, and I assumed the woman who created such an enduring heroine had to be just like Jo.

Then a few years ago, I ran across an intriguing little book called *Hospital Sketches* that gave me an entirely different view of Louisa, both as a writer and as a woman. Her account of her service as a nurse in Washington during the Civil War thoroughly gripped me, and I began reading as much about her as I could. I found a far more complicated person than I had expected—and that took me to the Houghton Library, where I began reading her letters and diaries and those of her sisters and her mother. I visited her home in Concord and could almost feel her moving through the rooms and up and down the stairs. Who *was* she? I was hooked.

2. *What elements of Louisa May Alcott's life particularly intrigued or challenged you, and what new light did you hope to shed on her story by writing this novel?*

It took courage for a sheltered woman like Louisa to volunteer as a nurse during the war. What she experienced in the hospital was brutal and sad, and I wondered how it shaped her. I also wondered why fame brought her so little happiness. Louisa's warm family stories made her a literary icon for the ages, and yet something inside her was trapped. Her recently unearthed "pot-boiler" stories hint at the depth of her repressed passion and reveal the contradictions and struggles between her literary and personal lives. I wanted to explore a possible route for her life journey—hoping to answer some questions about the choices she made in the context of Victorian images of duty and responsibility.

3. *How did the invention of Susan help you present Louisa in a fresh way, and how did she grow in her own right?*

Unlike her real-life contemporaries, Susan was free to ask questions. I also needed her to cast light on life with the Alcotts before Louisa's success and to be an intimate counterpoint to Louisa in Washington. But that wasn't enough for Susan. At a certain point, she stood up, brushed off her skirts, and declared herself a real character. I became quite fond of her, with all her frailties and contradictions.

4. *Is there any truth to Susan's story, or is she wholly fictional?*

She is wholly fictional, but I like to think she embodies some of the characteristics of women swept up in that tumultuous time.

5. *Why did you choose to add Clara Barton to the story?*

Everyone knows Clara for her work on the battlefield, but not many are familiar with her strenuous effort to locate dead and missing soldiers after the war. I certainly wasn't. So when the *Washington Post* story headlined FOUND: MISSING LINK OF CLARA BARTON'S LIFE caught my eye, I was intrigued. What a discovery, I thought—there it had been, this apartment abandoned for a hundred and thirty years as the world changed outside its windows. And now it was offering a new chapter of American Civil War history.

I couldn't get my mind off Clara after that. I was drawn to her vibrant personality and to her determination to bring some order to the war's chaotic aftermath by identifying the men who had been lost. She wanted to save them, dead or alive, from anonymity. This was a Clara different from the brave nurse tending the wounded out on the battlefield. I invited her into my book, and relished the privilege of imagining what life might have been like during that time—and in that long forgotten place on Seventh Street—for this remarkable lady.

6. *How did your experience writing* I Know Just What You Mean *with Ellen Goodman shape your work on this story of a lifelong friendship?*

Ellen and I knew from our own experience that female friendships do not survive on some kind of warm, fuzzy trajectory; the truth is, they are often shaped by challenges met and overcome. Sometimes you have to risk a friendship to save it— otherwise you sacrifice what made the friendship precious in the first place.

In this story, Susan hates the thought of spending the rest of her life lying to Louisa about her relationship with John Sulie, so she takes the risk of revealing the truth. We saw examples of that dilemma, in different circumstances, time and again in the lives of the women friends we talked to for our book.

7. *What challenges did you find writing historical fiction for the first time?*

It was a challenge to remember that the fictional part of the story comes first. I loved immersing myself in the historical material, but needed to balance accuracy with the demands of the plot. Historical detail must bring a tale alive, not engulf it. A hard lesson for a journalist!

8. *While writing, what kind of pressure did you feel to accurately represent Louisa? What liberties did you allow yourself to take? How did you think purists would respond?*

Louisa is an icon I've spent my life revering, and I wanted to be able to break through her carefully constructed persona (knowing she destroyed most of her diaries before she died to circumvent that possibility), while preserving the true spirit of a remarkable woman. I allowed myself to imagine her in love, and tried to show how difficult it would be for her to embrace any risk-taking that broke the Concord mold.

I don't know how "purists" would respond—I'm not sure who they are. Louisa's true story is rich with possibility and ambiguity; I hope those who care about Louisa are willing to imagine the unknown.

9. *What do you hope readers both familiar and unfamiliar with Louisa May Alcott's story will take away from this novel?*

I hope readers get a sense of what it was like for a woman to live as a participant in this historical era. Louisa isn't a historical cliché. She was a real woman, filled with the juice of life, living through extraordinary times.

10. *What will you be working on next?*

I am exploring a story based on the extraordinary life of Margaret Fuller, an early nineteenth-century journalist who was once one of the most famous women in America.